PENGUIN BOOKS

The Sacred Scroll

Anton Gill was born in London and educated at Chigwell School and Clare College, Cambridge. He has written on a wide range of subjects, especially contemporary European history, and published a series of thrillers set in ancient Egypt. Until recently, he has divided his time between London and Paris, but now makes his home in London again.

D1079851

The Sacred Scroll

ANTON GILL

PENGUIN BOOKS

PENGUIN BOOKS

Published by the Penguin Group
Penguin Books Ltd, 80 Strand, London WC2R 0RL, England
Penguin Group (USA) Inc., 375 Hudson Street, New York, New York 10014, USA
Penguin Group (Canada), 90 Eglinton Avenue East, Suite 700, Toronto, Ontario, Canada M4P 2Y3
(a division of Pearson Penguin Canada Inc.)
Penguin Ireland, 25 St Stephen's Green, Dublin 2, Ireland (a division of Penguin Books Ltd)
Penguin Group (Australia), 250 Camberwell Road,
Camberwell, Victoria 3124, Australia (a division of Pearson Australia Group Pty Ltd)
Penguin Books India Pvt Ltd, 11 Community Centre,
Panchsheel Park, New Delhi – 110 017, India
Penguin Group (NZ), 67 Apollo Drive, Rosedale, Auckland 0632, New Zealand
(a division of Pearson New Zealand Ltd)
Penguin Books (South Africa) (Pty) Ltd, Block D, Rosebank Office Park, 181 Jan Smuts Avenue,
Parktown North, Gauteng 2193, South Africa

Penguin Books Ltd, Registered Offices: 80 Strand, London WC2R 0RL, England

www.penguin.com

First published 2012
001

Copyright © Anton Gill, 2012
All rights reserved

The moral right of the author has been asserted

Set in 12.5/14.75 pt Garamond MT Std
Typeset by Palimpsest Book Production Limited, Falkirk, Stirlingshire
Printed in Great Britain by Clays Ltd, St Ives plc

ISBN: 978-0-241-95373-0

www.greenpenguin.co.uk

Penguin Books is committed to a sustainable
future for our business, our readers and our planet.
This book is made from Forest Stewardship
Council™ certified paper.

ALWAYS LEARNING   **PEARSON**

For
Peter Ewence,
with thanks for his
friendship and support;
11–16 September 2010,
and thereafter.

Prologue

Brad Adkins looked around the lab. He couldn't disguise his tension from the others and knew they were feeling it too.

They'd been working on the dig at Istanbul for three weeks now and they still hadn't found what they had been sent to look for. And time was running out.

The lab looked tidy enough to leave for the night, thought Adkins, watching his two colleagues carefully placing the boxes in the white cupboards ranged along one wall.

He turned to the deck of computer screens on the broad table and switched them off, one by one, methodically checking that all the information input that day had been properly saved. His colleagues had finished before him, and stood watching. Su-Lin, he thought, looked anxious to leave, but he refused to be hurried by the junior member of his team, even if she was there by order of their main sponsor.

'Almost done,' he said. Quite a dish, Su-Lin, but that'd be hunting a bit too close to home, and he didn't want to spoil the close professional rapport which the work on this project had created between the three of them. And God knows they needed it, he thought, given the pressure. He wondered how soon it would be before people would begin to get impatient.

'Let's get out of here,' said his Yale colleague, Rick Taylor. 'Another dead day – it's time to drown it out.' Adkins reached for the switch on the final screen. Taylor was hitting the bottle hard these days. He'd keep an eye on that. Taylor was right – they'd had another fruitless search. He tried to stay hopeful, but every day confirmed his growing suspicion that what they sought simply wasn't there. He glanced again at Su-Lin. Impassive now, she looked at her watch.

Adkins flicked off the last button. But as he drew his hand back and the screen went blank the door to the lab crashed violently open.

Five men in black, faces hidden by balaclavas, burst in, followed by a thin man and a plump woman dressed like tourists, wearing sunglasses large enough to cover their features.

It was the woman who spoke. English accent. Cut-glass. Polite.

'Sorry to disturb. We have some questions for you.'

'Who the hell are –?'

One of the men stepped forward and clubbed Taylor to the ground. He lay there without moving.

'Don't damage the goods,' said the woman. 'Don't damage anything.'

One of the men came towards Adkins. He flinched, expecting a blow. But none came. Instead, the man shoved a thick bag over his head and pulled it savagely tight at the neck.

Adkins felt panic begin to rise before the man hit him once across the nape of his neck. A clinical blow.

Then the darkness was total.

I

AD 1204

Constantinople, Monday 12 April, and at last an attack. First, I must write of the noise: the screaming, the thunder, the smell of burning tar and burning flesh, everywhere about us. It was as if the full wrath of the true Catholic Church had been unleashed.

The sun beat down that day, and it was windy. Huge buffets from the north, though at first it kept switching. But a good day for a battle, after so long a wait, and the wind at last swung round to a steady, harsh north, ramming our galleys and transports on to the shore. No way to turn back now, and there on the forecastle of the leading ship, Dandolo, ninety years old and blind, but with his helmet and breastplate shining, his sword aloft. By his side his trusted Viking, an old man too, but tough as hardwood.

We lowered the great assault ramps which were fixed to the prows of our ships so they fell against the two nearest towers of the city walls. We'd been wise to cover them with roofs of cowhide soaked in vinegar because, dark and hot as it was as we swarmed up them to the platforms at their tops, the coverings saved us from the fire and stones the bastards hurled down upon us. And we smashed our way to the top.

The smell of boiling pitch was everywhere in the dark

tunnels of the ramps and we were blinded by the light when we emerged. The first of us were cut to pieces by the Viking Guard, the wretched bunch of Saxons who protected the false emperor, but we kept coming and coming, and our ships spewed and squirted liquid fire through bronze siphons at the pitiful defenders. We watched the fire cling to them. They died screaming as they tried to wipe it off.

The walls of the city stood high and tall, but we knew they were not as good as they looked. They were crumbling; they'd had centuries of neglect, ever since the Great City came to believe itself impregnable, under the protection of the very wing of Gabriel himself. But we could see where the mortar was rotting between the stones and we planted brushwood soaked in naphtha in the hollows we found, and set fire to it to weaken the walls further.

There'd already been two conflagrations in the city during the attacks last year and they'd half destroyed the city then, though much of it was already falling down. Not that it wasn't magnificent still. It made our Paris look like a village. They said it had stood for nine centuries, ever since the Emperor Constantine had made it the seat of his new Christian Roman empire. It was the gateway to the East and the bastion for Europe against the Seljuk Turks who had taken the Holy Land from us.

Well, we'd deal with them soon enough. Once this business was over. The Byzantine Greeks who rule here still call themselves Christians, but they no longer show homage to the pope, and follow their own barbarous Eastern way of hearing the Word of God. Our job has been to put

4

that right – these people must be brought back into the True Fold, by force. And by Christ's Grace and the leadership of our good Lord Dandolo, we will do it!

In time, Pope Innocent will understand, and see why we have had to raise our swords against fellow Christians. He will see the Divine Justice of our action. We'll finish these bastard Greeks, now our blood is up. Bring them to their knees. Teach them to set themselves up against us, even to permit a mosque within their walls!

But it has been hard. After our very first attack on the Eastern Christians at the city of Zara, Pope Innocent pronounced us excommunicate! That lay heavy on us. Like a bullwhip, a thousand lashes, across your back. He relieved his dread sentence later, as he desired us to continue as Pilgrim Warriors to Jerusalem. And there were letters sent from Doge Dandolo. Those letters must have made him relent. But what power of persuasion could the doge possibly have over the pope?

Still, Innocent did not free the Venetians from excommunication. We marvelled, I remember, that they were unconcerned. Lord Dandolo even scoffed at it. We wondered what enabled him to dare do that. But he told us we had nothing to fear, and we believed him.

We couldn't disobey Dandolo, even though some of us murmured doubt. A few even tried to stand off from this present battle, but most were not resolute enough for that. There is something about the man, some power he has within him. He commands, and we must obey. And I am a simple Christian knight. I question not my leader.

It's always seemed a strange thing to me, but the fact is

we'd follow him anywhere. There were times when some of us wondered why. But you can't think about such things when there's a war to be won.

The Greeks used scimitars, that vicious sword they got from the infidel Seljuks they allow to live among them. It's a good sword though, cuts like a scythe, so when even a centimetre of that crescent-shaped blade is in you the rest follows through on the curve, increasing the cutting power, and it slices through bone and muscle without a hitch. My countryman and captain, Mathieu le Barca, lost his sword arm that way in the fighting on the first day. He fought on – the excitement raced through his blood on account of the wound and he felt no pain – but he was on his knees by the time I reached him and there were three men attacking. I brought my broadsword down on the closest, through the shoulder on the shield-arm from the collarbone down to the heart, cut him in two like a side of beef. The others tried to run then, but I got one in the middle of the skull, their Greek helmets no good against French steel, split his head in half, made me laugh to see the mouth open and shut in two bits like that. The third I headbutted with my own strong helmet. Made porridge of his brain.

But did any of us on either side pause to think, We are Christians and they too are Christians? We had gathered as Warrior Pilgrims under the Cross to drive the Turks from the Holy Land, to take back Jerusalem. That was our true mission.

It seemed we had a new mission now: to serve Lord Dandolo and be guided by him in the True Path. And we did not question. We obeyed. We were all in thrall to the old doge of Venice, and most of us trusted him.

6

As for the Greeks, they'd let things go to seed. They spent all their money on trumpery, nothing on arms and defence. They'd grown too sure of themselves, ruling the roost for nine hundred years. That's what Dandolo told us.

But I return to the battle. It was now at its height. There was no time for reflection. One of our ships, one that had not beached, we'd tied to one of the towers, but the sea's ebb pulled the ship back, and the tower was so rotten that it rocked, and we cut it loose for fear it would fall on us. We could see fear, too, in the faces of the Greek defenders on the tower.

The men on the beach sought weak gates, but the defenders hurled down stones and burning pitch with such fury that we had to find shelter, up against the very walls we wanted to bring down. Meanwhile most of our fleet, driven ashore and beached by the wind, disembarked thousands of men-at-arms, who ran up the ramps, stepping over the corpses, and gained a firm foothold. Lord Dandolo cried out that the wind which drove us on was the breath of the Archangel Michael, aiding us in our fight with the Great Satan.

And then we found a gate in their walls. We hacked at it with axes and iron bars and it splintered and fell open. We got some horsemen through, but inside they were ready for us. Brought down the warhorses, the destriers, with kitehead arrows – heavy diamond heads, cut through anything, right into the horses' flanks, severing muscle joining legs to body. I saw one come down, crush a kid, a little Greek boy there to watch the fun, couldn't get away in time, yelled like a banshee when his legs smashed. I went over to him and cut off his head. Put him out of his misery. But the horse nearly killed *me* then, with his hooves. He was in agony too, flailing, poor beast, but there was no saving him, and I cut the great veins in his neck to give him peace too.

With the horses down, the Greeks attacked our fallen knights, like the cowards they were. But we regrouped and we got in there and we fucking crucified them.

2

Constantinople, Friday 16 April, Year of Our Lord 1204

The monk who'd been reading the document aloud now put down his papers, eased his thin body in his black habit, stretched his bony feet in their soft leather sandals and took a drink from the cup of wine at his elbow. He peered across the room, its stone walls hung with tapestries, to where his employer sat. The stiff brocade robes he was wearing seemed to be all that held the old man upright. A candle guttered in its stand and a draught blew through the room, then the flame grew steady again.

Leporo could sense his master's feeble eye squinting back at him through the gloom. He had been with the old man for the last forty years, since he was a novice monk, well before the trip to Constantinople three decades earlier which had left his master all but blind. They hadn't managed to kill his eyesight as completely as they'd intended, back then. Leporo had seen to that. And what gratitude had he been shown?

Leporo prided himself on being one of only two men who stood close to the doge and enjoyed his confidence. Time was he had been the *only* one. He was Dandolo's confessor, but not that alone. He was his secretary, confidant, eyes and – often – ears. Not much got past him.

But he always remained one step behind his master. With

the passing years, that galled him more and more. Why should he be content with the crumbs which fell from the table when he might have the bread that was on it?

The problem was the other man close to his master. Leporo thought of him now, and hatred crept into his soul, its natural home.

But he kept his counsel. He knew how to bide his time.

'This knight whose memoirs you are reading from,' said the old man in a thin voice. 'Who is he?'

'Bohun de Treillis. A minor nobleman from Amboise.'

'He thinks too much. We need to trim his account. Blunt his quill. He reveals too many secrets and he has no business even guessing at them.'

'He is an ignorant man, *Altissima*. There is nothing to be feared. He writes in the dark.'

'I'll decide what is to be feared or not. Anything that bears a hint of my power must be excised. And, now – read on,' said the doge, peering uncertainly towards Leporo through the gloom. The monk saw the one good eye glint in the candle's flame.

He cleared his throat.

On the other side of the gate, there was a small square, streets leading off, and a crowd of people, staring at us, pissing themselves in fear. We put a few men in, and the people inside shrank back, all sorts, high and low, mixed up together in the streets, no fight in them, all gaudy clothes for the rich, though. They fell back into the narrow streets. Too narrow – too much risk of ambush. A man could easily get lost in this city; it was like a twenty-square-kilometre maze.

Our men followed the inside of the wall towards the sea, where a great chain had been stretched across the mouth of the big inlet, the Golden Horn, to keep us out. That'd been easy to smash. Bloody thing was half rusted away and, as for their fleet, the galleys were so rotten they were already sunk to their gunnels, and all their so-called grand admiral could muster was a few dozen cavalry who ran away as soon as they saw us!

How far into the battle were we? Six hours? Seven? The sun was at its height, beating down, and we would have boiled in our chain mail, but the wind cooled us. And now, at last – a real breach!

That was what was happening down near St Barbara's Gate, on the seaward side. Some of our men who'd got in by the small gate had managed to fight their way round to a big gate on the seaward side, where our transports were, and the Greeks melted before them. Vicious bastards – they ran away into the streets, sure, but that didn't stop them chucking anything they could find down on us from the rooftops.

Our lads got this big gate open, unopposed. It was wide and high; two, three, mounted knights could get through it at once. The transports immediately raised their anchors and beached themselves, throwing their foregates down so the big destriers, already caparisoned with their taffeta coats emblazoned with the knights' insignias, their steel head-protectors strapped tight, could be led out fast by the squires. The knights, helmeted and armoured, all the colours of the rainbow on their crests and surcoats, were soon ready for the fray.

We wore our own battledress because we were fighting

renegade Christians. We reserved the white surcoat with the red cross for the fight against the Infidel in Jerusalem. This, Lord Dandolo ordered us to do.

We stormed in. Right through that gate, the green sea glittering in the sun at our backs, the yellow sand, the high grey walls, the Greeks stampeding before us to avoid being crushed by the horses.

As for the defenders – well, they'd lost heart. And their new emperor, that traitor who'd killed the man we'd set up as their king – he'd gone AWOL. Well, he'd had his ten weeks. We'd been here the best part of two years, in this weird country, all hand-kissing and smells of strange spices; the unblinking sun in summer, the vicious cold and clinging damp in winter; all that silk and gold. Well, it was our turn now.

'Take that out,' said Dandolo.

Leporo nodded, and went on reading.

We were not such fools as to risk losing ourselves in the labyrinth of streets that connected the main squares and the palaces. We took up quarters on the Petrion Hill. We could see all around from there, and we smashed down a few of the wooden defence turrets the Greeks had built on top of the towers, just to let off steam. Evening by then. The officers told the men to bivouac: 'Busy day tomorrow!' But I couldn't rest. I kept looking out over the city. Like a sea it was, twinkling lights of fires here and there, moon drenching it in a greyish light. Looked like an open oyster – all you had to do was find the pearl.

We'd all heard tales of the treasures the city held – and

the Holy Relics too. Just a few of them ought to buy us our Christianity back all right, when we got home.

All that loot! Once we were done, we'd have more than enough not only to pay off our debt to Dandolo but to feather our own nests for life.

And in two weeks, we'll celebrate Easter here. *Our* Easter. Not theirs.

And then, the great Pilgrimage – to Jerusalem!

Leporo paused. He looked at Dandolo, brooding in his chair, and brooded himself about the hidden power the old doge had, and how long it might be before he, Leporo, could be master of it. But he took care to veil his thoughts. Who could be sure that Dandolo wasn't able to read them?

'Take out that stuff about Jerusalem,' said the old man.

'Why?'

'Because these Crusaders will never get there.'

Leporo wet his lips, not quite believing what he had heard, and not daring either to question or contradict. Instead, seeing his master's eyes flicker, he said, 'The looting and destruction have stopped.'

'Good.'

'It's as if the Pilgrims of Christ just ran out of breath, or suddenly realized what a steaming slaughterhouse they'd created – and that they were destroying things which could be of value to them. Now we have the business of restoring order and getting a new, Roman Catholic, truly Christian emperor on the throne. No more of this Eastern Church mumbo-jumbo.'

'*That* ought to shut the pope up. After all, that was

what Innocent wanted, all along. In the meantime, we have some history to rewrite. We must remove any un-favourable descriptions of the sack of the city that are appearing.'

'Do you want me to read any more of this?' he asked.

'Who wrote it, did you say?'

'One of the minor knights, as I told you. Bohun de Treillis. Not a man of importance.' The monk hesitated. 'And don't worry. He can't read or write himself. He dictated it to one of their French priests. His memoirs. Wanted to get them down while the memory was fresh. But the priest is also one of our spies. What do you want me to do with it?'

'How much more has he written?'

Leporo riffled pages. 'There's more about what we did after that first day.'

'About what the Pilgrims of the Cross did,' Dandolo corrected him. 'We Venetians did nothing.'

'We didn't destroy much, that's true. All we did was loot.'

Dandolo made an irritable gesture. 'Sometimes I wish you'd forget your Christianity.'

'I left it behind a long time ago. Perhaps that will be to my cost. But I am your loyal follower, as the years have proved.'

Dandolo ignored that. 'I wish I could see just well enough to read properly,' he murmured. Self-pity wasn't in Dandolo's nature, and Leporo, knowing this, eyed him keenly. After all these years, he still couldn't trust himself to fathom his master's darkest thoughts.

But it wasn't a ploy. Leporo knew what remained of

the old man's sight, ruined when they tried to burn his eyes out in Constantinople as a punishment for spying, was fading now, with every day that passed. His master was an old, old man. God alone knew how old he was, but he'd been in his mid-fifties when he had first taken Leporo into his employment as a secretary, four decades ago.

It was just a matter of time . . .

Leporo, whose own eyes had taken on a greedy glint as he thought of what was to come, what he might inherit, forced himself to return to the matter in hand. But the thought stayed at the back of his mind, and excited his soul.

'We are taking what is rightfully ours,' Dandolo went on. 'Venice has bent the knee to Constantinople for too long. No more!'

'We've done well here, no doubt of that. The Pilgrims have seized enough booty to pay us for the fleet we built them, *and* keep a tidy sum for themselves.'

'But how much have they destroyed?'

'Plenty.' Leporo picked his words. 'Works of art, from the ancient days. And they've burned down all the libraries. No profit in that.'

'The Pilgrims are all illiterate, so you can't expect anything else.' Dandolo paused. 'Beautiful works of art?'

'Exquisite. Irreplaceable. Fortunately, we've had Venetian squads out rescuing the good stuff to take home. To adorn St Mark's.'

'Pity about the libraries,' Dandolo said thoughtfully, but then a spasm pulled his face into a rictus of pain and his right hand, the good one – arthritis had turned the left into a claw – flew up to his eyes. When he sensed Leporo coming towards him, he waved him away impatiently.

'The headache?' asked Leporo.

'Of course the headache!' spat Dandolo. 'And why should I give a damn about their libraries? I cannot read any more. And why should I care about the beauty of their art? I cannot see it!'

'You remember it.'

Dandolo turned his milky eyes on his confessor, and Leporo saw their centres burn with anguish and rage. The glories of Constantinople were the last things his master had ever seen.

'Console yourself, my son,' said Leporo, taking refuge in his faith. 'You've got what you came for.'

'What do you mean?' said Dandolo in a dangerous voice.

Leporo shrugged. 'Revenge.'

'For my eyes? Do you think I would have waited thirty years if all I'd wanted was revenge?'

The monk fell silent. He knew full well why it had taken his master thirty years: he had been waiting for the opportunity and the means. Then, as if handed to him on a plate by God, they had come: a Crusader army – and the power to control it and bend it to his will. And now the time was drawing near when Leporo would seize that power for himself. He knew more about how the doge had controlled that army than his master could possibly guess. It had taken a lot of dissimulation, but he knew where the real power lay.

3

New York City, the Present

Jack Marlow looked up at the façade of the discreet hotel. It looked handsome in the pale sunlight of this early autumn day. It looked welcoming. Marlow hoped this would be a good omen. He needed a change after the bad business in Paris. This transfer was the answer to his prayers.

His mind took him back for a moment to the woman, a blonde lapse-in-judgement who worked in HR. It'd lasted three and a half years, and he'd thought it was the real thing at last. But he'd been wrong.

'What's the matter?' she'd said in response to his consternation when she dropped her bomb. 'We've had a pretty good run.'

Three and a half years. *A pretty good run*. And he'd been fool enough to think it was for real.

That'd been eighteen months earlier. An Achilles' heel he'd have to watch. Especially now. The first mission, from all he'd been told in his initial briefing, would need every gramme of concentration. But he'd kept his wound a tight secret. All that had happened was that he'd been used by someone who – as he discovered – had no conscience. And what should he blame for having been too credulous? Too trusting? The trace of Irish blood in his ancestry? Marlow smiled. No – allowing hope to get the better of reality, that was all. Bad news in his business. But nothing is wasted. Above all, he'd learned to know when there was nothing but darkness in another person's eyes.

He shook himself free of his demons and ran up the steps; at the entrance before the commissionaire had a chance to get the doors for him. The commissionaire didn't know him, and looked searchingly at the tall man casually dressed in a faded denim shirt under a black leather jacket. Marlow read the man's expression. The uniform was thinking, This guy doesn't look like our average guest. The clothes are good, OK, but he's dishevelled. Doesn't care about how he looks. Maybe too rich to need to. Maybe a music mogul? Give him the benefit.

Marlow swung past him. After all, the commissionaire was an innocent – he thought he was simply working for a hotel.

Two out of the five desk clerks knew better. The auburn-haired woman, a field agent once herself, returned his look and nodded him through. The look they exchanged wasn't entirely professional. There was remembered electricity in it for both of them. Real electricity, in their case. But Marlow was done with all that.

Running a hand carelessly through his dark hair, more unruly than usual thanks to the wind outside, he crossed the lobby, passing unobtrusive signs indicating the direction of the restaurant and bar, gym and pool. He didn't like the overstuffed *richesse* of the place, but it was good cover, and beat the hell out of the old import-export premises INTERSEC had used to hide its New York base

18

back in the bad old days of the Cold War. He remembered them like his first date. He'd been recruited after graduating in 1990, just in time for glasnost and all the shifting goalposts which followed.

He reached a red door beyond the lift area and went through it into what anyone else would have taken for a breakout space for the staff – vending machines and a couple of tables and benches, smell of poor coffee. Marlow glanced round – checking a space was second nature to him – then he spoke the magic words, a machine swung back, and he entered another world.

A minute later the steel-lined elevator deposited him in a modern, soundless lobby off which only one door led. An aluminium plaque on it read: *Richard Hudson*.

Marlow hadn't reached the door before it opened and Sir Richard himself stood before him. His new boss, though no stranger. They'd locked horns way back, in the London office, even before Marlow's Paris posting. Must have been sometime during his SAS secondment, thought Marlow. How tough that had seemed, back in the day. He hadn't thought he'd survive the disciplinary measures his insubordination had resulted in. But they must have thought him more of an asset than a liability.

Hudson was sixty-something now, the air around him carrying that odour of Lancero cigars and Annick Goutal cologne which only rich men in Savile Row suits exude.

He extended a hand. 'Jack. It's been a long time.'

'Sir.'

Hudson waved a hand. 'These days you must call me Dick. Everyone does. You and I are both Englishmen abroad, and here in America one dispenses with formalities.

I can't tell you how happy we are to have you on board. Chap with your qualifications. Especially now.' Marlow thought the man looked troubled.

'It's good to be here,' Marlow replied. There was a lot hanging on this appointment.

'It's a small team but a tight one. You've got Leon Lopez, as you requested. I gather you two go back a bit?'

'You could say that.'

'The girl's been with us a while but she's new to this field. And little field-work experience, beyond training. So you'll have to show her the ropes. Brilliant in her way. Hand-picked. But, of course, if she doesn't shape up, we'll take steps.'

'If she's got the qualifications I requested, that's good enough.'

'Partly why we put this team together so fast.' Hudson looked at him. 'As I mentioned when we spoke earlier, your first assignment is, shall we say, rather special.'

'That's what I'm here for.' Marlow shrugged lean shoulders, noticing the tightness return to Hudson's expression. But the man relaxed slightly then, and said, 'Yes. That's what you're here for.'

As they walked down the corridors, heavily carpeted in grey, and took a series of whispering stainless-steel lifts, Marlow, as he listened to Hudson filling him in on tighter firewall controls, thought about his time with INTER-SEC. INTERSEC, one of the few examples of successful international government collaboration, was known to very few people. But it spread its net wide. As far as Marlow knew, only a handful of rebel, unstable or minor states in the entire world had no representation in it, and within it the old guard, the USA and Western Europe, could just about maintain the balance between themselves and the new kids on the block: a transformed and dangerous Russia, and China and India. Just about. The game was changing daily. How much and how fast, Marlow reflected, he was about to find out.

'Here we are,' said Hudson, opening an unmarked white door. 'Room 55. Your new home.'

One end of the huge space they entered was partitioned off by a white wall, on which hung an original Matisse.

'From my own collection,' said Hudson, following Marlow's gaze. 'A good working environment needs tasteful surroundings.'

Marlow nodded, but he was picking up on the stress in his boss's tone, however hard the man tried to cover it. 'And beyond the wall?' he asked, looking at the sliding door, now closed, which punctuated it.

'Leon's domain – mainly computerized, but still part old-fashioned lab.'

The room they stood in was an open-plan workspace in which there were three large tables, on which stood the usual array of computers, and five telephones – four black, one blue. One wall was lined with bookshelves. The window had an open view across Central Park.

The door in the partition wall slid open and the familiar figure of Leon Lopez emerged through it.

'Jack! You old bastard. Good to have you back.'

Marlow had worked with him before, and there wasn't much about him he didn't know. Born in Kingston, Jamaica, forty-three years earlier, the oldest of four brothers, he'd been head of scientific research in the Special Operations Directive of INTERSEC for five years now.

'Going grey,' smiled Marlow, shaking his hand.

'But no paunch to go with it.'

Marlow knew there was more to the bespectacled, slightly stooping six-footer than just a back-room boy. Lopez's other job was senior lecturer in the History of Science at Columbia University. They'd first worked together in Honduras, when Lopez and Marlow were doing a spell with the Marines in what had been called an 'advisory capacity'.

'How's Mia? Still failing to teach you Swedish?'

'She's fine. And my Swedish has come on – even her mother approves.'

'And the kids?'

Lopez grinned. 'Alvar's thirteen now –'

'Which makes Lucia what – ten?'

'Exactly.'

'Surprised you're still doing this.' As he spoke, Marlow saw Lopez and Hudson exchange a glance. But then the main door opened and the woman came in.

'Jack,' Hudson said, 'this is Laura Graves.'

The woman looked at him levelly through clear blue eyes.

Marlow knew all about her. She was a native New Yorker, born thirty- years ago on Long Island, where her parents – Irish/French stock – still lived. An only child, she was unmarried, and she'd been recruited by INTER-SEC after collecting degrees from Yale, and Cambridge University in England. She'd then had a brief career in academic journalism.

Marlow took her hand. Her handshake was as cool as the look in her eyes.

He knew she spoke three living languages fluently – French, Arabic and Chinese, which complemented his own German, Italian and Spanish. In addition, she knew Latin and Greek, but her real expertise was in Sanskrit and Aramaic, with a working knowledge of the ancient Babylonian languages – Sumerian and Akkadian. Those were the skills she'd been picked for.

'Hello.'

'Hello.'

Marlow took stock of his new colleague. An intelligent face whose expression was reserved, though Marlow sensed humour beneath the surface, and in the fine lines at the corners of the mouth.

She was maybe 1.70m tall. High cheekbones, lips less than what you'd call full, a nose that just managed not to be aquiline, a delicate chin. All framed by the kind of long hair a model would die for, auburn. Lightly tanned skin, slight sunglass-paleness around the eyes. Her chunky grey sweater and black jeans couldn't disguise an athletic figure.

She gave him a faint smile now. Marlow, homing in on details, saw that her simple clothes were complemented by an emerald pendant on a silver chain, and an emerald ring on her right hand. On the little finger next to it was a minute, faded tattoo of what looked like a heart.

'Good to meet you,' she said.

'Welcome, all of you, to Section 15,' said Hudson, clearing his throat. 'Which, with Jack's arrival, is now complete. As you know, this section's been created in response to a special contingency of prime importance. As far as I am concerned, you'll report to me but I'll leave you alone. In fact, the fewer the people who know what you're doing, the better, even within INTERSEC.' He turned to Marlow. 'Sorry to be brief, but there's no time for a welcome party. I'll leave you to get acquainted. But don't take too long over it. Leon will fill you in.'

Marlow nodded, and Hudson left, trailing his aura of expensive cigars and cologne.

'So what have we got?' he said, turning to Lopez. 'A handful of missing archaeologists? They must be super-important.'

Then the blue phone rang. Marlow nodded again. Lopez picked it up, spoke briefly and passed it over.

Marlow listened intently, and hung up.

'Playtime over,' he said. 'Let's go to work.'

4

At a sign from his master, Leporo began to read from de Treillis's battle memoir again.

> We found no fugitives in the Palace. We found only the great ladies, the Empress Marie of Hungary, who was the sister of the Hungarian king; and the Empress Agnes, the sister of our own King Philip, both widows of late emperors of this city and this Eastern empire.
>
> I could see that the Italian, Boniface, one of our two leaders, had his eye on Lady Agnes from the first.

> They say that fifty years ago the emperor had a golden throne which was lowered from hidden heights down on to the dais which stood ready to take its weight. The emperor would welcome ambassadors here, in the great palace of Boucoleon, clad in his gold-and-silver clothes, capes encrusted with emeralds and rubies and sapphires. Next to the throne stood a plane tree made entirely of gold, in which clockwork silver-and-gold birds sang. And they say that either side of the golden throne were mechanical lions and griffins which by a secret device could be made to turn their heads, open their mouths and roar. And – wonderful to relate – after envoys to him

had prostrated themselves, the emperor, on a signal, would be hoisted up on his throne to those hidden heights, only to descend again soon afterwards, resplendent as ever, but now in completely different robes.

Even the Turks who came here in those days, they say, were cowed and impressed.

We found no such thing in the palace as that throne, but for all we knew it was there somewhere, in its many rooms – we stopped counting at five hundred, wary of getting lost, of an ambush even. But there was no sign of one.

We were blinded by the splendour. Where we use iron for nails and hinges, they use silver and gold. Where we have wooden or earth floors, theirs are marble; and that is only the beginning.

But I must speak of the fire.

It was worse than the ones that had gone before.

We had all hoped for rest that first night after the victory, though we were still cautious. I continued to look out over the city, thinking of its riches, when the glow of what I thought was one of the fires in Lord Boniface's camp some way off grew great, and spread. In minutes I could see that it was another great fire, ravaging the city. I found out later that it had been set by some of the Italians – Pisans – who were afraid of a counter-attack by the Greeks under cover of night. They were brawling drunk; they went to the mosque and picked a fight with the locals they found worshipping there. Wrecked the place and set it on fire.

There was a wind from the north. The fire burned all the rich quarter in its southward path, and it raged for eighteen hours. Lost a lot of loot that way.

A part of me felt sorry for the locals. They'd done nothing to harm us. They were only merchants. I saw one family who'd got out of their house but didn't run away, just stood near it, watching it burn. Their whole lives.

The rest of the city lay open. The emperor was gone, no one knew where, maybe out of the city with the rest of the rich, through the Golden Gate at the southern end of the West Wall. This was good, because the only troops left who were worthy fighters were his personal guard, the Warings – Vikings, and Saxons who'd fled from the Normans. They were confused, having no sense of direction or duty without an emperor to protect. We took them prisoner but handled them well. They were men like *us*, after all, men we could understand – not like the Greeks. Dandolo already had one of them in his pocket, a bloke who'd been with him for years. He helped smooth things over, but it was the old doge himself who won them over. How, I've no idea.

There was much to do. This huge city lay wide open to us, and we – and I mean us French as well as the Germans and the Italians – didn't hesitate to help ourselves to its riches. We were surely in the right, but it grieves me to report that in our victorious fury we respected nothing.

We did not respect the churches or the sacred images. And some of our men – not our own Frenchmen but the Pilgrims from Germany and Italy – attacked and raped men, women and children.

All sorts of atrocities and killings we carried out. The monasteries and the convents were looted and burned down, as well as the great houses. I saw our men tear the habits from nuns, young and old; two men would spread the women's legs while a third thrust in. They took turns, gouging the women till they bled, and then cutting their throats. I saw a monk try to intervene once, a young man, strong. They ripped his hairshirt from him and used a dagger to cut off his balls.

Leporo paused. Dandolo looked up.
'Why have you stopped?' he asked.
'There's a passage that follows which I do not wish to read.'
'Read everything.'

We rode into the great church of Saint Sophia on horseback, right up to the altar. We tore the vestments from the priests who stayed, praying, at their posts. The face of Christ in gold and in majesty looked down at us from the dome as we broke up the shrines and altars for the sake of their marble. We looted the sacristy and the crypt and the treasury. We needed money to pay the Venetians for the fleet we had ordered for the great venture to Jerusalem.

I'm a poor knight, but I'm a nobleman, and I could see the value and a bit of the beauty of what we took; but try telling that to the ordinary soldiers. They are farmhands from the kingdoms of the west who live in wooden shacks and mud hovels. They'd never seen anything like this. Half of them didn't have jobs when they joined up, were close to starving. This was their big chance. All they saw was stuff which could be melted down and turned into bullion and coin.

But it *had to be done*.

What I cannot support, and the memory lives with me still, is that they took one of the whores from the camp and got her drunk and sat her on the Patriarch's Throne in the great church. There she was, legs wide, and drinking, singing disgusting songs while a couple of sergeants pawed her. I left before I could see what else the men would get up to there. They were out of control.

It went on well after the fire had gone out, from Tuesday to Thursday in those last days before Holy Week. I say again that I had never seen such beautiful things as were pulled over and smashed up, if they were stone or marble, or melted down if they were gold, silver or bronze.

There was a statue of Our Lady in the Forum of the Ox near the city centre. They tore that down and within half a day it was molten metal, ready to be turned into coin, because she'd had the misfortune to be made of bronze. And that wasn't the only one, I can tell you. There was a massive statue of Hercules, and another one of Pegasus, the second so big that I counted ten storks' nests between the bronze horse's head and his crupper.

I was told of two others, one of Juno, and another, which we really should have spared – a statue of the Servant of the Winds, in bronze with the goddess so beautifully balanced on a rotating orb that she acted as a weather vane. And there was a statue of Helen of Troy which I *did* see before it was broken up and taken to the furnaces. I couldn't believe anyone would destroy such a thing; she was so beautiful you'd've thought she was alive. But nothing would stop them. We'd been farting around for so long, trying to take this city, better part of two years, and now, well, there was so much to get your hands on that the lads just couldn't stop themselves.

But the statues couldn't feel anything. It was the people I felt sorry for, and it was the little people who suffered. Most of the rich got away.

I managed to stop one soldier who'd heated the point of his sword and was about stick it into a little girl he'd picked up crying in the street. Had him arrested – hanged him later. Had the little girl taken to one of the convents in the suburbs. There, they had escaped the full fury.

When the anger simmered down, some of us looked back at what we'd done and wept. But it was too late. I reckon more houses were burned down than all the houses you could find in our three biggest cities back in France.

But there was still plenty to go round.

Leporo turned the last page. 'That's as far as he's got,' he said.

Dandolo gave a papery sigh. His right hand went to a pocket concealed within the tunic under his stole and closed round something hidden there. Leporo knew the gesture, and followed it with his eyes. He knew what his master was clutching so protectively. He watched, silently, covetously.

Dandolo was still. He closed his eyes. He stayed like that for a minute, so quiet that the monk peered to see if he could detect the rise and fall of the old man's clothes as he breathed.

He thought he could not. Cautiously, he approached.

He was within touching distance when the milky eyes snapped open. Leporo could see the old burns on the skin around them as Dandolo had struggled to keep his eyes away from the magnifying glass they had used all those years ago, in this city, to concentrate the rays of the sun on to his retinas, to burn them out.

Leoporo shrank back, but he wasn't quick enough. The doge's right hand shot out with surprising speed and seized his confessor's robe near the neck, pulling him down so the monk could smell the musty breath of age.

'What do you want to do?' said Leporo, playing the innocent. 'I've got a shrewd idea of what you want censored. Do you want to leave it to me?'

'I do the censoring. Bring me this knight. His thinking's too independent.' A new thought struck the doge. 'Is he *immune*, do you think?'

'Unlikely. Possible.'

'I'll censor his book today. Use my work as a model to censor the other stuff the Crusaders have written. Burn anything that delves too deep.'

'You have nothing to fear. History will be your judge. So long as you control the majority, the rest don't matter. Just give them a bone to gnaw on from time to time,' Leporo said.

Dandolo's face showed nothing. 'Bring me some wine. Then we'll get the work done. And bring Frid with you when you return.'

Leporo looked angry.

'Do we need him, *Altissima*?' Leporo hated Frid. That filthy Danish cuckoo in the nest. That brainless sack of

31

muscle. One day the Viking would be off guard and then
. . . Leporo fingered the thin knife at his belt. He'd already
wasted too many years in Frid's shadow.

The doge looked at him again. 'Are you still here?' he
said.

Frid doesn't know what I know, thought the monk as he slunk
away. *I have that advantage.*

5

Somewhere in the South-east European Hinterland, the Present

Brad Adkins thought, fleetingly, of his safe, comfortable home, of his wife and children. What was going through their minds? Did they even know what had happened? The images were strong enough to touch, but at the same time dreamlike. Yet the picture his mind held most firmly, him pushing little Sarah on her swing, wrenched his heart. Panic rose in knots from his gut to his throat.

Somewhere near him in the gloom Rick Taylor groaned.

'Rick?' he said tentatively, fighting down his thoughts, relieved that there was some kind of companionship again. 'You awake?'

'Wish I wasn't. Where the hell are we?'

'We've been drugged. How long have we been here?'

'They'll be looking for us.'

'How will they know where to look?'

Taylor stirred, his voice thick. 'Wherever it is, it's warm. Can't be far from Istanbul. Maybe we're still *in* Istanbul.'

'I don't remember any kind of journey.'

'Nor do I.'

'And where's Su-Lin? What have they done with her?'

Adkins remembered the young woman screaming, but from the moment they'd put the hood over his head, he recalled nothing more.

'Got her in another cell?' he said.

'Maybe she got away.'

'How could she?'

'Poor kid. Jesus, if they've got her alone somewhere –' Taylor said angrily. 'Christ, everything's a fucking haze since that bastard hit me.'

'They drugged us,' Adkins repeated emptily.

'What do they *want* from us?'

'Don't you remember? When they beat us? The hammering they gave us? The questions they asked? Christ, if they did that to Su–'

Adkins fingered the bruises on his arms and legs, praying that their colleague had come to no harm. Maybe she had escaped. Raised the alarm? Then his mind began to slump back into the lethargy he continually had to fight. Both men were naked, grimy, the stench of their bodies heavy in the confined space. At least now their captors had untied them. 'But none of the questions had anything to do with what we were looking for. They seemed to be after something else,' he said.

'Maybe they've got the wrong people.'

'Maybe we weren't told everything.'

'That's crazy.'

'They wanted more out of us than just archaeological skills.'

'That's even crazier. Jeez, my head –'

Adkins didn't answer. He was too tired to think any more. Despite himself, his brain was drifting back into a comfortable miasma. All he could think of, for some reason, was the deep sea, drifting over endless underwater dunes.

34

He shook his head to clear it. 'They'll be looking for us,' he said, echoing his colleague. 'They'll find us,' but he wasn't convinced, and neither, he knew, was Taylor.

Taylor had fallen silent.

'Rick? Still with me?' Adkins mumbled.

'Still here,' Taylor said. 'What the hell did they pump into us?' There was a pause. 'I could sure as shit use a drink.'

'Don't go there.'

Taylor croaked out a laugh. 'Don't worry – state I'm in, water would do nicely.'

It'd been – how long? – since they'd last been given anything; a couple of crusts of pitta bread and two plastic beakers of warm cola. And cola is no thirst-quencher, no matter what they tell you. 'If they want to keep us alive, they'll bring us something.'

'And if they don't?'

Brad Adkins's eyes flinched then as the dark cell was flooded with cold light from the lamps bolted into the ceiling. Soon afterwards, he knew, he would hear the footsteps.

He huddled protectively in his corner. He'd grown used to the filth, but he was still bewildered.

'Oh Christ, here they come,' growled Taylor, and Adkins saw that his reaction was different. Taylor was bracing himself.

6

Laura Graves sat uncomfortably across the desk from Sir Richard Hudson in his airy office two floors above Room 55.

'I called you in because I felt I owed you an explanation,' he began.

'If it's about the job –'

He looked at her seriously. 'I know you're disappointed, but this business landed on our desk in the middle of restructuring.'

'I understand, sir. Marlow has far more field-work experience.'

'But not your specific language expertise. The missing scientists have to be located, and that's where you're crucial. The job has top-level priority. And Jack is the man to lead an investigation like this.'

'Which is why you pulled him back from Paris.'

'I know you were expecting to take charge of the new Section 15 –'

'It was as good as damned well promised me.'

'– but, in our business, expediency is all. Later on, who knows? Situations change.'

Graves didn't answer that.

Hudson leaned forward. 'How much do you know about Marlow?'

'He and Lopez are old friends, I know that much.'

'I suppose you could call them that. Have you spoken to Lopez?'

'No.'

'That surprises me, considering you arrived before Jack.'

'I'm more of a newcomer than he is.'

'But you've been in this game almost as long.' Hudson leaned back. 'What do you think of him?'

She spread her hands, not knowing how to answer, then decided to fall back on a safe 'It's really too early to say.'

Hudson laughed briefly. 'You don't mean to tell me you haven't checked him out.'

'His files are restricted.'

'Tell me what you know.'

Graves didn't have much room for manoeuvre. In fact, in the short space of time since she'd met him, she'd thought long and hard about her new chief.

The research she'd been able to do was limited. She'd pulled a file which told her that Marlow was born in London. Now in his late thirties, he'd been educated at Winchester and the Sorbonne, where he'd read Archaeology and Anthropology.

The file also told her that he'd looked set for a career as an archaeologist, but something (not specified) made him change horses, and in a move which indicated to Graves an early recruitment to INTERSEC, he'd spent a year on the foreign desk of the *Guardian* before moving to *Time* and thence to a job with CNN. Cover jobs, in other words.

Just over ten years ago he had been in London, a field operative at INTERSEC's bureau there. Five years later, he transferred to Paris, a posting Graves envied. Like most people who'd never lived there, she equated Paris with romance and excitement.

'But you know all this,' she said to Hudson when she'd run through this information for him. 'Why ask me?'

'I wanted to hear how you described him.'

'Why?'

'Women are susceptible to him.'

Graves laughed scornfully. 'For God's sake!'

'Not that he's one to take advantage of that. In fact – certainly lately – he's been quite impervious.' Hudson looked roguish. 'I think Cupid's dart gave him a bad sting not long ago and he's retired from the lists. He used to be quite susceptible to women, too.'

'Why are you telling me this?'

Hudson shrugged. 'No reason. But there is one thing you could do for me.'

'Yes?'

'Just keep a sisterly eye on him for me, would you?' He looked at his watch. 'Now, you'd better get on. I've asked Marlow for an end-of-day report . . . unless you can give me a preview?' He raised an eyebrow a fraction.

'The only way to trace these people is to find out what they were after. But the gist is that it was a simple dig.'

'The Dandolo Project.'

'Absolutely. Marlow's got all the information available from the universities the three archaeologists work for – Yale and Venice. The two Yale boys are Dr Bradley Adkins and Dr Richard Taylor; the Venice academic is called Su-Lin de Montferrat, a Chinese-Italian.'

'And –?'

'Dandolo was doge of Venice, but he died in Constantinople in 1205. The archaeologists had discovered his burial site and were researching it.' She paused. 'Marlow will fill you in later. That's all I have.'

'Nothing special they were looking for then?'

'Nothing to show that yet.' She looked at him. 'But there must have been. Otherwise, why give this to us?'

'And why were they taken? This isn't some ad hoc terrorist kidnapping.'

'Too clinical?'

'Precisely.'

Hudson made a tent of his fingers. 'So it boils down to this: find out what they were looking for, and that tells us who snatched them. And be quick. We're keeping the Press away from this, but the families are beginning to ask questions. Understandably.'

'Shouldn't we make tracing the archaeologists top priority?'

Hudson swivelled his chair round to the window and gazed out over leaves still clinging listlessly to the trees in Central Park. The day had become as grey as a prison.

'There's interest in what they were looking for,' he said. 'And these days, it's sometimes hard to define what one's priorities are.'

He swivelled back, reached for a cigar, and lit it. 'You'd better be getting back downstairs,' he continued. 'And don't forget the little favour I've asked you.'

Graves made her way back to the elevators unsure whether she'd been given an order or not. But she felt less bad now about being passed over for Marlow. Slightly.

She thought again about the information she'd been able to glean on him. He certainly wasn't the easiest guy to read. Physically, not bad, she had to admit. Lanky, wore good clothes, carelessly green eyes, sad-looking, veiled, but buried humour there, if it ever got a chance to get out. Looked a little older than he was, but no doubt of a muscular, fit body. And, though she hated to admit it, he was sexy.

No details of his private life at all. Pity.

And no time to think about that now.

She punched in the code to Room 55 and entered quietly. The two men were at the other end of the room, backs turned, talking in low voices. She caught the tail-end of a conversation, and felt like she was snooping already.

'You're right,' Marlow was saying. 'It's a lesson I should have got by heart.'

Lopez looked sympathetic. 'But you've put that in the past.'

'It's still with me, like shrapnel. But as far as I'm concerned, the bitch is dead. And let's shut up about it. We're wasting time.'

Then he saw Graves and his expression changed. 'You're late,' he said, but he wasn't unfriendly. 'Where've you been?'

'Sorry' was all she said. To her relief, he seemed to choose not to pursue it. But he looked at her enigmatically and she wondered if he knew.

'What've I missed?' she went on hastily.

Marlow was already lifting a folder from his desk. 'This is it,' he said. 'Just come in. First section.'

He tapped the folder. 'The starting point here is our

three archaeologists. Standard missing persons in suspicious circumstances. Since the missing persons are foreign nationals, and two of them are Americans, there's more than the usual fuss,' he continued. 'It isn't just that they've vanished without a trace, but everything connected with them has as well. We're waiting on a report from the Turks who are handling it at the Istanbul end. Chase it up.'

'Do we know what they were on to?'

'Find that out and we find them.' His words, she thought, echoed Hudson's. 'Maybe.'

'I'll leave you,' said Lopez. 'I've got something to tie up. Tail end of a case. Just needs a last tweak.'

'Make it fast.'

Lopez disappeared into his lab as Graves picked up a black phone and dialled a number.

It took Marlow five minutes to digest the other documents in the folder. Background stuff.

The first was a printout of a *New York Times* article from 2001:

Last week, Pope John-Paul II visited Greece – the first pope to do so in nearly 1,300 years. In Athens he had a private 30-minute meeting with Archbishop Christodoulos, head of the Eastern Orthodox Church. When they emerged from the meeting the two prelates were stony-faced as the Greek archbishop read out a list of the 'thirteen offences' committed by the Roman Catholic Church against the Eastern Orthodox Church since the Great Schism of 1054 which divided the Church for the first time into its Eastern and Western branches. Among the thirteen offences, Archbishop Christodoulos made particular mention of the pillaging and destruction of Constantinople (modern-day Istanbul) by the crusading armies of the Fourth Crusade, inspired by Pope Innocent III and led by Count Baldwin of Flanders, Marquess Boniface of Montferrat and Doge Enrico Dandolo of Venice, in 1204, and bemoaned the lack of any apology for it from the Roman Catholic Church. He said: 'Until now, there has not been heard a single request for pardon for the maniacal Crusaders of the 13th century.'

Pope John-Paul responded by saying, 'For the occasions, past and present, when sons and daughters of the Catholic Church have sinned by action or omission against their Orthodox brothers and sisters, may the Lord grant us forgiveness.'

Archbishop Christodoulos immediately applauded this statement, and the pope added his opinion that the sacking of Constantinople was a source of 'profound regret' for Catholics.

Later, the pope and the archbishop met again at a place where Saint Paul had once preached to Athenian Christians. Here, they issued a common declaration, saying: 'We will do everything in our power to ensure that the Christian roots of Europe, and its Christian soul, may be preserved. We condemn all recourse to violence, proselytism, and fanaticism in the name of religion.'

The two leaders then said the Lord's Prayer together, an act which broke an Orthodox interdiction against praying with Catholics.

The next sheet contained a quotation Marlow recognized, from near the end of the New Testament, concerning the fall of Babylon. The sheet was a high-scan photocopy of a manuscript, written in a shaky but educated hand. There was a signature at the bottom, which started with a boldly penned 'L', followed by what looked like an 'e' and a 'p', but the rest of the name was indistinct. A typescript of the text accompanied it, and told him that the quotation was from the Book of Revelation:

And the kings of the earth, who committed fornication and were wanton with her, will weep and wail over her when they see the smoke of her burning; they will stand far off, in fear of her torment, and say,
'Alas! Alas! Thou great city,
Thou mighty city, Babylon!
In one hour has thy judgement come.'
And the merchants of the earth weep and mourn for her, since no one buys their cargo any more, cargo of gold, silver, jewels and pearls, fine linen, purple, silk and scarlet, all kinds of scented wood, all articles of ivory, all articles of costly wood, bronze, iron and marble, cinnamon, spice, incense, myrrh, frankincense, wine, oil, fine flour and wheat, cattle and sheep, horses and chariots, and slaves, that is, human souls.
'The fruit for which thy soul longed has gone from thee, and all thy dainties and thy splendour are lost to thee, never to be found again!'
The merchants of these wares, who gained wealth from her, will stand far off, in fear of her torment, weeping and mourning aloud,
'Alas, alas, for the great city that was clothed in fine linen, in purple and scarlet, bedecked with gold, with jewels, and with pearls! In one hour, all this wealth has been laid waste.'
And all the shipmasters and seafaring men, sailors and

all whose trade is on the sea, stood far off and cried as they saw the smoke of her burning,

'What city was like the great city?'

And they threw dust on their heads, as they wept, and mourned, crying out,

'Alas, alas for the great city, where all who had ships at sea grew rich by her wealth! In one hour she has been laid waste.'

Rejoice over her, O heaven, O saints and apostles and prophets, for God has given judgement for you against her!

Marlow glanced across at Graves, still on the telephone, and read on. Whatever all this was about the destruction of Babylon, it was linked to the disappearances, and the Dandolo Project. The photocopy was of a parchment dating from a good eight hundred years ago – he didn't need Laura to confirm that.

He knew who had copied it out, all those centuries ago. But why?

7

Graves watched Marlow as she waited on the phone and he read.

He was about 1.85m, she reckoned. He looked as if he worked out, but that was unsurprising in an INTERSEC field officer. His body movements were lithe and keen – in a word, she thought again, sexy.

The face was more interesting than handsome, but attractive. Regular features – straight nose, clean-shaven, chin firm but not chiselled. Dark hair. Guarded eyes, as she'd already noted; but it was there that the attractiveness lay.

There was also something restless in his attitude as he sat there, brow slightly furrowed, reading with swift concentration.

She hoped they'd work well together. She was aware she was Sir Richard's appointment, not his.

She listened to the voice at the other end of the phone for a few seconds then hung up. Marlow was nearing the end of the file on his lap. From the lab came muted, metallic sounds.

Marlow flipped the folder shut and glanced at her. She walked over to him.

'Anything?' he asked her.

'On its way.'

He handed her what he'd been reading. 'Take a look at the biblical stuff.'

She read it quickly.

'It's from a document the archaeologists turned up in the State Archives in Istanbul. Copied out by a man called Leporo, who had something to do with the doge of Venice. Quite why, since he would have had easy access to a Bible, we've no idea.'

'Obviously important to him.'

'The description isn't far off what the Crusaders did to Constantinople,' said Marlow.

'Doge Dandolo was one hell of a guy.'

'Dandolo was already an old man, and – some say – blind.'

'How old?'

'For those days, almost supernaturally old. We don't know exactly, but he was probably around ninety-five.'

'Not possible!'

'Perfectly possible.'

'But if he was doge of Venice, what was he doing getting involved in a Crusade? I thought the Venetians put trade and commerce well above war?'

'And so he did. That's why he got involved. Constantinople at the time was a big trade rival to Venice.'

'But Constantinople was a Christian city,' she said.

'Nothing gets in the way of business.'

Graves looked at him as he smiled sardonically. 'You're not going to tell me that he diverted the Crusaders to Constantinople?'

'That's exactly what he did,' he replied.

'How?'

'That's easy, at least on the face of it. The Crusaders were mainly French and German. Small nobility and

farming stock, most of them. They were country bump-
kins by the standards of Venetians – and Greeks, for that
matter. They were far more sophisticated. The Crusaders
ordered a fleet from the Venetians because their plan was
to sail to Egypt and attack the Holy Land from the south.'

'Were they sailors?'

'No – but the Venetians were. What the Crusaders
didn't know was that Venice had just concluded a peace
agreement with Egypt, which supplied them with grain,
and a trade route to the East. Alexandria was to be a big
centre of commerce.'

'But Egypt was already a Muslim country.'

'What did I just say about business?' said Marlow.
'Egypt was weak at the time, there'd been a civil war and
the Nile had failed to flood for five years in a row, so food
was scarce. The Egyptians didn't want a crusading army
marching through their country. Dandolo was prepared
to guarantee that that wouldn't happen, in exchange for
the advantages I've just mentioned.'

'I still don't see how –'

'Dandolo came from one of the oldest Venetian families – one of the ones which founded the city. He was
already an old man when he was elected doge – in 1193.
His one *overriding* ambition was to make Venice controller
of European commerce. He wanted a monopoly. To that
end, he needed to knock out any trade rivals, and he'd
stop at nothing to do it. But apart from that' – Marlow's
voice darkened –'he had other ambitions . . .' He turned
to the newspaper report he'd been reading. 'Well, he succeeded. "Pillaging and destruction" . . . "Maniacal
Crusaders" . . .'

'You mean –'

'You should read some of the reports of the people of Constantinople who were writing at the time,' Marlow went on. 'There was one guy, Nicetas Choniates, who was a senior official there. He wrote a whole history of the siege of the city, and the sack of it which followed. The Crusaders burned down his library, along with others. Countless classics of antiquity must have been lost to us for ever. But not only that, they melted down or smashed up priceless statues and monuments, just to turn it all into ready money. They ran amok, in other words. Only the Venetians had the sense to hang on to some of the good stuff to ship back home as prizes. Look at the horses on St Mark's in Venice. They're just one of the trophies looted from Constantinople in 1204. And there were religious relics too – the Catholic priests who'd gone along with the Crusaders weren't slow to snap up everything they could find. There are churches all over Europe today which display stuff – pieces of the True Cross, heads and limbs of saints, that kind of thing – which all came from the looting of Constantinople – the greatest city in the world at the time.'

'I remember something about that,' said Graves. 'Louis IX of France bought the Crown of Thorns from the Venetians, in 1239, I think. He spent half the country's GDP on it – 135,000 livres – and built the Ste-Chapelle to put it in.'

'So what were the archaeologists looking for? What had they found?'

'I think I read something in the background study about Nicetas,' said Graves, catching some of Marlow's urgency as she skimmed through notes of her own. 'Here it is: *They have spared neither the living nor the dead. They have insulted God; they have outraged his servants; they have exhausted every variety of sin.* That takes some beating.'

'They did a thorough job. Even two hundred and fifty years later, when the Ottomans under Sultan Mehmet II finally took the city, it was still a kind of ghost of its former self. Mehmet was only twenty-one years old when he rode into Constantinople, and its ruin moved him to quote an old Persian poet: *Now the spider weaves the curtains in the palace of the Caesars. Now the owl calls the watches in the towers of Afrasiab.'*

'But what has all this to do with us? And what's the connection with these missing archaeologists?' asked Graves.

'That's what we've got to find out. But I told you – Dandolo was after something more.'

'World domination? Again?' Her tone was bordering on sarcastic.

'Why not? He was one of the first to see beyond Europe and Asia. He knew – somehow – that the world was bigger than that.'

Graves paused, not able to believe it. 'You mean the Americas? But he lived nearly three hundred years before Columbus!'

'It's exactly what I mean.'

She shook her head. 'But where are you going with this? You haven't answered my question about how he diverted the Crusade.'

'That's crucial. Dandolo must have had a means – a surefire means – of holding on to all the power he wanted, and the *way to get it*.'

'Is that what —?'

'How do you think he managed to control and divert a whole crusading army to suit his purposes? It wasn't just economic leverage. So — *what power did he have over them?*'

'So what now?'

'Get Leon in here. I don't care if he's finished or not.'

8

'Let's go over what we've got,' Marlow said fifteen minutes later. 'Laura?'

'Taylor and Adkins are both married men in their forties, and research fellows at Yale University. They started their research in Venice back in 2004 – the year of the eight hundredth anniversary of the Fourth Crusade. The project was joint-funded by Yale and Venice universities. Su-Lin de Montferrat is the 33-year-old daughter of an Italian father and a Chinese mother who'd been resident in Genoa for years, but who died within days of each other five years ago. We need more on Su-Lin, but she'd been a senior research student at the time she was co-opted from research in Venice to the Dandolo Project. With a bursary from MAXPHIL – which was also the main sponsor of the dig.'

'And MAXPHIL is the philanthropic arm of MAX-TEL.'

They all knew about MAXTEL. Everyone did. MAX-TEL was a household name.

'The guy who runs it is Rolf Adler. He was born in Cottbus, in what was East Germany, the German Democratic Republic, in 1959,' said Marlow, scanning through a secure file on his terminal.

'Tough town,' remarked Lopez, remembering a rare field trip he'd made there years ago. 'Remember?'

'Don't live in the past, my friend,' said Marlow, but he remembered too. That time, Lopez had saved his life. He turned from the computer and rapidly went on, not needing to refer to notes. 'MAXTEL was founded in 1991, so Adler didn't waste any time after Germany was reunited. He got some capital together and started selling reconditioned TV and radio equipment, then went into cars, Mercs and BMWs mainly, then branched into the media. Started a small local radio station in 1992, but Cottbus isn't that far south of Berlin, so he had access to a biggish audience – if anyone was interested in what he was pumping out.'

'What was he pumping out?' asked Graves.

'Western pop, pretty old stuff, and some soft-political right-wing material – nothing Nazi, but some people thought there might be undertones. That's when the first files on MAXTEL were opened.'

'Where'd he get his money?' asked Graves.

Marlow shrugged. 'Basket of backers. Some pointers to the Russian mafia. Kept its head down when Gorbachev was in power, but grew a little bolder under Yeltsin. The rest is history.'

'Any proven connection?' Lopez pursued.

Marlow shrugged again. 'Adler was already wealthy by the mid-nineties, and he was one of the first East Germans to put investment feelers out towards the West. He was never one of the true in-crowd, but no one could accuse him of not being pushy.'

'I remember working on this,' said Graves. 'He went from strength to strength to strength but kept his sheet clean. By the end of the nineties the papers here were calling him the Murdoch of the East.'

Marlow nodded. 'One or two of his competitors sold out to him without any argument, even when their own market share was strong. But there's nothing definite. Except that their acquiescence was sudden – dramatic, even. Boris Isarov of Global Technology was flying high when Adler shot him down. Global started to lose ground, senior executives peeled off – all of them, in fact, except one, Vladimir Bilinski, Isarov's right-hand man and a hard nut, ex-KGB colonel, all that.'

'What happened to him?' asked Lopez. 'I remember the name.'

'He went off to the Moscow office in his Volvo with his chauffeur and his bodyguard one morning as usual, after kissing his wife and kids goodbye, and that was it. None of them was heard of again. The Russian and the German police looked into it, not very hard. Isarov launched an investigation himself. Whether he found anything out, nobody knows. But soon afterwards his own family was killed in a fire at his house. Wife and four children, oldest twelve, youngest two. Isarov sold his majority share in Global to MAXTEL soon afterwards and went into retirement.'

Graves and Lopez exchanged a look.

'I know what you're thinking, but don't forget Eastern Europe and Russia in the 1990s were like the Wild West. Adler wasn't the only guy to play dirty. And there is nothing at all to link him to any of this. Isarov and Adler were close friends, and remained so. He went to the Isarov family funeral, there were photos on the front pages of *Isvestia* and *Die Welt* that spring showing him comforting Isarov, and he invited Isarov to his villa near St-Tropez that summer. The autumn following the accident, Adler paid generously for his interest in Global.'

'Where was Adler when the tragedy struck?'

'In Dallas, closing a deal for a radio station there.' Marlow looked back at the screen. 'Later on, he dabbled in derivatives and credit default swaps, collateralized debt obligations, special-purpose vehicles, and all that sort of banking finagling, even sub-primes, but managed to steer clear of trouble when the financial balloon went up in 2008. He got rich and he stayed rich, and now he controls a network of TV and radio stations across the globe, as well as a clutch of newspapers, mainly here in the States, but he's also got a toehold in India and China.'

Marlow scrolled rapidly down a page. 'Nowadays, he's one of the good guys. A Maecenas where charities are concerned, especially in Africa, where he's got a lot of goodwill; and he's endowed university chairs all over the place, from Nigeria to Nebraska. Backing research undertakings like the Dandolo Project is a hobby of his. And he leads a simple life. Widowed – his wife died young – never remarried. Lives in Lausanne, and in the grounds, in a glass case, is an East German Trabant car, the first thing he treated himself to when he began his ascent. He's had the thing gold-plated. He doesn't spend much time in Switzerland – just enough to secure residency requirements.' He sat back. 'That's it, but if we're going to take a closer look at him, we need more on his background.'

'I can help,' said Graves.

'Go on.'

Graves scanned her own screen. 'I've got this much. His father was a technician at the Boxberg power station. Mother was a housewife, did some cleaning for a local politician's family. Adler had an older brother, who died aged seventeen in some kind of hunting accident, in 1974. Adler went to a local school, then got a scholarship to Humboldt University in Berlin. He read physics, switched to economics.'

'Any more on his business training?' asked Marlow.

'Nothing formal. I think he saw his opportunities when the Wall came down, and went for it.'

'He was thirty-ish then. Late starter by the standards of a lot of the new boys.'

'He spent 1982 to 1988 teaching in a *Fachhochschule* back in Cottbus. Travelled in the East a lot after his wife died. No children.'

'So, what led him to take an interest in the Dandolo Project specifically?' said Marlow.

'It's just one of several, on the face of it.' Graves looked at the onscreen notes. 'MAXPHIL is involved in investigating ways of salvaging the damage done to Iraq's cultural heritage, for example, and another venture has to do with a research programme into the history of the origins of mathematics and astronomy. Both university-run projects. The principal one for the Iraq undertaking is Houston, the other is Humboldt, his old *alma mater*.'

'All very respectable.'

'Yes,' said Graves evenly, locking the file she'd opened and snapping it off. She took her glasses from her nose, and pinched the bridge.

The blue telephone rang. Marlow spoke briefly then listened, his expression changing as he did so.

'So soon?' he said. 'But I haven't had time to brief them fully –'

The voice at the other end interrupted him.

'I see,' he said. 'OK.' He listened some more, his expression changing again, to one of incredulous surprise. 'Yes, of course. At once.'

He put the phone down carefully and stood up before speaking. 'That, it goes without saying, was Sir Richard.'

'What's he handing down from the mountain now?' asked Lopez.

Marlow looked at Graves. 'You and I are flying to Istanbul tomorrow. We've a meeting with Detective-Major Haki, Turkish security service. He's handling the disappearance that end.'

'What a way to start your job,' grinned Lopez. 'No such luck for me, I gather.'

'You know you hate travelling,' said Marlow. 'You've got to clear your decks completely for anything we send you for analysis. Premier urgency.'

'What've they found?'

'They'll give us the details when we get there, but there's a coded email coming through now,' he replied. 'But right now, Hudson wants me in his office. He has a visitor who's keen to meet me.'

'And that is?'

'Rolf Adler.'

9

Marlow filled Graves in on the meeting with Adler on the way to the airport.

'Why was he there?'

'God knows how much influence he has to have reached us in the first place,' replied Marlow, 'but he knew all about the archaeologists, and offered his services in helping to locate them. Hudson was non-committal, but it's obvious that Adler's got some pull.'

'What's he like?'

Marlow shrugged. 'He's got that patina the very rich have: a kind of sheen, a kind of confidence other people just don't possess. Looks younger than he is, obviously works out a bit. Grey hair, hooded eyes. Too much bling, but all of it's there to make its point – cufflinks, rings, tie-pin, watch – all signalling that his corner shops are Asprey's, Cartier and Tiffany's.'

'But you didn't pick anything up from him?'

'Sixth sense, you mean? No.'

'Anything to bring us closer to the archaeologists?'

Marlow didn't know Graves yet, and one instinct which was strong in him, especially now, was never to show his hand to anyone until he was sure of them. He knew his own weaknesses and he also knew how, even with his guard up, they could still take him by surprise. There'd been times when he'd thought he'd give up, hand in his resignation, but each time he'd hesitated, and now his career had taken him beyond that option, and what he'd been deluded enough to believe was the love of his life had gone. What was left to him – all that was left – was his work. And a chance to redeem himself.

Graves went on. 'How does he want to help?'

'How do you think? By throwing money at the problem.'

'But he'd want to know what we know too?'

'Didn't seem to concern him.'

'Does that concern you?'

'What do you think?' said Marlow, with a slight smile. He was sitting close to her in the car, and Graves felt the warmth of his thigh along hers. She was wondering if that was intentional or not when he shifted slightly in his seat, and moved away.

'Do you think they're still in Istanbul? Adkins and his friends?'

'I doubt it,' he replied, still smiling that faint smile.

Istanbul was dark and rainy. Streetlights dazzled, along with the lights from dozens of tiny shops, filled with everything from coffee pots to carpets – from simple kelims to ornate Persian silk rugs selling at $50,000 apiece. Everything doubled itself in reflections in the glossy, rain-slicked tarmac and cobblestones. The area in and around the grand bazaar of Kapari Carsi glittered red and gold.

They checked into the hotel near Sultan Ahmet Square, and made their way west across the European side of the city in a yellow Hyundai taxi, after the usual debilitating argument with the driver about the fare. The impression they'd got of the Grand Bazaar had been fleeting.

Driving at the usual breakneck speed of the Istanbul cabbie, they sped through the Sehzadebasi district, and took a right up Kimyagar Dervis and Vezneciler, passing university buildings, turning left before they got as far as City Hall, to reach an unassuming street just north of the Laleli Mosque.

Letting their driver drop them not far from the address they'd been given, and making sure he'd driven off, muttering darkly for their benefit about the size of his tip, they walked back through the fine rain to a building with a plain façade and a scattering of brass plates by its forbidding street door to indicate the professions of the occupants. They sheltered under the entrance awning. A row of bell-pushes on one door-jamb were identified by numbers only. Graves pressed number five.

It didn't take long for the buzzer to click the door open, but Marlow looked up and down the empty street while they were waiting. Just to make sure. But there was nothing to indicate that they weren't alone out there in what had now become freezing drizzle.

A young man with a black moustache stood in the vestibule. He was dressed in the international secret service uniform – dark suit, white shirt, dark tie – and had the kind of features – regular, unexceptional that you'd immediately forget. It had occasionally crossed Graves's mind that a lot of her colleagues might have been recruited on the basis of such looks, so perfect were they for the job.

He greeted them gravely and led the way along a dimly

lit corridor to a door at which he knocked softly before opening it immediately and gesturing them to enter. Then he melted away.

The room they found themselves in was large and bright, and a chaos of untidiness. The books that lined most of one wall were in disarray, many spilling out on to the floor, others, mingled with buff folders, tottering in uncertain piles on the fine Isfahan carpet, which they half smothered. The other walls were dotted with a collage of maps, graphs, children's drawings and one or two reproductions of dark Rembrandt portraits. A table bore an old Dell computer, evidently not often in use and half buried by more paperwork. An ornate desk stood in front of the tall windows. A closed MacBook Air perched precariously on one corner, in danger of being shoved to the floor by another Manhattan of what looked like ledgers but might have been law books.

The man behind the desk rose to greet them. He didn't look unlike the middle-aged Rembrandt himself. He was clean-shaven, with a plump face, and a body to match. His nose was bulbous and his greying hair wispy and unruly. The eyes were small, grey and shrewd, and his expression a mixture of humour and sadness – the face of a man who'd survived a lot by taking stuff on the chin, but never letting anything floor him. A man, thought Marlow, whose company you'd probably enjoy but whom you'd never take anything other than seriously.

'Welcome!' he said, in English as he bustled round the desk to shake hands with Marlow, plant discreet kisses on Graves's cheeks, and introduce himself. 'Have they offered you tea? No? I'll see to it.'

But he didn't. He hastened instead to clear more mountains of books from two gilt armchairs, and made a little clearing around them so that Marlow and Graves could sit down. 'I should have done this earlier – it's not as if I didn't know you were coming, after all . . .' He pattered on, retrieving his own seat and facing them, elbows on the desk and fingers pointed together at the tips. 'Have a good flight?'

They thanked him.

'Good, good. Taxi OK? I'd have sent an official car for you, but we don't like to draw attention to ourselves in this department,' continued Detective-Major Cemil Haki. 'But have no fear – the taxi was one of ours. And the driver. Did you guess?'

He laughed at their silence. 'Orhan is one of our best couriers. He loves to play the cabbie. A little too authentically sometimes. But the safety of our guests is always paramount in his mind.'

'That's reassuring,' said Graves.

'And we keep our counsel. In all messages to the outside world from this department, in fact, we like to present ourselves as simple policemen. You'll understand, won't you? Trust is such a rare commodity that's it's always a shame to waste it.' His tone turned briefly regretful.

Marlow was looking at a framed photograph on the wall behind the detective-major, between the two windows, and the one thing on the walls that hung straight as a die on its hook. It was maybe seventy years old, and showed a slim, thin-lipped, distinguished-looking man in an immaculate light-coloured suit, a cigarette in a holder dangling from elegant fingers.

The detective-major followed his gaze. 'Recognize him?' he asked.

Marlow shook his head. 'But he looks familiar . . . '

'It's my great-great-grand-uncle, the famous Colonel – later General – Haki.' The detective-major smiled. 'I don't take after him. Except perhaps in my line of work.' He paused before going on. 'He was involved with the British a couple of times at least – there was a famous business involving a gangster called Dimitrios at the end of the thirties, and in 1940 a British engineer called Graham got his fingers burned tangling with some German agents – the Germans always like to meddle in Turkey, you know; it was almost a kind of unofficial colony for them, and of course they hated the Russians, who were also trying to put their oar in . . .' He trailed off, letting the faint suggestiveness in his tone hang in the air. 'Asia Minor, the Cradle of Civilization, the Sick Man of Europe – all that kind of thing.'

'I knew your name was familiar,' said Marlow.

'I thought you might know it.'

Haki became businesslike, sweeping the pile of ledgers away so brusquely that it collapsed – an event he ignored – and drawing the pencil-slim laptop to the centre of his desk. He flipped it open and busied himself with its keys and trackpad for a few moments.

He grunted in satisfaction then looked up, the glow of the screen giving his face a slightly sinister illumination. 'We have found no trace of them yet,' he said.

'Have you got *anything*?' asked Graves, ignoring a warning look from Marlow.

'We would not have invited you into our inner sanctum

for nothing,' replied Haki, his own voice remaining politely neutral.

'Tell us what you know,' said Marlow. 'What were they after? We have to find them.'

10

'As you know,' the detective-major said, 'our friends were investigating the burial place of the Venetian leader Enrico Dandolo.' He gestured them to look at a picture he had summoned to the Mac's screen. 'This is his monument in the great basilica of Hagia Sofia, only a short bus ride east of where we are sitting. The building is almost as old as Christianity itself, and it was a church until we Muslims took over this city in 1453, when it became a mosque. Four hundred years later it changed its nature again, and became a museum. But its original function as a place of worship – the house of God, of Allah – still sanctifies it in the eyes of many.'

'Its being a cathedral didn't stop Dandolo from desecrating it,' observed Graves.

'Ah, the fury of those Crusaders!'

'So why is there a memorial to him there?'

'For many years it was thought to mark his tomb; but it is in fact an embellishment of the nineteenth century.'

They looked at the grey marble stone, set into the floor of one of the church's galleries and virtually indistinguishable from its surrounding flagstones except for a simple carved border and the incised words: HENRICUS DANDOLO.

'So where is the grave itself?' asked Marlow, as he thought: And why is it so important? Why have the Turks involved their secret police in a missing persons enquiry?

'Apparently a mystery,' replied Haki. 'Until your archaeologists made their discovery. It seems they were the first
to find it. At any rate, there's no record of anyone else
having made the discovery, though there's some evidence
to suggest that German archaeologists were sniffing
around the site early in the twentieth century.' He swept
his hand over the computer's trackpad. 'Here.' He tapped
the screen. 'This is the Church of St Irina. It's not far
from Hagia Sofia, just a little to the north, but it's much
older, founded by the Emperor Constantine himself. This
is one of the oldest Christian buildings in the world. There
was a Roman temple there before. Constantine built a
church on top to make a point.'

'And Adkins and the others found the grave there,' said
Marlow.

'Yes.'

'How did they know where to look?'

The smile died on Haki's face. 'Nobody will know that
precisely until we find them, but we do know that there
were some papers in the city archives in Venice, and it
certainly *looked* as if no one had seen them for centuries.
Whatever the case, those documents must have contained
a clue. It's the only possible explanation. Dandolo made
his mark for his city, and he was extremely old when he
died, so there was bound to be *some* clue – the odd thing is
that it wasn't discovered long ago.' He looked thoughtful.
'Who knows?'

'What did they find?'

Haki shut the computer and leaned back in his chair. 'I
haven't given you any tea yet,' he said, 'and you must be
exhausted.'

'Never mind. Tell us what you can.'

The Turkish agent spread his hands. 'They were on to something, that's for sure, but in view of what's happened to them, it seems they weren't the only ones to know about it, though they thought they were.' He leaned forward, elbows on the desk again, but this time his hands made fists, which he clenched and unclenched, gently but insistently, as he spoke. 'No one knows exactly how old Dandolo was when he died – but, as you know, he was at least ninety-five. A stupendous age for his time.'

'A stupendous age for ours,' said Graves.

'He died here in Constantinople – I mean Istanbul – in 1205. He'd come to power late in life, he was already in his seventies, and he was hungry to use it. Maybe that hunger was what kept him going. As you probably know, he was also blind, or at the very least he had seriously impaired vision. No one knows why, possibly he had an accident or a disease of some kind, but it struck him when he was about sixty, thirty-odd years before the Fourth Crusade, and it seems to have struck him – here.'

'In this city?' asked Marlow.

'In this city.'

'What happened?' asked Graves.

'We don't know. But a standard punishment for serious crime in the Byzantine empire was – blinding. They took a magnifying glass and burned out the eyes, using the light of the sun, just as a boy burns holes in paper.'

'My God,' said Graves.

'As you say,' replied Haki. 'Perhaps the public executioner who was charged with the task botched the job and left the future doge of Venice with some vision left. I think he can't have been totally blind because he couldn't possibly have achieved what he did if he hadn't been able to see at all. A blind man in his position would have to have had absolute trust in at least a handful of people, and trust, as I have said . . .' Again, his voice trailed off.

'But nobody knows for sure,' said Marlow quietly.

'None of the accounts written at the time agree.' Haki rummaged on the desk until he unearthed a small brass handbell, and rang it. It emitted a tinny sound which didn't seem loud enough to penetrate beyond the room's walls, but apparently it did, for Haki explained: 'I'm ringing for tea. I want some even if you don't. All this talking . . .'

A young man in a white jacket appeared with a brass tray holding a pot with an elegant spout, a smaller one, three tulip-shaped glasses filled with steaming tea, a bowl of brown sugar lumps, and some dried white figs stuffed with walnuts. Haki popped a lump of sugar behind his upper front teeth and took up a glass. He slurped noisily and happily through the sugar. 'Better!' he said.

Marlow followed suit, without the sugar. Graves found the glass too hot to hold comfortably.

'Forgive me,' said Haki. 'You aren't used to it. There are napkins on the tray.' He passed her one.

'Adkins and his team,' he resumed, 'were fascinated by the skill, given his age and disability, which Dandolo showed in manipulating an entire foreign, powerful army and diverting it from its true goal – Jerusalem – to direct it against the main trade rival of Venice – Constantinople – under the thinnest of pretexts. Of course he was helped by our natural propensity for greed and gain, but he was asking them to attack fellow Christians, and they weren't just any bunch of mercenaries – they were a crusading army, which had the blessing and the encouragement of the pope himself. The whole thing had been pretty much Innocent III's idea in the first place anyway.'

'And did he succeed?' asked Graves.

'Yes,' added Marlow. 'At the expense of breaking the back of what remained of the Greek empire.' He thought for a moment. 'And *how* did he do it? That's what Adkins and Co. were trying to find out.'

'I'm not sure that I follow your train of thought,' replied Haki. 'But what I have to say is relevant. What was left behind, as the victors parcelled out the land between them amid much squabbling and more blood-shed, was a fractured and unstable political structure – a kind of pastiche of what it was like in Western Europe at the time, little kingdoms wrangling with each other, nobody turning his back on anybody. It was a kind of vacuum, and – even though it took another two hundred and fifty years – it laid Europe open to us, the Turks. The Muslims.'

'A vacuum which Dandolo was responsible for,' said Marlow.

'Yes. Not, I think, that he would have cared.' Haki sipped his tea. 'Sacrificing the future for short-term gain is nothing new. And in every department of our lives, plenty of us don't mind who else we hurt, as long as we get what we want – whether it's a new business or a new lover. People do what they want to do. No one has any control over what anyone else chooses to do with his or her own life, no matter how much we sometimes like to think we have. Acceptance can be a bitter thing.' He drained his steaming glass and grimaced. 'Already getting cold,' he remarked. 'More?'

They shook their heads.

'Do we know if the archaeologists found anything which answered their questions? Anything in the tomb?' persisted Marlow. 'Their disappearance is linked to something they found in the grave.'

Haki agreed. 'I think they discovered more than they bargained for.'

'What?'

'Dominance of the Mediterranean trade and the routes to the south and east wasn't all Dandolo was after,' said the detective-major. 'I need to do just a little more digging myself, but I'll show you tomorrow. And the rest of the story can be explained better when you see for yourselves what we've got.' He looked at his watch. 'But not tonight. I have preparations to make, and other business to attend to before I wend my weary way home to my wife and family.' He raised a hand to silence their objections. 'Please. You are – as I think you say – on my turf now, and you must allow me to be the best judge of how we proceed. We will need hours tomorrow, and even people like us cannot function efficiently without rest. I'll send you a mail which will be on your laptops by the time you return to your hotel. I hope you left them in the safe there if you didn't bring them with you. This can be a very light-fingered city. Yes? Good.' He rang the bell again and the first discreet young man immediately materialized. 'Zafer: organize some transport for these two good people back to the Four Seasons.'

It was a different yellow cab this time – a Toyota – and

a different driver. This one drove steadily and did not speak, nor was any fare discussed. But he kept glancing in the rear-view mirror, and from the expression on his face he saw something he didn't like. He took a couple of turns down side-streets which clearly weren't leading them by any direct route to the hotel, and looked in the mirror again.

'*Boktan*,' he muttered. Without looking at his passengers, he added in English, 'Sit tight.'

It had stopped raining, but the roads were still slick and wet, and the pollution in the air which the rain had caught in falling had made them slippery too. The driver picked up a little speed, then abruptly did a handbrake turn, spinning the car round 180 degrees before steadying it among a fanfare of angry horns from other vehicles and, ramming it into a lower gear, roaring off up Babiali Cadessi in the direction of the Galata Bridge.

But the black van that was following them was fast too. It swung in behind them. There could be no doubt now.

Their driver turned west again on Nuruosmaniye and then south, crisscrossing the network of streets in Emin Sinan and Mimar Hayrettin, tearing down them as the people on the streets scattered and yelled. The van hammered behind them, smashing into a trader's stall in a cascade of fake Rolexes. They continued on, hurtling through streets barely wide enough to take the vehicles, the lights of their pursuer shining into their car as Marlow and Graves hunched down and pulled out their guns.

Marlow manoeuvred himself to look out of the rear window and could see a figure leaning out of the front passenger window holding what looked like an Uzi sub-machine gun, but as he levelled it, the van hit a pothole too deep even for its tyres to take. The big vehicle jolted and the gunman, braced hard against the window frame, snapped like a twig, dropping his weapon. The van swerved on to the pavement, rending its side on the stone-work of the buildings which lined it, then swung round in a skid and came to a halt.

Their cab pulled off down a dark alley which twisted so much it hardly seemed possible for the car to take its turns, but after a while it broadened. The driver rammed the car round a corner into a courtyard, jammed on the brakes, killed the engine and doused the lights.

All three of them sat silently, catching their breath and listening to the uninterrupted roar of the distant traffic. The driver turned in his seat, pistol out, and watched keenly through the rear window. Then the tension left his shoulders.

'Got the *amciklari*,' he said, though his voice was still tight. He looked at them. 'Better get you some other transport. This car's no good now.'

He dug out his mobile phone and punched a key and was soon talking urgently to someone at the other end.

Twenty minutes later, at a quarter past midnight, a dark Mercedes limo dropped Marlow and Graves at the bright and expensive hotel in the busy tourist district, which they'd chosen precisely because of the crowds and the anonymity.

'Drink?' asked Graves, motioning towards the bar. She was feeling shaky, the tiredness had caught up with her, but she was trying to digest what Haki had told them, and to second guess what he had in store for them the next day.

'Rooms first,' said Marlow, keeping the urgency out of his voice. 'Need to check.'

Graves collected their laptops from the concierge's safe and followed him upstairs. They had a suite with bedrooms and bathrooms opening off either side of a large central salon, equipped with all the WiFi and broadband necessary to any tourist or businessman who might stay in this kind of hotel. Graves was about to place the laptops on the coffee table when Marlow stopped her.

'Just a moment,' he said.

She watched as he went into his room, returning with a simple extendable metal tape-measure. On the coffee table, on one of the bedside tables, and on the desk which stood under the windows, with their spectacular view over the Sultanahmet Camii and the Sea of Marmara beyond, a number of casually arranged books and magazines lay. Moving swiftly, Marlow measured the exact distances from the edges and corners of the magazines and books to the edges of the surfaces of the tables. After the first three measurements, he relaxed, but that disappeared after he'd worked on the coffee table. He checked again. Then he re-measured the distances on the desk. He stood back.

'Check your room, Laura,' he told Graves. 'Carefully.'

She did as he asked and returned. 'Nothing missing,' she said.

'Everything as you left it?'

'Ye-es –'

His disquiet was beginning to affect her. She wanted to relax. She cast a glance at the mini-bar. 'What's the matter?'

'The magazines aren't as I left them,' he said. 'A centimetre out of place. We've had visitors. And those guys sure as hell weren't following us just to check we'd be coming back here. Whoever they are, they know about us.'

I 2

Constantinople, Year of Our Lord 1171

Thirty years before the Fourth Crusade attacked the great city of Constantinople, affairs in Venice were not going well.

They were not going well for the Venetians who lived in Constantinople either.

That was why a fleet had been organized in Venice. A war fleet. The doge, Vitale Michele, had divided the city into six districts, the better to raise the taxes needed to pay for it. But where in hell had it all gone wrong? Vitale Michele wondered. They'd had good relations with Constantinople for years. The emperor of the Byzantine Greeks, Manuel, had been westward-leaning and friendly, even when, in the past, his domain had to put up with crusading armies passing through on their way to Jerusalem.

Recently, he'd been getting ambitious. He was reducing the privileges of the twenty thousand Venetian business-men who lived in and around Constantinople and favouring instead their rivals from Amalfi, Genoa and Pisa. And he'd taken a huge chunk of the Dalmatian coast from Hungary. It was worrying.

The crunch had come early in 1171.

The fourth day of February, the Feast of St Isidore,

was always considered an unlucky day for the world. Tradition had it that on that day babies were born without a conscience – people who had no hearts. In the small hours of St Isidore's Day that year, families in the Genoan community near the Golden Horn were awakened by a commotion in their streets.

The Genoans clutched each other in their beds, gathering their children to them. There was thunderous hammering at their gates then the splintering of wood and hinges as doors were staved in. Torn howling from their homes, men, women and children were driven into the streets and hacked down by hooded men, heavily built, much bigger than the average Greek, some on horseback, the majority on foot.

Fires were started and became ferocious conflagrations as the keen breeze from the north encouraged the flames. By dawn, the Genoan community was no more. Just a few buildings and streets remained intact. Most of the district was reduced to ashes.

Manuel I Comnenus, fifty years old and a seasoned ruler, stroked his beard thoughtfully. The thing had been unpleasant but necessary, and it had been a complete success. Even his grand vizier, who, he knew, had his own network of spies, was in ignorance of it. The last piece of the mechanism in his plan to crush those upstart Venetians was in place. Rumours about who was responsible for the atrocity were already in circulation. Meanwhile, nothing had been spared to give help and sympathetic succour to those Genoans who'd survived. Genoa would be grateful. They'd be eating out of his hand.

'They say it was the Venetians who did it,' continued the grand vizier smoothly.

'Well, they've gone too far this time,' replied the emperor.

The grand vizier watched his master's face. There were a lot of Venetians in Constantinople, and to move against them might be – unwise.

Manuel's face was impassive as he continued: 'They've been getting above themselves for too long. This, we cannot tolerate.'

'What do you intend to do?'

'Listen closely.'

It took a little time to prepare, but when the Greek blow fell, it fell heavily. On 12 March Manuel's soldiers moved against all those Venetians who lived within his territories. There was very little destruction this time, and almost no slaughter, but the effect was devastating.

The following day saw a long caravan of Italians, the few possessions they'd been allowed to keep piled on handcarts or carried in bundles, streaming westward out of the Golden Gate. They had no horses with them, nor donkeys; not even oxen.

'Was it wise to expel them without anything?' the grand vizier had wondered.

'Certainly! We have to teach these dogs a lesson,' replied Manuel. 'They can count themselves lucky we didn't kill them.'

'But their homes and all that is in them – their ships, their goods, *everything*?'

'Confiscation is confiscation,' said the emperor.

'Besides, you should be pleased. It'll be a little something to top up your coffers.'

They were watching the stream of refugees from a tall tower above the Gate. One of Manuel's concubines fed him sherbet figs as he looked down on the slowly moving column of people. He sucked the sweetmeats idly. He and the grand vizier shared a common thought: most of those straggling along a hundred feet below them would never reach their home town.

They both knew, too, that Venice would not take such an affront lying down.

'They will come for us,' said the grand vizier.

'Let them. We'll be ready for them.' Manuel Comnenus stroked the hair of the girl who was feeding him. Everything was falling perfectly into place.

13

Venice, the Same Year

'They've done *what?*' snarled Doge Vitale Michele when the news reached him.

His right-hand man and head of special operations, the hawk-eyed sixty-year-old Enrico Dandolo, spread his hands. 'We cannot say we did not see this coming. But we were over-confident.'

'It'll be a disaster for trade. Already the city of Zara has rebelled against us and sided with the Hungarians. And as if losing our principal port on the Dalmatian coast weren't enough, now we face the enmity of the Greeks.'

'We must seek other routes to the East. Egypt –'

'Too far! Too costly! Anyway, they're not even Christians, and now that bastard Saladin's virtually in control down there . . .' The doge lapsed into a brooding silence. Saladin. Not a man to trust. Far too ambitious. Far too intelligent. Wouldn't get *him* to kowtow to anyone. God, he thought, just when everything was going so well – what was the world coming to?

'Then what do you suggest, *Altissima?*' Dandolo's smooth tones interrupted his chain of thought. He pulled himself together and came to the decision his mind had been leading him to all along. Venice would have to crack the whip. Get these dogs back into line. It was then that

Vitale Michele gave orders for a war fleet to be made ready. The Venetians would moan about the extra taxes, but if they could be made to see the long-term benefits, they would acquiesce. He would lead the expedition himself.

'And you'll come with me,' Vitale told his aide. Dandolo was a man he preferred to keep under his eye. Another one who was far too ambitious and intelligent for his own good. But the man was also a master spy. He'd have his uses in the East.

By the autumn, they were ready. The armada sailed out of the lagoon in September but, after a ten-day voyage, anchored well to the south of their goal, at the island of Chios, to prepare themselves for the assault. While there, they had news that Manuel wanted to open negotiations which might – who knows? – lead to some kind of deal being hammered out without the need to fight.

'Don't listen to him' was Dandolo's advice.

'Of course I'll listen to him,' the doge snapped back. 'If we can save ourselves the cost of a war . . .'

'He's playing for time.'

'Even if he were, he'd be no match for us. There's no one in the world who can defeat Venice at sea.'

Dandolo demurred, and suggested that at least a mission might be useful – a secret mission, of course – to the Kingdom of Jerusalem. The Christians had been in control of the Holy Land for nearly a hundred years and, small though their resources were, it might be worth getting the kingdom on the side of Venice.

That made sense to the doge, and Vitale gave his permission, but not without extracting an undertaking from his underling to return, no matter what, the moment he was summoned. Dandolo took three ships and sailed south and east on the very same day the Venetian ambassadors sailed north to meet the Greek leaders at Constantinople. Meanwhile, the Venetian fleet at Chios lay up, and waited.

14

Istanbul, the Present

'There've been bomb attacks here very recently, and who knows when there will be more?' Major Haki was saying. 'But we can find nothing so far to link this case to Islamist terrorists. After all, there have been bomb attacks all over the world now; most major capitals and towns have experienced something of the kind. But this ... this is somehow different.'

'You're telling me you think the men who followed us, searched the hotel, weren't terrorists,' said Graves, kicking herself immediately for being over eager. She remembered what Hudson had told her: too clinical for terrorists.

'Does it look like that to you, Laura?' said Marlow, impatiently.

'We are not ruling it out,' said Haki. 'We are ruling nothing out. But we need to be certain of what we've got to go on before we go in that direction. There has been no announcement from any recognized group, no ransom demand, no tapes on YouTube, nothing.'

'So what *have* you got?' said Marlow.

'We found the van where they'd left it. Bloodstains, but nothing else. They'd taken their gunman with them – injured or dead – but we're working on it.'

They'd already seen the archaeologists' laboratory at

Istanbul University. It was empty – so empty it looked as if it had never been used. Major Haki had left Marlow and Graves to it, and they'd gone over the place with a fine-toothed comb, but there wasn't a fingerprint, a hair, to indicate that the lab had been in constant use a week earlier. They sent what details they had, together with police photos of Dandolo's tomb, back to New York, where Lopez was cutting through whatever bureaucracy it took to reach the right people at Yale and Venice universities to extract the findings the archaeologists had sent before their disappearance.

Now, they were driving to the Pera Palace Hotel in Galata, where Adkins, Taylor and de Montferrat had been staying.

'Don't expect too much here, either,' said Haki, as their car pulled up.

The three rooms were situated side by side along a corridor on the hotel's third floor. They were large doubles and they had been left exactly as they had been found after the disappearance had been reported.

They might as well have been serviced by the hotel after guests had left. The only difference was that the courtesy soaps, shampoos and all the paraphernalia placed in hotel bathrooms worldwide had not been replenished. But there were no half-used or discarded plastic bottles, discarded combs or shower-caps to be found either, and all the towels, and the sheets and pillowcases from the beds, had gone.

'Whoever abducted them had a tidy mind,' said Graves.

'If they were abducted,' said Marlow, as a new thought struck him.

'Why go to all this trouble otherwise?'

Marlow said, 'Why go to all this trouble at all? We know that these people's findings and their computers and whatever was on them have disappeared into thin air. Either their abductors wanted to make sure the trail would be as cold as it possibly could be, or . . .' His voice trailed off.

'Or?'

'Or this is some kind of red herring.'

'Perhaps they were tidy-minded Martians. For all we've got to go on, they might as well have been beamed up in a saucer.'

Marlow looked at her. 'Whoever it was, they've left someone around to keep an eye on us.'

'Haki's men are watching our backs.'

'There's still the visit to our hotel. They thought they were being meticulous there too. But they didn't get anything.'

'They didn't get us. They'll be hanging around until they do.'

'They want to find out what our next move is. And how much we've found out. They must have guessed that our friends would have sent work back to their universities. They wanted to frighten us off. Crude tactics. Gangster tactics.' Marlow thought for a moment. 'They're in a win-win situation.'

'How so?'

'They've covered their tracks perfectly. This looks less and less like a terrorist op. Those people aren't concerned about leaving footprints in the snow.'

'We don't know for sure. There's no fixed MO for these groups.'

'We get what we can here, and go back to base. Fast. We need to find out what Adkins and his friends found, because someone else wants that info badly.'

'Leon should be sending us full breakdowns on the archaeologists' backgrounds any time now.'

They were interrupted by Major Haki. 'If you've finished, my friends,' he said, 'I'll send you back to the Operations Centre. Your colleagues in New York have forwarded new information there.'

'Are you coming with us?'

Haki smiled. 'I have some small details to settle here before I leave. But I will be only, perhaps, fifteen minutes behind you. And I mean that in terms of Anglo-American time, not Turkish time. In other words, when I say fifteen minutes, I mean fifteen minutes.'

In the OC, where Haki had set up in a suite of rooms above his office, Marlow watched Graves open her laptop and consult the secure email file.

'The additional background you requested.'

'Good.'

'Adkins first. There's a better photo too.'

She swivelled the computer round. Marlow looked at a fair-haired, brown-eyed man with a dimple in his chin. A lot of information followed which might or might not matter: Adkins was married with one daughter, long-term domestic situation settled but there'd been the odd affair. Democrat. Not hugely ambitious, but had published widely respected papers, particularly in relation to ancient Mesopotamia.

Marlow picked up on that. 'Mesopotamia. The cradle of civilization,' he said thoughtfully. *Babylon. The first civilization. The Egyptians, the Romans and the Greeks all learned from it. All modern society, in all its aspects, is just a development of what was established in Mesopotamia many millennia ago.* 'Is there a connection there?' he said.

Graves shrugged. 'Could be. It was where Iraq is now. There was a fertile crescent 8,000 years ago, and out of it came pretty much the first of everything: written language, organized religion, urban society, economics, mathematics, art and architecture, structured warfare and, above all, an understanding of astronomy. Mind you, they used that in order to predict the future. The civilization took thousands of years to develop, and power passed from Assyria to Babylon and back during that time; but its roots were in the truly ancient civilization of Sumer. But Mesopotamia lasted the better part of six thousand years. Towards the end, the Chaldeans, who were great astronomers, were making calculations which are virtually unmatched to this day, despite all the advances and technical developments made since.'

'What's Adkins's main field?'

Graves scrolled through, frowning. 'Mathematics and astronomy. Here's a note of one of the papers his reputation's built on. It's about a Babylonian, a Chaldean called Kidinnu, who was active around 325 BC.'

'What about him?'

'He was one of their greatest astronomers. But the paper focuses on one particular discovery he made. He managed to calculate the duration of the solar year with an error factor of only four minutes and 32.65 seconds.'

'Impressive.'

'He was more accurate than the next-best effort, which

85

was made by a Czech astronomer towards the end of the nineteenth century. He's barely been improved on, even today.'

'How did Kidinnu do it? Do we know?'

Graves looked at him. 'We don't. But then, we don't know how the Egyptians illuminated the tunnels inside the pyramids, for example. There's no sign of soot from burning torches, and yet there must have been a light source for them to work.'

'And Kidinnu had no telescopes.'

Graves was serious. 'Yet he managed calculations we can only match with the most powerful radio-telescopes available. The Chaldeans would have been a match for the best astrophysicists of our age. And they lived over two and a half thousand years ago.'

'At the end of a civilization –'

' – which had already been growing for almost six thousand years.'

Marlow looked out of the window at the gleaming modern buildings of Istanbul. He was wondering what an expert on ancient science was doing on a dig concerned with the early Middle Ages. Then he turned back to the computer and scrolled down to the new information on the other two.

He looked at the photograph of Rick Taylor. It showed a handsome man with grey eyes and a neat beard.

'He's also married,' said Graves, looking over his shoulder. 'Scandinavian stock, a couple of years older than Adkins. Three kids, all from his second marriage.'

'And he isn't just an archaeologist either, is he?'

Graves consulted the notes. 'It's interesting, Jack.' It

was the first time she'd used his Christian name – involuntarily – and she glanced at him to see its effect, but read nothing in his face.

She went on. 'He *started* in archaeology and anthropology but switched, and it's an interesting switch. He took his doctorate in astrophysics. He also studied quantum mechanics, looking into the dual particle and wave-like behaviour and interactions of energy and matter.'

'Which tells us what?'

'I don't know.'

'The effect of energy on matter . . .' Marlow looked thoughtful. The ghost of an idea was occurring to him. For the moment he dismissed it as too fantastic. He would come back to it later.

'But, basically, his interests, and many of his papers, concern the physical properties of celestial bodies. He's also done in-depth research on Copernicus and Galileo,' Graves went on.

'Much later than our friend Dandolo,' Marlow pointed out. 'Copernicus was born sometime around 1470, and Galileo a century later.'

Graves nodded. 'But they were involved in the same kind of research and, according to one paper by Taylor there was another guy working on the same theory as theirs – that the earth and the planets orbited the sun – but this guy was one hell of a lot earlier.'

'Go on.'

'His name was Aristarchus of Samos. He lived around 300BC and he had a theory that the earth and the other planets revolved around the sun, rather than everything revolving around the earth.'

'What happened to him?'

'His teachings were suppressed by the Church later, just as the Church suppressed the findings of Copernicus and Galileo which pointed to the same thing.'

'Well,' said Marlow, 'the Church always quashed anything that called its own authority into question or what's written in the Bible: "The Lord set the earth on its foundations; it can never be moved . . . And the sun rises and sets and returns to its place." That's why scientific research had had such a hard time.'

'True enough,' Graves agreed. 'Anyone like Galileo, under the sway of the Catholic Church, was suppressed.'

'But ask yourself – what has all this to do with Dandolo's tomb?'

Graves shrugged. 'Someone out there thinks there was something pretty important hidden in it.'

'Maybe.'

Graves looked at him. Marlow wondered if she knew he wasn't taking her wholly into his confidence. It would be a mistake to underrate her intelligence. He would have to tread carefully.

'Look,' she said, picking her words. 'Both these guys are *grounded* in archaeology. I can see that they also had very specialized knowledge which might have been applicable to this project, but –'

But Marlow was already looking at the information on Su-Lin de Montferrat.

'What a woman,' he said, in a voice which Graves unaccountably found irritating. 'Why the hell isn't there a photo of her? But listen to this: fluent Italian, Chinese, German and English. Good French and Spanish.

88

Working knowledge of Russian.' He paused. 'Private life: very little to go on. Disastrous marriage to a French academic, which ended in tears. Seems to have devoted herself to work since then.' He paused again. 'Finished her education at Venice, reading Chinese before switching to history. Specialized in the early-medieval period, concentrated on archive work, manuscripts and so on, but before that, and this interests me, she wrote an essay on egotism which won a prize in her first year, based on some of the teachings of Lao Tzu, and arguing from them.'

'And?'

'She discusses self-absorption as part of Borderline Personality Disorder.' That was a condition Marlow knew about; he'd fallen victim to someone in its grip.

'Yes?'

'This could be important. Think about what we know of Dandolo, and imagine the kind of person whose ego is so powerful and unrestrained that it takes over everything else. The sufferer can *invent and believe in a persona for themselves* which suits his or her purposes in life at a particular time. People around them can be completely taken in by it, but if and when circumstances change, the sufferer can switch it off, ruthlessly discard anyone or anything which no longer suits them, and invent a completely new persona which suits them better, conveniently rewriting the past in their minds in such a way that they can exonerate themselves from any responsibility or blame. Like a snake shedding its skin. And it's possible for them to go through life completely plausibly – they almost never get found out, until it's too late.'

Marlow stiffened. He knew all about that, but he

remained silent. If they could be controlled, these would be very useful qualities in certain professions, his own included. And he felt the bit of shrapnel twist in his heart. All he said was, 'Details?'

'Well, there are pages of pretty much academic stuff – original and insightful, that's what won her the prize – but then she goes off at a tangent, and I highlighted this, because I found it fascinating. Listen: Lao Tzu was referring to egoists when he described people who, without the need for ropes, *bind* themselves. That's the drawback of the condition. It limits you, confines you to a bubble you've created around yourself. Such people become their own unconscious prisoners, largely because they're incapable of experiencing, expressing or understanding normal emotions. That's why they can be so ruthless when it comes to self-protection, self-interest. In a way, they don't know what they're doing.' Laura looked over her glasses at Marlow then returned her gaze to the screen. 'But – and this is what Su-Lin argues – self-interest motivates *all* animals, and that includes us.'

'Meaning?'

'We think some fierce or dangerous animals – like crocodiles – must have a good side because they're "tender" towards their young. That's pure sentimentality. All they're really doing is looking after the future of the crocodile race. It's self-interest. Only mankind, and possibly a handful of higher orders of animal, like dolphins, can show real altruism – putting other people before themselves. And even that is rare.'

Marlow shrugged. 'Sounds about right.'

'It explains people who have the kind of ambition

Dandolo had – utter ruthlessness in pursuit of their goal. And that could be important to us.'

'Let's find these people first.' Marlow looked out of the window again. The street below was deserted except for a dark Porsche SUV which slowed up slightly as it passed the building. He watched it drive out of sight. 'These three guys we're looking for had qualifications additional to, but way away from the ones they needed just to investigate the tomb of someone who died in 1205,' he said. 'And it was a big project. Well funded. In these cash-strapped times.'

'What are you thinking?' asked Graves, watching his face.

Marlow shrugged. 'What are *you* thinking?'

Graves closed the lid of her computer. 'I'm wondering who they were *really* working for.'

15

Kingdom of Jerusalem, Year of Our Lord 1171

'You'll come with me,' said Dandolo.

His right-hand man was a monk of the new Cistercian Order who'd been his personal assistant now for nearly ten years, since Dandolo had plucked him from his novitiate and pressed him into his service. Brother Leporo preferred life on the outside of a monastery, but he'd never let go of his ties with his religious colleagues and so had contacts among the priesthood working in the Kingdom of Jerusalem – one, in particular, who'd been doing pretty well out of the local slave trade.

'If it is your wish, *Altissima*,' replied the monk, smiling quietly to himself at this further mark of his master's favour, and at the advantages he saw in it for himself.

It was from the Jerusalem contact that Leporo, some time earlier, well before leaving Venice, had got wind of something the Knights Templar were guarding.

The man wasn't specific, he couldn't be, since the Templars played their cards very close to their chest. But the word was that it was something of inestimable value, of incredible power, something of unimaginable age that had come into the Templars' hands by unknown means.

'But they say it is not for everyone's use,' the slave-trader monk had said.

'Meaning?'

'There is word that one of the Templars, back at the time it fell into their hands, tried to master it.'

'And?'

'He was a sensible man, a cold man, a master administrator' – the monk looked at Leporo – 'a strong mind.'

'What became of him?'

'He became withdrawn, neglected his work. Obsessed with the thing. Trying to make it work for him. The Grand Master, without his knowledge, had it withdrawn from his custody and sealed away. He recognized that here was a power to be respected, if not understood.'

'And the administrator?'

'They found him one day on the beach, scrabbling among the pebbles. Any stone the size of a small book, flat, rounded, he put in a sack he had with him. They took him back to Jerusalem, prayed for him, but he wailed day and night in his cell, dashing himself against its walls.' The monk paused. 'Until one day there was silence.'

Leporo was silent for a moment before asking. 'But didn't the Templars try to find out what he had been searching for? In this thing?'

The slave-trader looked at him. 'The Templars are not fools, Brother. They took it to be a Holy Relic, and treated it with the respect they felt it deserved.'

'But they knew of its power?'

'They knew of its value. Its market value. The Templars are good at valuation. They have abandoned God for mammon. They did that long ago . . . as did I. As have many of us, out here, stuck between the sun and the sand.'

And now, fifty-odd years since their foundation, the

Templars of the Holy Land were badly cash-strapped. Twenty years earlier, they'd begun to concentrate less on guarding pilgrims to the Holy Land than on looking after their property and their money in return for a fee. This venture into banking and insurance hadn't turned out too badly, but the Knights hadn't forgotten they were warriors too, and it was the warrior arm of the sect of soldier-monks that was costing them money. In battle, Templars never retreated. They would rather die. A bad war therefore could cost them 90 per cent of their manpower, and recruiting and training replacements was costly.

'The Knights might be persuaded to part with this artefact,' Leporo's friend had told him, 'if the price were right.'

And they had it right there, in their headquarters on the south-eastern side of the Mount of the Temple in Jerusalem. Leporo had shared this information with his master – he'd never have had the money or the clout to get it for himself, he reasoned, but once it had left the Templars' hands, who knew . . .?

But, on the voyage there, they'd thought they'd never reach the Crusader port of Acre.

The sails of Barbary Coast pirates appeared about a kilometre to the south as they were passing Cyprus, and there'd been panic on board when the pirates changed course and started to make for them. The Venetians had the wind in their favour, thought they could outrun them, but it wasn't to be.

The pirates had two sleek dhows, big ones, which cut through the smooth waters of the White Sea like knives. They came abreast with the swiftness of wolves and lay, one alongside the port and one along the starboard side of the Venetian galley. The brightly clad Moors threw ropes with heavy grappling irons across and pulled their ships close to their large, lumbering prey.

The battle was fierce and bloody. Thirteen Venetians had fallen, including the second envoy, the Marquess of Verona, before the Italians managed to replace panic with discipline and their marines closed with the pirates. The Moors, though skilled fighters, were fewer in number and relied on surprise and fear as their greatest allies. They fell back under the heavy blows of the Venetian broadswords and scuttled away, retreating to their own ships, trying to cut their grappling ropes clear and make their escape. The captain would have let them do it, but Dandolo stayed him, ordering raking crossbow fire at close range to slaughter as many of the pirates as he could.

The rest surrendered, offering what booty they already carried from previous attacks as ransom for their lives.

Dandolo stared at them, kneeling, bloodied, beaten.

'Kill them all,' he ordered. 'And sink their ships. But first . . .'

And to the astonishment of the captain and crew, but not to Leporo's, he had the pirate chief brought forward and kneel on the deck of the galley. Taking a sword from one of the marines, Dandolo hacked off the man's arms.

'Throw him into the sea. Let him feed the sharks.'

They reached Acre two days later, enriched by the pirates' booty.

On the long journey overland, south from Acre to Jerusalem, hot and dusty though it was, they could relax a little.

King Almaric had the road well policed, and there was scant risk of any attack on the tight-knit caravan of Dandolo's entourage.

At length they arrived at the gates of the Holy City.

Almaric, a tough man in his thirties who spoke Arabic as fluently as his native French, and passable Italian, gave them a courteous, though guarded, welcome. But Dandolo wasn't interested in making an impression on the king. Dandolo didn't want to rock any boats, but he knew Almaric needed to keep Constantinople on his side – a fact Dandolo had conveniently failed to mention to Doge Vitale.

It was the doge's own fault if he hadn't realized as much himself. There was about as much chance of getting Almaric to side openly with Venice as there was of finding a miracle cure for Almaric's son's leprosy.

Brother Leporo, of course, knew all along that what Dandolo was interested in was the Templars. Relics of any kind were useful, and if he could collect a powerful one to take home, it would be a political feather in his cap. As a monk, Leporo was well aware of the growing hunger in Europe for things which had once belonged to the founders of Christianity – Christ and His disciples. If those things belonged to martyrs, so much the better. Ownership of a lock of hair, a finger, a splinter from the True Cross, could impart status to its possessor, whether he was a king or an abbott, and, more important sometimes even than status: redemption from sin.

Leporo also knew full well that his master had an eye on the doge's cap of office – the *corno ducale* – for himself.

'There's no harm in making friends with the Templars,' Dandolo told him.

'Of course, *Altissima*! Their banking network stretches all over Europe. They're not only exempt from local taxes, but immune from local laws, everywhere. The pope himself has given them what amounts to free rein. They own property all over the place, and they've established thousands of branches, from Cadiz to Calais, from Albi to Aleppo.'

'But despite all that their profits are not enough! They need cash in the Holy Land, and that's the Achilles' heel which we can take advantage of.'

'Still, they are, in terms of what they control and what they own, richer than many kingdoms.'

'*And they are above nations.* They are' – and Dandolo relished the new expression he had coined himself – '*multi-national.*'

Leporo was right. Dandolo dreamed of becoming doge and turning Venice itself into a power to rival and surpass that of the Templars. He did not feel old, but he was sixty. How many years were left to him? He was impatient, but he knew he had to be the opposite, if all he lusted for was ever to come to fruition. Still, he vowed he would do what he could with whatever period of life God vouchsafed him. He'd fulfil his dream, with God's help or without it.

Perhaps, in time, he could even control the Templars themselves.

But, for now, they would be useful friends to have – if he could persuade them to it.

16

Dandolo rose before dawn on the morning of the fourth day, had himself dressed in his most expensive robe and set out for the Al-Aqsa mosque. Since the triumph of the Christians in the First Crusade, the Templars had taken it over as the centre of their military and banking operations.

Al-Aqsa was one of the most sacred sites of Islam. Here, the prophet had dismounted from his magical steed, Al-Buraq Al-Sharif, to pray at the Rock which bears his footprint. Now, under the Templars, its cool offices, corridors and open spaces, all traces of Islam whitewashed over or removed, the building was a model of secular efficiency, although there was something of the monastery about it too. Plain crucifixes hung on the walls, and costly illuminated volumes of the Bible were placed on lecterns in the assembly hall, once the *musalla*, and elsewhere. Cells for the knights' accommodation were arranged round the vast central atrium.

Dandolo and his retinue, including Leporo, two interpreters (one in case of need, and one to correct the other if anything should, accidentally or by design, be lost in translation) and a discreet half-dozen of his bodyguard, were greeted at the main gate by two tall, austere-looking young men in plain brown garments marked with a discreet red cross. Dandolo wondered if this muted dress was designed to send him some kind of signal – where were the resplendent white robes emblazoned with the great red cross on chest, back and upper arms? Had they sent *underlings* to welcome him?

But whether the affront was real or imaginary, he swallowed it, and allowed himself to be escorted across the atrium, already growing hot in the sun despite its well-watered lawns and palms, to a cluster of small, domed buildings which had once been designed for the use of senior priests and scholars of the *Quran*. The Templar attendants paused at the door of one then entered. They emerged again within moments and took up places on either side of the door, admitting Dandolo, the interpreters and Leporo. The bodyguard would remain outside. So much for disguising them as monks, thought Dandolo irritably; but the Templars hadn't got where they were by being stupid.

The modest exterior of the place he'd entered was not belied by the room he found himself in. It was simply furnished, only distinguishable from a monk's cell by its size, for it was large, dim and cool. The only decoration on the peeling white walls was a simple wooden crucifix, and there was no bed. Instead, two plain wooden tables and, on a rack, a suit of chain mail.

Two men were seated behind the tables. One of them rose and surveyed his visitors with distant eyes of startling blue. A gaunt man, with a leathery face browned and lined by the sun, he was dressed in a black robe woven of light wool. The other, small and wiry, whose eyes were black and intense, wore the black habit of a Cistercian under the brown cloak of the Templars who had accompanied Dandolo's party from the gate.

'Enrico Dandolo.' Dandolo spoke into the silence. 'Special Envoy of the Doge of Venice.'

'I know who you are,' replied the man in black, in perfect Italian. 'I am Odo de St Amand. At your service.' His smile was as arid as a desert.

Odo de St Amand. What was *he* doing here? Dandolo had thought him to be in Paris. And what honour was he being accorded in being received by the Grand Master himself?

'What can we do for you?' continued Odo in the same level tone. He did not introduce his companion. 'And, as you see, we have no need for your interpreters,' he continued. 'Unless you prefer me to continue in French. You may find fault with my Italian. It is a little rusty.'

'Your Italian leaves nothing to be desired.'

'Good. Then you may dismiss them. And your other man.'

'By your leave, he stays.'

After the slightest of pauses, Odo nodded. The interpreters withdrew, to join the rest of Dandolo's party outside.

Once the four men were alone, Odo gestured to Dandolo and Leporo to sit on the simple wooden chairs in the room. There was no other furniture, except for a stout cabinet which stood against a wall. No refreshment was offered, not even water.

Odo relaxed slightly. 'It is, I am sure you will agree, better that we keep our discussion open to as few ears as possible.'

Dandolo watched him. How much did the Grand Master already know about the true nature of his mission?

'I am gratified that you grace us with your presence here.'

'Why not the Hospitallers?' interjected the other Templar, his tone edgy.

'Because the Knights Hospitaller do not quite share . . . all . . . your interests,' replied Dandolo, with an equal measure of veiled aggression in his voice. What was this man driving at?

'You mean they are not as interested in money?' continued the brown-garbed man. He might have gone on, but Odo stilled him.

'What have you come for?' he asked the Venetian.

'To express my admiration for your work – I fully intend to do the same for the Hospitallers, by the way, since by your prowess both Orders have helped secure and maintain our Christian Faith in the birthplace of Our Lord. And to extend the hand of friendship from Venice, on behalf of my master, Doge Vitale.'

'What makes you think we need your friendship?' the other Templar asked coldly.

Odo said, 'Be quiet, Thomas.' Turning to Dandolo, he said: 'You must forgive him. He is here, if you like, to make sure I do nothing rash.'

'Come to the point,' put in Thomas, adding reluctantly, 'If you please.'

'Certainly,' said Dandolo. Glancing at Leporo, he continued. 'We think you may have . . . something for sale. If so, we might be interested in acquiring it.' To himself, he thought, *they already know.*

17

'And what is it that you are interested in acquiring?' asked Thomas.

'A relic.' Leporo spoke for the first time. 'You are a fellow Cistercian, Brother Thomas. You will understand our eagerness. A Holy Relic, which we should like to acquire for the protection and the greater glory of our basilica of St Mark, and our city.' He hesitated. 'We find ourselves in troubled waters, and we have need of the Lord's protecting arm.'

'You mean your confrontation with the Greeks of Byzantium,' replied Thomas brusquely.

Was there nothing these people didn't know, thought Dandolo. He must handle them with subtlety. But in order to gain what, exactly? He only had Leporo's word for it that they had some thing of great value. True, he trusted his aide, and Leporo's judgement in such matters was seldom false. Well, he had come this far, and he wasn't going to pass up any opportunity which presented itself for his own aggrandisement. And he had more than enough money at his disposal to satisfy even these money-conscious warrior-monks.

He guessed, too, that the presence of the Grand Master and the aggressive nature of Friar Thomas were good indications of what they were prepared to put on the table.

'We seek to do God's will,' he replied simply. 'But to do so justly, we poor humans need all the help we can get.'

There was silence in the room then. You could hear the breeze rustling the leaves of the palms outside, and the muted talk of Dandolo's men as they waited in the shade outside.

The two Templars exchanged a look. Odo, Dandolo guessed, was for taking the negotiations further; Thomas against.

Then Odo walked over to the cabinet, unlocked it, and from it produced a leather bag, which he placed on the table between them.

It was a small bag; the leather was rough and well-worn. Odo's lean fingers undid the strings which held it closed.

He drew out a small iron box and a key, attached by a leather thong. He placed the box on the table, fitted the key into the lock and turned it in a complex series of clockwise and anti-clockwise movements which Dandolo found hard to follow. No doubt Odo would tell him the secret of the manipulation if a deal was struck. At last the lock clicked open. Odo raised the lid with great care.

The box was lined with grey wool. Lying within was a clay tablet, about the size that would fit comfortably into your palm. One side was covered in a crowded series of symbols, but they bore no relation to any alphabet or numeric system that Dandolo had ever seen. The other side was blank, though Dandolo could make out a thumb-print, no doubt pressed into the clay when it was still moist by whoever had written on it.

Just behind him, Leporo could not suppress a sigh of disappointment. Dandolo kept his face expressionless, however, as Odo laid the tablet down next to the box. He looked at the casket again and saw that there was an inscription of some sort on it, and another on the shank of the key, but he couldn't make them out.

Friar Thomas grew tense as the tablet emerged, and Dandolo noticed that the monk's eyes grew keen with – what? – something like craving? Desire?

He had noted the reluctance of the Templars to part with this unimpressive-looking piece of baked mud. As he glanced at Odo's eyes, fixed on the tablet, he saw something there too. Regret? Indecision? Second thoughts? But then the eyes lifted to meet his own.

Dandolo didn't want to meet those eyes – yet. He looked at the writing – for that was all he could think of it as – on the rough piece of terracotta. As he did so, he flinched. He couldn't be sure that he wasn't imagining it, but it seemed to him, fleetingly, that the letters, which looked as much as anything like the footprints of tiny birds – seemed momentarily to glow dark red, like blood.

He glanced at Leporo to see if he had noticed anything, but Leporo's face was impassive. Dandolo pulled himself together. Odo, he realized, had been watching him.

'An interesting piece,' he said.

'Isn't it?' replied Odo.

'Not much to look at,' remarked Leporo.

Odo ignored the comment, while Thomas shot thunderbolts at Leporo with his eyes. But the monk collected himself, and said: 'I agree with Brother Leporo. It is, indeed, a small thing. Perhaps not worth your attention. We can only apologize.'

Dandolo raised a hand to silence him. He kept his eyes

on Odo. 'Tell me about this . . . thing. I have to say, it is not quite what we expected.'

Odo gave him another thin smile. 'I know. You are disappointed in its size. Or you thought at least the box might contain the head of the spear which pierced Our Lord's side at Golgotha, or the jewelled fingerbones of the apostle who touched the wound made by that spear – Doubting Thomas.'

'Those would be great and Holy Relics indeed.'

'This thing is older than either of them.'

Dandolo looked again at the tablet. He could see, without being an expert, that it was old, very old indeed. It seemed as old as Time itself.

'May I touch it?'

Odo spread his hands. 'Of course. But be careful. There are things about this tablet of which we are not entirely sure.'

Dandolo stretched out a tentative hand.

The clay felt as cold as death, so cold it burned; and hard, hard as adamant. He did not dare pick it up, but withdrew his hand instead. He wanted it, that much he knew. But at what price? He thought of his bodyguard outside, and the heavy casket of Venetian florins borne by one of the packhorses in their charge. He would pay anything . . . but then it was better not to show himself too avid for it. He would start the bargaining at half the amount he had with him – already a far higher sum than he'd intended.

He remained silent.

'It was made a time long before the arrival of Our Lord Christ on this sorry earth,' Odo continued. 'No one knows exactly when. Nor where.'

'How did it come to be in your care?'

Odo stole a look at Thomas. It was strange, but it seemed as if he were asking permission to answer. 'It has been in the possession of our Order for many years. It was bequeathed to us by the heirs of Bishop Adhemar of le Puy. They say he discovered and acquired it in Alexandria shortly before his death, after the success of the very first crusade against the Fatimids and the Seljuks, when we drove them back out of the Holy Places. The tablet is referred to in Adhemar's letters. He calls it the Sacred Scroll. Perhaps he thought it was a printing-block, and tried to use it to print its meaning out on parchment. But we do not know.'

Dandolo knew of Adhemar. The bishop had been one of the main instigators of the crusade which had ended so successfully at the close of the previous century. A man of extraordinary power and influence. It was said that, had he come earlier into prominence, the Holy Places would have been won and held for ever. The story of how he rallied one hundred scared and disoriented men against five thousand Saracens on the plains below Masyaf, and routed the enemy completely, had passed into legend. Some told that the Saviour Himself had descended from heaven to come to his aid. Others – in quiet voices – spoke of demons.

'Why did he bequeath it to you?' The question was out almost before he had articulated it in his mind, but Dandolo corrected himself immediately; he had been too direct. 'I mean, did he intend to redeem it?'

Odo hesitated before replying. 'What you say is true. He believed a powerful force for good lay in this modest piece of clay. But it was his descendants who gave it to us for . . . safekeeping. Our correspondence with them, decades after the bishop's descent into madness, indicated that they felt it needed to be kept . . . secure.'

Odo's hand went out to the tablet, took it and placed it back in its box, closing the lid and reaching for the key. 'Perhaps we are, after all, being hasty,' he said. 'We cannot say that it is a Christian relic. It will not redound to the glory of Venice. A poor thing, in fact. We may have other —'

'But it plays a role, a key role, in our Christian heritage,' said Thomas suddenly.

'Adhemar mentioned something in his letters,' Odo said. 'We cannot fathom it. He refers to the Book of Revelation. "When the Lamb opened the seventh seal, there was silence in heaven about the space of half an hour." You know the piece. It covers the eighth to the tenth chapters of the book.'

Dandolo knew it. He looked again at the tablet, and thought of the seven angels and what the blasts from their trumpets summoned forth. A hellish hail of fire and blood; destruction of the seas and the life in them; a blazing star poisoning all fresh water; the wreckage of the heavens; and the further horror which the last three trumpets invoked. *Woe, woe, woe, to those who dwell on earth, at the blasts of the other trumpets . . .*

It was as if a voice from the centre of earth were reciting the words to Dandolo: *. . . he was given the key of the shaft of the bottomless pit . . . and from the shaft smoke rose like the smoke of a great furnace, and the sun and the air were darkened with the smoke from the shaft. Then from the smoke came locusts on*

the earth, and they were given power like the power of scorpions of
the earth; they were told not to harm the grass of the earth or any
green growth or any tree, but only those of mankind who have not
the seal of God upon their foreheads; they were allowed to torture
them for five months, but not to kill them, and their torture was like
the torture of a scorpion, when it stings a man. And in those days
men will seek death and will not find it; they will long to die, and
death will fly from them . . .

Dandolo thought of the locusts, the demons with human faces and long, flowing women's hair but with teeth like a lion's and their bodies scaled like armour, and he thought of the Four Horsemen released next by the blast of the sixth angel's trumpet; and of the terrible silence of the seventh angel, whose trumpet's sound he still awaited, but would hear at the very last.

18

Dandolo stared at Odo. 'What does it mean?' he asked.

'We cannot fathom it,' replied Odo. 'But we know that the bishop believed that this thing has the power to give man a force which man himself should not have. A force which man cannot control.'

Dandolo's rational mind dismissed it, but despite himself he was fascinated and – was it the right word? – awed.

He pulled himself together. Were they trying to pull *more* wool over his eyes? But the faces of both Odo and Thomas were deeply serious.

'That is why we have kept this thing a closely guarded secret for so long,' continued Odo. 'But – and I make no secret of this – we need cash now if we are going to keep the Holy Places secure. And if we ever lost control here, we would not wish this thing to fall into the hands of the Saracens. In Egypt, the power of Saladin grows by the day.'

'There is another story' – Brother Thomas spoke slowly – 'which you should know of.' He looked across at his master, who, after a moment, nodded his assent.

'It is said,' began Thomas, 'and Bishop Adhemar believed it, that it was with this tablet that the Dark One tempted Our Lord in the wilderness.'

The Templar paused while the Italians listened attentively. At length he continued: 'Matthew, Mark and Luke describe the temptations of Christ; Matthew and Luke in detail. That He should make bread out of stones to feed Himself; that He should hurl Himself from the pinnacle of a temple, trusting to the angels to bear Him up and save Him, and that He should have dominion over all the nations of the earth in return for His allegiance to the Dark One himself. Matthew makes this the last temptation of Christ.' Thomas paused again. 'And Christ refused: *It is written, You shall worship the Lord your God, and Him only shall you serve.* He would not touch the tablet Satan offered him, the tablet which would give him ultimate power. Because He knew that if He could not convince people of His doctrines by His own power and persuasion, they would be worth nothing. There is no short-cut to Grace.'

'By using this tablet? The Devil himself made it?'

'That is his thumbprint on the reverse,' said Thomas simply. 'We believe that if the symbols written on this piece of clay could be properly deciphered and interpreted, the man who had that knowledge would hold the key to the ability to move nations.'

'Then it *could* be used for great good.'

Thomas looked at Dandolo severely. 'Never would that come to pass, if an ordinary mortal controlled it.'

And Adhemar ended mad, thought Dandolo, looking at the tablet, and seeing the characters written on it glow red once more.

Then the vision passed. He realized that the Grand Master and the monk were watching him expectantly.

He measured his words. 'I humbly acknowledge the wisdom of your decision that such a thing should be kept as safe and as secret as is humanly possible, and that it should be kept out of the hands of the Saracens at all costs,' he said. 'If the mantle of such a responsibility should fall on the shoulders of Venice, then I am the last man to turn away from it. If, at the same time, I may be of some material service to the brave and noble Order of the Knights Templar, the greatest bastion of our Faith in the East, then the privilege and the honour is doubled.'

'And what price do you put on this privilege?' asked Odo, after leaving a polite pause to mark the gravity of what all present knew to be a purely political speech.

Dandolo didn't look at Leporo when he replied, without hesitation, 'Fifteen thousand Venetian florins.' The calculation seemed to have taken place without him. It was three-quarters of what he had with him. And he already knew that if they pushed the price above 20,000, he'd give them letters of credit to match the amount. An expensive punt, but the money he'd brought with him came from his private coffers. He had to have the scroll, as Adhemar had called it. Whatever it cost. He'd deal with the doge and the Venetian Council later, and get the money back from them. He knew damned well that Doge Vitale's expedition against Constantinople would founder, and the doge would then need every friend he could get. All Dandolo needed was patience, and time. In time he would achieve his ends, he knew that now.

19

An hour later, the Templars had settled for 25,000. A fantastic amount, which caused Leporo to look at Dandolo askance when the four men stood up and shook hands.

The tablet was returned to its box, the casket locked, its key retied to it, and handed over to Leporo, who stowed it in his satchel with extreme care. Now, at last, Odo rang a bell on his desk and offered the Italians food and drink. It was eleven in the morning, and the sun was reaching its zenith. The Venetian party turned down an invitation to stay the night and set off on the return journey to Acre. Dandolo, quietly triumphant, as something deep within him, something he could not identify, was stirred, was eager to return to Chios now, and as there was a full moon, he elected to travel through the night. They would leave Jerusalem late in the afternoon.

Before they ate, Dandolo told Leporo to ensure that their men drank no wine before travelling, a necessary precaution, since the Templars, surprisingly, had tried to ply them with the stuff. The Venetians stayed with light beer – water was not to be trusted: it contained disease.

In the event, they were wise to do so.

The attack came at three in the morning, when the Venetian caravan was already some kilometres into the desert north of Jerusalem. The attackers came from the eastern hills, the moon behind them, riding horses and wearing black robes. Their headdresses covered their faces, leaving only their eyes visible.

Dandolo was glad they did not find him unprepared. His men, on a signal arranged in advance, quickly drew their pack animals into a circle which formed a living wall. All their valuables and provisions for the journey to the port were placed within it, and the bodyguard, twenty men only, but armed to the teeth with lances, javelins, swords, axes and bows, took up their positions behind the nervous mules. The horsemen numbered about forty, and first circled the corralled Venetians, taken aback that their attack had been anticipated.

But they were not put off. Ten of them rode in hard, wielding longswords and flails, hacking at the bucking and kicking mules where they could, but failing to reach the group sheltered behind them. Then they withdrew and let their bowmen take over.

'Who the hell are they?' Dandolo's captain of the guard yelled. 'Desert pirates? There should be none on this road! The Templars have cleared it.'

'Don't think we can rely on the help of a Templar patrol,' replied Dandolo, seizing a javelin. The archers had reined in a short distance away and were even now taking aim, but they were close enough to be within the throwing range of a strong man, and Dandolo was still that. He took careful aim himself, allowing for the dim and deceptive light of the moon, and hurled his javelin, watching it arc in the air and seeing it land deep in the neck of his target, where it joined his upper chest. The woollen folds of the man's garment were no protection in the face of the heavy blade of the Venetian's descending weapon.

The man leaned slowly forward on to his mount's crupper before toppling to the pale-grey sand, on which a dark stain quickly appeared as he clawed futilely at the ground in a last vain attempt to rise.

Encouraged by this, the Venetian bodyguard let fly a volley of javelins as the black-clad swordsmen rode in for another assault. Many of the spears found homes, burying themselves in horses' flanks or attackers' thighs and torsos, and taking five more men out of the skirmish at one stroke.

The defenders cheered, but the attackers remained eerily silent. They regrouped, once again riding around the corral to encircle it, and taking care to remain outside javelin range. The archers fitted arrows to their short bows and drew them, firing a volley which killed two of the mules and three of the bodyguard, the black-fletched arrows falling like rain from the sky and jabbing into unprotected eyes and necks, their shafts glittering in the silver light. The stricken mules kicked at the heavens as they shrieked like banshees in their death agony, while grooms strove to hold down the rearing and screaming survivors, taut reins cutting into their hands and drawing blood.

Another deathly volley followed fast, before the defenders had time to react, most of the hissing arrows digging into the sand this time but several still biting into human and animal flesh. Two of the mules broke loose and galloped away, dragging their wounded handlers across the desert behind them until they were lost to sight, swallowed up by the darkness.

Dandolo had had enough. He moved swiftly to his nervous horse, which stood by the baggage in the centre of the ring, and mounted it, drawing his own sword. He jumped his horse over the backs of the remaining mules, which had been drawn in to form a tighter circle, and rode straight at the man who seemed to be the attackers' leader. The masked figure whirled a flail menacingly round his head, looking for a place to bury its spiked ball, either in the Venetian's thigh or in his horse's neck, but Dandolo crouched low in the saddle to avoid its arc and, coming up fast and close, drew his sword up high just as the flail swung past his head, and brought it down with all his strength into the man's body, cleaving it on the right side so that the whole of the torso, from neck to waist, was split open.

The sword wouldn't loosen from where it had bitten into the pelvis, and Dandolo was pulled from his horse, bringing his opponent down with him. They rolled together on the sand, but the man in black, whom Dandolo feared still had enough strength left in him to get a grip on his neck, started to twitch and throw his remaining good arm around in a frantic effort to regain equilibrium. Dandolo kicked himself free and clambered to his feet, watching as the man, whose right side was now all but torn free of the rest of his body, writhed on the ground beside him.

He could hear the fight continuing behind him but seemed oblivious to it, and to all danger of getting a lance or an arrow in his own unarmoured back. After what seemed an eternity, he swung round in time to see the black riders making off towards the south, leaving a scattered mess of dead and dying men and horses behind them.

The corral broke up and the surviving Italians, in shock, began to take stock.

The captain of the guard came up fast. He took Dandolo by the shoulder. 'Are you all right?' he asked.

'Winded, but I'll live,' replied Dandolo grimly.

'What shall we do? Go after them?'

'No. We've stung them badly enough. They won't be back tonight.' But he thought: They'll try again. We must travel day and night until we reach Acre, whatever happens. It was too far to go back to Jerusalem and seek Almaric's aid. Besides, if the attackers were who he thought they were, such a move would be a vain one.

He bent over his assailant, whose convulsions had now reduced to a few agonized spasms, and, holding what remained of his upper body steady with his boot, taking care to get a good foothold so as not to slip on the blood, he unravelled the woollen headdress which covered his face.

In the moonlight, the almond-white visage of Brother Thomas glared up at him, the black eyes crazy with hatred. But as Dandolo watched, the eyes glazed, the irises turned upwards and disappeared under the lids, and all expression went out of the face. Suddenly it looked almost peaceful.

'What were they after?' asked the captain of the guard.

Dandolo gave him a look. 'I have no idea,' he said.

'What shall we do? Shall we bury them?'

Dandolo laughed at that and, remounting his horse, turned it north and rode on.

20

Istanbul, the Present

It was mid-morning when Detective-Major Haki arrived back and ushered them into his office. One table and an area around it had been cleared, and on the tabletop lay a series of neatly arranged folders.

'This is everything we've been able to collect,' Haki said. 'Together with the latest material sent to you from Professor Lopez in New York. Material he's been able to glean from Yale and Venice, I imagine. Of course, that stuff's in your encrypt on the computer, but I've transferred it to my laptop – if I can find it –' Here, he broke off to rummage on his desk among papers under which his MacBook Air had easily become buried. 'That's the trouble with such a discreet little thing,' he grumbled. 'Mind you, I can remember the days when computers were the size of suitcases. Doesn't seem that long ago, either.'

'It isn't,' said Marlow, wondering how much of Haki's behaviour was an act. Had the detective-major attempted to decipher Leon's material? But the urgency of the situation left him no time to reflect on that.

Haki said, 'I'll leave you to it,' going over to his desk and busying himself with other paperwork. He had no intention of leaving the room.

Marlow had to trust him. He picked up Haki's laptop and flipped it open. Quickly accessing Leon's material, he confirmed that it contained indications and confirmations of what the hard-copy material transferred electronically from Yale and Venice contained, together with a gloss and some preliminary observations of Leon's own. He committed it all to memory, and deleted it from the laptop. He knew from its own built-in safety measures that the encryption was intact – no one else had attempted to access it.

The hard-copy material in the folders showed details of the open tomb, as it had been when Adkins, Taylor and de Montferrat disappeared. There were some general photographs, which showed an underground chamber lined with some kind of hardwood which had survived down the centuries, though the painted scenes – presumably from the late doge's life – had long since peeled and faded. There were the remains of what looked like flags bearing coats of arms lying on a stamped-earth floor. The bronze coffin lay on a low stone plinth. Its lid had been removed and the corpse within was visible, clad in a faded brocade robe, so stiff that it had retained its shape after the body it encased had shrunk, for the body, as far as Marlow and Graves could judge from the photographs, had withered, rather than rotted, away.

The next folder contained detailed photographs.

'I see Adkins, Taylor and de Montferrat were careful to leave artefacts and items of jewellery in place,' said Graves.

'No doubt prior to removal to the Topkapi Museum.

They were accompanied and supervised by Turkish colleagues at all times,' said Marlow.

'The site was placed under heavy guard as soon as the excavation began,' said Haki from his desk.

They studied the photos, scanning them for any clue which would answer the question of why Brad Adkins and his team had vanished. There was nothing obvious. Something they had taken with them then? Or which had been taken from them?

'What the hell did they find?' asked Marlow.

'Something that someone else was after?'

'That much is clear. And who wanted it?'

'We can't hold the press off this much longer. And the families are getting more and more anxious. We're running out of excuses to give them.'

Marlow turned back to the photographs again. They showed the corpse in detail. Gold and ruby rings hung loose on shrivelled fingers to which the traces of purple gloves still hung. The face, the only other part of the body clearly visible, was a shrunken ball, almost a skull, covered with a thin layer of deeply tanned skin, its nose reduced to two oval holes, the mouth a gaping hole and the eyes vacant sockets. Six photographs showed details of the face, especially of the skin around the eyes, where burn-scars were still faintly discernible. And there were photographs, in a third folder, of the hands.

'Look at the right hand,' Marlow said, after studying one photo intently and handing it to Graves. 'What do you see?'

She looked hard. 'It looks like a claw.'

Marlow handed her another picture. 'And look at this one, of the left.'

Graves gazed down at the high-density colour photograph, and compared it with the first. She laid them side by side on the table. The left hand, or what was left of it, was open, as if relaxed in sleep, the long fingers bent, but with nothing of the agony in them which characterized the fingers of the doge's other hand. 'Maybe he had arthritis,' she suggested.

The right hand looked as if it had belonged to someone in a torment of pain.

'That's not arthritis,' said Marlow.

He had seen a hand like that once before, in London. It had belonged to a former East German double-agent who had managed to escape from the Stasi, but not before he had been badly tortured by them. He'd talk of that with Lopez, who'd been with him at the time.

All the fingers of that man's right hand had been systematically broken. Marlow looked across at the detective-major. 'I need to see the remains personally,' he said. 'Something's been missed. Find it and we find them.' He was thinking, Even the faintest clue, an impression in the soil, something left behind by Adkins, Taylor or de Montserrat – something which to anyone else would seem unimportant and which a photographer, however thorough, might have missed or discounted.

Haki picked up the telephone and made three calls in quick succession. He seemed to be passing from one office to another until he got the official he needed to get the permission he sought, for with each call his tone became more peremptory, more impatient. But the whole process took fewer than five minutes, and by the end of them a smile was back on his lips again.

'We'll take my car,' he said.

The interior of the Church of St Irina was plain and bare, but the force of the worship that had taken place there down the eighteen centuries of its existence, almost until very recent times, struck Marlow like a mallet. It was closed to tourists and surrounded by a military guard.

The place was empty except for two bored young soldiers armed with Kalashnikovs, who stood near a large oblong hole in the ground on the south-east aisle. It was cold inside the church, and the two men obviously hated the posting.

Everything in the tomb was in place, and only plastic sheeting covered the artefacts and the body inside to protect them from dust. Above it wooden poles supported a corrugated-iron roof. Between the poles, more plastic sheeting was stretched. Haki led the way, pulling aside two sheets and descending gingerly into the pit by a short stairway attached to one side. The three of them stood over the body, and Marlow bent forward, looking keenly at the corpse's right hand.

There was no doubt about it. Someone, at some time well after Dandolo's death, had been here and broken all the fingers and the thumb.

'Why do that?' asked Haki, his voice hushed.

Marlow stood back and answered briefly. 'To prise them apart,' he said. He glanced at Graves. 'Seen enough?'

'Yes.'

'Then let's get back and see what other treats Leon has in store for us.'

Haki's mobile rang and he spoke into it briefly.

'There's something else,' put in Haki. 'It's expected back from our own lab – any time now.'

21

Year of Our Lord 1171

I need a better man to captain my bodyguard, thought Dandolo once safely back at Chios, remembering the battle on the sand. But there'd be time enough to arrange that.

He congratulated himself on having been able to second-guess the Templars' duplicity, and on having kept the nature of the transfer of money secret from all but Leporo. He also congratulated himself on having kept the secret of how to open and close the lock to the casket even from the monk, but he had the knack of it himself, practising with the box empty – the tablet itself, wrapped in a silk handkerchief, securely tucked into a sleeve of his gown.

Both the box and the key, each made of iron, were the work of a master locksmith, who must have worked for Adhemar, for they were old, but not that old, perhaps seventy years or so.

The inscription on the key made no sense to Dandolo – it appeared to be a series of numbers, in a script which may have been Aramaic.

As for the writing on the box, that was in Latin, in a code so simple that it took him less than a day, on the voyage from Acre to Chios, to decipher. The *sense* of what was written was another matter: it told of a dark eagle descending on the earth, its talons outstretched. Nothing could prevent the onslaught of the eagle, the script ran, unless . . . But the end of the riddle was missing.

Once he had mastered the lock, Dandolo took to leaving the box shut but empty. The key and the tablet he kept with him at all times. He couldn't carry the box about with him everywhere he went, but he found he was uncomfortable if the tablet wasn't permanently under his hand. Besides, the locked box provided a useful decoy, and no one, he knew, and nothing, could open it without the key. It was so skilfully made and fitted together that no crowbar could force it. He was sure that not even the grey exploding powder they said the Chinese made could dent it.

As he'd foreseen, the embassy to Constantinople had become mired in futile negotiations. Doge Vitale needed him to join the other Venetians there, and see what, if anything, could be salvaged. And there was a hidden agenda: Vitale needed Dandolo to set up a spy ring. Venice would have been mad not to seize such an opportunity to take stock of the real might of this potential adversary. Vitale hadn't ruled Venice wisely and well for fifteen years not to have learned a trick or two: he knew that before he launched such an operation he needed to lull the Greeks – already convinced of their own intellectual superiority over the Venetians – into a sense of security. The moment they thought they could trust the legation, the time would come to betray that trust.

Dandolo wasn't sorry to be leaving Chios again so soon. The winter of 1171 had given way to the spring of

1172. Now, the weather was hot and humid and, though it was contained for the moment, the plague had broken out on one ship during Dandolo's absence in the Holy Land. In daily increasing numbers, men broke into heavy sweats, before the telltale blisters appeared in their groins and under their armpits. After that, death came within days.

The ship had been towed to a place apart from the rest of the fleet, and the crew quarantined, but things didn't look good, and the long wait was clearly preying on the nerves of the Venetian task-force. Dandolo toyed with the idea of having the ship burned, with its crew in it, but dismissed it. He calculated that such a measure would serve only to undermine morale within the fleet more, and morale was already at a low ebb.

A new voyage, then. Dandolo prepared for it by having his most resplendent robes placed in his trunks – he knew what suckers the Greeks in Constantinople were for pomp, though he doubted if the finest show Venice could make would go far in impressing them. Oh, the riches of that city!

There were three days' sailing ahead of him. The sea was calm throughout, glittering gold under the sun during the day and silver under the moon at night. The winds were balmy and cool, and more often than not in their favour. Dandolo spent the time closeted with Leporo, going over their papers, and what new plans and offers they could bring to the negotiating table in the Palace of Boucoleon.

Here, perhaps, their first chance would come. There was no doubting the power the tablet had, if only he knew how to harness and use that power. But that knowledge would come. In the meantime, Dandolo considered how best to play Vitale and the Greeks off against one another. With the right planning, and Vitale discredited, there would be only one man to step into the breach.

'Your star is rising,' Leporo said, reading his thoughts.

Dandolo, immersed in his thoughts, did not answer. If he showed himself too proud, too soon, all might founder.

They arrived on the morning of the fourth day.

Dandolo's party found the Venetian legation quartered in
the vacated mansion of a rich compatriot who had lived
in Constantinople for half his life. To reach it, they had
passed through streets paved with white marble flagstones. Everywhere in this quarter the houses' façades
were faced with the same white marble.

The city looked as if it were on permanent holiday.
Gold and silver were everywhere in evidence, from the
threads of the women's dresses to the decoration of the
staffs even men of quite modest rank carried. The colours
of the garments worn, and of the awnings over shops and
restaurants and even the studios of the craftsmen, were
yellow and green and purple, and the city appeared to be
in the grip of a great energy – everywhere, people were
engaged in their activities, from doing business to having
fun, with an intensity which staggered the more restrained
Venetians.

Money passed freely from hand to hand, and if there
were poor districts in the vastness of this capital of the
East, they were well hidden. The streets were clean, and
no unpleasant smells hid in them. Huge statues of bronze
and marble graced the broad squares, figures of the saints
and Our Lady, huge ornate crosses, as well as groups
depicting heroes of Ancient Greece – discus throwers
and wrestlers, runners and javelin-throwers, as well as a

mighty Herakles, and a Bellerophon riding Pegasus. Four magnificent horses dominated the entrance of the hippodrome, where crowds thronged at the thrice-weekly race meetings.

The worst you could say was that the scent of perfume sometimes hung too heavily in the air, and the interior of the churches was equally heavy with incense. In the city centre, two mighty buildings presided over the glittering press of people and buildings: the white wedding-cake of the Boucoleon and the brooding, vast basilica of Hagia Sofia, to the north of which stood the more discreet city mosque.

The immense and overwhelmingly ornate Palace of Boucoleon was a place designed to strike awe into the heart of the proudest foreign visitor, with its doors of pure cedar and its locks and bolts and fittings – even the humblest gutter – all of gold or silver. But Dandolo's sharp eyes noticed cracks in the plasterwork here and there, or dust swept into a corner and not cleared; and if that was the case here, in the city's golden heart, what else lay hidden which did not chime with the gaudy confidence the city exuded? Every place had its Achilles' heel, just as every person did. Dandolo would make it his business to find it out. But he also saw that, as things stood, Constantinople was, from the point of view of a potential enemy like Venice, all but impregnable.

As a first step, he decided to cultivate the legation's host, the silk merchant Tonso Contarini, who was living in his country palace just outside the Theodosian Walls, on his estate to the west of the city, while the Venetian legation occupied his town house, but he spent most of his time at his offices, above which he maintained an opulent apartment.

Contarini, originally from Pisa, had lived so long in the Great City that his Greek and Arabic were now better than his Italian, which had a slightly old-fashioned edge. His slang was twenty or thirty years out of date.

He was about the same age as Dandolo but his dyed hair, makeup, and well-toned body belied his years, and his tanned hands and neck were bedecked with gold and turquoise necklaces and rings. Most of the remaining Italian expatriates had not gone so far in adopting Greek excess, but Contarini had lived here longer than any of them, and they viewed him as the father of the community. He had an open face which it was hard to imagine could possibly belong to the shrewd business mind that dwelt behind it. His pale-blue eyes seemed the very emblems of frank honesty.

He accepted Dandolo's discreet overtures of friendship with an apparently open heart, and before long the two gave the impression of being inseparable companions, Contarini even offering his compatriot the run of his House of Women – another Greek custom he had adopted, which had in turn been adopted from Muslim friends and colleagues within the city.

Meanwhile, the Venetian and Greek diplomats remained cloistered in conference and deadlock. The Italians didn't appear to have noticed, or, if they had, paid any attention to, the shipbuilding work going on in the long, broad inlet of the Golden Horn. Dandolo had not wasted time in organizing, from among his own men, five agents to roam the city and ferret out whatever information they thought might be useful – from trade to internal politics to armaments. Five men in such a gigantic place was a tall order, and Dandolo, disguised, had secretly gone to the Horn himself, to make an estimate of the Greek naval force. He counted a hundred and fifty war-galleys in good fighting order, and many more which, by contrast, left a lot to be desired in their state of repair.

He would discuss the matter with Doge Vitale.

Contarini knew everyone, and arranged a dinner party in Dandolo's honour, though nominally it was given for the doge. There were two hundred guests, mostly Greeks, but also Muslim business associates and the most important members of the legation, mingling with Greek generals, admirals and civil servants from the office of the Grand Vizier. In such a dazzling array of people, only the emperor himself was missing – but he was away on a hunting party in the country north of Galata, and it was, after all, an informal occasion.

Also present, Dandolo had noticed, was a handful of massive men from the far north, almost all of them red- or fair-haired. They wore their hair long and braided, and each man also wore a large, looping moustache, some also braided. Their earrings and pendants were of agate or amethyst with complex geometrical designs, and their bronze bracelets were carved with hunting scenes – wolves, bears, deer or boar baited by dogs, while the hunters stood nearby in thickets, ready with bows and short stabbing spears. Many of them wore slim gold or silver headbands. Their dress, despite the mild weather, was leather or fur jerkins and leather trousers tucked into soft boots. They kept themselves to themselves. Most of them were already drunk, though the food had not yet been served.

'Who are they?' Dandolo asked his host.

Contarini cast an eye over them. 'Ah. They are the chiefs of the emperor's Varangian Guard.'

'Unusual men.'

'Yes. All from the far north. England and Scandinavia – places so cold and barren you need to be tough just to be born in them, let alone survive there.'

'What are they doing here?'

'Oh, they've been guarding the emperors here for generations. Some of this lot were born here, though you wouldn't think it to look at them. They keep themselves to themselves and they have their own women. Newcomers flow in from the north, and every so often a shipload or two of new countrywomen of theirs, just to keep the bloodline fresh, is imported. They bring them down the River Dnieper in Rus, to the Black Sea, and then sail south to here.'

'What brought them here?'

'The usual. Business. Well, that's why they came here in the first place, though the first Englishmen turned up about a hundred years ago, I'm told, after the North French invaded and took over their country. They couldn't stand being ruled over by a bunch of Normans, so they emigrated to their friends in Scandinavia at first. Then they followed the long trade routes south from there, and those that didn't find roots along the way, ended up in the Greek Empire.'

'Do any of them speak Italian?'

'No, but their officers speak Greek.'

A thought crossed Dandolo's mind. 'I'd like to meet them,' he said.

'You won't find them easy,' said Contarini, looking at his guest carefully.

'Nevertheless . . .'

'Don't try to suborn even one of them,' continued Contarini, with a lightness of tone which belied his insight. Dandolo stiffened inwardly. He'd thought he had Contarini on a string. He'd been wrong.

'What do you mean?' he said, laughing, and drinking his wine. 'I'm just curious.'

'They're employed because of their loyalty. It's unquestioning. And it's directed towards the emperor. Only him.'

'And if the emperor dies?'

'Then they switch to the next emperor.' Contarini spread his hands, and relaxed slightly. 'It doesn't matter if the new one's a usurper. It doesn't matter if the new emperor has murdered the last one to get where he is. If he's successful, he gets the loyalty of the Varangians.'

'Sounds like a weakness,' said Dandolo. 'Being able to switch your loyalty on and off, like that.'

'Like the worst kind of woman,' replied Contarini, with a laugh. 'But seriously, their job is to protect the office of the emperor, not just any individual who holds it: so their allegiance is to the throne, if you like, rather than whoever happens to be occupying it at any one time.' Contarini looked across at the knot of five Vikings, who stood in a bunch, detached from the gaudy and gossamer throng around them. Their noses seemed to pinch at the scent of rose petals, wine, spices and perfume that hung like an all but palpable veil over the vaulted, golden-walled hall in which the party was being thrown. 'There's one, anyway,' he continued, 'who speaks good Greek and, now I come to think of it, even some Italian. He has an Italian mistress, a Pisan, a countrywoman of mine, here in the city. The other Varangians frown on that, but they're generally an easygoing lot, among themselves. And to outsiders, well, they're like hunting-dogs. Fierce, but, once you've got their trust, devoted to you. The problem is winning that trust in the first place.'

Dandolo followed his companion's gaze. 'Introduce me,' he said.

Spring was dragging its feet towards summer. The Venetian legation had left three weeks earlier, with the faint makings of a truce in their hands, to return to Chios. Dandolo had warned Vitale of the incidence of plague in the fleet, and that it had been contained; but no more news had come from the island. Dandolo and his own men had stayed behind, to tie up loose ends, as he'd explained to Contarini, pretty sure that thus the news would reach Greek ears, but they themselves were due to leave the following week. The matter had become urgent.

'I'm not happy,' said Leporo. 'We should have left by now.'

'I know,' replied Dandolo. 'But it won't be long.'

'I don't see why we couldn't have left with the rest of the legation. It's time we quitted this, this – Babylon.' He looked around, into the shadows, fearful of hidden listeners.

Dandolo looked at him. 'Unlike you to be so – how shall I say? – spiritual. I take it you refer to the Whore of Babylon when you liken this city to a den of vice?' Dandolo shook his head. 'This city is not a beautiful woman who entrances you, takes everything from you, and leaves you with nothing.'

'My duties may include temporal ones,' replied the Cistercian, 'but first and foremost I am a man of God. This city is nothing more than a cesspit. And it is exactly like a faithless whore.'

'A very profitable one.'

Leporo shook his head impatiently. 'You know what I mean.'

'You mean,' replied Dandolo evenly, 'that it is less like a faithless and abandoned woman, than a place of danger for us.'

'You place too much trust in Contarini.'

'I place no trust in him at all,' snapped Dandolo sharply. 'But as long as I can use his friendship, I will.'

The Greek fleet had sailed only a matter of days after the departure of the legation. Its destination was secret, but it wouldn't have taken a Pythagoras to work out where it was bound. Only diplomatic immunity – or the need to ensure that Venice got a report of the rout of the Venetians at Chios – had, Dandolo felt certain, spared Dandolo's party from arrest. The Greeks would send him home as the bearer of bad news. They, no doubt, thought that their victory at Chios would be decisive. They were just as good mariners as the Venetians, and their fleet was bigger by thirty galleys.

His time had served him well, thought Dandolo. His men had gathered much useful information, and he would leave a network of contacts in the Italian community, men suborned by a mixture of money and the gentlest of hints concerning what might happen to their friends and families back home if they did not comply. Vitale already had some of the information, but not all. Dandolo didn't want the doge to return to Venice with too many bargaining chips in his hand.

Dandolo had always been certain that the Greeks had no intention of holding to any truce, but would make all haste to send their fleet to Chios and drive the Venetians back westwards with their tails between their legs. Their navy was strong. On the other hand, their army was underfunded and undermanned. The Greeks felt themselves to be so strong that they could afford to neglect their defences. Another few years of that, he reflected, and Constantinople would be an apple ripe for the plucking.

Dandolo had never had any intention of rejoining the Venetian force at Chios, and agreed with Vitale that he should make his own way back to Venice, as soon as he had wound up his operations in the Great City. The plan was that Vitale would follow with the expeditionary force at the end of the summer, if the truce looked anything like holding.

But then news reached Dandolo which worried him greatly.

'Somehow,' Leporo reported to him one fine morning, 'Emperor Manuel's got wind of the fact that we've brought back some kind of powerful magic totem.'

Dandolo clasped the sleeve where he carried the scroll with him at all times now. That, the Greeks would never have. Though he didn't yet know how to harness its power, he sensed it, instinctively and without question. It was his, but it possessed him as much as he owned it. He would die before he would be parted from it. It was almost, he felt, as if it had chosen him.

He shook himself. Superstition, he reflected, was cunning, baffling and powerful. If any magic that existed in the tablet, surely it lay in a man's ability to interpret and act on the information in the mysterious writing on it.

The tablet was valuable, of that he had no doubt, the more so since the Templars had tried to cheat him of it so violently, so desperately. He pressed it to his side with his arm, feeling its unnatural cold even through the heavy brocade of his gown.

The cold burned him.

But a nagging doubt ran through him. No sensible man would deny the force of the supernatural, after all – and the rational man would say that the supernatural was simply that which has not yet been discovered. Whoever had made the 'scroll' – and he didn't believe that guff about the Devil – had been, surely, a rational being, aware of what he was doing.

At that moment the door swung open to admit the young Varangian Guard, Frid, whom Dandolo had had himself introduced to at Contarini's party.

'What do you think, Frid? Do you think we should bring our departure date forward?'

Leporo glared at the young Varangian. He had hated him on sight, and now he hated him more for the sudden manner in which Dandolo had taken him into his confidence.

It had been a terrible two weeks for Frid, involving a great change in his life, and an intense struggle within himself, a struggle which he still hadn't resolved.

24

Shortly after Contarini's dinner party, Frid had been summoned to the quarters of his chief, the leader of the Varangian Guard, the *akolouthos*, John Nomikopoulos himself. Not a Viking, but a Greek, Nomikopoulos nevertheless had to bow to the customs and prejudices of the foreign rank-and-file. He told Frid that he was in line for promotion, a high honour, but that in order to qualify, he would have to abandon all ties with his Genoese mistress, Margareta.

Frid was twenty-six years old. A wife had been selected for him among the Norsewomen in the Varangian community, and he was expected to do the right thing. But Frid, faced with a choice, discovered almost to his surprise that he wanted Margareta more than he wanted anything else. He spent days and nights on his knees in his cell-like barracks room, praying for guidance, and none came. His heart and mind, however, remained unchanged.

Perhaps that would not have been the case if it hadn't been for a new factor in his life, which had been subjected to some bewildering buffets in the space of the last fourteen days. Following his summons to the office of the *akolouthos*, Frid had accepted another invitation – to go in secret to the home of a Danish arms dealer in a distant quarter of the city, near the Palace of Blachernae in the north-western sector.

There, the Venetian special envoy was waiting for him.

It quickly became clear to Frid that Dandolo knew all about his situation and was in a position to offer him a way out. If he left the Varangians – a thing unheard of but not forbidden – Dandolo would offer him the post of captain of his own guard and, as far as that was concerned, the special envoy had no objection to his bringing Margareta to Venice with him. Matters had already been squared with Margareta's family, and if he so chose, Frid could be married without delay by the special envoy's own personal assistant, an ordained priest and Cistercian monk.

'Of course, you are under no obligation,' the Venetian had said, 'but you should make your decision without delay, as we will soon be leaving the Great City, and you and Margareta will have only this one opportunity of joining us.'

Loyalty was paramount in Frid's mental makeup. He had been trained to it and instructed never to give or change it lightly. It was bred in his bones from childhood onwards. And his loyalty since he had joined the guard nine years earlier, as a raw seventeen-year-old from Gotland, had been to the Emperor Manuel.

But he'd known Margareta now for a year, a long time to keep her waiting, and during that year his feelings towards her had grown. What would he not have done for her sake? And this seemed to be a truly God-given chance to change the place, if only once in his lifetime, the place where he set his allegiance and his trust.

And he would be taking Margareta back to her homeland. Well, to Italy, at least. As for the atrocity against the Genoans at Constantinople, Frid knew who the true culprits had been. Duty had obliged him to be a member of the detachment of Varangians detailed to kill the Genoese so that blame could be placed on the Venetian community.

Frid would never tell a soul about the betrayal. But he owed Margareta something on account of it. Pisa had been a close ally of Genoa.

Within five days he had made his decision and acted on it. Two days later, he had a new uniform and a new master, and he was a married man. He knew he'd have problems imposing his will on the Italians of Dandolo's bodyguard, but he had no doubt of his own authority. He was less sure of how he would handle the monk Leporo, who had performed the marriage ceremony with the minimum of grace and who, he sensed, resented having to share Dandolo's confidence with him. But that, he was sure, would be settled by Time.

25

'So –?' Dandolo asked again. 'What do you think?'

Frid was not used to having his opinion sought. It was enough getting used to speaking Italian and not Norse. But he knew his mind. 'We should go,' he said. His changed circumstances made him eager to finish the job, to leave the city he'd spent the last nine years of his life in. Dandolo looked across at Leporo. 'You've been seconded,' he said drily. 'Make the arrangements.'

'You wouldn't take *my* word for it,' Leporo said.

'Make the arrangements,' repeated Dandolo.

Leporo was on the point of leaving when there was a furious hammering at the door.

'Open it,' said Dandolo.

One of the Venetians of Dandolo's team entered. The man was out of breath, haggard.

'What is it, Francesco?' Dandolo demanded.

'I've come from the port,' replied the messenger, steadying himself against a table and struggling to breathe evenly. 'The news is bad. A Greek ship has just returned from Chios –'

'Yes?'

'Our navy has been smashed. The attack came at dawn, when no one was prepared. We've lost twelve ships – sunk or disabled. They set the flagship on fire with all hands. They showed no mercy. Eleven more ships were captured.'

Dandolo blanched. He would have expected the Venetians to have put up more of a fight, caught on the hop or not. Each ship represented a capital outlay of perhaps 1,500 florins. 'What happened?'

'They're saying that the same wind which was behind the sails of the Greeks blew round after the attack started and scattered our ships. They couldn't regroup and counter-attack. The Greeks lowered sails, used their oars to power their ships, and picked us off – those of us they could catch – one by one.'

'But what were we doing? Why weren't we ready? What were *our* oarsmen doing?' Dandolo spoke as a great cry of triumph went up from the direction of the port.

'Most of our ships only had skeleton crews aboard. All the rest were ashore. There was no time to muster them. Vitale had trusted in the truce, and besides – '

'Besides *what?*'

'The plague,' gasped the man. 'The plague had taken hold. They'd set up a *lazaretto* and quarantined the sick, but they couldn't stop the spread. Half our manpower was dead or dying by the time the Greeks struck.'

The sounds of victory had grown louder; it was as if the Greek triumph were now pounding on their door. One of their ships must have anchored and its crew was spreading the news.

Dandolo thought fast. 'Gather our men,' he ordered Frid. 'Tell them to pack everything and be ready to leave by tonight. By my authority. Check the tides. Go with him, Francesco. We'll get out by the dawn flood at the latest.'

'They'll detain us if they want to,' warned Leporo.

'Let them try,' retorted Dandolo. He was thinking, the

142

only use we are to them now is as emissaries to take the bad news home. But he wasn't taking any chances. The safety of the tablet took precedence over everything else in his mind.

He made his way down to the Galata quayside where their own three ships were moored, but was stopped by a contingent of the Greek Imperial Guard.

'Enrico Dandolo, Italian Envoy?' its captain demanded.

'What do you want? How dare you accost a Venetian diplomat?'

'You're under arrest.'

Dandolo was taken immediately to the Palace of Boucoleon but rather than being ushered through its gates he was bundled roughly down an alleyway along one side and thrust through a side-entrance. Everything happened in silence.

Here, there was no white marble, no gold, no silver, no finery. Black stone walls hedged him in. He was shoved along a corridor and down a long staircase, carved through rock into the depths of the earth.

The staircase ended in a hallway lit by torches which guttered in their sconces. The stench was suffocating. Five wooden doors, black with soot and grease, opened off this space. The prison guards who'd taken charge of him stripped him roughly, but even in his panic Dandolo noticed that one of them, taking charge of the garments, folded them carefully and placed them on the table which was the hall's only furniture. Then they unlocked one of the doors and flung him into the dungeon beyond it.

He was alone in the semi-darkness. The cell was window-less, and only a little grey light came from the gap between the door and the wall. The cell was clean and free of vermin, and the straw in the palliasse equally so, and dry. Apart from the straw mattress and the rough wooden bed on which it was placed, there was a chair and a table, and a half-barrel for him to piss and shit in. He knew what they were up to.

He marked out three days, No one spoke to him, and they brought him no food. Water was delivered once a day through a hatch, in a wooden beaker which he was obliged to return empty whenever the hatch opened, always at irregular times of day or night. The hatch remained open only for a few seconds, and if he missed it, he would get no chance of anything to drink until the next day. Yes, he knew what they were up to, but he refused to crack.

Dandolo spent hours listening, but heard no sound except for the banging of the hatch – not distant voices, not the wind, not a footfall, nothing. He tried to pray, but mostly he thought – would he get out? What would they do? Why was he here? Were they after the tablet, Adhemar's sacred scroll? Had his double-dealing been discovered? His network of spies? Had he been betrayed by one of them, or was it Contarini who had given the order?

The scroll was always in his mind. It haunted him, it tormented him like an itch he could not scratch. The absence of the tablet's familiar icy cold against his skin racked him like the memory of a lost love. It had been tucked deep into a loop of the sleeve of his inner robe when they arrested him.

The key and the box were in his baggage with Leporo, but Leporo could not open the box.

Had the scroll fallen into another's hands? That was the thought that tore at his spirit.

He could bear his physical state. Though he was hungry, cold and naked, he was spared other abuse. He could only think that some kind of respect for his diplomatic status restrained his gaolers.

On the fourth day, the door was unlocked. Two men entered, bringing a lamp with them, whose unaccustomed light hurt Dandolo's eyes. He rose from his chair as the door swung shut behind them.

The men were in their mid-thirties, tough-looking, bearded, with intelligent, cold eyes. Faces from which you could expect nothing – neither mercy, nor humour. The faces of people to whom there could be no appeal.

They motioned him to sit, still, without speaking. Dandolo did so, aware of how weak his limbs were.

No sooner was he settled than one of the men moved fast, unexpectedly, and kicked the chair brutally from under him. He fell sprawling on the floor, grazing his elbows and knees, twisting his foot badly. A shooting pain told him that one of his toes had fractured, snagging on the edge of a loose flagstone.

He thought they would kick him then, urinate on him, smash his head on the stones, but they kept their distance. Only as he attempted to rise did the first man push him back down, with the toe of his boot.

'You Venetian dog,' said the second, but his voice was mild, without malice, as if he were stating a simple matter of fact.

Dandolo started to get up again, and this time they let

him. The first man retrieved the chair and held it for him to be seated once more. Dandolo hesitated.

'Sit down, you filthy Italian spy,' the man roared suddenly, his voice splitting Dandolo's ears. He took him by the hair and slammed him into the chair with such force that it rocked, and its struts split.

Angered, Dandolo started to speak: 'What do you want from me? Do you know what will happen when Venice –?'

'Venice will do nothing!'

'Tell us what you have found out,' said the quiet man, perching on the edge of the table, drawing off one glove and playing with it with his other hand.

Dandolo said, 'I don't know what you mean.' His first and overwhelming sensation was one of relief: *they are not after the tablet. They do not know.*

26

But then his nightmare was realized. The man with the gloves dug into a purse at his belt and produced the tablet.

He laid it carefully on the table. 'What is this?'

Dandolo hesitated before replying. 'A talisman. A family heirloom. I carry it with me everywhere.'

'A lucky charm?' the man asked, but he wasn't sneering.

'If you like. It is of no value.' He struggled to keep his voice calm.

The other man unhooked a dagger from his belt and, holding it by the scabbard, hefted it in his hand. Its pommel was in the shape of a lion's head, in iron. 'Then you won't mind if I smash it,' he said.

Dandolo controlled his breathing. They'd notice the slightest sign of tension. 'It is of value to me,' he said.

'Then tell us what you have found out, if it is of value to you,' the first man almost whispered. 'We don't want it. We'll let you have it back.'

'It's in code, isn't it? Were you planning to take it back to Venice with you, or were you going to send it?' questioned the first man.

'If you were, you're out of luck,' said the man with the dagger. 'Your ships are impounded and your men confined to their quarters on board.'

'Who?' Dandolo asked quickly, a glimmer of hope in him.

'Your men! The Varangian you recruited, and your guard, and your sailors. Everyone except some monk who got away – buggered off back to his monastery – that's what they always do at the first sign of trouble.'

Dandolo let out his breath. They hadn't got Leporo.

The other man dropped his glove on to the table and stood up again. He leaned forward and brought his face close to Dandolo's, while the other pinioned him to the chair.

'Tell us what you know or we'll twist off your balls with wire.' The voice remained soft. To hear him, you might have thought he was seducing a woman. 'And that will be just the beginning.'

'You can kill me,' replied Dandolo evenly. 'But Venice would never forget such an insult. My city will reach out and tear the heart from your body.'

'Ah,' said the man. 'It is not our custom to execute criminals such as you.'

Relief flooded him. *Not our custom to execute . . .* Then, he might be facing a year or two in prison, at the worst, while he waited to be exchanged. He was important enough!

The first man straightened. 'This is a waste of time,' he said decisively. 'We will arrange a confession and have it signed for you. And we'll send it back with you, hung around your neck. We know you've been spying on us. Your network here has been smashed.'

He had been betrayed, then. Who had he been foolish enough to trust? Who had he underestimated? He had answered his questions within seconds. Apart from his own men, there was only one man in the Great City who could have found out about his secret mission.

Contarini. A fellow countryman but not a Venetian; a man who had lived away from home for so long that by now he was more Greek than Italian.

Dandolo cursed himself for his confidence in the man. Had he not learned by now that you can never know what is in the heart even of your dearest friend? Henceforth he would trust in only one thing.

But there was still room for manoeuvre: 'You'll send me back?'

The man spread his hands. 'Of course.' He paused. 'But we will also put you in a dungeon from which you will never escape.'

Then Dandolo understood. He remembered what the standard punishment for treachery was in the Greek empire. Tears of panic and rage stood in his eyes.

27

They came for him in the middle of the morning of the next day. They had bathed and clothed him, and as soon as he could he had placed the tablet back in its hiding place. They had offered him meat and fruit, and wine, but he touched nothing but water, and little of that. He had not slept, wanting to keep his eyes open for as long as he could.

'Wash him and dress him,' he heard the quiet voice of the man with the gloves say. 'And prepare him.' Dandolo smelt the man's musky perfume as he leaned close and whispered. 'We will let you keep your talisman. You will need it.'

The rough clay tablet was placed gently in his right hand. He closed his fingers tightly round it. Nothing mattered more, he told himself, than that he had it back again. If it was with him, nothing they could do, beyond killing him, could stop him.

He drank in everything he could see, no matter how unimportant, from the plain beaker which held his drink to the patterns the light made on the irregular stonework of the walls.

But then they put a black hood over his head. He was led from the cell and bundled into a cart of some kind, seated, then trundled through streets filled with jeering crowds.

They went a long way. When they stopped and he was pulled out of the vehicle, he heard the lapping of the sea, and felt the sun on his hands. It was a hot day, and he sweated under his robes, though he felt calm, almost dead, within himself.

He was made to mount some stone steps. At the top of them a soldier removed the hood, and he looked around him. At first the light dazzled him. The sun was almost at its zenith, and burned white in a hard blue sky. Not a cloud tempered it.

He stood on a broad platform, which must have been placed high on one of the fortified southern towers punctuating the walls which ran along the coast between the city and the Sea of Marmara. The platform was made of white marble, the stones so exactly placed together that they seemed to form one unbroken surface. At the far end was a long raised dais, on which a number of Greeks in official robes were seated. Dandolo squinted to see who they were. At the centre sat the Grand Vizier; the emperor was not present. Near the Vizier Dandolo picked out the figure of Tonso Contarini. For a moment their eyes met. Contarini lowered his.

The two flanking sides of the square were crowded with onlookers, for this was a public spectacle. Dandolo scanned the faces there, and his heart gave a leap of hope when among them he saw Leporo. The monk had exchanged his black habit for a modest Greek tunic. Leporo and he exchanged a brief look. The monk discreetly sketched the Sign of the Cross in the air.

At the centre of the platform stood a table, big enough to take the body of a man laid prone. Dandolo saw that it was fitted with leather, buckled restraints to go round the ankles, thighs, arms, wrists, torso and neck. A kind of leather pillow, narrow, with raised sides, was ready to take the head and hold it firmly. Above it was fixed an apparatus of some kind – a tripod with an adjustable arm at its top, in turn equipped with a slot into which something must fit.

Dandolo steadied himself as he felt his legs weaken. Two soldiers supported him as they led him to the table where another man awaited him, flanked by two assistants. The three were clad in black *tschalvar*, but their upper bodies were bare. Each wore a leather cap and mask.

It seemed to be happening to someone else. Dandolo's spirit hovered over his body as he was handed over to the assistants by the soldiers. They were burly men. One held him down as the other arranged and tightened the straps around him. He allowed them to do this without a struggle, and when they were finished he found he could not move. The sweat ran over his body under his robes.

They fitted pegs to his eyelids to hold the eyes open. His hands clawed the air.

Now the assistants drew back and the third man stood over him. Gimlet eyes, eyes of steel, looked into his. The man disappeared from Dandolo's view then reappeared holding a magnifying glass in a bronze frame, which he fitted to the slot in the arm above the tripod.

It was a burning-glass. Dandolo watched as the man adjusted it so that it aligned with the sun. His eyelids strained to shut against the pegs which held them. His body writhed against the fetters.

A concentrated beam of sunlight bore through the lens and briefly scorched his face as the man moved the glass across it, towards his eyes. The man covered the glass with a black cloth until he had positioned it correctly.

The right eye first.

Dandolo flinched as he watched the man's steady hand guide his instrument. Pain was near which would be like no pain in the world had ever been before. The white sun screamed into his eye as the imperial executioner burned it out. Dandolo could feel it bubble and burst, and the agony was like a boiling iron spike thrust hard through his head. His forehead poured sweat and he could feel another, more viscous, liquid running down his cheek towards his mouth. He did not know whether he was screaming or not.

The glass moved slowly across the bridge of his nose towards his left eye. The eyelids fought against their restraints, the muscles that controlled them instinctively urged to protect.

And now, a miracle! His surviving eye saw the executioner glance around for a moment. No one else was near. And the man reached up, and tilted the lens slightly so that the sharp beam was diffused. When he set to his work again, the beam that bore through his pupil into his retina hurt him indeed, but it *did not sear out the eye*.

Now he heard himself scream. Now he felt his body arch and stretch vainly against the leather straps. And his left eye saw, after a long minute, huge amoebic shapes of purple and blue and gold float up against it, bumping into one another as they crowded into a narrow space.

The executioner stood back, businesslike, and un-screwed the lens from its slot. The assistants came forward and undid the straps before roughly bandaging the wrecked eyes, then hauled the sobbing Venetian to his feet as he dribbled and spewed down the front of his apparel.

Dandolo closed his eyes, squeezing them shut until multicoloured stars appeared on the insides of the lids, as he was thrust forward, down the steps, and on to the cart again. No hood was necessary now. Sightless, he was taken north through the city, across the Horn to Galata, and deposited at the quay where his ships were moored. He heard troops coming to attention, and the rattle and clat-ter of their weapons as they did so.

Then a voice. A clipped, official voice in the darkness of his world. The first voice he was to hear that belonged to a face he imagined he would never see.

'You have been escorted to your ships. You will sail on the first tide to Venice. Reasons for our sentence and its execution will be despatched with you. Be this a warning to your city never again to spy on us.'

He was left alone. He heard people receding and, after-wards, silence except for lapping water and the screaming of gulls. Everything in his head throbbed. He could not bring himself to open his eyes. He could not move. He dared not. He felt himself swaying. But after an eternity there was an arm on his, guiding, and the familiar smell of a man he knew, and a voice he knew too.

'Lean on me,' said Leporo. 'The gangway is close by. We have an apothecary. Once on the ship we will attend to your eyes.' Leporo placed his head close to Dandolo's.

Dandolo could feel the man's lips touch his ear as he whispered: 'I bribed the executioner. We will bathe your left eye and anoint it. I could not persuade him to spare them both – the job had to be seen to be done properly. But with God's grace, you may be able to see again – not perfectly, but in part. With God's grace. In time.'

Ah, thought Dandolo. Time . . .

Then an urgent thought struck him, and his right hand delved into his sleeve. He sighed, despite his pain, luxuriously.

It was still there.

28

Istanbul, the Present

They were looking at the last photograph in the batch Marlow had ordered Lopez to extract. This one had not been taken at the site of the tomb but in the laboratory which Adkins had been using at the University of Istanbul.

It was a picture of a key. Not a very large key, though it was of great antiquity.

It was 7cm long, with a diamond-shaped bow and complex teeth; and on its shank an inscription was incised. The key, which looked as if it were made of iron, the metal pitted with age but not rusted, had been photographed from both sides, lying on a matt white surface. The inscription was carried over from one side of the shank to the other.

But the photograph was poor and the writing barely legible.

'This seems to have been the one artefact removed from the tomb,' said Haki.

'Where is it now?' asked Marlow.

'We don't know,' Haki replied. 'It must have been taken with the other material that disappeared along with our friends.'

'Can you make anything of the inscription?' asked Graves.

'Major Haki, have you a magnifying glass?' Marlow said.

After rummaging in his desk, Haki came up with a small plastic one. 'This is it,' he said apologetically.

'Thanks.'

Marlow pored over the photographs for a long time. At last he straightened. 'It's not writing, it's numerals,' he announced. 'And if I'm right, it's in Aramaic.' He handed the photo to Graves. 'They invented a numeric code, and this may be an example of it, but we need a better picture.'

'There's something I don't understand,' said Graves. 'This key, by the look of it, by its design, must date from . . .' Her voice trailed off in puzzlement.

'Yes?' Marlow prompted.

'Early medieval. Eleventh century, maybe a little later.' She looked thoughtful then continued, 'Aramaic died out as a living language and was replaced by Arabic in the seventh century – three hundred years before this key was made.'

'What the inscription says may solve that.'

'As soon as we're back in New York.'

They were interrupted by a knock on the door.

'Ah,' said Detective-Major Haki. 'At last!'

One of the dark-suited aides came in quickly. He was carrying a plastic box. Haki took it and placed it on the table. 'This is what I wanted to show you,' he said. 'The one artefact – if you can call it that – which our people recovered from the tomb itself after Adkins and his friends were abducted. But we had to verify it before passing it on to you.'

Haki opened the box and withdrew something soft, wrapped in tissue paper. This he pulled delicately aside to reveal, further wrapped in sealed transparent cellophane, a pair of dirty white cotton gloves.

'We found them under the plinth on which Dandolo's coffin rests. Look.' Without removing the cellophane, he turned them over.

'I needed to know if they had been left behind by your scientists,' Haki continued. 'But they looked too old for that. I'm amazed that Dr Adkins and his friends – or anyone else – missed the gloves. But we had more time, and we were looking not for ancient artefacts, all of which were clearly in view in the tomb, but for modern clues – so we delved a little bit deeper.'

'Yesterday, you said that Adkins and the others were the first to discover the tomb,' interrupted Marlow.

'I said that that was how things *appeared*.' Haki spread his hands. 'I am no archaeologist. I thought I had better have our experts date them. Now, I hope, we shall see the result of their labours.'

He took out a manila envelope from the box and opened it, taking out a single sheet of A4 paper. He read it quickly.

'It seems that someone did get there before your people,' he announced. 'About a hundred years before.'

29

Later that day, having taken their leave of Detective-Major Haki, and back at their hotel – a new one, closer to Atatürk International Airport – Marlow and Graves took stock. As he pondered, Marlow found himself looking at Graves's hand on the table before him. She was wearing her heavy emerald ring, but his eye was attracted to the tiny faded heart tattoo on her little finger. It looked as if someone had tried to erase it, and certainly she should not have had any such easy identifier on her body. He wondered what the story behind it was. Well, it was her story, and broken hearts were not uncommon.

'Now for the hard part,' said Graves, failing to read the thoughts etched on Marlow's face.

'Haki's very charming, but he hasn't a clue what's happened. Maybe he isn't that concerned. Turkish Security hasn't been breached.'

'True, but it's not as if we're going away empty-handed.'

'We've come away with a basket-load of questions, and we're no closer to what's happened to Adkins and his team. But there's nothing more for us here. Maybe back at base we'll be able to dig out more on *why* they vanished.'

'They've told Adkins's and Taylor's families. But they've been muzzled.'

'When's our plane?'

'Six-thirty in the morning.'

Marlow looked at his watch. 'Get the new data to Leon. Maybe he'll have some ideas on the code on the key.'

'That's my department and I'm already working on it,' said Graves, irritated. Marlow and Lopez might have gone back a few years, but she wasn't going to be treated like some intern.

'The gloves too.'

'Those goddamned gloves! They give me a headache.'

Marlow shook himself. He was tired, and he knew that his companion was too. They hadn't eaten since breakfast early that morning. And when he was tired he had to fight harder to keep at bay the black thoughts which assailed him, which never left him. 'The key, the broken hand – everything points to the reason for Adkins's disappearance.'

'Haki will keep us posted with anything new.'

'Do you trust him?' asked Marlow.

Graves was nonplussed. 'What choice do we have? His credentials check out.'

'He ruled out Islamists,' said Marlow thoughtfully.

'What are you driving at?'

'There's nothing in any records at all about what might have been buried with Dandolo. He was a major figure in Venetian history. He brought huge prosperity and financial stability to the city-state. New trade-routes, dominion over Egypt and Crete, and that at a time when the Seljuk Turks had pushed the Christians out of the Holy Land.'

'All very interesting, but it has nothing to do with our mission –' Graves broke off. She was getting too tired to think, Marlow saw; and that was a dangerous thing.

'Let's eat,' he suggested.

*

The hotel was modern and functional. Its restaurant was cavernous, gloomy, fashionably stark and underlit. It wasn't any more attractive than the sanitized Turkish food it served. And the thought of eating there, followed by a couple of hours' work in one or other of their severely furnished rooms, depressed them both.

'Let's find a proper restaurant,' Marlow decided. 'This place is like a morgue.'

Graves, new to fieldwork and anxious about security, agreed with the idea in her heart, but her head questioned the security risk, and she said so, adding, 'Isn't there a good chance that we haven't been able to shake off whoever it is who's so interested in us?'

'There's a place down the road. It's safe. You can see it from here.'

He pointed. A short distance away, red and gold lights flickered along a jazzy frontage.

But he checked his gun. A Heckler & Koch USP Compact 9mm. Light and inconspicuous, it'd do enough damage at close range. He drew his jacket open just enough to let Graves see it. She nodded, patting her shoulder-bag. Good, he thought. Not such a novice after all. Their computers were in the hotel safe, in concealed compartments within their briefcases. Everything was covered.

Like the outskirts of most airports, the streets and buildings around the hotel shared its bleakness. The restaurant was an oasis, owing its existence to airline staff tired of plastic food.

It was dark by now, and lights from streetlamps, and

from the hotel's façade, were mirrored in the polished surfaces of cars as they made their way across the hotel car-park to the road. Occasional buses, trucks and cars drove past at speed to and from the city centre, but the principal sound punctuating the night was the noise of aircraft engines, coming in with a whine or taking off with a roar.

There was a metallic, dusty smell in the air.

They were halfway across the car-park when Graves saw the first figure, out of the corner of her eye. If the man hadn't moved, she wouldn't have spotted him at all, and even the slight, stooping movement he made as he started to run towards them she mistook at first for a trick of the light.

Marlow caught her reaction immediately and jerked his automatic out of its holster, holding the firearm steady as they stood back to back, his eyes straining to pick out the figure again, Graves following his gaze.

But there was nothing. The man had disappeared.

'He was there,' Graves breathed. 'I know it.'

'Let's move. Back to the hotel.'

They retraced their steps. There was no one about; the hotel doorman had disappeared into the dimly lit foyer. If there was any assailant out there, Marlow thought, he'd make his move now.

Suddenly there was a flurry of movement behind them, to the left and right. The men must have been hiding behind cars. How long had they been watching the hotel, waiting for just such a chance? How had they managed to spring this ambush?

There was a gentle thud – the noise of a silenced gun

162

– and a bullet hissed past his right ear. Graves was already crouching, her pistol up and ready, swinging this way and that. Marlow turned quickly and got a shot off in the direction of the man who'd fired at him, a hooded figure in black fifteen metres away. He went down, but Marlow hadn't time to make sure, as the sound of a scuffle and the dull crack of a gun behind him made him turn again. Three men, similarly dressed in black, hoods pulled over their heads, had taken Graves and were dragging her fast towards a black Porsche Cayenne SUV which stood nearby with its doors open and its engine running.

Jack started to run towards them as another bullet flew past him. He ducked as he heard the soft sound of a third muffled shot.

30

Venice, Year of Our Lord 1201

They'd had a hard journey. It had rained for days, and all the roads were mired, slowing their horses and bringing their three baggage-wagons to a complete halt so often that they'd been on the point of abandoning them. The whole countryside, marshland and sullen farmsteads, slouched under the weather, and all colour was drained from the trees and the grass. Even the clinging mud, which got into everything, from their sodden clothes to their hair, looked grey.

'Look there!' Geoffrey de Villehardouin cried suddenly.

The others turned their gaze in the direction he was pointing.

Across the bleak plain of the Veneto they could see the pale outline of the city on the horizon. They breathed a sigh of relief. But the hard part – the negotiations – was still ahead of them.

Geoffrey de Villehardouin, one of the group of ambassadors – six French noblemen and generals – paused to reflect on their mission. They'd stopped in the light drizzle which was falling on their aching bones to look at Venice, barely discernible through the thin mist. Somewhere high above, there was a hint that the sun was struggling to break through. They set up a makeshift camp to await the return of the couriers they'd sent ahead earlier to announce their arrival.

It had all started a handful of years earlier. A crusade led by the kings of England and France and the Holy Roman Emperor had failed to take Jerusalem, lost to Saladin's army fourteen years before, back from the Turks. That was a thorn in the side of Rome, which conveniently ignored the fact that Jerusalem was also the holiest city in Islam after Mecca; and the energetic young man who'd taken over as pope in 1198 wanted to wrest the city back. The problem was getting there. The Kingdom of Jerusalem had been reduced to a few coastal towns, and they were clinging on by their fingernails.

The leaders of the new crusading force which was being organized in response to Pope Innocent's appeal, Count Baldwin of Flanders and the Marquess Boniface de Montferrat, wanted to attack from the south, using grain-rich Egypt as their operations base. And for that they needed a fleet to get their army across the Mediterranean.

The best shipbuilders were in Venice and Genoa. Genoa wasn't the better bet. Hence this embassy to Venice.

It was all taking time. Things weren't well organized, thought Geoffrey. He hoped the eloquence of at least one of his fellow ambassadors, Conon de Béthune, would help swing things. He'd heard that the doge of Venice, Enrico Dandolo, though very old and, it seemed, blind, drove hard bargains.

Within a few hours the couriers returned with the news

that the doge and his council awaited them at their convenience and extended to them the warmest of welcomes. Warm, dry lodgings and fresh clothes had also been made ready for them.

To the bedraggled Frenchmen, it seemed almost too good to be true.

Having bathed, changed and eaten, warm at last and rested, there followed three days of the usual diplomatic tiptoeing around under the guise of hospitality and bonhomie. Everyone was testing the water – but that was to be expected. There was a difference, however, and Geoffrey wondered if he were the only one to have noticed it.

He sounded out four of his companions, but they were unaware of anything out of the ordinary. They even enjoyed the necessity of bathing – a formality they weren't used to – before visiting the courtesans who'd been placed at their disposal.

But Geoffrey de Villehardouin was not reassured. His apprehension grew worse. Something strange seemed to have crept into his soul.

After some hesitation, he shared his fears at last with Conon, the most aloof and, in Villehardouin's view, intelligent, of the six Frenchmen.

'Seigneur de Béthune, a word –'

'Speak, Lord Marshal.'

Villehardouin hesitated, not knowing quite how to formulate his words, but he could no longer keep his doubts to himself, however uncertainly he expressed them: 'Do you feel that – somehow – we are beginning to think ourselves *in complete accord* with the Venetians?'

De Béthune eyed him keenly before replying: 'You've eaten too much good food and drunk too much good wine, Geoffrey. We all have. And it's the rest and warmth after our hard journey.' He waited a moment. 'Don't worry. We'll be on our guard when the time comes.'

31

At length, the deputation was summoned to the Council Chamber of the doge's palace. The huge vaulted interior impressed the northerners with its grandeur, no less than the solemn ranks of the forty-six councillors in their red-and-gold gowns trimmed with ermine.

At their centre sat Dandolo. Despite his ninety-one years, he sat ramrod-backed on the ducal throne, the gnarled fingers of his left hand grasping the arm of his seat, his right concealed within his robe. He was clean-shaven, and you could see that there was still flesh on his bones. He exuded a vitality which seemed unnatural in a man of his years.

Only his eyes appeared to have no light in them, though Geoffrey could have sworn he saw a ruby glint in the left one.

After the preliminary courtesies and introductions were out of the way, Conon began.

'My lords,' he said. 'We have come to your noble city and court as envoys of the chief barons and knights of France, who have taken up the Holy Cross in order to take vengeance on those who have outraged Our Lord Jesus Christ by the usurpation of the City of Jerusalem, and, if it be God's will, to recapture it for the Church.' He paused for effect. He realized he was anxious – more anxious than he had imagined – to get the sober ranks of big businessmen seated before him on his side.

He would do anything for them.

He noted, too, that all of them kept looking towards the doge to gauge his reaction. Clearing his throat, he continued, 'And since the great lords of France who sent us know that nowhere in the world exists a nation better fitted to aid them in this great enterprise, they entreat you, in the Name of Our Lord God, to share the pity they have taken on Jerusalem and the offence caused to God by its capture by barbarians, and most graciously to do your utmost to supply us with a fleet to the purpose, both ships of war and of freight.'

There was a long pause, a pregnant silence during which the stony faced council regarded the envoys who stood isolated in the middle of the chamber.

'And how do you suggest we set about this laudable task?' the doge asked at last.

'In any way that you care to propose,' replied Conon immediately – and to his consternation. It seemed *not to be his voice* that was speaking. He cast an eye at his colleagues, who were nonetheless smiling and nodding their approval. 'As long as our leaders can meet your conditions and bear the cost,' he added, mastering himself.

But as he continued, he found himself playing entirely into the Venetians' hands, losing any sense of playing his hand, of bargaining, and trading on the responsibility Venice should show unhesitatingly towards the Church.

'I see,' said the doge. He looked around his council and exchanged whispered words with those nearest to him. Then, grasping the armrest of the throne with his left hand, his right hand still firmly tucked within his robe, he stood up. An elderly Cistercian monk at his elbow hastened to assist him, but he shook the man away. Finding his balance, he looked – Conon was sure he *looked* – piercingly into the ambassador's eyes and went on. 'Your French leaders are asking much of us. This is an ambitious enterprise, not to be undertaken lightly. We will debate the matter and give you our answer in one week's time.'

Conon started to speak, but the doge stayed him with a gesture. 'Do not be surprised at this delay. It is an important matter. It requires our full consideration.'

With that, he bowed stiffly, and made his way, the monk in close attendance, towards a door set in the wall a short distance behind the throne. He seemed to know his way. Near the door stood a huge, red-headed, battle-scarred man in late middle age, whose outstretched arm the doge leaned on. This man – no Italian, thought Conon, noticing the furious look the monk shot at the giant – led the doge through the door. The rest of the assembly broke up without further ceremony. The audience was at an end.

32

Dandolo knew there was no need to convince his council what to do. His good eye glittered as he dismissed Leporo and, to the monk's irritation, drew his bodyguard, Frid, into secret conference. They were cloistered together for a long time.

'It's time to put our plan into operation,' said Dandolo.

Frid's loyalty to Dandolo had not wavered once in the thirty years he had been in his service. Indeed, after the death of his wife, Margareta, of the water-sickness, one year after their arrival in Venice, in 1172 – the year of the fall of Doge Vitale after his disastrous expedition against Constantinople – which was swiftly followed by the death of their infant son, Frid's loyalty had increased to a dependency. Dandolo became his only family, and he thought no more of returning to the Northlands than he would of flying to the moon.

But Frid was a Viking, and hadn't forgotten the expertise of his ancestors. He knew the art of building ocean-going ships.

Over the years, Dandolo had gradually let him into the secret of his great plan. Together, they had developed it.

It had needed enormous patience, and that they both possessed, the more so since, after nearly three decades of study, and fighting off encroaching Death with a will of iron, the doge had emerged triumphantly from his study one spring day in the last year of the last century, his left eye glittering madly.

Dandolo had at last unlocked the secret hidden in the mysterious tablet, the great secret he had always been convinced it held. It gave him the key to exercise the greatest art of all. All he had wanted was the occasion. And, now, as if God had placed it in his lap, in the shape of this crusading army of boorish Franks, he had the means of using this art and the vehicle, to make himself the Master of the Earth.

'We will build them their fleet, and they will pay for it. But it will be our fleet,' Dandolo breathed when they were alone in his study.

'They are going to demand a big fleet – far bigger than they need,' said Frid.

'Exactly,' replied Dandolo, with the ghost of a smile.

Frid went to a locked chest, opened it, and from it drew a number of rolls of paper. The designs.

For a long time they went over them together.

'Ships such as the world has never seen before,' breathed the doge.

'People will know.'

'I will mask their minds,' said Dandolo. 'I will mask the minds even of the shipbuilders, and they shall do what I desire, without question.'

'The power and the glory will be yours,' said Frid.

Dandolo looked at him sharply. 'No. It's for the glory of Venice!'

33

At the end of the time the doge had set, the envoys were summoned again to confront the council.

'We have duly debated your request,' the doge began. 'And by the grace of the city, we have agreed to assent to it. You, for your part, must determine that you accept our terms and can bear the cost our work will incur.'

The ambassadors exchanged glances – again it seemed as though they were incapable of doing other than the doge suggested.

Conon de Béthune and Geoffrey de Villehardouin, though they looked at each other, found no trace of disquiet in their minds. They read nothing but quiet accord and triumph in each other's eyes.

The doge signalled to the Cistercian monk Leporo, who was always at his side. The man of God stood, unrolled a parchment which was handed him by a herald, cleared his throat, and began to read: 'We undertake to build freighters to carry 4,500 horses and 9,000 squires; other ships will be constructed for 4,500 knights and 20,000 sergeants of infantry. The contract we offer will include nine months' worth of rations for the men and fodder for the animals. Our price' – the monk paused here, impressively – 'is 89,500 new Venetian grossi.'

This was a huge sum, but the envoys nodded their assent immediately.

'Moreover –' the monk was about to continue, but Dandolo himself took over, rising and grasping the wooden rail in front of his throne with his left hand.

'Moreover,' he declared, his voice trembling with emotion, 'we shall abide by this covenant: that for a twelvemonth after we have sailed on this great mission from Venice, we shall ourselves act in the service of this holy war and in the service of the God who holds His shielding hand over it. For the love of this God, we ourselves shall supply a further fifty armed galleys at our own cost to the fleet, with only this proviso: that all spoils of war shall be divided between you and us, half and half, resulting from whatever our successes by land or sea may be.'

'We agree,' replied Conon. Geoffrey de Villehardouin looked at him, a last dying flicker of doubt in his mind. But when he tried to recapture that doubt and focus on it, it vanished like a dream.

34

To give polish to the solemnity of the occasion, Venice held a High Mass in the cathedral of San Marco, to which the great and the good of the city thronged.

Looking back on it later, Geoffrey de Villehardouin still marvelled at it.

After the elevation of the Host, he remembered, the six French envoys appeared before the high altar and knelt, unable to hide their emotion, in front of the citizenry of Venice. Their tears flowed, and soon the doge, and all the people assembled there, wept too, filled, as many said later, with the Mystery of the Holy Spirit, and a profound sense of the justice of the enterprise in which they were about to partake.

At the very moment when feelings were running highest, Dandolo climbed the steps to the pulpit and looked out over the shining crowd which filled every corner of the church, whose mosaics dazzled in the light of ten thousand candles.

Mastering himself, the doge, gripping the pulpit's edge with his left hand, fixed the envoys with his strange eyes and declaimed to his subjects: 'Citizens of Venice! Witness the honour God has paid you in inspiring the finest nation in the world to forsake all other peoples and all other matters of worldly trade and commerce, and choose us to join with them in such a high enterprise as the very deliverance of Our Lord Himself from the yoke of the Saracen.'

The formalities over, Leporo met the Frenchmen in a private office, where they went over the fine details of the voyage to Egypt. Once this had been settled, the doge, who, the envoys gathered, had been busy at his prayers, joined them.

'And what are we to say of the date for our gathering here for embarkation?' Geoffrey asked.

Dandolo had already made his mind up on the matter. 'We have a fleet to build, and you have an army to muster,' he said. 'It is now Friday 9 March,' he said. 'The Feast of St Antony. Easter Sunday will be in sixteen days . . .' He calculated for a moment.

'We all need time,' he continued. 'I believe that we should set the date for the Feast of St John next year. Let that be the date by which we are all foregathered here, and in readiness.'

Once again, the ambassadors from France found themselves unhesitatingly assenting.

Dandolo smiled. 'And now it only remains for the business of the charters based on our agreements before God to be drawn up and signed.'

'There is also the matter of the down payment, too,' said Leporo, smiling too.

'A mere detail,' added the doge. 'I know you have not brought such a large amount as the agreed sum of 5,000 grossi with you, as the generosity and extent of the gifts you have brought us would not have permitted of it in your baggage train. But rest assured that we have banks able and willing to extend the amount to you as a loan on the most advantageous terms.'

Borrowing from us in order to pay us, thought Leporo, proud of the plan, which had been his contribution. *And the interest which falls on top will benefit our Holy St Benedict, patron of my Order.*

Two days later, Geoffrey, Conon and the rest put their signatures or made their marks on the documents of agreement, which their attendant secretaries, members of the Order of the White Monks, had read through to them.

Now, they were preparing to depart. But, as he handed the envoys their copies of the charters, heavy with seals and ribbons, the old doge suddenly fell to his knees.

'Let me swear once again, by the Holy Gospels and by the body of our own patron saint, Mark, that I shall carry out faithfully all conditions set down in these weighty agreements.' He groped his faltering left hand in the direction of the envoys, but Geoffrey could have sworn that once again he saw the man's left eye glow red.

Conon stooped to grasp the hand. He felt a grip of frozen iron.

'And let me enjoin you to honour your side of the bargain too,' Dandolo rasped in a voice of high emotion.

'We so swear, *Altissima*,' Conon replied.

Visibly reassured, allowing himself to be aided by Conon, the doge got to his feet, one hand straying to a large, ruby-studded crucifix he wore over his robe.

Conon was surprised to find tears in his own eyes, and saw that his fellows were weeping too.

But they were tears of joy.

'We will send letters of this matter to Pope Innocent,' he said.

'And so will we,' said Leporo, as Dandolo, apparently made frail by his feelings, was led away on the arm of his giant bodyguard.

The next day, the Frenchmen took their leave.

Alone at the balcony of his study, Dandolo watched them depart. His vision went in and out of focus. He shook himself and squinted. He had fought off Death to live this long, in order to achieve his purpose.

He had fought off the decaying sight of the eye, which Leporo had saved by bribing the executioner at Constantinople all those years ago, long enough to crack the code of the tablet. It had taken the most secret scholarship to do it, and one elderly Armenian Christian, in particular, to aid him. The Armenian had been versed in ancient Chaldean rites, and had proved himself invaluable, but was now dead – a tragic drowning.

He prayed fervently to God to let him live another few years, let his remaining sight not fade for another few years, and he would have his heart's desire.

His thoughts turned to Constantinople.

I am returning, Great City, he thought. I shall not see you again, not with these eyes; but I am coming back. And I will have your glories burned out of you until nothing remains of them but charcoal and hissing water. I will burn out your great, golden, pampered eye, and leave nothing but ashes there.

35

Berlin, the Present

A sharp wind blew down Unter den Linden from the east. It was six o'clock in the morning and from the picture window of his office on the fifth floor of the MAXTEL building, Rolf Adler watched a sheet of newspaper skeetering along the deserted pavement until the wind lifted it and banged it high up against the trunk of one of the lime trees which lined the street, where it flapped vainly like the wings of a wounded bird. It was warm in the office, and the lighting was soft, in sharp contrast to the neon-lit outer room where three secretaries were already bent over their computers or on the telephone, waking up troubled administrators at the universities of both Venice and Yale.

Adler usually took four hours of deep, untroubled sleep – these nights, alone more often than not, since he found sex less and less interesting, and women increasingly boring.

He hadn't slept any longer since his teens. That was in the days when, instead of waking either in his Berlin penthouse on the top floor of the MAXTEL building here on Unter den Linden, or in his mansion in the hills above St-Tropez, or in his London, Paris or New York apartments, he'd woken to cold darkness in a corrugated-iron shack, or in the mean little house of his brutal childhood in Cottbus. *Get up early to get ahead*, his father had admonished him, between bouts of knocking back bottles of supermarket schnapps and thrashing his nervous little mother black and blue.

The previous night's sleep had been irritatingly fitful, but now, dressed in what he liked to think of as his armour – a 5000€ Billis & Dunn charcoal-grey suit with a crisp, white Egyptian-cotton shirt and a dark, discreetly patterned tie by Elizabeth Miranda – he considered the day's work.

He liked this moment of quiet, though this particular morning he was feeling anything but calm. But he also liked to take care of his investments, and that included his non-profit-making ones.

Something had gone seriously wrong with the Dandolo Project. And that project carried a lot more weight than mere philanthropy.

He leaned across the black surface of his desk and touched a key on a screen set into its surface. Seconds later, a thin blonde, her hair loosely gathered in a black velvet bow, entered the room. She was in late middle-age, once pretty, but now getting scrawny in her attempts to fight off the years with remorseless dieting. Timid, dark-brown eyes. A nervous, evasive manner. But completely trustworthy.

He'd stopped sleeping with her years ago, when he'd noticed that the games were getting a little rough even for her to take, and besides, her husband had beaten her when he'd noticed the deep scratches on her back; but Adler hadn't fired her.

Such dog-like devotion was a rare commodity; it was the one strength in all her weakness.

His tone was even. 'What is going on, Frau Müller?'

'We've just been on to the dean's office at Venice.'

'Yes?'

'He wasn't very happy about –'

Adler stepped forward and stood close to her. She flinched, expecting a blow, but none came.

'I don't give a fuck about his feelings, Frau Müller,' he said quietly. 'What have you actually achieved?'

'He's sending over all the information they have immediately.'

'That's better. Yale?'

'We've been putting pressure on them for days. But our people there have reported progress at last. Apparently there's been an embargo –'

'Yes, yes, I know all about that.' Adler tuned back to the window testily. Frau Müller had already ensured that the MAXPHIL executives on the East Coast had made it clear to the academics processing Dandolo Project material at both universities that they wouldn't just be losing funding if they didn't comply to the letter with what their benefactor required of them. A near tragic accident suffered by the six-year-old son of one of them – the little boy had narrowly escaped death when he'd fallen foul of a savage guard-dog which had inexplicably slipped its chain and found its way into the family's garden – had been enough to shake things up there. With luck, however, and the right hospital care, he should be able to walk again quite soon.

Adler smiled. Good Frau Müller. She may have been

scared of life, but she was good at obeying orders. Any orders. She'd even arranged for the hospital bills to be taken care of.

He dismissed her and sat at his desk, forcing himself to breathe deeply and regularly. He mustn't let his anxiety get the better of him, however much was at stake.

His chair was too soft and too comfortable. It irritated him. He stood up again and paced the room, his dark-grey loafers noiseless on the teak parquet.

His anxiety had led him to take an enormous risk a few days earlier, and he'd been fool enough to take it on his own doorstep. At that moment a dozen of his men were out on the streets, putting things right. But until he knew that the matter was settled, he couldn't rest.

He bit hard into the knuckles of his right hand, so hard that the flesh grew red and white around the marks. The skin of his right forefinger was hardened and permanently creased from such treatment down the years.

But Adler remained ill at ease. He wasn't getting the full picture and, despite his own personal efforts, he worried that someone else was.

36

Forty-eight hours earlier, a car swung north up Wilhelm-strasse from the direction of Pariser Platz. It was a big, dark saloon and its driver had a little difficulty squeezing it into a parking space in a quiet street in Pankow. He'd driven the short distance from central Berlin, where they'd been keeping the prisoner isolated in the sequestered sub-basement of the office building.

Now, the prisoner was chained and gagged on the floor in the back of the car.

He had arrived a little early and the minders he was expecting to meet him hadn't yet arrived, but it was still before dawn and the streets were empty. Not far away stood the dilapidated apartment block, a leftover from the bad old days of the German Democratic Republic, which would be his cargo's final destination.

He'd been distracted by the parking business and, after all, this was a routine delivery, he'd done five or six over the past year, never asked questions, just took the wad of euros at the end of the day and went off to the betting shop and his favourite Irish pub.

So it took him completely by surprise when he heard the clink of chain somewhere close to his left ear, and then felt cold metal links wrapped round his throat and pulled tight.

Graves had been instantly and heavily drugged the

moment the Porsche SUV had roared away from the hotel parking lot in Istanbul, and when she had awakened in a featureless, windowless room, harshly neon-lit when the lights were on and pitch dark when they were not, she had no idea where in the world she was. She had only the vaguest memory of travelling any distance at all, though she could remember the rhythm of a small plane; but that might have been anything from between a week and a year ago. She hadn't seen her attackers, and only remembered a glimpse of a European couple, a man and a woman. She could hardly be sure even of that.

But they'd left her alone in the room, after throwing ice-cold water over her and kicking her around a little, just to bring her to her senses. Much later, they'd brought in a heavy wooden stool with holes in its seat through which they ran nylon ropes in order to bind her to it. After that, the hooded and anonymous men – she knew they were men, from their smell and their strength – had covered her head with a thick sack, tied it close around her neck, and left her.

She was terrified. She thought she would tell whoever it was who had abducted her everything she knew, just for the sake of a glass of water. There'd be no need to torture her, she told herself, surely they wouldn't think of doing that.

When the interrogators came into the room they did so very softly. She thought she heard the door click open, and felt the faintest breeze on her ankles where her jeans had ridden up over her ankle boots – they hadn't stripped her, that was something, and they had allowed her to perform her natural functions, so she was in no physical discomfort, apart from the ropes cutting into her arms and legs. She was fully conscious and her head was clear, but that was small consolation for no longer being able to see. She could only hear tiny sounds from an indeterminate number of people, which seemed to come from all around her.

Without warning, the stool was brutally kicked over and she fell helplessly with it, banging her left arm and leg on the concrete floor, and grazing her temple through the sack. Someone grasped her head and hauled her and the stool upright, twisting her neck and making her ears ring. A voice with an unrecognizable accent whispered close to her ear, speaking English:

'*Where is it?*

Before she could answer, someone struck her across the head with a baseball bat, just hard enough to topple the stool again. This time she fell on to her right side.

The assault went on for a long time, and with such intensity that the inner core of her mind, which had so far managed to keep her sane by remaining detached from what was happening to her, began to cave in.

The same question, the only question they asked, was repeated over and over again. Bleeding, weeping despite herself, and running her tongue round her mouth to reassure herself that her teeth were still intact, she found herself finally let alone.

The door clicked open, someone left the room, and it clicked shut. But she was aware that she was not alone. After an hour of silence, in which she could only hear the breathing of the other people in the room and the pages of a magazine being turned, the door opened and closed and immediately a murmured conference took place, in which she could distinguish a new voice, calmer and more cultivated than the others.

The language spoken was German. She didn't understand much of what was said, but she thought that at least some of the conversation came from people who were not native German speakers.

Finally the new voice silenced the others. 'She knows nothing,' it said impatiently. 'Dispose of her.'

37

There was a good deal of activity then. Graves was untied, and the blood in her veins stung as it found itself able to circulate freely again. She stretched her buckled legs and tried to set her mind in operation, to calculate, to assess, as she had been trained. It was true that she hadn't had enough field experience, but her training had taken such situations into account, and she should be able to cope with it. She pretended to be weaker than she was – not a difficult task – and allowed them to chain her up without offering more than the token resistance which they might have expected.

They did not remove the hood from her head, but she'd noticed that the string which held it in place had loosened slightly during the course of her torture and, though bruised and shaken, she took note that her body was not badly damaged. They hadn't broken any bones.

She was still wearing the clothes she'd had on when they'd kidnapped her – jeans, shirt, boots and a sweater – though her short leather jacket and her shoulder-bag were gone. Jack Marlow would have retrieved her laptop and other luggage from the hotel and he would have alerted Haki and INTERSEC. But nobody knew where she was – she herself had no idea. Unless . . .

They laid her on the cold floor and went away, returning moments later dragging something which rustled. The next minute she was being zipped into a body-bag.

They carried her through the door and into a lift, which took an interminable time to finish its journey. Inside the bag, in addition to the fact that she could see nothing, she felt claustrophobic, and had to fight down panic. She realized that she did not even know whether it was day or night and, within the bag, she had no sense of temperature either, so she only knew that they had left whatever building they'd been holding her in.

She heard a car door open. The bag was unzipped – it was too bulky to fit between the front and rear seats where they now crammed her, the space so narrow that she could barely move, though once they had left her alone she managed to squirm into a more comfortable position. She could now smell the plastic-and-petrol interior of the car, and she could hear more clearly again, but she still had no clue about where she was, or about the identity of her abductors, whose communications with one another now were monosyllabic and guttural.

The driver's door slammed. The car drew away. She was sweating, and she could smell her own body, stale and a little rank after her days of captivity. She longed for a shower and squirmed some more to see how much she could move – her limbs longed to be able to stretch – and as she did so realized that the chains were looser than she'd thought, and that her own sweat, even within her clothes, made her able to slide a little within the hold her bonds had on her.

She experimented, infinitely slowly, infinitely carefully, for she knew that too much movement and too much sound would alert the driver. But she also knew that she was alone with him.

There wasn't much traffic. The car was moving smoothly along, though they weren't going fast. She had no idea how much time she had before they reached their destination. She had to be free by then.

After what seemed an age she had worked one arm loose.

38

She hadn't finished by the time the car drew to a halt. Her legs were still trapped, but she had both arms free and had managed to rid herself of the hood and work herself into a position where she was half sitting on the floor. If she rose any higher, the driver would see her and realize what had happened. She concentrated on her timing. After the car had stopped, she waited a full twenty seconds. She didn't dare wait any longer, whatever the consequences might be. In one movement then, she hauled her torso upright and swung the free chain over the driver's head and round his neck, hauling it tight with all her strength, and keeping a desperate pressure up until the man, who bucked and pulled, went limp at last.

Graves looked around through the car's windows but through the entire 360-degree spectrum she saw no movement at all. There were three lorries parked end to end some way down a bleak treeless street which could have been anywhere. Tall, cheap apartment blocks built in the late 1950s stood back from the street, fronted by frozen, sandy patches of soil in which a few sparse areas of grass grew, and clumps of stubborn weeds. The blocks looked deserted.

Graves pulled herself up on to the rear seats and hurried to free her feet of the chains. She kicked them free, glad that they had let her keep her boots, and looked up and around again. Then she noticed three heavy-set men in overalls emerge together from the nearest block, a hundred metres away, making their way towards the car.

Graves saw that the driver was still in a sitting position behind the wheel, but she didn't know whether she had killed him or not. There was no time to find out now. She wriggled across the seat to the offside door, unlocked it and opened it, half falling out and trying to stand on legs which trembled and all but refused to support her weight. She forced herself to stand and went into an immediate half-crouch.

She wondered if she could run. Peering above the window's rim, she saw now that the men had noticed something amiss and had broken into a shambling run. It was now or never. Gritting her teeth against the shooting pains in her legs, she hurled herself in the only direction she could go – away from them.

39

She didn't look back and, as she got into a rhythm, her circulation returned quickly. She picked up her pace and developed it into an even lope. She was lighter and, she guessed, fitter than her pursuers, but they weren't light-headed from hunger, they weren't parched by thirst and, above all, they knew where they were.

The street ahead was endless, and there was no cover, but at last it debouched into a square where there were a few people about and, by the grace of God, a large, gleaming, yellow bus. She read the indicator: *Hauptbahnhof*.

Central Station.

She looked over her shoulder. The men had reached the other side of the square, still perhaps fifty metres from her. They hadn't slackened their pace, and one was reaching into his overall pocket, bringing out a small dark metallic object which glinted in the first sunlight of the day. An automatic.

She had no money. Her mobile phone was long gone. She looked as if she'd spent long nights sleeping rough. She had no idea where she was. But she knew that, wherever it was, it was a German-speaking country. Which meant she could get by without drawing too much attention to herself. The bus door was open and passengers pushed past her to get on.

There was only one hope, but it was slim. There was no use depending on it.

The men were closing in. Just as the doors began to hiss shut, Laura leapt on to the platform.

She moved down the bus and hoped that the driver wouldn't notice that she hadn't stamped a ticket in the machine. She took a seat near the back and looked behind her in the direction of the receding square. The men had come to a halt and were conferring. They'd know the route the bus took.

She needed to get somewhere central – somewhere she could get her bearings. If she could make it to the main station, she might be able to blend into the crowd; buy time.

At the third stop, one of her pursuers got on. He didn't look at her and took an available seat two rows behind her. The bus was filling up, and soon there were no places left.

They were travelling down a wide boulevard when Graves decided it was time to get off. She had a plan.

She made her way up the bus past where the man was sitting on an aisle seat, near the exit doors. She manoeuvred herself behind him and, digging the tips of her index fingers hard into the hollows behind the base of his ears, jabbed hard. The man didn't have time to register surprise before he slumped forward. Graves pushed through to the door. She was on the street before anyone on the bus had noticed what she'd done.

The morning rush-hour had started and the shops were raising their shutters. She made her way in what she thought was an easterly direction and crossed several other streets before she came to what she was looking for, since by now she'd gathered that, wherever she was, it was a city of some importance and size. A metro station. Over its entry staircase, its name: Tiergarten. And not far away, the instantly recognisable tall column of the Siegessäule in the middle of the park.

I am in Berlin.

The next thing was to make her way to the INTERSEC contact point but, because of international cutbacks, some of the agencies had been re-defined, or closed down altogether. Berlin had been a prime location during the Cold War, but times had changed, and focus had shifted. INTERSEC's presence in the city had been reduced to one official representative within INTERPOL.

She had no idea what day of the week it was, even. But she could orientate herself now.

She jogged painfully down Strasse des 17. Juni and had just reached the Brandenburger Tor at Pariser Platz when exhaustion hit her. She bent down, resting her hands on her knees, steadying her breathing. One last push, she told herself. But as she straightened up she saw three men dressed in black tracksuits and trainers emerge from behind the line of trees on the north side of the avenue she'd just left. They started running towards her.

Oh, shit, she thought, forcing her body forwards once more. She crossed the broad square to the east of the triumphal arch and set off along Unter den Linden. There were plenty of people about now, but Laura knew that her pursuers wouldn't be deterred by the thought of shooting in a crowd. She kept going.

Up ahead she saw a red neon sign on one of the new office buildings. MAXTEL. A glimmer of hope lit up in her. She knew she wouldn't be able to make it to the safety of INTERSEC now, but MAXTEL might spell some kind of safety.

The three men were closing in fast, and the glimmer went out. She knew she didn't have a hope of making it to the office block.

At that moment, as she drew to an exhausted halt, a blue Mercedes CLS 63 AMG shrieked to a standstill at the kerb next to her. The driver leaned over and pushed the passenger door open.

'Get in!' he ordered.

Graves did so, fast. Behind her, her pursuers had drawn their automatics. The car screamed off, to an outraged fanfare of car horns.

Graves turned to her rescuer, shocked and relieved as she recognized him.

The thin hope had paid off.

Jack Marlow smiled at her. 'You're safe now,' he said.

40

New York City, the Present

'Your timing was almost perfect,' Graves told him later.

She hadn't had much faith in the chip they'd implanted in her upper left arm before the Turkish operation had started, and they'd explained that the system wasn't fool-proof, but, safe back in New York now, she had reason to be grateful. If Marlow had arrived even a minute later, she would have been dead meat.

'We lost the signal on GPS several times, and then when they took you to a second-level sub-basement it went altogether, but we'd pinpointed you to Pankow, though where you were before that, we don't know. Maybe they'd second-guessed us and were able to put a block on the signal. We picked you up again when you escaped and I shadowed you from there. I'd have picked you up sooner but we lost you again on the bus. I'd noted the route, how-ever. Picked you up again when you got off, though it took a while to reach you then.'

'Why Berlin?'

'That we don't know.'

'I saw a sign for the MAXTEL offices just before you rode up in your shining armour.'

Marlow shrugged. 'Doesn't mean anything. Adler was most anxious to locate you too – offered all the help he could.' He shook his head. 'Not out of sentimentality, though – he wants to know what happened to his three missing archaeologists just as badly as we do – he thinks his reputation's on the line.'

'Why's he involved in this anyway?'

'It's his project. MAXTEL put a million dollars into the Dandolo Project through MAXPHIL, and that gives him a right to be more than a concerned bystander,' Marlow replied, but he didn't sound comfortable. 'He's clean, anyway. Cleared with Sir Richard and God knows who else higher up the chain.'

Leon Lopez had entered the office as Marlow was speaking, a sheaf of papers in his hand. 'He's probably funding INTERSEC too,' he said. 'Practically everything else is privatized now – why not us?'

'He's a businessman. It's second nature for him to want to know what's happening to his money,' said Marlow.

'He's not the only one,' said Graves.

Marlow turned to her. 'I want you to think again. Can you tell us anything more, anything at all, about these people?'

'If you're still thinking along the lines of a group like al-Qaeda, no. I think there was a European couple there at first, and I'd also say the methods these people use aren't typical of terror groups. There remains that question they kept asking me. Over and over again.' Graves shuddered at the memory.

She rubbed her bruised arms. She'd been back in New York three days now, she'd just been released from INTERSEC's hospital wing, and she'd been warned that it'd be a month before she was fully recovered.

'If they are the people who got to the tomb first – if they are the people who picked our scientists' findings clean and then disappeared Adkins and the others – they must know we haven't found anything they might have overlooked,' said Lopez.

'That doesn't follow,' said Marlow. 'Whatever it is they're after, they're desperate to locate it. We have to assume that Adkins, Taylor and de Montferrat haven't been able to help them, or they wouldn't have come after Laura. But they have no guarantee that we – or Haki's people – haven't found what they want.'

'Meanwhile, we do have this to go on,' said Lopez, placing the papers on the desk in front of them. What they had was a set of refined, high-definition prints of the missing key. The inscription along the sides of its shank was now clearly visible, the etching as clear as it had been on the day it was incised.

Marlow took a long, hard look at it.

At eleven the next morning he called a meeting. The three of them went over his findings together.

'I guessed this was some kind of numerical code,' Marlow began. Graves was leaning close over him, and her hair brushed his cheek.

'This is Aramaic script,' he went on. 'So it's either a conscious use of an archaic language, or the key itself is very old indeed. We can't know that until we have the key and can date it, but Aramaic was being replaced – gradually – by Arabic as the *lingua franca* of the Middle East by the seventh century after Christ.'

He looked round at them. 'The history is very important.

As I told you, Aramaic's an old language, dating back to Babylonian times. We don't know where it came from originally, but the Aramaens were a people who settled in northern Mesopotamia and spread from there, as the old empires of Babylon and Assyria fell into decline.'

Marlow broke off, thinking about the specialities of the scientists involved in the Dandolo Project. Then he realized the others were watching him expectantly.

'What we've got here,' he continued, 'is a code based on gematria. It's an ancient practice of assigning numerals to letters or groups of letters either directly or by association. It can operate on various levels of complexity, but this one isn't too difficult. What is hard is to make any sense of the meaning of the words the numbers relate to.'

'And what does it say?' asked Graves.

'The first side describes a dark eagle descending on the earth. An eagle, maybe a vulture. Its talons are outstretched to clutch, and its beak is ready to tear, the world. And it cannot be stopped, unless –'

'Unless what?'

Marlow reached for the second photograph, which showed the other side of the key's shank.

'*Unless I open the box and you choose to be saved.*'

The three of them looked at one another.

41

Jerusalem, the Present

Geoffrey Goldberg stood at the door of his electrical goods shop on Misgav Ladach, a short way west of the al Aqsa mosque. Like everywhere else, business was slow, and he whiled away his time standing in his doorway, watching the world go by.

The young woman had caught his attention two days earlier. At first, he'd taken her for just another Japanese tourist trying to find her way to the old town – either she must have been one of the few independent travellers from that country, or else she'd got separated from her group.

She certainly looked lost.

It was when she passed by the shop for the third time, always dressed the same, gradually becoming more dishevelled, that Geoffrey, a kind man and a pillar of the local Rotarians, began to take more serious notice.

There was a vulnerability about the young woman that tugged at his heartstrings. He was convinced that she was in need of help.

Seeing her pause in the street just opposite his shop, looking wistful and sad as the people bustling by jostled her, Geoffrey's heart melted.

Crossing the road, he was soon level with her. He was

naturally a shy man and once he was close to her he was unsure what to do. But the eyes that met his seemed forlorn and questioning, so he pulled himself together.

'Can I help you?' he said in English.

She looked at him blankly. 'Sorry?'

'You seem to be – ehrm – in need of help. Can I help you?'

Her mind seemed to engage with the present then, for her eyes lost their blankness and she looked at Geoffrey gratefully. 'Help me? – Oh, yes please!'

'Have you lost your way?'

The blank look again.

'Come over to my shop.' Geoffrey took her arm and steered her back across the road. Once inside, he sat her in a chair and went behind the counter to the cubby-hole which contained a kitchenette and the means to make coffee.

He handed her a cup and leaned with his own on the counter near her.

'What seems to be the matter?' he asked, feeling awkward.

'I don't know.' She was the verge of tears.

'Have you lost your party?'

'I don't know!' she wailed suddenly. 'I don't know where I am! Where am I?'

Geoffrey was surprised. 'In Jerusalem. The Old City. Near the al Aqsa.'

'Where?'

'Jerusalem. In Israel.'

'Oh –' But she continued to look confused.

He tried a different tack. 'What is your name?' he asked.

She looked at him in wide-eyed panic. 'My name?'

Geoffrey had realized by now that something was seriously amiss. He saw that the girl had broken into a sweat. Part of him began to wonder if he hadn't been rash in getting involved, but the woman seemed unfortunate rather than mad. 'I wonder if you have a passport,' he said gently.

'I think so.' She rummaged in her bag but then let it fall to her lap as she gazed dully into space. 'I don't know who I am or where I am or how I got here,' she said flatly.

But Geoffrey could see the corner of a passport sticking out of an inner compartment of the bag. 'May I?' he said.

She didn't react, and so he delicately extracted the document and opened it. It was an Italian passport, and there was her photograph, date of birth, and name. An unusual name. Su-Lin de Montferrat.

Geoffrey picked up his phone and called the police.

42

General Erich Ludendorff had been very reluctant to undertake this assignment. Germany was a year into a deadlocked war, and he felt that his proper place was in either Berlin or at the Front, not stuck here. Of course he knew that the Fatherland had to maintain a firm controlling influence in the crumbling remains of the Ottoman empire, and that if it didn't keep a hold on Turkey, the Sick Man of Europe, Russia would fill the gap; but surely that could have been left to the diplomats.

Nevertheless, when the renowned archaeologist, and his fellow-countryman Robert Koldewey had wired news of his findings in the Church of Saint Irina, he obeyed orders to go and evaluate them, as well as providing a bit of military muscle and senior presence to back up the efforts of the German Navy. And the informal request of his friend and superior officer Marshal von Hindenburg had actually been a thinly veiled order as, after thirty-three years in the army, he'd been quick to recognize.

Istanbul – Constantinople, as it was still called by most people – was a jewel a lot of people were interested in; but the British were putting their foot in it, with their usual grandiose we-rule-the-waves high-handedness, and the French were havering about on the sidelines – again, as usual. The Germans, on the other hand, had two battle-cruisers in port, the *Goeben* and the *Breslau*, and their own man, Admiral Wilhelm Souchon, in place and ready to become the Ottoman empire's naval commander-in-chief.

Turkey was in Germany's pocket, but the Germans trod carefully, deferentially renaming the warships *Yavuz Sultan Selim* and *Midilli*. And Souchon wore a fez with his uniform.

Still, it was a balancing act. Everyone knew that the Ottoman empire under Mehmet V was on its last legs, and that there was a powerful nationalist movement, the Young Turks, under a new leader, Kemal Atatürk, waiting impatiently in the wings. And the Germans had to pretend that their military were under Ottoman command.

Ludendorff was a soldier first and last, but he hadn't risen to number two in the High Command without having learned a few other aspects of the game. If Koldewey had something the Fatherland could use to its advantage, well and good. And it wouldn't hurt, Hindenburg had suggested as they parted company in Berlin, to play the violin under Atatürk's window as well.

Koldewey, five months Ludendorff's junior, carried weight. Grumpy and anti-academic, dour and misogynistic, he'd never held a university position. He'd studied architecture and art history, but hadn't shone in either. His archaeology was largely self-taught, but his dogged determination when directing a dig had earned him an international reputation, especially for his work in Turkey and those parts of the Ottoman empire defined by the rivers Tigris and Euphrates – ancient Mesopotamia. He'd not only located the famous Hanging Gardens of Babylon, but also the Tower of Babel and the Great Gate of Ishtar, and he also had the ear and the personal support of Kaiser Wilhelm himself.

Ludendorff wasn't a man to be fazed by others, but he looked forward to his first meeting with the crusty scholar with trepidation. Certainly no one in the world matched Koldewey in knowledge of the most ancient civilization on earth.

Koldewey hadn't had any problem in persuading the Ottoman administration to let him prod around in Istanbul, and his reading and research had led him to the Church of Saint Irina, where he'd started a careful excavation which uncovered, not the ancient temple he was hoping to find below the church's foundations, but a tomb of much more recent date. It was here that Ludendorff was bidden after the two men had first met in the smoking room of the Pera Palas Hotel, two days previously.

It was 05.00 hours. Koldewey liked early starts.

The church was surrounded by a military guard, but only Koldewey and five assistants were to be found in its interior.

'Welcome, Herr General,' said the archaeologist.

Ludendorff grunted, his eye drawn immediately to a set of sturdy wooden shelves to one side of the large rectangular hole in which Koldewey stood. On them various artefacts had been carefully arranged.

'We'll come to those in a moment,' said Koldewey, following the general's gaze. 'First, join me down here and look at this.'

Ludendorff gingerly descended the narrow pine staircase which had been set into one wall of the dig.

In the centre of the excavated grave, an ornate coffin stood on a plinth. Its lid was off, and within Ludendorff could see a richly robed corpse, laid out in great state.

'Put these on,' said Koldewey, handing the general a pair of white cotton gloves. 'We have to be careful not to contaminate anything.'

'What have you to show me?'

'This.' Koldewey bent over the corpse and pointed to something held loosely in the body's right hand. 'I wanted to show it to you *in situ*, as I found it.' He took a small clay tablet, about the size of a notebook, from the hand. It came away easily. 'It was held in so tight a grip that I had to break the fingers to prise it loose,' explained the archaeologist. 'Not a job I like doing, but it had to be. I didn't want to risk breaking the tablet. In the event, I needn't have worried – it's as hard as basalt. Only a sharp blow with a hammer would shatter this.'

'What is it?'

Koldewey looked at the general. 'I came here thinking I might find something under the church's floor. I'd seen something in the archives in Venice which attracted my attention to the place. But I was expecting a Roman temple, a Temple of Mithras, perhaps, or, if I was lucky, something earlier. There's been a place of worship here since time immemorial. But *this*!'

He placed the tablet carefully in the general's gloved hands.

'What is it?' Ludendorff asked again, seeing only a greyish, roughly shaped piece of terracotta, covered with indecipherable markings not unlike the footprints of a small bird.

Koldewey was silent for a long moment before he spoke again. In that silence, Ludendorff sensed something of the man's excitement - and something else, which he recognized with surprise as – fear.

'If I'm right, it is the key to a power which, up until now, we have only been able to dream of.'

Ludendorff didn't understand. What Koldewey had said sounded more than melodramatic, but his tone was deadly serious. 'Explain yourself, sir,' he said. He was hot in his uniform, despite the early hour, and he didn't like this bearish, shirt-sleeved man with his unruly hair and tousled beard.

'I haven't yet had time to make a full study of it, but I can read enough to know what the spell encompasses.'

'Spell?'

'Incantation, invocation, theorem – tract, maybe. But I'm sure enough already that whoever can comprehend this and interpret it properly –' Koldewey broke off. 'It's too early to say,' he concluded guardedly, and changing tack.

'What are these markings?'

'It's an ancient script – cuneiform. It was first used five thousand years ago, and I can already tell that this is a very early example. It's written in the language of Sumer, the most ancient civilization we know.'

'And it's important?'

Koldewey's eyes glittered, and his expression was impatient. What a dolt this general seemed to be! Even so, the archaeologist knew he needed the man's support if he was to get the tablet back to Germany without anyone else's knowledge. 'It's fortunate that *we* found it,' he said tersely, reaching out to take the tablet back.

Once in his own hands, he transferred it to a small calico bag, and from thence to the pocket of the jacket which he now put on. 'You can take the gloves off now,' he said. 'And I'll show you the other pieces we've found.'

Ludendorff took off the gloves with relief. They chafed his hot hands. He threw them to the floor of the tomb irritably, kicking them under the plinth.

43

Among the other objects taken from the tomb and ranged on the shelves there was one other article of significance. A small iron box, highly decorated and locked.

'We think this was made at a much later date to house the tablet,' explained Koldewey. 'But we can't be sure. And we haven't been able to find a key, so we can't open it. We have searched everywhere, but our time here is limited.' Koldewey shrugged. 'I think the key is lost for ever.'

'Force the box open. Blow it open, if necessary.'

Koldewey glared at Ludendorff. 'We have tried every means of unlocking it without damaging it, but it is as if it were sealed shut. Without the key, there is no chance of getting it open. It's as tightly closed as an oyster.'

'You open oysters with a knife.'

'Do it in the wrong way and you can cut yourself badly. And there are some oysters which will never open.'

'You haven't yet told me whose tomb this is. Or how he got hold of this thing.'

'The first part of your question I can answer. The second, I cannot. But I think he knew what it was. He went to his grave clutching it as if his life depended on it, and that grip hadn't weakened in seven hundred years.'

That evening, the two men sat over cognac on the terrace of Ambassador Freiherr von Wangenheim's residence, looking out over the thin mist that clung to the Bosphorus, making the lights of the ships ghostlike and indistinct.

'Two things,' said Koldewey.

'Yes?'

'We must close the tomb carefully, and we must ensure that it looks as if it had never been opened. All traces of our excavation must be eradicated. No one, ever, must know what we have discovered.'

'There are the guards, and your assistants.'

'The guards have no idea what they have been watching over. My assistants . . . can be dealt with.'

Ludendorff locked his fingers together. 'And the second?'

'We must get the tablet – and the box – out of here, to Berlin. I can make a thorough examination there, in peace.'

'Easy enough.'

'But the Turks must not know of it. They must think we have taken nothing away. I have made a list of all the artefacts found here, but I have omitted these two.'

'What's the great secret?'

The strange look of excitement mingled with fear came into Koldewey's eyes again. 'I have told you all I know and all I suspect. You must trust me for the rest. Germany must trust me.'

Ludendorff was aware of Koldewey's standing in the Kaiser's eyes, and he nodded briskly. 'When?'

'Tomorrow at dawn. I will travel with the articles personally.'

'The Ottomans –'

'The Ottomans have already been advised that my work here is at an end. They need us. They think we will protect them from the Russians and from their own revolutionaries. They do not present a problem.'

Ludendorff nodded again, finished his cognac, and started to rise. Koldewey stopped him, placing a hand on his sleeve. Ludendorff, hating physical contact, forced himself not to recoil as the archaeologist fixed him with his eyes. 'Tell no one anything of this. Tell your aides-de-camp only what is necessary for them to make the arrangements.'

'The secret is safe with me.'

'It is of paramount importance that it remain secret. Neither Hindenburg, nor even the Kaiser, must know.'

Ludendorff was suspicious, but something in the man's manner convinced him he was right. 'What will you do?'

'Plumb the mystery. I will consult Einstein and Max Planck. I'll need their expertise, but they won't have to know the full truth. You and I will meet in Berlin and –'

Koldewey broke off and turned his gaze to the waters which divided Europe from Asia. There were things he knew which it was not yet safe to confide even in Ludendorff – perhaps especially not in the general.

If he was right in his suspicions, a power lay in his hands which other men could only dream of.

44

Venice, Year of Our Lord 1202

Nobody likes to starve.

Doge Enrico Dandolo had just celebrated his ninety-second birthday. It was early summer, and the Army of Pilgrims for Jerusalem had been penned in, on the Island of San Niccolò. The completed fleet rode at anchor down by Castello, and the new ocean-going ships within it were indistinguishable, to the uninitiated eye, from the ordinary galleys, warships and transports which made up the bulk of the vessels. Nobody questioned anything.

The doge had seen to that.

Dandolo gripped the cold tablet with the curious writing on it tightly in his right hand, under his robe. There was a special pocket in his right sleeve where he could lodge it, but he had learned that it was at its most powerful when he had it in his grip. He had only to think the words written on it and he could feel the minds of men glaze as they passed under his control.

The most powerful weapon in the world. But he had also learned that it had to be used with discretion, and that it needed a strong will to control it. He could not think that it had a will of its own, but he knew enough to respect the force within it. *It wasn't in the clay itself, but in the writing.* But only the most perfect copy could ever replicate that.

And who could possibly make a duplicate of anything so complicated? Only someone deeply familiar with the original. The old Armenian? He was dead. The only other people who knew of it were Frid and Leporo. Frid was so loyal he might as well have been part of Dandolo's own body. As for Leporo . . . the monk was a follower, not to be trusted as far as you'd trust your own limbs; but he knew only as much as it was necessary for him to know. And his hatred of Frid had endured for decades; it was under control.

The tablet had served him well so far. The army he needed was gathered. Now it was time to put it to the test.

Dandolo turned to his companions, wincing as he willed his failing left eye to bring them into focus.

'Is everything going according to plan?' he asked.

'Yes, *Altissima*,' Leporo replied. 'We have stopped the supply boats taking food to San Niccolò. It's been a week now. They have water, but not enough, and with the weather growing warmer, it will be growing stale in the barrels.'

Dandolo held up a hand. 'We don't want to push this too far,' he said. 'Biddable is what we need, not resentful. Replenish the water. And keep an eye out for disease. We must tread carefully. Let Frid take charge of it. They trust Frid. He is more like them than we are. Let them continue to want for food. We need dogs that are hungry enough to fight.'

He nodded at Frid, who stood by the door. The Norseman inclined his head in return, and left. Leporo watched him go. He showed no deference to the doge, and yet the doge treated him more cordially than he had ever treated his faithful monk.

But his time would come.

'And now,' said Dandolo, interrupting his thoughts. 'Now for Zara.'

Leporo half shrugged. 'You'll never get them to agree to that.'

'I'll get them to do anything I want. Assemble their leaders.'

Dandolo considered. The game of chess was going as he wished. Since Eastertide, the Crusaders had been arriving in Venice, and the Venetians had billeted them all on the barren little island of San Niccolò. Once there, there was no means for them to get food and drink except by boat – and the Venetians controlled the boats.

The Crusaders had another problem. As he had planned, the great numbers of men the French leadership had expected had not materialized. There were not enough people to fill the fleet Venice had built for them, let alone pay for it. Even by handing over all their money, and all their gold and silver plate, all their treasures, everything except their horses and what they needed to fight with, Leporo calculated that they were still 35,000 grossi short. But the Venetians had a contract and it had to be honoured.

No one disagreed with that and, as for the Venetian Council, they ate out of Dandolo's hand. In the meantime, if the Crusaders refused to join him in his expedition against the City of Zara, he'd keep the money they'd paid him, and the fleet, and they could go hang.

But they wouldn't refuse, he reflected with satisfaction as he hugged the tablet, so hard that it bit into his palm. It was as if his hand bore the physical imprint of its symbols. They couldn't so much as get off the island without his ships. He'd quarantine the place and let them all starve to death, animals and men, knights and squires, cookboys and trollops alike, if they even so much as attempted to stand against him.

Zara was a Christian city. Dandolo was well aware of how the pope would react if he attacked it. But that didn't worry him. He knew how much Innocent III wanted this crusade. The tablet – the sacred scroll of Bishop Adhemar – had seen to that. The doge thought of the bishop, who had died locked away from the world. Adhemar had tried to crack its secret but only partially succeeded. And that knowledge had driven him mad.

He smiled. The beauty of the thing was that he was able to make men do precisely what he wanted them to and, with a little set-dressing and a little acting from him, they did it without ever being *aware*.

45

Dandolo didn't need the council for this. Flanked by his guards, in their uniform of silver and yellow, he was dressed in black satin robes with a white ducal cap embroidered with gold thread on his head.

He stood by his throne on a dais in a private audience chamber, lined in dark oak and hung with icons of the Passion of Christ. Leporo sat at the secretary's desk. Frid stood to the right behind the throne. Incense hung in the air. The high windows let in little light. The precious metals, jewels and the gold leaf on the icons flashed and glittered in candlelight.

Impressive. Daunting.

The atmosphere would serve its purpose.

The Crusaders were ushered in, but found no seats in the central area before the dais. Two of the original ambassadors, Geoffrey and Conon, stood in the company of the leaders of the enterprise, Baldwin and Boniface. They looked shabby. Two months on San Niccolò with no water for washing had seen to that.

Both the leaders were so tanned they no longer looked like the aristocrats they were. Baldwin – tall, thirty years old, with cold eyes of a blue so pale they were almost white, heavy chestnut hair and beard. Boniface – stocky like a peasant, twenty years older, a seasoned warrior. Someone had once given him a bad wound on the face – a scar testified to that. His black, shrewd eyes were those of a man to be watched. Not a trace of grey in his black hair or beard.

Dandolo exaggerated, groping as he seated himself on his throne. Make them think he was stone blind. Add to the pathos. These sentimental northerners fell for that, he'd discovered.

He smiled at them, a smile of wounded sympathy, of pained understanding. Their response to the Zara proposal was exactly as he had planned: confused acceptance. But he saw that he would have to work on them a little more.

There were powers still within the tablet he had not yet been able to tap. He needed to draw on his own resources now to deliver the coup de grâce.

Clutching the tablet, running his fingers over its uneven surface, he went to work.

'I can understand your reaction, but I beg you – reflect! This city of Zara was ours, and we treasured it. It was – it is – the most precious jewel of the Dalmatian coast, and it was crucial to our trade route to the East. We nurtured it, we poured our love and affection into it, we aided it, we shed salt tears over it. But –' the doge made a gesture of regret in the air with his left hand. 'But, like an ungrateful mistress, the city spurned us and, twenty years ago, rebelled, declaring itself independent and, to make matters worse, sending emissaries to the pope and to the King of Hungary, begging them, and backing up their supplications with lies, to give it their protection. But control of that city is ours by right, and *we will have it back*.'

'It is a Christian city,' Count Baldwin said.

'So it is, and so you have pointed out. But was their action Christian? I think not.' Dandolo sat back. 'My lords, you know us. We keep our word. Look at the fleet we have prepared for you, dedicating all our resources to the work for these eighteen months past. But my people have sacrificed much to achieve this, and they are still wanting tens of thousands of grossi from you. You must pay us the money you owe.'

The Crusaders looked at one another. Marquess Boniface spoke firmly for them all: 'We are in agreement with you, *Altissima*. But we have given you all we have. All save what we need to fight with, and –'

'If you don't, I must tell you that you won't move one foot from San Niccolò. And you won't find one boat come to provision you. Not even with water.'

'If there were some way –'

Dandolo leaned forward. 'There is. Help us get Zara back. We can't do it alone, or we would have done so long ago. But with your help, we can, and will.'

The Crusaders bowed their heads. It was as if their will were not their own.

46

'We will be *excommunicated*.' Leporo said later, when they were alone together. Despite his neglect of his vows, the monk felt a chill run through him at the thought.

'Pah!' said Dandolo. 'Let the pope bring on what he will.'

'I'm thinking about the Pilgrims of the Cross.'

'They will do nothing I do not want them to do!' snapped the doge. 'Look: we take Zara. We split whatever we take from that city fifty-fifty with the Pilgrims. With their half, if it's enough, they pay us the balance of what they owe. Then they have their fleet, and we can overwinter in Zara. In the spring, they'll be rested, refreshed, full-bellied, they'll have fucked themselves fit on those Dalmatian whores, and we can pack them off to the Holy Land – or wherever else we may want to send them.'

'What about the Papal Legate?'

Dandolo eyed his sidekick narrowly. 'Cardinal Peter can fuck himself,' he snarled. 'The man's as effective as a bladder on a stick, set against an iron mace.'

'But when news of this reaches the pope, or if you defy the cardinal –'

Dandolo gestured impatiently.

'Innocent has already given the Lord of Zara a letter promising instant excommunication on anyone who attacks the city.'

Dandolo looked at Leporo with contempt. 'Let him do his worst. A letter! Let's be modern, Leporo! A letter from that overdressed cretin in Rome isn't going to send even a rat kicking down to hell. Now listen. Once I have the Pilgrims' agreement signed and sealed, send them some food and wine – not much, and not good. Pigs' trotters and the cheapest Veneto you can find. In barrels, not bottles. They can have the good stuff later. And arrange a Mass in St Mark's. Get the Pilgrims' leaders to attend.'

'What's the Mass for?'

'I'm going to take the Cross.'

Leporo could barely restrain his laughter.

'I'll kneel weeping at the altar as the archbishop himself sews the red cross on my cap. Or perhaps I'll have a blue one. Blue suits me better, I remember. I'd be surprised if half the population of Venice doesn't take the Cross too.'

'Would that be good?'

'Think, Leporo. We need to leave someone behind in Zara to make sure Emeric of Hungary doesn't try anything after we've moved on.'

'Moved on?'

'Never mind! Do as I say. I want that Mass at dusk tomorrow. Plenty of candles. Adds to the mystique. And incense.'

'*Altissima*.' Leporo saw hell's mouth gape before him.

Left alone, Dandolo considered. This bit of theatre he had planned was icing on the cake. He pushed aside the gloomy thoughts of mortality. Now, he felt rejuvenated. After all, he reflected, everyone reaches his last Christmas, his last Easter, his last fuck, his last plate of meat, his last glass, his last shit. But until that happens, you get on with it.

There was much to do.

Zara. Zara would fall, and be punished for its presumption. He'd kill every pox-ridden Dalmatian he could get his hands on. It'd be good to see this bunch of French louts put through their paces – see what they were capable of. A few of them would die, but the cause was in his interest, and this would be a rehearsal which also brought practical rewards. After they had brought Zara to heel, they could turn from the puppy and curb the dog. Constantinople would cower before him.

His penis stirred at the thought, a tortoise-head nodding from its antediluvian shell.

47

Conon and Geoffrey watched the hurried preparations.

'The Blessed Mary is to be thanked for this! Fever and disease treated, and the camp cleaned up!' said Geoffrey, hardly able to believe the sudden change of fortune.

Conon shared his relief. The captive army was still kept on San Niccolò, but they'd been given good wine and the best meat, and whores of course, clean ones, checked and changed every week by the nuns of Santa Clara. The horses got the best oats and the purest spring water, brought in by a never-ending chain of ox carts from the Dolomites. The Pilgrims themselves were galvanized into activity after the long, uncertain, half-starved wait, and any murmur of dissent was absent. Everyone threw himself body and soul into the great victory soon to be gained.

'It will be good from now on,' Conon said. 'I feel it.'

'Pray God it be so,' replied Geoffrey, now more thoughtful again. He was still, deep within himself, unsettled by the secrecy he sensed from the Venetians. Trapped on the island, they had no news of the outside world except what they were fed by the city.

'We must trust Venice,' said Conon, reading his thoughts. 'And be of good cheer. Neither Rome nor Zara has the ghost of an idea of our plans.'

*

In the autumn all was ready. October crept into Venice from the lagoon, but there were still days of crisp sunshine when the sea was tranquil and the offshore breeze blew into newly rigged sails which flapped eagerly, as if impatient to be off. The sails were white in the sun; the crests painted on them glowed fresh and clean. There wasn't a heart not full of restless energy.

At last the final victualling was done, the men marshalled aboard. The vacant places in the ships created by the shortfall in crusading men were filled with volunteers from the bleak Veneto farmlands and from the Serene City itself. There were favourable winds coming from the north-west. The sea rolled itself out like a carpet.

On the eve of All Hallows the fleet was ready for the voyage south-east to its goal.

The tide it would take rose at dawn.

48

On Monday 11 November, they anchored off Zara, a prosperous city, with white towers and red roofs, lying snug behind stout walls. The bells had already started to ring out their warning before the last of the fleet, nearly five hundred ships strong, heaved to. The doge's galley, painted vermilion, rode nearest the shore, about a kilometre off. Under a red awning, the doge sat, warming his bones in the autumn sun. In response to the bells from the city's towers, cymbals clashed and trumpets sounded from the prow of his ship, from many of his ships.

But apart from sounding its bells, the city did nothing but hunker down. Dandolo smiled at the thought of what must be going through the governor's mind as the man scanned the fleet anchored on his doorstep.

Zara could do nothing against such a force.

Perhaps they would surrender without a fight. Part of him hoped they wouldn't. These people needed to be punished. Resistance would give him the excuse he needed, and he wanted to see what these Crusaders were capable of. Above all, he needed proof that they would obey him without question. He was not yet confident of his power.

He wondered what the feelings of the people of Zara were when they saw that Venice had the backing of an army of Christian pilgrims. He wondered how much faith they placed in the pope's letter now. But even if they didn't, and sent couriers to Emeric of Hungary for help, it would be too late.

Nothing could save them.

The next few days saw the transports taking horses, men, and siege-machines – petraries and mangonels for hurling rocks – to the shore. There were battering rams, and wooden tunnels covered with heavy hides soaked with water to protect those using them from the boiling oil and Greek Fire which would be hurled on the army from the tops of the walls. There were scaling ladders, and towers on huge wheels to be rolled up against the walls for the final assault.

For another few days the air was filled with the noise of hammering and sawing as the carpenters assembled these, while the troops set up their camps around the walls and honed their weapons. Ladders were mounted on the prows of several ships, which were brought in to invest the seaward walls.

The governor of the city requested a parley. A side gate opened in the western wall, and he and his party rode out and down to the shore to the Venetian encampment.

Dandolo was waiting for him.

'What do you want?' he asked the governor.

The governor, a young man, frail-looking, spread his hands. 'Peace,' he said simply.

'You'll give up your city, just like that? For those are my terms.'

'Zara is a rich city,' replied the governor, his pride stung. 'We will pay you a reasonable bounty.'

'But you would be paying us with what is ours by right anyway.'

'We can withstand a siege.'

'For how long? You have eyes. You see that our engineers are already undermining your walls on the seaward side. It would be a pity to see such a fine city as yours crushed like a roach.'

The governor bowed his head. 'To withstand you would be as futile as sweeping leaves in the wind. At least order your sappers to stop until we have negotiated. We have seen them set wood for fires. We can smell the naphtha.'

'I have given you my terms.'

The governor was sweating. His ceremonial robes hung heavy on him, and chafed. The sun was high in the sky and there was no wind. You would have thought the year was just being born, instead of dying.

'At least give us time to evacuate the city in peace. Our people are guiltless.'

'Those under the age of twenty may depart. The rest must take the consequences of your rebellion: those who were alive when the city rebelled against us and arrogantly claimed independence, only to seek the protection of another master.'

'How long?'

'Today is Friday. On Monday, open the city to us, or face the consequences.'

The governor retired.

As he rode back to the city with his retinue, he thought, There are many faces a monster can assume: that of a saintly friar, of the woman of one's dreams, of a Templar banker. Too often one gladly accepts a pretty box, only to find that it contains nothing but shit.

Dandolo's face was the face of a martyr from an icon. Too holy to be true.

49

Paris, the Present

Laura Graves sat in the Grizzli café at the lower end of the rue St Martin, drinking an espresso and thinking about the information she'd received from Lopez. And about the breakthrough they'd had with the reappearance of Su-Lin. Minus her memory, which hardly helped.

It set up another hurdle for them to jump. She'd talk to Marlow about it. She was impatient, but needed to sort a few more things out in her mind first. She'd come out to clear her head, but that wasn't working. Her mind chafed. She still bore resentment against Marlow for leading this mission, taking the job which she had assumed was hers; but at the same time there was something about him she found hard to resent. Graves was unused to being unsure of her feelings. She didn't like it.

She fiddled with the emerald pendant she was wearing again that day, and leafed through *Libération* without taking in a word; the headlines about the collapsing economy, student demonstrations and the president's plummeting ratings were hardly news. She was so absorbed in her thoughts that she had scarcely been aware of the other people, tourists mainly, taking coffee under the awning on the terrace around her. Now, she glanced at them with second-nature professionalism. Among them were an elderly, fashionably skinny blonde with a slightly younger American who was obviously her lover, an argumentative quartet of French students, and an elegantly dressed middle-aged man who looked as if he'd be more at home in the Café de la Paix, and who spoke French with a German accent when Damien came over to take his order.

Graves gave up, dropped enough euros for the coffee on the tabletop and walked round the corner to INTERSEC's HQ.

Paris isn't always a pretty city. It can be grey, miserable and dark. It was like that now, and it had been just the same a week ago, on the day they'd flown Su-Lin into the recently refurbished but still horrible CDG airport and driven her to the INTERSEC office on the boulevard de Sébastopol, a once-genteel, now commercial thoroughfare that leads from the river all the way up to Strasbourg-St Denis.

The INTERSEC office was at the southern end, near Châtelet, in a Haussmann building on the east side. There were a lot of lawyers' offices in the vicinity, as it was a few minutes' walk from the central courts on the Île de la Cité. Often the offices occupied what had once been mansion flats. INTERSEC's was no exception. It was big, two apartments knocked into one, and soundproofed; the discreet brass plaque on the dark-red door read: Boyer-Fogel & Associés, Avocats à la Cour.

There was no accompanying plaque on the wall facing the street, and no name next to the doorbell, one among many, in the entrance foyer.

They'd sent the Lear jet to Jerusalem to fetch Su-Lin de Montferrat as soon as word reached them.

Jack Marlow had chosen Paris for her because, by INTERSEC standards, it was quiet. It was also where much of INTERSEC's most important and secret work was done. There was a disused newspaper kiosk outside the door, a battered public phone booth, and a Morris column with posters for the latest films and theatre productions. Nearby, the rue de Rivoli cut its long line east–west across the city.

Marlow was leaning out of the window of what had once been the main drawing-room. He was looking south at the clock-tower on the quai de l'Horloge, and the narrow black spire of the Ste Chapelle beyond it, but he was lost in his thoughts.

Part of his mind still harked stubbornly back to the time he'd spent here before INTERSEC had moved him to New York; bad memories, but Paris would probably always have that effect on him. Most of his attention, however, was occupied with the problem posed by de Montferrat's memory loss.

'We've little to go on. She had the clothes she stood up in when she was found in Jerusalem, but apart from a packet of Kleenex and a little loose money in the pockets, nothing else – no wallet, no documents apart from the passport,' he said, turning to Graves. 'Nothing hidden at all. What have we got on the bag? Forensics?'

Graves consulted a list. 'It had a lipstick in it, some other makeup, a pen, a pack of Camels with one cigarette left, a Bic lighter, an Italian passport which is certainly genuine – and a handkerchief. And there were no house or car keys, no hotel card, no receipts, no tickets – nothing to indicate any recent background or trail at all. We know the authorities in Jerusalem contacted all likely hotels and tour operators, and they came up with nothing. *Too* clean.'

'So clean we might never have heard if they hadn't sent the details to EUROPOL.' Luckily the guy on the Secure Desk there made a note of it and passed it to INTER-SEC. The communication was routed straight to Section 15 because of the Dandolo Project. It had been a near thing, and he didn't like it. He wondered if someone was trying to obstruct him. He also wondered if he could confide in Graves, but didn't. He knew she'd wanted his job. She'd moved the emerald ring to her little finger to cover the old tattoo, he'd noticed. Had she seen him looking? The ring was loose on that finger.

'Has Leon reported back from Venice?' he asked.

'Due back in New York today.'

'Why didn't he file direct from Venice?'

'Didn't trust the encryption facility from there.'

Jack let that go. 'Tell me as soon as you hear.'

The cold city air cleared Marlow's head. It had been a long time since he'd drunk any Jameson's, but the night before, as he'd struggled with the problem of what to do with the archaeologist, who was still suffering from the amnesia that'd affected her when she was discovered in Jerusalem, he'd done more than damage to a bottle. Today he was paying the price.

He thought about de Montferrat. Attractive woman, intelligent, keen to help if she could. There was a warm look in her eyes, though they still managed somehow to be enigmatic. Perhaps that was due to her loss of memory.

Jack couldn't be sure. But there was no doubt that she was intriguing.

It was too cold for comfort, and a fine rain had started to fall, slicking the grey pavements and the busy road along which the one-way traffic streamed north. The leafless plane trees which lined the boulevard swayed gently in the light breeze, last autumn's fruit, little rough-skinned brown balls, still clinging to the outer limits of the uppermost branches. He closed the window and turned back into the room.

It was a large and light, with white walls that matched most of the furniture. Paintings and screenprints by Allen Jones, Hannelore Jüterbock and Mark Upton hung on the walls. Graves was at her desk at the far end, facing the two tall windows near which Jack was standing. For once, her Mac was switched off, and she was buried in a large hardback book, from which she was making cross-references to a blue file. She looked up as he turned, and took off her reading glasses. Fully recovered, in a crisp business suit, she looked fresh and bright.

But she also looked worried.

'What the hell do we do with her?' she asked.

He sat down in the black Wassily chair near the bank of computers ranged on a low console which ran along one wall. 'Let's see how her memory goes. But I have a question.'

'Yes?'

'It comes from what you've been researching. De Montferrat. May lead nowhere, but it's an odd enough name to make for more than a coincidence. What have you got?'

She flicked her hair back from her face with a quick gesture and looked up at him. When their eyes met they both knew that there was still tension between them that mustn't be allowed to get in the way of the job. 'I've checked family trees, and God knows they don't go back in a clean line that far, but –' Graves broke off to flip back a few pages in the book she'd been consulting. 'Here we go: Boniface de Montferrat, born 1150, died 1207, son of William de Monferrat and Judith von Babenberg. Big man in Europe in his day. His court was one of the most cultured in the world. But listen to this: his cousin, the King of Swabia, was married to Irina Angelina – the daughter of a Greek emperor, Isaac II, who had his court at Constantinople.'

Marlow looked at her. 'There's a link?'

'We know Boniface was one of the leaders of the Fourth Crusade. Irina's father was deposed in a coup. No tears for him, he wasn't such a great guy, but once the Crusaders had taken Constantinople for Dandolo, they put Isaac back on the throne, with his son Alexius as co-ruler. They didn't last long, but –'

'There is a connection, then. But far-fetched.'

'I don't know so much, and you shouldn't be so quick to jump to conclusions. If anyone might have shared Dandolo's interest in getting control of Constantinople, Boniface is your man.'

'And you think that Su-Lin is descended from him?'

Graves shrugged. 'I can only trace the de Montferrats up to about 1900, but I don't see why not.'

Marlow thought about this. 'And that's her connection with the Dandolo Project? Of course, her colleagues must have known about it.'

233

'It could just be a coincidence.' She shook her hair again.

'We'll get Leon to look into Su-Lin's father. Wealthy businessman, wasn't he? Something to do with industrial chemistry?'

'Something like that,' Graves replied. 'Haven't you done your homework?'

'Sorry, miss. I'll talk to Su-Lin about it too. It might jog something.'

Graves looked quizzical. 'You never know.'

'Why are you looking at me like that?'

'Nothing.'

Marlow said, 'No it's not.'

He's calling her Su-Lin, she was thinking. Not de Montferrat. A small thing, but . . . 'This memory thing,' she said aloud. 'It brings me to my second question. She hasn't lost her ability to read, has she?'

'No.'

'Then she must have been able to read the name on her passport.'

'We've been through that. The psychologist working with her says she can read, but not necessarily perceive. She can *read* the name, but she can't *connect* it with herself. Not yet.'

'She still worries me.'

'She's completely clean: she's had a full medical. No bugs or devices, embedded or otherwise. Why should she have?' But Marlow looked thoughtful. 'The important thing is to find out what happened to her and Adkins and Taylor. And why. God knows it's taken us a hell of a lot of diplomacy to placate the families.'

234

'Who are worried sick.'

'That isn't our principal concern.'

'Come on, Jack – you're not that cold.'

He looked at her, said nothing.

'We've got to get into her memory somehow. It's the best lead we have,' she went on.

He looked at his watch. 'I'm going over to interview her again now.'

Graves looked worried. 'Who might know that she's with us?'

'You ordered a press embargo the minute she'd been located and identified.'

'Yes, of course. What else are secretaries for?'

'Look, it worries me too. We're holding off on Venice University for the moment. We've informed Hudson, but –' Marlow hesitated before confiding in her, but he had to trust her at least in part her to work with her at all, and now he had no choice: '– I haven't disclosed her *precise* whereabouts, even to Sir Richard.'

Graves looked at him sharply. 'Didn't he object to that?'

Marlow smiled thinly. 'He hit the roof. I told him it was a matter of *ultra*-security. It needs to be kept within Section 15 alone.' He paused. 'Leon knows, of course, and as far as her shrink is concerned, she's a subject for debriefing. That's it.'

'Don't you think Hudson will get to it if he wants to?'

'He's got to trust me if this is going to work. Christ knows who we're up against. Whoever came after Adkins, Taylor and Su-Lin, and came after us, and got you – those people mustn't have a second chance.' He looked at Graves. 'I want you to keep your head down too.' He still hadn't told her everything he suspected. She was new to him. She had been Hudson's appointment. She was clearly Hudson's blue-eyed girl, and a part of him was furious to have had her foisted on him.

She looked rebellious. 'Crap. It goes with the territory.'

'Next time we mightn't be so fortunate.'

'I'll take my chances.'

The blue phone rang.

'Ultra-secure from Group Head,' the voice on the line told Marlow.

He looked across at Graves.

'Summons?' she asked.

'It's happening faster than I thought.'

'Are you still there?' said the voice on the phone impatiently. 'Sir Richard wants you. *Now*.'

50

Zara, Year of Our Lord 1202

The fine weather held, but the sun shone on a cruel scene as those citizens under the age of twenty began their enforced departure from Zara.

'Some of the young people have refused to leave,' Geoffrey de Villehardouin told Conon uneasily.

'It doesn't surprise me,' replied Conon uncomfortably. 'It means parting from lovers, parents, employers, protectors.'

'We could have shown more mercy.'

'But Dandolo ordered us . . .'

'I saw men and women in tears after the troops formed the corridor outside the North Gate. There was a couple, a boy and a girl – she couldn't have been more than fifteen, but he was twenty-one. They clung to each other as if they were made of one flesh. They broke away as our men tried to separate them, made a run for it.'

'What happened then?'

'They got them back,' Villehardouin anwsered. 'The doge wanted an example made of them. They nailed them to crosses. Set fire to them.'

'It's going well,' Leporo told him.

It was working. Dandolo didn't believe in magic but, even so, the effectiveness of the tablet awed him.

What was it the old Armenian had told him?

He'd explained that the key to the writing on the terra-cotta slab showed him when the thing was at its best to use. Something to do with a correct conjunction of the stars and the sun.

He'd told how the Babylonians had calculated that different stars had different physical properties. They had begun to think about the effect of interaction between energy and matter.

Dandolo hadn't bothered with much of this; his focus was narrow: enough knowledge to make the tablet work. As long as it did what he wanted it to. But if there were more . . .

However, the old Armenian's thinking was dangerous, and Dandolo kept what he'd learned to himself.

He'd had Frid take the old man out on a boat, and drown him.

The doge relaxed, and looked out over the fleet now drawn up in the harbour of Zara. His eye picked out the great ocean-going ships which he'd promised himself for the adventure over the vast sea to the west of the Mediterranean. It was still a wonder to him that no one but Frid and he could see them for what they were. If all went well, with the money he collected from the vast, rotting city of Constantinople, that adventure would soon be his to undertake. If God still gave him the time.

But first, Zara had to fall.

51

The governor listened gloomily to the report. He had been given from dawn to dusk on Saturday to clear the young from his city, and as the sun sank below the western horizon that day, the bells of the churches began to peal. That was the signal; at the end of the ten minutes the bells would cease and the gate would be closed. It was shut amid cries, as some young enough to leave were still left inside, and some parents fought each other to push their children through the closing doors at the last.

'In the struggle, three people died – one, a five-year-old boy, crushed by the gate. We lit the torches on the walls of the city soon afterwards, and the silence was like no other the city has ever known,' the garrison commander told him.

The governor looked up. He wasn't hearing anything new, but the garrison commander was conscientious, and left nothing out. 'Can we win?' he asked.

The garrison commander was silent.

'I want no damage,' the doge told the Crusader captains. 'The property is ours: the more the soldiers wreck, the more we deprive ourselves of profit, and it is out of your share that you repay us what you owe, and gain your independence for your great enterprise.'

'Amen to that,' said Baldwin of Flanders. 'We will obey the order.'

'Tell your sergeants to keep a close watch on your men. And as for the people . . .'

'Yes?'

'Kill them all. Every one. Whether they resist or not. I don't want to inherit a population of traitors.'

'We need to keep some. Able-bodied men. As labour. We'll have to repair the walls – we can't avoid damaging them, if they put up a fight,' objected Boniface, the scar on his forehead showing white.

'No,' Dandolo said decisively. 'Round up teenagers for that from the hills when it's over. They won't have gone far, and they'll come home without objecting. Winter is on us; the hills provide no shelter.' Dandolo paused. 'And make sure your men don't destroy any fuel in the city – log piles, candles, they must be spared. We must hope they don't use all the oil they have by boiling it and throwing it down on us. Hang anyone who disobeys.'

'What about the women – we'll need some of them,' said Baldwin.

'Get them from the hills,' said Dandolo. 'Enough to go round. We want no fights over women.'

'How will the city be divided once we've taken it?' Boniface wanted to know.

Dandolo had considered that. 'We are attacking from the seaward side. We will occupy the port and the southern districts. You take the northern.' He looked at them. 'Do you agree?'

Did they know that the southern part of the city was by far the richer? But he knew what their answer would be.

'We do,' the leaders replied, unhesitatingly.

*

On Sunday they went to Mass, though the bells in Zara remained silent. There was some activity on the walls, but otherwise little movement within the city. On Monday 18 November, at dawn, they went to war.

The catapults hurled rocks at the battlements as the Crusaders stormed the walls from the landward sides and the Venetians attacked the seaward fortifications. The engineers dug under the foundations, working with picks and shovels, sweating under the cover of canopies of wet hides, which protected them from the worst of the boiling oil, fire and rocks thrown down from the battlements on to them. Three times during the first two days the attackers were repulsed. The people of Zara had good archers and there were plenty of able-bodied young men in the city who had not neglected their military training. They couldn't ride out, but they could push away scaling ladders, and they defended with such ferocity that the attackers couldn't bring in the assault towers.

But the weather held. If it had rained, the wheels which supported the towers would have slipped on rock or sunk in mud. But the battle was fought under a mild, late-autumn sun. Winter was tardy here.

The comfort was that the governor hadn't ordered the city itself set on fire. But, Dandolo had reasoned, if the governor destroyed the place, where would his people flee to? If he didn't, he might believe that he could negotiate for their lives, if he lost. It was for that reason that Dandolo had not chosen to try his power on the governor. That, and the need to see how the Crusader fought. But it had been a calculated risk.

At the moment it looked as if the governor had no intention of losing. Or of facing the inevitable. For the city would fall.

52

On the third day one of the south-western towers, where the sea-wall met the western-landward wall, came down, collapsing on itself and killing all within it, as well as perhaps fifty of the sappers who'd undermined it. One breach was enough. The panic of the defenders was palpable, and that day the attackers pushed the assault towers right up to the walls on all the landward sides. The fighting on the battlements was furious, and many of the attackers who climbed up never returned. If they did, it was minus a hand or an arm.

As far as Dandolo was concerned, they might as well have been dead. Maimed, what good were they to him?

That night, fires started in the city.

'We must take it before it kills itself,' Dandolo said to Leporo. 'How are our people doing?'

'Frid says we'll be inside the city by tomorrow at dusk. If he isn't exaggerating. They're cutting off the heads of the dead defenders who've fallen outside the walls and catapulting them back inside tonight. Weakens morale. Plenty of husbands, fathers, brothers and boyfriends there.'

'Good.'

'The fires aren't spreading. They're controlled. They're burning away rubbish so they can clear the streets when it comes to fighting in them.'

'Frid will break in from the south with our forces. I have every faith in him.'

'Swordplay is what he excels at,' agreed Leporo, hoping the Viking would be cut down in the first assault. He would watch the battle tomorrow with interest; it would be good to see the kind of power he himself would one day wield, once Frid was out of the way and Dandolo, lacking his protection and increasingly infirm, dead.

The fury unleashed on Thursday was without pity. This day, the battlements were taken, the attackers and defenders both using axes and maces. No room for the finesse of swordplay here, or time. The Venetians had an easier task, as most of the defenders were occupied with the larger Crusader force attacking from the other three compass points. The smell of blood, burning flesh and hot oil, and the smear of smoke and flame, blended with the screaming of injured animals and the anguished cries of women and children as they tried to escape, seek hiding-places in cellars or sanctuary in the churches, whose bells rang defiantly until they were silenced by the crash of a projectile into a steeple.

And as Frid had promised, by sunset the Venetian Navy and the Army of the Holy Fourth Crusade commanded the battlements and the gates, and what was left of the walls and towers of the proud city of Zara.

Friday was the worst day. Dandolo summoned Frid personally to make his report.

The Viking, unused to talking much or for long, spoke slowly and deliberately. He stood at uneasy attention before Dandolo's table, the two of them alone in the room. Leporo was busy elsewhere, supervising the loot that had already been seized. Dandolo had not wanted him at his elbow every waking minute.

'The fighting in the streets was hard and vicious, this day,' Frid began. 'Our men kept losing themselves in the tangle of narrow streets and finding themselves cut off or ambushed; and the defenders were a people living at the broken edges of what, a week earlier, had been a tranquil life. Now they were fighting with the ferocity of people who have nothing to lose.'

'Go on.'

'My platoon was cut off from the rest of the Venetian force. We'd taken a wrong turn and found ourselves penned in a little square with a well at its centre. Some of my men are professionals, but the bulk's made up of seamen and volunteers who'd taken the Cross because of you.'

'Because of me?'

'You inspired many when you had that blue-and-gold watered silk crucifix sewn on to your cap by the archbishop of Venice in St Mark's cathedral, shortly before the fleet sailed.' Frid hesitated before continuing. 'But that enthusiasm was wearing off, and weakened further as they saw that taking Zara wasn't the walkover they'd been led to believe it would be.'

'You speak plainly.'

'It is the truth.'

Dandolo laced his fingers. The plain truth would not hurt.

'As the enemy closed in from the streets which led into the square, I told my people to close ranks,' Frid continued. 'I had a dozen crossbowmen with me, armed with pull-lever

245

weapons which were quick to reload, and iron bolts, though only twenty or so of each.

'I ordered them to form a ring round the well and to fire volleys.'

'Evidently you were successful.'

'*Altissima*.' Frid bowed stiffly. 'The first fusillade brought down a dozen men – a hit-rate which made the attackers recoil, and left their dead and wounded scattered in their blood on the floor of the square. One man had taken a bolt to the neck, another full in the sternum. I heard the crack when the bone shattered as the bolt smashed its way home. Two others were hit in the thigh, another in the belly. One poor bugger had caught it in the groin, and his screams drowned out almost every other sound. Those killed were the lucky ones.'

Dandolo nodded. There'd be no prisoners, no patching up by the Venetian barber-surgeons, and he knew Frid wasn't going to waste time on coups de grâce.

'My men wanted to break out after the foe, but I told them to hold firm. I watched the Zarans to see what weapons they had. Swords, axes, daggers, but no bows. We were lucky. It's hard to use bows in street fighting any-way, but they might have had men on the roofs. I watched the roofs but there was nothing. How many of the bas-tards were left, I didn't know.'

Frid took a breath. He was getting old for this. His knees still ached, and his chain-mail had irritated him, despite the buckram tunic he'd worn beneath it.

'Then I saw a movement on the roof on the west side of the square, then another. They had short-bow men there after all.

'"The roofs! Aim at the roofs!" I yelled, as a first volley rained down on us, the arrows taking out five of my men, but luckily none of the soldiers with crossbows. The Zarans were shooting ragged.

'"Break up!" I told my lads. "Hand-to-hand! Bowmen, target the roofs!"

'We ran fast to grapple with the regrouped enemy in the square, cutting at hands, wrists, legs and faces. Soon the whole narrow space stank of blood and sweat. I stayed by the well, bracing myself against its low wall. I watched the progress of the fight. My volunteers were being sliced apart by the Zarans, but the Venetian seamen and professionals held fast, and there were still more than twenty of them in the melee.

'But more of the enemy were pouring into the square.

'I made a decision. "Get some of our people up to the roofs," I said to the sergeant at my side. "As many of the crossbowmen with them as you can muster."

'The sergeant ducked his head in acknowledgement and went about his business. Before long the fight had broken out above their heads and I could see that it was going our way. A Zaran bowman, his guts spewing out behind him in the air, crashed heavily to the ground, falling on two of his fellow citizens who were stabbing a crouching Venetian – a good, brave lad; I knew him well – in the square below. More followed, and then the hail of fire from above changed its aim. Now, more Zarans were falling, picked off by crossbow bolts.

'I saw our advantage and pressed it, bellowing to my men to close with the faltering defenders.' Frid felt a rush shame at the memory. 'As I did so, two young, burly

247

Zarans closed on me. My sergeant was gone, supervising the action on the rooftops; the rest of my men were heavily engaged, cutting down those of the defenders who were not already dead, wounded or fled. The battle was almost over, but these two weren't going to leave without taking me down.

"'Fucking Viking pig,'" one of them spat at me.

"'Say your prayers, granddad,' the other sneered. And without warning he swung his sword and knocked my helmet from my head.'

Frid paused, remembering what he did not say. He did not tell Dandolo because, for a moment, the clear belief he had in his leader had left him. What had he said to the Zarans? "Only obeying orders"? He was ashamed. And he couldn't drive away the memory of his shame:

His red hair, streaked with white, was still thick, and the sword had struck a glancing blow. He'd felt the flat of its blade, though, and that sent him reeling. He clutched the well wall to stop himself from falling. But he still went down on one knee.

His attackers roared and moved in quickly. Men of maybe twenty-five years old. One kicked him hard in the face.

'I saw you at the north gate. You sent my wife and children out, penned me in here. You're going to die slow!'

'Shouldn't have done that,' said the other.

Frid was breathing hard, but he was back in control. These two talked too much, and moved in too close. Still braced on one knee and with his back against the wall, he pretended to be more badly injured than he was.

'Take pity,' he begged. 'Only obeying orders.'

'What pity do you show, fuckface?' said the second young man. He was younger and lighter than his companion, and looked less

248

cocksure despite the advantage he thought he had. Frid lunged forward, grabbed his legs under the knee and, once he was off-balance, tipped him over his massive shoulders and into the well. The man didn't even have time to yell. It must have been five seconds before they heard him crash into the water at the bottom.

The other man, recovering from the unexpected shock, dropped his sword and grappled a mace out of his belt, a solid one, not on a chain, and took half a step back, raising it. Frid might have been an old man now, but he was still fit, and the tip of his little finger knew more about fighting than his opponent had in his whole muscular young body. He had a seax at his side, an old Viking machete, its heavy iron blade worn by use to half its original width, but the edge sharp enough to shave with. There was room to manoeuvre to cut with it, which would have been its best use; but Frid had seen that the man wore only a mail tunic and leather leggings. His lower belly and his private parts were protected by just a wooden codpiece. As the young Zaran raised his mace, the tunic he was wearing lifted, and then Frid pushed himself up and forward from his bent knee, which screamed in pain and protest, and thrust hard, just above and to the right of the man's prick. The seax would have gone right in if he'd wanted it to, for the flesh was soft there and he'd avoided hitting bone, but Frid let it penetrate only eight centimetres before pulling it out and, as the man dropped his mace and brought both hands down to the wound and bent his broad back as well, in the instinctive gesture of defence Frid had expected, the Norseman stood up, stepped back, and raised the seax to swipe through the nape of the neck and sever the head from the body. The head rolled away and the body jerked convulsively for a long moment before it fell to its knees and then, still writhing, to the ground.

'What happened then?' Dandolo cut in.

'When?'

'After you lost your helmet,' prompted the doge.

'I got them in the end. Then I looked round. There must have been fifty corpses in the square. The only men still standing were my own. I led them in a cheer, raising my seax, dripping blood, above my head. Then I wiped it and sheathed it, shoved my fingers through my beard to untangle it, wring some of the blood from it, shook myself. So much for Zara, I thought.'

The rest was easy, though how Dandolo got the French to do it was a mystery whose secret was fully known only to Frid, and knowing it did not mean that the Norseman understood it. Leporo, for himself, kept his counsel.

The women, the children and those too old to have fought, and the surviving warriors of the city, were pulled out of the looted churches and the cellars and wherever else they'd been hiding, brought down to the beach and corralled in pens constructed of tightly woven withies. There were a thousand of them, and it took a day and a night to slaughter them. The Crusaders and the Venetians did it with spears. Then they threw brushwood over the bodies, seasoned it with naphtha and set fire to the make-shift pyres. Black smoke rose. The fires didn't burn out until Sunday evening, and the stench was appalling. By then, Zara, that vile, treacherous bitch of a city, was theirs, and most of it was intact.

But it wasn't over.

53

'They've done *what*?' Dandolo snarled at Leporo. Three days had elapsed since the victory.

'It wasn't the fault of our men. The French started it.'

They were standing in the reception hall of the governor's mansion in the south-east quarter of the city, Dandolo's interrupted morning meal spread out on a table under one of the windows overlooking the harbour.

'The Pilgrims think they've got a raw deal.'

'So they started fighting *us*?'

'Some of the men only. Their leaders are putting down the insurrection.'

'Send for them,' Dandolo growled. 'I turn my back for one *night*, and this happens!'

Baldwin and Boniface, shamefaced, arrived an hour later. Everyone had been billeted according to his rank, and patrols had been sent out to scour the hills to the north for young men and women suitable for the purpose to which they were to be put, in repairing the walls and servicing the men of the Fourth Crusade. Everything had seemed calm. The plan to overwinter in Zara and in the meantime assess and divide the spoils had been agreed. But then fighting had broken out between some of the French and the Venetians over loot from the principal church, and it had spread to the streets.

'Frid's been out there too, and it's dying down now,' said Boniface.

Dandolo was aghast. Why had there been this disobedience? Had the tablet failed him? Had he lost concentration? It was a shock to discover that to exert his will over this army of what he was beginning to think of as his slaves, he could not relax for one moment.

He clutched the tablet tighter. It seemed to nestle in his hand of its own volition, as if it were a living thing. Did he really have power over it, or had he gone too far – was it beginning to have power over him?

He shook the notion off. It was preposterous. He was in control, and he alone.

'But that's armies for you – especially ones made up of nations that won't agree,' Geoffrey de Villehardouin said to Leporo later, when the fighting had died down and the two men were alone together.

'I saw little of it,' said the monk. 'What happened?' During the brief skirmish between the allies, Leporo had been cloistered with Dandolo in the mansion, making an audit of the city's assets.

'Baldwin and Boniface set about restoring the peace almost as soon as the trouble broke out. But as soon as they managed to put a stop to it in one quarter, it broke out in another. Three hundred men have died needlessly. And that in fighting which took place on a single night!'

'May God preserve us!'

'It's over now. The ringleaders on both sides have been arrested.'

'That much I do know.'

'And do you know what punishment will be meted out to them?'

'There are fifteen main troublemakers. The doge in his wisdom had determined that their punishment be exemplary. He has ordered them taken to the shore at dawn, and crucified.'

Geoffrey breathed hard. But he said nothing more than 'Let us pray to God that our internal conflict is now over for good, and that we can go forward on the great enterprise we have before us with renewed vigour in the spring.'

'There's enough work to do to keep the men busy until then,' said Leporo. 'We have to rebuild the damage done in taking this place.'

'And rest. And divide what we have gained. Then we will have our fleet fully paid for.'

Leporo smiled. Dandolo and he had calculated that, dividing the spoils fifty fifty, the Crusaders' share was still not enough to cover their outstanding debt. They would still be in the power of Venice, and they could not rebel.

'Let us pray that it is so,' he said.

54

Paris, the Present

Ben Duff, the psychologist in charge of Su-Lin's treatment, met Marlow in the entrance hall of the special flat they'd placed her in.

The secure apartment INTERSEC maintained was round the corner from HQ, in the rue Pernelle. The glass in the windows was bulletproof. The front door was made of battleship-grade steel. A rear entrance was concealed in the kitchen, and the door to a panic-room set into a wall of the entrance hall was similarly disguised. The place had been designed and modified in the days when INTERSEC still had a grown-up budget.

'It's going slowly, but not badly,' Duff told him. 'I'd have been happy with progress like this if it'd happened a month from now. And we've had a breakthrough since we last talked. Overnight, in fact.'

'Good.' Marlow kept the irritation out of his voice. 'Slowly' was not what he wanted to hear, and he was preoccupied with the conversation he'd just had with Sir Richard. The INTERSEC top brass were drumming their fingers.

'There are some aspects that'll need looking at further, but I think we're on the right track.'

'I need to talk to her alone.'

Duff looked doubtful. 'Not yet,' he said. 'I must be in attendance at this stage.'

'Give me half an hour.'

'Ten minutes. And only if I decide it's appropriate.'

But Marlow was impatient to interview the woman without a third party present. He needed to be alone with her to understand her.

Dr de Montferrat lay on a chaise longue by the shaded window in the living-room. She stirred when the men came in and sat up on its edge, swinging her long legs round with unconscious elegance. INTERSEC had organized a new wardrobe for her, most of which she liked, and now she looked very different from the lost tourist Geoffrey Goldberg had rescued outside his shop in Jerusalem. She was dressed in a close-fitting charcoal silk roll-neck, a matching cashmere suit and black patent-leather shoes with low heels, which increased her height by a couple of centimetres. She'd eaten about half the light meals they'd given her, but she'd put on a little weight since she'd been found, and from Duff's notes Marlow had seen that she weighed 45 kg.

'Light for her height,' Duff had told him. 'Could be malnourishment while she was out there.'

She had a boyish figure; narrow shoulders, neat, perfectly proportioned breasts, slim hips; and her straight black hair was just long enough to frame a pale face which, if you didn't know anything about her ancestry, you'd have found hard to attach a nationality to. The almond eyes were dark brown, and she had high cheekbones, but her lips were full and generous and her chin strong; her nose was delicate and – Tennyson's words came to Marlow's mind – 'tip-tilted, like a flower'.

She seemed glad to see the two men, and Marlow noticed that Duff had hit it off with her. An easygoing man whom she found easy to handle, he guessed.

She looked as if a train of thought had been disturbed by their arrival, though she must have been expecting them.

'It's good to see you,' she said. A light voice, attractive. She put as much feeling into her voice as she could. She liked the look of the tall, slightly dishevelled policeman with the dark, troubled eyes who accompanied her doctor.

The apartment was spacious, the walls painted in light colours; the furniture was modern and finished in white or cream. But the inner courtyards it looked on to on one side crowded out daylight, and most of the lamps were on.

She gestured them to chairs. 'Something to drink?' she asked. 'Lemon tea?'

'Jack wants to hear your news,' said Duff. 'And no lemon tea, thanks.'

She looked at Marlow; he too shook his head.

'What news there is,' she said to Duff. Her English accent was virtually faultless. Only variations in inflection and faultless grammar betrayed the fact that she was not a native. 'Where shall I begin?'

'Tell him about the dream,' said Duff.

De Montferrat thought for a moment. 'I was a little girl again. When I woke up, I wondered where I was. I wondered how I had got here. I seemed to have passed weeks of my life in complete darkness. But it all seemed so real.'

'Ben mentioned that a long blackout period would have been part of your condition,' said Marlow. He glanced at his watch, hoping this dream story would lead to something concrete.

She smiled at him shyly, giving him the full benefit of her eyes. 'I was playing in a garden. Then I went inside and looked at the aquarium I'd been given by my parents a couple of years earlier for my birthday. The pretty gleaming fish under the lights. The sunken castle, the pirate shipwreck. The fronds of the water plants moving in the ripples made by the air bubbles.' Her tone was unemotional. 'I thought that I was tired of the fish. I switched the aquarium off. Then days seemed to pass. I went out, I played with my friends. They were all boys. They all admired me. I forgot about the aquarium. Later, I looked at it again. Dark and empty. Some fish had risen, dead, to the surface. I scooped them out and threw them away. I supposed a few might still have been alive in there, somewhere.'

Marlow wondered if this was a true memory. Few people are capable of such unconscious cruelty, but they do exist.

'Is that the end?'

'Almost. I didn't think about the fish any more. I went out to play again. There was a pretty garden, and a view over fields and open countryside, with trees, but this time I was alone. All the boys had gone . . .When I woke up, I was confused. But I know that I questioned my surroundings – these surroundings – for the first time. I was aware of them. And I was aware of myself. I knew who I was.'

'And your memory?'

She struggled to find the words. Duff came to her

rescue. 'There are still significant gaps,' he said. 'No rec-
ognition of your parents, for example, is there?'

'I only know they are both dead. I know I grew up in
Italy, mostly. But when you showed me photographs of
my parents they might as well have been strangers. I have
only your word for it that they are the people you tell me
they are.' She paused. 'All I have of my childhood is that
dream, and it doesn't feel real at all now.'

'What about recent memories?' asked Marlow, ignoring
a warning look from Duff.

'I do remember my work at Venice. I remember all I
was taught. I remember all my training. And I remember
the Dandolo Project.'

Marlow locked on to that. 'When did these memories
come back?' he asked Duff crisply.

'Less than an hour ago,' said Duff. 'I needed that time
to confirm.'

'But when I talked to you earlier, Dr de Montferrat –'
he started, then interrupted himself. 'When did you have
the dream you told me about?'

'Last night. But everything was still misty this morning.
I was frightened that what seemed to be coming back to
me was just an illusion. I wanted to wait. I needed to talk
to Ben first . . .'

She was becoming agitated. Duff put a restraining hand
on her arm. She calmed down quickly, but he left his hand
there.

'Would you have any objection if we talked alone for a
while?' Marlow asked her.

Her eyes widened a fraction. 'No. Not at all.' But she
turned her gaze to Duff.

'OK,' he agreed reluctantly, frowning at Marlow before turning back to Su-Lin. 'Relax. Don't forget what I told you before Jack arrived – you have to be patient with these things. I think we've turned a big corner today. But healing takes time; it can't be hurried.'

She gave him a sad smile.

After the door had closed behind him, she leaned back on the chaise longue, and her dark eyes met Marlow's. 'What do you want to know?' she said.

'What you haven't told Duff.'

She looked surprised. 'I have kept nothing from him.'

'What happened after the dig? What happened to the others – Adkins and Taylor?'

Now she seemed furtive, scared. 'I don't know. I would have told Ben.'

'Something happened. Something bad. Try to think. Try to remember.'

'I can't! It's horrible!'

'What's horrible? Tell me.'

He looked at her. She'd sunk back again. She was breathing heavily, holding him with her eyes, but he could read nothing in their depths.

He waited. Then he said carefully, 'Let's start with the Project. How did you become involved with it?'

'You must have checked that. You probably know better than I do.'

'I'd like to hear it from you.'

She looked thoughtful, questioning herself, but said, 'I will help you as much as I can. You must be patient with me.'

'Think, then. The lives of your colleagues depend on it.'

'I know.'

'What did you find – can you remember that?' he tried, more gently.

'If I could remember, I'd tell you.'

'Where were you when it happened? In the lab? In the hotel?'

'I don't know!'

'Maybe the lab?' Marlow knew that was the more likely place. Harder to get people out of a busy hotel than a quiet university department. It would have happened late in the day ... early evening, when the archaeologists would have been packing up for the day.

Maybe.

'Try!' he persisted.

But there was nothing in those enigmatic eyes.

Marlow looked at her long and hard. If there *were* anything in those eyes, it was loneliness. Loneliness. That was something he was getting close to becoming an expert on. He thought about that. It was something with which he could empathize. Maybe that would be the way to get through to her.

It wasn't in the rule book, but he reached across and took her hand.

55

Mid-afternoon, Marlow reappeared in the fourth-floor office.

'How's it going?' Graves asked, as he hurried in.

'With Su-Lin? She recognizes where she is and who she is. Our problem is her recent memory field.'

'The one that counts.'

He ignored that. 'You?'

'Mixed bag.' But she was finding it hard to keep the excitement out of her voice.

'Spill.' Marlow was about to sit down in the chair across from her desk, and she pushed her computer aside, ready to talk. But then his BlackBerry rang. He checked the incoming number before turning aside and leaving the room again.

Graves watched him go, slipped on her reading glasses, and picked up the file she'd been working on, the one she'd need for the conversation they were about to have. She was looking forward to it.

She thought about Marlow despite herself. She thought about him too much.

They'd been working together for weeks. She prided herself on her ability to find out what made a person tick pretty quickly. It made it easier to work with them. Leon Lopez had been a pussy-cat. Easy, friendly, open-hearted to those he trusted, and humorous. It hadn't taken long for them to get each other's measure. Since they'd been away from New York, she'd missed Leon.

Of course, no one ever knows what's going on in another person's mind, but you've got to recognize where you can repose trust.

Graves was trained to do that only with extreme caution. Everyone has a chink in their armour, and that can be exploited; but Lopez was a co-worker Graves felt she could lean on.

Marlow was different. It wasn't just his reserve. He was a man who kept his gloves up. On the defensive.

Against what?

Something must have happened to him to make him like that. Something which had hurt him, or some professional slip, buried in his past, which caused him to build such walls around himself.

She thought of his dark eyes, and the wariness in their depths.

She heard him raise his voice slightly, outside in the corridor. What he was saying was indistinct, though she could tell he was speaking French. Then he hung up and there was the sound of his footsteps on the parquet as he returned.

She shook herself back to reality. She couldn't deny that her interest was personal, any more than she could deny that she was attracted to him, but anything in that direction would have to wait. There was work to do, and it was nothing short of crazy in their line of work even to think of a personal relationship with a colleague. Death and betrayal were always too close for that.

But she had something here which she could really impress him with.

'Sorry about that,' he said in a voice which gave nothing away.

She flipped back into her professional mode without missing an outward beat, and opened the file.

'There's good news and bad,' she began.

'Bad first,' he said, sitting down but not relaxing a muscle, arms forward, leaning lightly on the desk.

'Leon's back in New York now. Venice turned up some interesting stuff.'

'He's sent his report in?'

'It's what I've been working on this morning.'

'Shoot.'

'OK – bad news first.' She looked at him. 'Leon took a thorough look at the Archivio di Stato in our area of interest. He searched documents dating from 1160 to 1210.'

'Took his time.'

'Those archives go back a thousand years. There's seventy kilometres of shelves.'

'Point taken. And the bad news is?'

'We know Dandolo became doge in 1192, when he was over eighty, and died in 1205. But he was politically active for years before he took over as leader of the city-state. There's some minor stuff dealing with him between 1160 and 1169, but after 1170 – nothing.'

'Computer files? Microfilm?'

'Leon was on to that – the cupboard's bare.'

'Just the material on Dandolo?'

'Just Dandolo.'

Marlow considered this. 'Destroyed. Or someone's taken it.' He filed the information in his mind.

Graves gave him a look. 'How long do you think it'll take to get anything concrete out of Dr de Montferrat?'

'Duff thinks another five days.'

'Has he drawn any other conclusions about her?'

'Like what?'

'I don't know – anything at all.' Graves hedged, deciding to keep any reservations she had to herself.

'So – the good news?' But Marlow's face remained closed.

She picked up the file and drew a sheet of paper from it. 'Look at this.'

It was a high-definition photocopy of an ancient manuscript, but what was written on it was completely indecipherable. Tiny, crowded-together incisions which looked like the jumbled footprints of small birds. The printing covered a very small physical area – barely larger than the surface of his BlackBerry. The ground was grey; the letters – or symbols – stood out in white. So whatever it was had been printed from something bearing incised markings, not raised ones.

'What is this?' he asked.

'That's what I'm working on.'

'Did Leon find it?'

'No – I did.'

'Tell me.'

She'd been impatient to do so ever since she'd confirmed what she suspected when first examining the document. 'I don't suppose anyone's looked at the original since it was filed in the archive. There was a note attached to it dated 4 February 1849: "Indecipherable. Cuneiform script? Language: Sumerian? Or Akkadian?

No date. Possible date: *c.* 1000BC?" No one's bothered with it since. And you can imagine how long it took to get the museum officials to authorize a proper copy. French bureaucracy sometimes seems stuck in the nineteenth century itself!'

'What archive?'

'The archive in the Musée de Cluny. Just down the road from here. The Museum of the Middle Ages.'

'Go on.'

'It was a long shot, but while Leon was looking in Venice, I thought, why not look here too? It's just as well that I did.'

'But why here?'

'Because Bishop Adhemar was French!'

56

Marlow knew immediately that his assistant had made a breakthrough. 'Begin at the beginning,' he said.

'OK.' She took a deep breath. 'Bishop Adhemar is mentioned in some of the research documents Adkins and his team managed to communicate to Yale before they disappeared. It was Leon who dug him out first. Dandolo mentions him two or three times.'

'So what's the connection?'

'Adhemar was one of the leaders of the First Crusade, around 1096. Adhemar travelled widely in the Middle East. He even spent time in Constantinople. He died in the Holy Land in 1098.'

'He was in Constantinople, you say?'

'Yes.'

'What's his background?'

'He was bishop of Le-Puy-en-Velay. There're various stories about him, one of which concerns a visit he made to Egypt. Shortly after that trip, he became obsessed with something – something he'd found there, something, the legends say, which had the ability to impart supreme power to anyone who possessed it.'

'Some object?'

'Yes.' Graves's eyes gleamed. 'God knows when this document found its way to the Cluny Museum, but there it is. It wouldn't have gone to Venice, because, as I said, *Adhemar was French*.'

'Where is this leading?' Marlow could already guess.

'Adhemar had a huge influence on the management of the First Crusade, and even after his madness and death many of the rank-and-file soldiers insisted he was still alive, still watching over them, controlling them. There were stories of the bishop walking among them, encouraging them.'

'Don't waste my time with ghost stories, Laura,' said Marlow, but he was intrigued.

'Don't forget that people who lived nine hundred years ago or so were less cynical than we are. They believed *literally* in the miracles which Holy Relics could work, for example. And if you believe something hard enough, you can make it happen – or at least *think* you've made it happen.'

'And you're saying that this bishop had found some sort of relic in Egypt?'

'In Alexandria, yes. Except that I don't think it was a relic.'

'Go on.'

'I did some more research. Some of the papers Adhemar left behind apart from this one – and there aren't many – have references by him – obsessive references, I'd say – to a "*sacred scroll*".'

Marlow looked at the photocopy he was holding.

'It was something he never seemed quite able to figure out how to use,' Laura went on. 'He knew what it was and what it could do – but he could never manage to make it work *completely*. If he had any success, to judge from his writing, it was hit and miss, random. What ate him up was that he knew there should be a system, but he couldn't work out what it was.' She leaned forward, tense with excitement. 'Just today, while you were working with the de Montferrat woman, I think I nailed it.'

Marlow continued to study the paper.

'The original manuscript is ink on vellum,' Graves went on, 'and it's in a poor state of repair now – much of what's written on it has been eroded by time, and so the meaning of the whole is incomplete. But one thing's for sure: what's on that parchment hasn't been penned by hand – it's been *printed*.'

'But people like Gutenberg and Caxton weren't born until the fifteenth century.'

'Printing existed before them – it's been around for three thousand years. Adhemar travelled widely in the East. Printing was known in ancient Mesopotamia, what's now Iraq. But there's more to it than that.'

'This script has nothing to do with the Roman or Greek alphabets, which would have been the two used in Dandolo's time – and Adhemar's. And, as I remember, the inscription on the pictures we have of the key the archaeologists discovered –'

'Now lost –'

'It isn't Aramaic either.'

'You're right! This script must be much earlier. It probably *does* date from around 1000BC, the time the curator at the Cluny Museum suggested when he wrote his note in 1849. But it *may* be much earlier even than that.'

'So what is it?'

'This *is* written in cuneiform, as the curator at the Cluny guessed.' Graves couldn't resist going into an explanation which Marlow didn't need. 'It's a kind of proto-alphabet, used by the priests and the priest-kings who ruled ancient Babylon. It was still in use for secret and ritual purposes, well after it had been supplanted in everyday use.'

'OK – but what does it say?'

'Nothing. It's nonsense.'

Marlow looked at her sharply. 'What do you mean?'

'Or rather, not quite nonsense. I said that what you can see here was printed.'

'Yes.'

'Well, Adhemar must have got hold of something almost a thousand years ago, when he was in Egypt, that he thought was a printer's block. He knew roughly how old it was, and he knew that ancient peoples of the Middle East had mastered the art of printing. He didn't worry about the fact that the characters were incised, not raised. He only knew it was valuable, he knew it had some power, so he printed it out, to produce his "sacred scroll".'

Marlow had caught some of her fire. 'But – it *wasn't* a printer's block?'

'No! That's what had me perplexed. What we have here – and it's impossible to make out its meaning fully, because the parchment it was printed on is so decayed – is a *mirror-image* of what was cut into what I guess was a small clay tablet. That's what confused Adhemar. That's why he couldn't use it correctly. Only some of the symbols and phrases have the same mirror-image as the positive one.

That's why his reading of it must have been incomplete. His "sacred scroll" – this parchment in the museum here in Paris – wasn't the real thing at all!'

57

Marlow was silent for a moment. 'Then what was?' he said.

'The Babylonians wrote on clay tablets. They stamped, or cut, the letters on the clay when it was still moist. When the clay dried, they had a permanent record of what they'd written. And they used small tablets, convenient enough to hold in the palm of one hand. Portable, easy to use – you hold the thing in one hand, you use the other to "write" on it.'

'So –' Marlow knew what this was leading up to.

'Of course, they had far larger tablets and columns for writing, say, lists of laws, but for most purposes they used these little clay tablets. The Babylonians used them for everything from schoolbooks to shopping lists, but there are also hundreds which contain sophisticated mathematical and astronomical formulae. Hundreds of thousands have come to light since modern archaeology began in the region, right up to the time of the Iraq War, when everything came to a halt. And a hell of a lot has been destroyed since 2003. But the heyday for archaeologists was the second half of the nineteenth and the first half of the twentieth centuries. One of the greatest of the researchers was a German called Robert Koldewey, who died in 1925, aged seventy.'

'So the real sacred scroll is actually a small clay tablet.

The same size as the area covered by the printing on this photocopy of Bishop Adhemar's manuscript,' said Marlow. And there are hundreds and thousands of these?'

'There are thirty thousand still waiting to be *catalogued* in the vaults of the British Museum alone. Most of them have been there for a century.'

They fell silent.

'Dandolo managed to divert an entire foreign army from its original purpose and use it to smash Constantinople, the greatest trade rival Venice had,' Marlow said. 'Are you telling me that somehow he got hold of this – thing – and worked out how to use it to control a Crusade?'

'Why not?' she said. 'He was in Constantinople in about 1170. And he travelled in the Holy Land from there. As the Venetian envoy. After he'd made his copy, Adhemar would certainly have left the original tablet somewhere for safekeeping.'

'And if he left it in the Holy Land, or someone did, after he went mad?'

'The Templars began to hold property as surety or simply in safe-deposits. They became bankers. They were the equivalent of a Swiss bank. Dandolo had dealings with the Templars nearly a century after Adhemar's death.'

Marlow shook his head. 'Too far-fetched.'

'Have you a better hypothesis?' asked Graves.

Marlow thought some more. 'What if this tablet still has the power to do what it did for Dandolo – if it did anything – if it still exists?'

'There's no reason why it shouldn't have. It won't be some kind of magic spell. It'll be a scientific formula. The

Babylonians were interested in the movement of the con-stellations and the effect the various changing positions of the stars had – or might have – on their people, and what might happen to them. That's what they were chiefly interested in – observing the stars, and reading clues from them – in order to control the future. You could say that they were astronomers by accident. What they were really interested in was astrology. But that doesn't devalue what they discovered about the stars. They were scientists first and foremost, and it's possible they knew more than we do, even today. Einstein and Max Planck both took their findings – as they came to light – very seriously. Einstein was a pioneer of astrophysics. Planck was the founder of quantum mechanics.'

'The physical properties of celestial bodies; and the interactions of energy and matter,' said Marlow, remembering the special qualifications, over and above those of archaeologists, of Adkins and Taylor.

'Adkins and the rest weren't just working on Dandolo's tomb for the sake of early medieval history, were they?' said Graves.

'It doesn't look like it now,' replied Marlow slowly. 'If you're right, they were looking for this – scroll.'

'But their interest wasn't purely archaeological.'

'So, who – beyond Yale and Venice – were Adkins and Taylor really working for?'

'And de Montferrat.'

'And who *else* was interested?'

'What do you mean?'

'If they were abducted, kidnapped – *taken* – the people who did so certainly weren't the ones they were working for!'

'Maybe they thought they were simply working for their universities. Maybe we're reading too much into this.'

'I don't think so. It explains why we're involved.'

'We've still got to find them.'

'Get all this to Leon,' Marlow said. 'Top secret – *ultra-secure*, as we have to say these days. He's to follow up with Yale and Venice. Very discreetly. No one else in on this. No one. We've got to find out what's behind the mask.'

'Check.'

'And well done. You're a star.'

'You're welcome.'

They looked at each other. Then Marlow's expression changed: 'There's still the question of that key,' he said.

'Yes,' she agreed.

'It's a small key, wherever it is.' He looked abstracted. 'Remember the inscription on the key? – "*Unless I open the box . . .*"'

Graves looked at him. 'That would work,' she said.

'Some kind of casket! The same date as the key. Made of – ?'

'Iron, probably. And designed to contain . . .?'

His face cleared. 'Something about the size of a Black-Berry. Or a Palm?'

They looked at each other.

'But where the hell is it?' she said.

'Wherever it is, somebody has the key to it.'

'The question is, who?'

'We have to find the box,' said Marlow. 'We have to find the key.'

58

It was after 11 p.m. The night staff had already checked in. Marlow was the last to go – as always, he reflected. But life at the moment held nothing for him outside his work. He remembered something Boris Cyrulnik had written in *Talking of Love*: 'Someone who is wounded cannot come back to life immediately. It is hard to dance when your legs have been broken.'

But he found his thoughts trailing towards Su-Lin.

The blue phone rang. He returned reluctantly from the door to pick it up.

'I know it's late, but I thought you'd like my conclusions on that dream as soon as possible,' said Ben Duff.

Marlow sat back at his desk.

'I had another talk with Su-Lin before I left. I think the experience was real. But she disagrees. She says she would never have done anything like that.'

Marlow thought about that. 'Well, why doubt her?'

'Young children haven't yet learned not to be selfish. But the rules most of us learn, and become second nature as we mature and live with other people – to take our place in society, in other words –don't get fully absorbed by some people.'

'And you're saying she's one of them?'

'All I'm saying is that she may actually have committed this bizarre act in her childhood. It may sound like a small thing, but it's worth considering. There are people who go through life protected, as it were, by their egocentricity, which goes hand in hand with their emotional immaturity. It never leaves them. And they'll always write a script in their head which places them as the blameless party in any situation, even situations they've created themselves. Bad ones, especially.'

'Go on.'

'The thing is, such people are very difficult to spot, unless you're a victim of one. They can function perfectly normally in every aspect of life until they're confronted with something they can't cope with, and then they kick out at it – in one way or another. Their disadvantage is that they're often not aware of it when a normal person has seen through them – but most of the time they get away with things. It was recognized long, long ago. Lao-Tsu was writing about it 2,500 years ago. He described egoists as people who, "without ropes, bind themselves". Duff paused. 'I'm sorry. I'm getting a little obsessive here. Nothing to do with memory loss.'

Marlow's tone was brisk. 'What we need to find out, before anything else, is how she ended up in Jerusalem after disappearing in Istanbul, and what the hell happened to her, and the others.'

Duff's voice sounded more businesslike now. 'She's making good progress, even since you saw her last, and certainly she's up to another session with you.'

'When?'

'Tomorrow?'

'Early.'

*

Marlow's Paris apartment was a small, anonymous duplex owned by INTERSEC, in the Quartier de l'Horloge, just north of the Pompidou Centre.

The minute he'd closed his front door, the exhaustion hit him, as did the familiar loneliness, somehow worse since he'd met Su-Lin.

But the loneliness ran deep, and it was like an ocean he didn't have the strength to swim across. Little warnings flickered in his brain about how vulnerable this made him, but they weren't strong.

He looked round at the bleak, white space, with its spartan furniture and poor insulation, through which the north wind blew and sometimes moaned with insistent vigour. He sighed, and pulled off his coat, slinging it on the coat-stand in the narrow hallway, from which an unsteady wooden spiral staircase ran to the upper floor.

He took a leak in the draughty lavatory, washed and changed in the adjoining bathroom and bedroom and climbed the stairs to the living area with its open-plan kitchen. He switched on the television. He zapped between a couple of American crime series dubbed into French, an interminable political discussion programme, and an old movie – Chabrol's *Le Boucher*.

He switched the thing off again. Well over a hundred channels, in several languages, and nothing he could face.

He looked hard at the remains of the bottle of Jameson's. Maybe a quarter of it left – not enough to do him any serious harm. But something he couldn't put his finger on was bugging him, and he resisted the whiskey, making coffee instead.

He went out on to the small terrace, to look at the view

of Sacré Coeur to the north, St Eustache to the west and, twinkling away like a giant, kitsch sparkler for its ten-minute long, on-the-hour lightshow, the Eiffel Tower; but the raw wind from the north drove him inside again. He picked up a novel – Fred Vargas's *L'Homme à l'Envers* – but even it couldn't engage him in his present mood.

He thought of the woman who'd brought his life to a standstill a year ago. He had to shake himself free. But nothing in his training manuals said anything about how to cope with heartbreak.

Work was the thing. The only way back.

Finally, he sat at the marble-topped table which sepa-rated the kitchen from the living room and worked on the questions he needed to ask Su-Lin. At about 4 a.m., he sighed, blinked pricking eyes, and made his way down to the bedroom.

But his night, what was left of it, was sleepless.

59

The weather showed no sign of relenting the next day. Marlow made his way south down the rue St Martin early, cutting across the place Michelet, where he bought a *Guardian* from the ginger-haired man at the kiosk. He knew he wouldn't have time to read the paper, and threw it on his desk when he arrived in his office, switching on his computer and checking emails before turning his back to the room and looking across the courtyard it faced, towards the windows of the flat where Su-Lin was under surveillance.

He tried to put himself in her position, into her mind, but the exercise was impossible, and he abandoned it, looking at his watch. Fifteen minutes to go before Duff was due. He picked up the paper and leafed through it after all, but, as he'd anticipated, he took nothing in. He felt impatient. He wasn't enjoying being back in Paris.

He suppressed the bad memories which were still clouding his mind from the night before and concentrated on the questions he'd prepared. He hadn't been working for more than a few minutes when there was a knock at the door.

Ben Duff was early, but Marlow was relieved to see another face.

'I've visited her already,' said Duff, 'and she's ready to talk to you alone again.' He didn't seem happy. 'I know you have things to ask her about which don't concern me, but I'm still going to sit in for a while. If it's going well, I'll leave you to it. But not for long – say, an hour. She won't be able to take more than that.'

Marlow nodded assent.

They made their way to the apartment. There was the same offer of lemon tea, which this time they accepted.

Marlow had decided to start his questions with Jerusalem, and work backwards from there.

She answered him with evident difficulty, but she seemed keen to be as helpful as possible. She was also nervous; but that was to be expected. Marlow watched the delicate movements of her hands and body as she prepared the tea, making the humdrum task into a ritual.

There was something vulnerable about her, too. He needed to be on his guard. He had been played that way before.

She remembered nothing about travelling to Jerusalem. She knew she was lost, but whether or not she had known the city previously, she couldn't say – she hadn't been able to remember any cities at all. She'd instinctively kept her bag with her because something told her that its contents might provide a clue to her identity, but she hadn't recognized the passport for what it was, let alone known it was hers.

'Might you have been in Jerusalem in connection with something in the past? Something you were researching?' said Marlow.

She looked nonplussed. 'I'm sorry?' she said.

'You remember what you were doing in Istanbul?' Duff put in, prompting her lightly. Marlow glanced at him. His eyes were very clear as he looked at her. It looked as if his concern for her might go further than his professional care.

'Of course I remember Istanbul now, and Dr Adkins and Dr Taylor, but after that . . .' She looked distressed.

'Let's focus on Jerusalem first,' Marlow said, as gently as he could. 'What might have been happening there at about the time of the Fourth Crusade – or a little earlier?'

She was able to deal with historical facts. 'It was a Christian city. The centre of the Kingdom of Jerusalem, which lasted for two hundred years from the year 1099, when the First Crusade took the Holy Land from the Seljuk Turks,' she said, as if reciting. 'In 1291, the Kingdom's last city, Acre, was destroyed by the Muslim Mameluks. That was the end of it.'

'But Jerusalem itself?' Marlow pursued. 'Say, just before the Fourth Crusade?'

'It was a Christian city. There was a Christian king,' she said.

Duff looked at Marlow and nodded his approval. It was good to keep her on home ground.

'Go on,' said Marlow.

'Until it fell to the Saracens under Saladin in 1187. Saladin took over most of the country, except the coastal cities.' She looked at both of them, uncertainly. 'All this I remember. Shall I go on?'

'Yes,' said Marlow.

'The fall of the city shocked the Christian world,' she said. 'And a Crusade was launched to recapture it, two years later. That was the Third Crusade. The most famous.' She looked at Marlow. 'The one which had Richard the Lionheart as one of its leaders.'

'What happened to the Christians in Jerusalem when Saladin took over?'

'Those who could fled to the safety of the cities on the coast. Some were sold into slavery. But there were no atrocities. Saladin was not that kind of man. Unlike your King Richard.'

'Were there . . . Knights Templar among them?'

'You are good at history!' she cried, smiling at Marlow, who smiled back. 'Yes. There was an important banking and trade centre, along with the military barracks. The Templars took over the Al-Aqsa mosque as their head-quarters. They moved their operations to Acre when Saladin got too close to Jerusalem.'

'And what happened to the Crusade?'

'It dragged on until 1192. But its leaders fell out, and they never retook Jerusalem. There was a truce in the end. The Christians kept a coastal strip as their kingdom. Saladin allowed unarmed Christian pilgrims to visit the Holy City unmolested. The Templars stayed on, protecting the pilgrims, taking care of their money and property, as they had always done, since they were first founded in 1119. But by the time we are talking of, they weren't really warriors any more – they were bankers.'

Duff sat back in his chair, sipping his tea. He looked at Marlow sympathetically. It was going well, as far as he was concerned. Marlow was impatient for him to leave.

'Tell me – before Saladin invaded – when there was still a Kingdom of Jerusalem throughout the Holy Land – when the Templars still had their HQ in the Al-Aqsa mosque complex – might Dandolo have been there?'

Su-Lin looked puzzled.

'He was in Constantinople in about 1170, wasn't he?' Marlow prompted.

Su-Lin looked thoughtful. 'He might have been,' she said hesitantly. 'I don't know.'

That sounded odd to Marlow. 'Might you have gone to Jerusalem to find out?'

'I don't know . . .' She was beginning to show signs of distress again.

'Did you learn all this when you were doing your doctorate, or was it later, when you got your MAXPHIL grant for the Dandolo Project?'

Though she tried to cover it, she baulked at the mention of MAXPHIL. Didn't look like an act, either. 'What –?' she said. 'What are you talking about? You're confusing me.'

'Never mind,' Marlow replied quickly. 'I've seen Dandolo's tomb,' he went on, changing tack. 'Fascinating.'

Her eyes brightened again. 'Isn't it?' Then she looked troubled again. 'But the dig is over now.'

'Not necessarily. If we find your friends safe and well.'

'What can have happened to them?'

Marlow hesitated, cast a glance at Duff, who nodded encouragement. 'We'll find them,' he assured her, wondering if they would. People stayed missing for years. He tried not to think about that.

Duff coughed politely. 'I think at this stage I'll leave you to it,' he said, more to his patient than Marlow.

Su-Lin nodded. The doctor rose, looking at his watch. 'Another half-an-hour,' he said to Marlow. 'I'll come back then.'

They fell silent after Duff had gone, looking at each

other. Marlow broke it by saying, 'Can you tell me what you found in the tomb yet? Can you remember?'

He leaned forward in his chair, leaned close.

'Yes, I do,' she answered at last. 'Quite clearly.' She reeled off a long list of artefacts, almost by rote. But there was no mention of a medieval box, or a Babylonian tablet. Or a key.

'That's all I can tell you,' she concluded. 'I may have missed some things out.'

'I wasn't expecting a comprehensive list,' he lied. He considered telling her that he had one, just to challenge her, to show her his question had been a test, a trap; but he didn't.

She had leaned forward too. Her eyes were candid. He could smell the scent she was wearing – a clean, fresh smell. He recalled that a bottle of L'Eau d'Issy had been on the list of things she'd asked INTERSEC to buy her.

She'd clearly remembered her own preferred scent.

Marlow hadn't forgotten Graves's request. The face so close to his was clear and confident. 'There's something else I need to ask you,' he said, straightening up.

'Yes?'

'About your name.'

She gave an embarassed smile. 'It's an awful mixture, isn't it?'

'I'm thinking about your family name.'

Was there, fleetingly, something in her eyes? But she was ready for the question. 'You're thinking of the connection with Marquess Boniface,' she said.

'Is he an ancestor?'

She laughed in a relaxed way that irritated Marlow. 'I

don't think we go back quite that far,' she said. 'Even my mother, who was a great snob, could only trace her ancestors to 1800. I don't think my father bothered. He was too busy making money.'

'But it's quite a coincidence.'

'Isn't it? Rick and Brad used to tease me about it.' Her face clouded again. 'I'd give anything see them again, Jack. Safe. Anything.' She looked at him. 'I want to help in every way I can.'

Marlow was taken aback at the vehemence with which she spoke. She had even leaned forward and held his knee. Now, as if coming to her senses, she withdrew her hand, slowly.

'But it must have crossed your mind that there might be a connection between your father's family and Boniface,' Marlow went on. 'Your business is research. Didn't you look into it?'

'Oh yes. As soon as I learned about the Marquess!' She laughed. Her laugh was like windbells. 'I got as far as 1900. But it was harder to find a trace, before that. What was left of his line petered out over a century ago. And my father was born in 1949.'

Marlow remembered what Graves had said about Boniface's family tree. This corroborated it. But he hadn't time to chase chimeras now.

He hesitated, remembering how distressed the subject had made her. 'Can you remember nothing about what happened?'

The clouds appeared again in an instant. 'I have tried!'

'What's the last thing you *do* remember?'

'If you knew how hard I have tried to remember!'

The intensity returned to her voice. Marlow contained his impatience, and sat silently, as she composed herself.

'We have got to find them! Only you can help us!'

'Oh God!' she complained suddenly, sitting upright. 'All this. Why did it have to happen?' She darted a look of fire at him. 'And you – who are you? Why are you keeping me here? Does anyone else know where I am?' She burst into tears – immediate, uncontrolled floods of tears, as if all the tension that had built up in her since she had reclaimed her memory needed to break out. 'This awful place – I can't go out – it's like a prison! I can scarcely even see the sky. Please! I want to go home. They will be missing me.'

'Who will? Where's home?' he said brutally.

She gave him a bitter look then turned her face to the window.

Marlow followed her gaze out at the sullen, concrete-grey Parisian heavens. The room had grown dark as yet another downpour threatened. He found himself reaching across to comfort her, but she shook him away.

He wondered if he should call Ben Duff back, but that would conclude this interview. He didn't want that. He sat and waited for the bad moment to pass.

He had another fifteen minutes. At the end of that time, he had got no further. But he had made a decision.

Precisely half an hour after he had left, Duff returned, and immediately registered the tension between his patient and his employer.

*

'She's made a remarkable recovery, hasn't she?' said Duff guardedly, when he and Marlow were alone together in the corridor outside.

'Truly remarkable,' Marlow replied, his thoughts elsewhere.

60

During the next three days Marlow saw little of anyone except Su-Lin and, after the first morning, Duff, pressured by Marlow, reduced his presence to the first few minutes of each interview. He was never further away, however, than his office and, every time he took his leave, he reminded Su-Lin that she had only to press the button that connected to a buzzer in his office and he would intervene.

This procedure annoyed Marlow, but it put a rein on his impatience, with the result that he was able to restrain himself whenever he came close to pressing his subject too hard. And the result of *that* was that he got more out of her than he might have done otherwise.

It was a question of gaining each other's trust. Marlow allayed her fears and suspicions, and told her as much as she needed to know about his organization.

She was convinced that she was in the hands of INTERPOL, and Marlow showed her fake documents to back this up.

'We have to keep your location secret, or your abductors might try to recapture you,' he explained.

That made sense to Su-Lin.

He was certain that her motivation – to get to the bottom of whatever had happened to her colleagues and find them before they came to any further harm – was sincere.

'But can't I go out at all?'

'It's too risky.'

'Just for a while – to get some air? I know I'd be safe with you.'

'We have to concentrate on where Brad and Rick might have been taken. The slightest memory. The longer it takes, the greater the danger.'

'I know.'

'Let's get on.'

She took his hand and smiled.

But the information she gave stayed incomplete, and was surrendered only reluctantly by Su-Lin's mind.

'It's natural,' Duff explained to Marlow. 'The mind's protecting itself by blocking out the major trauma which has placed her in her present situation.'

That made sense, frustrating though it was. The more Marlow tried to bring her back to the subject, and however obliquely, the stress it caused forced him to back off.

'When did it happen?' he asked her.

'At night, I think, or late evening. We were just finishing at the lab.'

'How did they get in?'

'I don't know.'

'Did you see them?'

She hesitated. 'Not really. There were five or six of them. All men. Maybe one woman, but I couldn't tell. One minute we were alone, discussing the day's work; the next –'

'How were they dressed? Do you remember that?'

'No! . . . Maybe, dark clothes. All dressed the same, I think. They had guns, knives. They tied us up. I think they hit Rick and Brad first, to knock them out.'

'Did you scream? Call for help?'

'It all happened too fast. I may have done. But after they tied me up, they hit me, too. I must have lost consciousness. After that, I . . .' Her voice trailed off mournfully.

Marlow felt what was dangerously like compassion. But he'd got no more out of her than those sparse details. Nor did she remember how she might have escaped, or how she had ended up in Jerusalem.

At first. But some traces of memory surfaced as their talks progressed.

'They kept us somewhere – dark. There was a concrete floor. I don't remember any windows.'

'Were you tied?'

'Our hands, yes – at the front, so we could eat when we were given food. Our legs, no.' She looked at him with sudden clarity. 'They kept us in blindfolds most of the time. They didn't speak to us.'

This was a breakthrough. He pursued it. 'Anything else? It sounds like an impossible place to escape from.'

She thought hard. 'There was a window in the bathroom. They let us go there. A narrow window.'

Marlow looked at her slim figure. She was as slightly built as a girl. He let the thought develop in his own mind: her captors might not have considered that she would have been able to slip through such a window. But with her hands tied?

'Did you escape through that window, do you think?'

'It was high in the wall.'

'*Could* you have?'

'I don't know! I can't remember!' She looked at him pathetically. A lost look. He changed tack.

'Tell me about the dig.'

She was on surer ground here, and talked more freely, though Marlow noticed the look of sadness that crossed her face every time the names of Adkins and Taylor came up. But he kept her to the details and the facts concerning the artefacts they had discovered. There were still big gaps in her memory. No matter how deviously he tried to trick her into revealing something she might not want to reveal, she always looked blank when it came to any information about a box or a clay tablet.

The box and the tablet would have stood out a mile, if Adkins's team had found them. Marlow came to the conclusion that the archaeologists hadn't discovered either, though he thought he could detect a look of disappointment buried in her eyes when the objects came up in his questioning.

But he resisted hammering the point. No need to panic her. No need, either, to make her too aware of their importance.

He wondered if either of the other two had found the artefacts and concealed them from his colleagues. Always at the back of his mind was the discovery that all three of them had specialist qualifications, beyond the field of archaeology. But any attempt to trip Su-Lin up over whom they might have been working for, apart from Venice and Yale universities, met with failure.

'Do you remember finding a key?' he asked, coming

back to the subject on the third day, as he had on the preceding two.

'You've asked me about that. No.'

'It was small, iron, medieval, with an inscription on the shank.'

She shook her head.

On that third day, he decided to show her the photographs of the key. She took them, looked at them with keen interest, and handed them back. 'No. I would like to know what the inscription means. Is it Aramaic?'

'Don't ask me, I'm just a humble policeman.'

Suddenly, she looked at him hard, and took his hands again. Her own little hands disappeared into his.

'Please help me,' she said. 'I feel so alone.'

61

At the end of the third day, Marlow called a meeting with Graves, Lopez joining them via the secure link from New York. It was 6 p.m. there, midnight in Paris.

Marlow read a digest of the notes from his interviews with Su-Lin, and a resumé of Duff's findings. He added the information he had on the lack of a family connection between Su-Lin and Marquess Boniface.

'Even if there were,' he added, 'it'd be of no more than sentimental value, after eight hundred years.' He added, aiming this at Graves, 'Maybe we should check out her mother's side. Perhaps our subject goes back to Shi-Huangdi.'

Graves ignored him. They sat close together, side by side, their knees almost touching.

'So where do we go from here?' asked Lopez from the screen on the glass tabletop.

'We can't keep her cooped up indefinitely,' said Marlow, taking out a file and rummaging through an untidy sheaf of papers.

'You say the photos of the key meant nothing to her?' said Lopez.

'Yes,' Marlow replied.

'But she must know about it. We know the archaeologists took those photos,' Graves snapped.

'I don't think so. Duff bears me out.'

Graves looked scornful. 'She remembered one hell of a lot of other stuff.'

'But not everything.'

'You'd have thought the key would stand out,' said Lopez. 'As far as we know, it's the only significant thing they took.'

'Her memory still isn't perfect.'

'Or maybe it's just selective,' said Graves.

'She doesn't believe they were working for anyone other than the universities,' Marlow told them.

'Perhaps she didn't know,' said Lopez. 'It's still possible that one of the others was – or both of them.'

Marlow sat back. 'We've got working theories but no facts.'

'There's the fact that I was kidnapped and almost killed,' said Graves.

'But who's behind it? Who knows – beside us – what the hell that clay tablet has written on it and what it has the power to do?' said Lopez.

'For Christ's sake, how many people do you imagine know about this thing? It's been buried, a secret, for centuries,' Graves snapped back.

'Except for whoever owned those gloves,' replied Marlow. 'The ones Haki found.'

'But if they found out a hundred years ago what the tablet could do, don't you imagine there'd be some evidence of its use, somewhere in the world, during the twentieth century?' asked Lopez.

'Two world wars to choose from,' Marlow said. 'A ton of other smaller ones. Stalin's Russia. Vietnam. Year Zero in Kampuchea. Al-Qaeda. Take your pick.'

The other two were silent.

'I've made a decision,' Marlow continued. 'About Su-Lin.'

The others looked at him expectantly.

He turned to Graves. 'We can't keep her here for ever. So I'm recruiting her.'

Her reaction was immediate. '*What*?'

'Limited informational access, of course. And she thinks we're INTERPOL.'

Graves remained unconvinced, but Lopez looked thoughtful.

'We can't let her go. We've got to keep her secure. We might as well make some use of her. She wants to help find her friends; clear up this mystery. She's bright, she's on our side . . .'

'She's had no security clearance whatsoever.'

'Jack – you sure this is such a great idea?' said Lopez

'Otherwise what do we do with her?'

Over the TV connection, Graves and Lopez exchanged a look.

'Maybe we should talk about this, Jack,' Lopez said tentatively.

'Maybe you should,' added Graves, more crisply than she'd intended. She fiddled with her ring, not the emerald today, and scratched the tattoo hidden beneath it.

'I've told you, Laura, she's clean,' said Marlow tersely, running a hand through his hair and closing the subject. 'Leon, can you fill Laura in on Su-Lin's father?'

'Nothing dramatic.' Lopez turned to some notes in front of him. 'Marco de Montferrat. Major industrialist. Bad press in Italy during the Berlusconi years because he described the politician as a dangerous little prick. Some enemies, as you'd expect, but all of them straightforward business rivals. No Mafia connections. Big charitable foundations in India and China. Died in his bed in 2005, aged fifty-three. Heart. Wife died a year later. Killed herself. Grief.'

'So Su-Lin's a rich woman,' said Graves.

'Not necessarily. Most of the money that didn't go to the taxman – and, admittedly, not much did – went to the foundations. Some unaccounted for, sure. I've had my people look into one or two of the computer files of his banks in Switzerland, and they're harder to crack than the Pentagon's. We'll find it, but wherever it is, he's covered his traces well.'

'How much do we think?'

'Not a lot – 10 million.'

'Dollars?'

'Swiss francs.'

'Sounds enough to me,' said Graves.

'From her background, Su-Lin doesn't live life on the high side,' commented Lopez.

'Dig up anything more you can on her. I'm not letting her in too deep before we've covered everything. See what you can get on the MAXPHIL connection. They gave her a grant for the Dandolo Project, but she couldn't open up on that.'

'Or wouldn't,' said Graves.

Marlow glared at her.

'OK. And now I'll leave you two lovebirds to it,' grinned Lopez.

'See you in two days,' said Marlow.

'I'll grill you a stripsteak,' said Lopez. 'Nothing like down-home cooking.' The screen flashed CLOSE and went black.

'We're going back that soon?' asked Graves.

'Sir Richard's champing at the bit. Taylor's wife's got it into her head that they've been kidnapped by a Turkish fundamentalist group, and she's been to the *New York Post* with it. I have to throw him a sop.'

'Are we taking her with us?'

'What do you think? Where we go, she goes.'

'New York in two days, then?'

'That's right.'

Marlow, relieved at the prospect of leaving Paris and the dark memories the city held for him, couldn't have imagined how wrong he was.

62

Conversation among the mainly male audience, though there was a scattering of young women, too, sitting around the tables in the club, died down as the houselights dimmed. The only illumination now came from candles in black holders. The stage was bathed in an orange glow cast by spotlights high in the ceiling.

The stage held two saltire crosses equipped with restraints for wrists, ankles and waist, and a black table to the rear on which some kind of equipment was concealed under a cloth.

Music came from speakers hidden around the room. Into its rhythms were woven the eager, submissive cries and whispers of women.

Four men dressed in leather breeches and executioner's hoods appeared, dragging between them two girls, one an ebony-black blonde, the other an almond-white brunette. The girls were buxom and broad-hipped, and filled their overly tight dark-red leather bikinis. Their legs were sheathed in thigh-high boots.

The girls feigned terror. The acting wasn't great, reflected Rolf Adler as he watched, but it would satisfy his clientele, who weren't here for the art, after all.

He looked on from the plate-glass window which gave

on to the clubroom from his office above, and sipped a cognac as the girls were divested of their bikinis and strapped to the crosses. Their moaning became more terrified.

They were getting better at it, thought Adler, thinking he'd pay a bonus to the wannabe actress he'd hired as their coach. It had been nothing short of a miracle. The black girl had been lifted from Somalia barely a month earlier, and the white one was a Ukrainian schoolteacher's daughter who'd run away to the New World in search of a better life. Neither had what you would call perfect English. But they'd shown promise.

Not that it mattered any more. All they'd had to do so far in their performances was writhe and moan under the fake lashes of soft leather scourges. What they didn't know was that tonight was special.

There would be real whips. Their blood would really flow. Their cries would soon require no acting.

Afterwards he'd have them patched up, see to it that they were paid $100 apiece, have them driven way into the country and thrown out into the middle of nowhere. No point in killing them. Messy, and a waste of time and money.

There'd be other girls; he put on a show like this for selected guests. The rest of the time his club, Zara la Salope, down an alley off Mott Street on the Lower East Side, not to be found in any directory or anywhere on the web, provided upmarket porn to a tiny membership rich enough to afford the fees. Only one couple in the room were not regulars, a middle-aged English husband and wife, she – plump, with waist-length dyed dark hair, wearing a miniskirt twenty years too young for her and 10cm too short; the man gaunt, greying, wet-lipped and long-jawed, blue eyes so pale they were almost white, his suit hanging on his bony body as it might hang on a scarecrow.

Valued employees. Pip Trotter and Evelyn Sparkes.

Adler waited as the young men flung the cloth from the black table, to reveal, as the audience gasped in anticipation, a selection of truncheons, canes and flails. He watched the first minute or so of the show to ensure that his customers were getting their money's worth then touched a button in the panelling. A velvet curtain slid across the window. Another button, and the sound from the clubroom cut out.

He returned to the meeting he'd convened.

The office, perched on the mezzanine above the clubroom, had no windows. The whisper of filtered air was now masked by the soft tones of the Mozart piano sonata which had replaced the hungry whimpering of the girls. It was teak-lined in a manner which Adler believed reflected the best taste of cultivated, opulent class; hung on them were paintings of moist-eyed girls by Romantic sentimentalists such as Jean-Baptise Greuze. There was a heavy desk with gold pen-sets and stationery holders. The telephone and the computer were concealed, as their harsh modernity jarred with Adler's preferred overall impression of imperial grandeur.

The desk had a leather chair behind it. To one side sat Frau Müller, thinner, if possible, than ever, her blonde hair almost white and held up by a black elastic velvet band, clear of her forehead. Her pale skin, her eyes, furtive and dark brown, her tilted nose, her slight overbite, her thin but hungry lips – Adler found it hard to imagine how this woman could ever have appealed to him. What had their nicknames for each other been? The Wolf and Red Riding Hood. The memory embarrassed him.

But her loyalty and discretion guaranteed her position at his side; and, as long as she feared him, she was a dependable factotum, ready to do whatever was demanded of her.

Her makeup just failed to mask a bruise on her left temple.

The floors of the room were strewn with silk carpets from Iran. There was a heavy bookcase holding, among worthy but untouched tomes, a set of leather-bound telephone directories; and a low, ornate table, on which a handful of untouched copies of *The New Yorker*, *Country Life*, *Paris-Match*, *Haus und Garten* and *Manager Magazin* was tastefully scattered.

The place had been carefully planned. The room was not just the club's office. It was the seat of MAXTEL's unaudited operations in the New World. Only half a dozen people knew of it.

Around the table were arranged a low chesterfield and three club armchairs, all upholstered in red leather. On the table with the magazines was a cluster of silver-stoppered decanters, an ice-bucket and tumblers by Riedel. Nuts and cornichons lay in silver bowls next to pristine linen napkins. Additionally, there were glass ash-trays, a cedar box of Cohiba Lanceros and a tall silver match-stand.

Ignoring most of this proffered hospitality, though each had a frozen Grey Goose martini before him, three men occupied the armchairs. They were dressed in grey suits, pale shirts and dark ties. Their eyes differed. One pair was black, the next chestnut brown, the third, ice blue.

The meeting had gone well. Everything was in place. And the three men – the Chinese, Indian and Russian representatives of MAXTEL's operations in their respective countries – had made satisfactory reports on their operations.

Except for one thing.

'I need to know where it is,' said Adler, coming immediately to the most important point, the thing that nagged at his mind day and night and would not let him go. 'I need to know fast. I am so close.' In the pocket of his plum-coloured velvet dinner jacket, he caressed a key. He was never without it.

The three men shifted in their seats. Adler regarded them. Guang Chien, Vijay Mehta and Sergei Kutuzov had been with him for years, and were the best and the most loyal executives on his staff. Which was why they ran MAXTEL in their countries – the most important countries – for the business. The markets and the potential, and the political fragility, offered Adler everything, except one last item.

Their influence and contacts stretched throughout the Middle and Far East. If what he sought had been in Asia, they would have found it.

'We must continue our search' was all he said.

'We have done all we can,' said Kutuzov, turning his glass in his hand.

'Our principals begin to grow anxious,' said Chien. 'I speak for all of us.'

'They've invested heavily in this project,' added Mehta, noticing the expression which had crossed Adler's face. 'And they've invested on trust. After all, MAXTEL is copper-bottomed. But even so –'

'They want to see a return. Progress,' growled Kutuzov. 'A bone to gnaw on, anyway. Otherwise –'

'I am aware of that,' Adler replied, uneasy at any hint of rebellion. But he knew Kutuzov's manner was bovine, and let the surliness in the man's tone pass. 'I intend to cast the net a little wider.'

Indeed, he already had. But Western Europe had yielded no results yet, and Paris remained a work in progress. As for the Americas . . . Nothing more was to be had out of anyone at Yale or Venice without showing his hand too much. Two apparent suicides on campus and three missing archaeologists was enough.

But Adler was not a patient man. He hadn't been patient since he'd learned, on a cold autumn day in Venice three years earlier, about the existence of the object which had empowered a doge of that city. A man whom he'd never heard of previously but whom he had come to enshrine as his ultimate role model.

At first he'd been cynical, but then delved deeper, tapped into the city's archive, a bribe here, a bribe there, extracted what he needed, covered his tracks, left enough behind to encourage the curiosity of others, sent out pointers in the right directions. Academics seemed the safest bet. Good cover, and a quite logical, unquestionable means to his end. As far as Adler had been able to ascertain, the secret he'd discovered was shared by no one else, except his original informant, an intelligent man, but a hopeless drunk, now dead, alas. And MAXPHIL was ideally placed to finance such a valuable research project.

He smiled at his colleagues. He liked to think of them as colleagues. After all that communist nonsense he'd endured while he was growing up, he thought of himself as a good friend of democracy.

'Have another drink.' He smiled. 'And I'll explain . . .'

Half an hour later, Adler brought the meeting to a close. He opened the curtain and switched on the sound. They had unstrapped the girls and were dragging their torn bodies offstage as the music rose to a crescendo and the lights cut to blackout. In the clubroom, the lighting rose and the audience beckoned East European waitresses, dressed as schoolgirls, to refresh their glasses.

'How much do they pay for these shows?' asked Guang Chien, as the meeting broke up. 'These special shows?'

'More than they should,' smiled Adler.

'$5,000 a seat,' said Kutuzov. 'But we include a bottle of Taittinger.'

'Pocket money,' said Adler.

It amused him to run the club, and its exclusivity guaranteed his security. There wasn't a single member whose own position in life wouldn't have been drastically compromised if he or she divulged its existence.

'What made you choose such a name?' asked Mehta. 'Zara la Salope? Zara the Slut. Isn't that rather a giveaway?'

Adler gave him a thin smile that promised nothing. 'Private joke,' he said, thinking of a city which, long ago, had been brought to its knees by his hero.

His hero had sought to conquer the West. Apart from the obvious jewel of Brazil, Adler's ambitions lay in the opposite direction.

Conquer the East, and the problem of the West would take care of itself.

But he needed the box which the key in his pocket fitted. Within the box, he was convinced, lay the secret. And with the secret in his grasp, he could achieve more than his hero had ever have dreamt possible.

After his associates had left, he turned to Frau Müller. 'We need to speed things up,' he said.

'Yes.'

'Tell them what to do. We've wasted enough time on that line of enquiry.'

She nodded, but he could see that she was hesitating. He waited.

She looked at him diffidently. 'Shouldn't we give it a little longer? It seemed so promising.'

'If there was anything to get out of them, we'd know it by now. I want the thing aborted. Send them back to do it personally.'

She nodded, fear in her face. He always liked to see that, it reassured him, and he knew that in some twisted way she enjoyed it. Then she left.

He turned and sat at the desk. His mind turned to the next meeting, the one tomorrow morning. The one which he had really come to New York to attend.

The one with friends in high places.

63

Early April, just before dawn, and it was cold. Erich Ludendorff stood near the front of locomotive Hk1.293, flanked by a semicircle of five general staff officers. All were wrapped in stiff, high-collared greatcoats. All were tense. Their breath plumed in the freezing air.

Ludendorff hated the assignment, but it was necessary if the war, already abandoned as hopeless by his colleague Tirpitz two years earlier, had the faintest chance of being won.

Russia had to be neutralized, so Germany could concentrate on the Western Front, and this was the only way of achieving that aim. By good fortune, protests among the Russian people had spread. The hardships the country was enduring as a result of the war had forced the tsar to abdicate. Russia was now a leaderless country on the brink of revolution.

There was a new leader waiting in the wings, a leader who'd been in exile a dozen years. And that leader was living here, in Zurich.

The German officers waiting at the central railway station drew themselves up as, from the dark entrance to the platform, a group of thirty Russians emerged. At their head was a stocky, balding, middle-aged man with a goatee. He was pale and underfed, but his Mongolian features and his hard eyes made him instantly recognizable to Ludendorff, who stepped forward to greet him.

Neither made a move to shake hands. For his part, Ludendorff had a horror of everything which Vladimir Ilyich Lenin and his Communist Party stood for. But there'd be time to deal with them later, when they'd achieved the desired effect and plunged Russia into civil war. Russia would then no longer be a threat to Germany. On the contrary, Russia would be grateful.

'Is everything in place?' asked Lenin, looking at the locomotive. The engine, with its flanged smokestack and its sturdy cattle-bar, looked tough enough for a long journey, but the single first-class carriage it drew looked frail and vulnerable.

'Yes,' Ludendorff ground out.

'The train enjoys extraterritorial status?'

'As you stipulated.'

'Good.' Lenin looked around. His open overcoat had a fur collar, but he was bareheaded, and under the coat Ludendorff could see that the man's suit and shirt were threadbare. Lenin looked round at his companions and then back at Ludendorff. 'We will go,' he said, in a voice used to command.

Ludendorff didn't like his tone.

'My people will sit in the front half of the carriage, you Germans, segregated, must take the back two rows.' Lenin looked keenly at the general. 'But I will need to have some conversations with you,' he added.

His German was good, his accent thick.

Five minutes later than the appointed time of 4 a.m.,

the train rolled out of Zurich *Hauptbahnhof*. It was still dark. There was frost on the inside of the carriage windows, but this quickly thawed with the heat of the bodies of the passengers. Ludendorff didn't like the smell of the Russians, either metaphorically, or – as he was coming quickly to realize – physically. It was going to be a long few days, getting this lot to Berlin. From there, Lenin and his followers would make their way across Sweden and Finland and end up at Petrograd's Finland Station. St Petersburg, which the tsar had renamed Petrograd two years earlier, was in the hands of the Bolsheviks, and from there Lenin could create whatever havoc he wanted, thought Ludendorff; just as long as it kept Russia out of the kaiser's war.

Long before then, though, Ludendorff would have handed the Communist leader over to his fellow revolutionaries. His job ended at Berlin's Stettiner Station. His part of the mission would be over. Thank God.

He bunched his hands inside his gloves to try to warm them further.

They crossed the border into Germany later that day, and the Russian exiles, watching through the grimy windows of the carriage, commented irritatingly on the absence of men at the stations they rolled past in the fields, and in the towns. The only males they saw were elderly, teenagers, or children. Any man between sixteen and sixty was fighting in the trenches of Belgium and France. Ludendorff hoped the German situation didn't look desperate to his unwelcome charges.

On the second day, Lenin moved from his usual seat to place himself next to Ludendorff, who sat alone, apart from his officers, as his senior rank dictated. He smiled sociably at the German general, who nodded back guardedly.

'I love Beethoven' was Lenin's unexpected opening remark.

'Really?' replied the general, uncertain of himself, disliking the man's guttural accent as much as he disliked the scent of violet cachous which came from his mouth.

'Yes,' continued the Russian reflectively. 'But some of his music, I cannot listen to.' He paused, looking at Ludendorff, and when the general remained silent, unable to formulate any kind of response to that proposition, he continued, 'Especially the piano sonatas. Especially the *Appassionata.*'

Ludendorff shifted in his seat. 'And why might that be?' he asked helplessly.

Lenin's eyes became distant. 'Because it engenders emotions in me which I cannot afford to have.'

Ludendorff looked at him blankly. There was an awkward pause, after which he said, 'I hope they're feeding you well. Looked like you and your friends needed a bit of that.' He spread his hands. 'No shortage of food in Germany, as you can see. I gather they have a problem with that in Russia.'

Lenin ignored him. 'I cannot afford emotions which make me wistful and sad. I need to concentrate on things which are solid, which are material. But I also need' – his voice became more confidential and he leaned forward; Ludendorff could smell the violets strongly on his breath – 'I also need to be able – without fear of making any mistake – to sway the minds of men.'

The thought of a man like Lenin ever feeling wistful and sad made Ludendorff want to laugh, but he suppressed it. 'You have the support of the German state,' Ludendorff assured him, his official voice switched on. He'd read some of Lenin's writings, had even ploughed through *What is to be Done?* He couldn't make much of it, but he'd done enough research to know what to say: 'And your ideas will fall on fertile soil.'

'I hope so,' said Lenin. 'But I need to be sure.' In the silence that followed, broken only by the repetitive rattling of the train, he shifted his position so that he was sitting in the window seat opposite Ludendorff.

The two men looked each other straight in the eye. All around them, fellow-passengers were reading or sleeping. There was no conversation except for desultory exchanges between Lenin's wife, Nadya Krupskaya, who looked to Ludendorff like a codfish, and her companion. A nib scratched on paper as one of the officers behind Ludendorff compiled a report.

For a time, Lenin turned his attention to the monotonous farmland the train was passing through. It was a grey day, and the countryside lay sullenly under a sky the colour of cement. 'And if *I* am sure,' he continued, as if the silence had lasted a matter of seconds rather than minutes, '*you* can be sure that Russia will be out of the war. Your Eastern Front will no longer exist, and you can transfer the forces that become available to defeat the British and the French. You'll need all the men you've got. Hasn't the United States just joined in – finally – on the Allies' side? Silly of you to sink that liner. They might have stayed out of it.'

Ludendorff pursed his lips. The man was well informed. 'You have our full, disinterested support,' he repeated guardedly.

'But the faster I move, the faster you can, no?' said Lenin.

Ludendorff didn't know where the conversation was going, but something within him didn't like the turn it was taking. He remained silent.

'My friends in Berlin – *a* friend, I should say, a professor of ancient history at Moscow university, currently in exile on account of his political views – has been most enthusiastic about the discoveries made by his colleague, your compatriot, Robert Koldewey,' Lenin continued, looking out of the window as if fascinated by the dull view.

'Not my field,' said Ludendorff. 'Know nothing about it.'

Lenin turned to him, raising his eyebrows. 'Now that *is* surprising. I'm told you were with Koldewey in Istanbul only two years ago.'

'Official business, that's all.'

'Of course.' Lenin paused, but could not conceal his impatience. It was as if he were trying to pace himself. Ludendorff waited, hoping to be able to counter whatever was coming next. Damn it, how much did the man know?

'I hear you brought some trifles back from Koldewey's dig to Berlin,' Lenin continued, his voice less light. 'Among them, something of great value – great power.'

'A handful of artefacts, yes. I left all that to Koldewey. He's the expert.'

'This . . . this thing I'm thinking about,' Lenin went on insistently, and there was no doubting the gleam in his eye now. 'It seems that it's being kept under wraps. But if it were in the right hands, it might be – how shall I say? – of enormous practical and political value.'

'To you?'

Lenin spread his hands. 'Who else? And don't forget, my friend, that my success is your success.'

'You want us to give you this thing?'

'My friend Professor Kaschei has had several conversations with Dr Koldewey. Discreetly. They have drunk vodka together. My friend the professor assures me that this is a line well worth pursuing. And if nothing comes of it, no harm will have been done.'

'And if something does come of it?'

Lenin smiled. 'As I said, if I win, you win. You needn't think for a moment that a grateful Russian Soviet Republic, with all the might of our natural resources and a truly motivated workforce, wouldn't be eternally grateful to our friend, benefactor and ally, Imperial Germany.' Lenin looked at him. The eyes were bright and dark, and bored through the general. There was something of genius and something of madness in them.

'But I have tired you,' said the Russian, stretching and rising to his feet. 'I will rejoin my companions and sleep. You should sleep too. There is little else to do on this train except eat, read, and try to keep clean.' He turned to go but something made him turn back. The eyes fixed Ludendorff. 'All I ask is that you think about what I have proposed. We could change history together, you and I.' Lenin relaxed. 'We will talk again,' he said in parting. 'We still have a day, I think, before we reach Berlin.'

*

Left to himself, Ludendorff closed his eyes. But he didn't sleep. His mind was not in turmoil, it never was that, but he was disquieted, and there was no one to consult. Nor would there be, for there was no time. The schedule of the journey to the Finland Station was tight, and it was crucial that it be kept to. He tussled with the idea Lenin had put to him for two hours.

But by the end of that time, his decision was made. Whatever else Herr Lenin might say to him in the twenty-four hours in which he was forced to remain in the Russian's company, nothing would sway him from his course.

64

Edirne, the Present

It felt as if they had been walking for days, not hours, and the ragged landscape burned under the high sun. Rocks cut their feet in the depths of the remote valley, they were still blinded by the light after so long a time in the darkness of their prison, and yet they stumbled along, hauled upright, pushed and shoved whenever either of them showed any sign of collapse.

But they were out, away from the torture. And the blindfolds had been taken from their eyes when the black SUV had come to a halt after a long drive.

They didn't know where they were, or what country they were in. Somewhere hot, somewhere southern. But the rocks, tussock grass and sparse shrubs, among which lean goats foraged, gave them few clues. There were no villages, no people. But, drugged and beaten though they had been, they knew they couldn't have travelled far – they had never completely lost consciousness, even if most of their recent experience had unfolded like a dream. How many days or even weeks was it since their abduction? Five? Ten? Fifteen? Time eluded them.

What they had never been able to understand was how

to answer the one question the man and woman – they knew them only by their voices – in charge of their kidnappers and torturers had repeatedly put to them:

'*Where is it?*'

They knew it must have to do with the dig they'd been working on. They had, in desperation, invented answers which might please their gaolers, but these were never satisfactory. Now the two Americans had other things on their minds.

At last they halted. Their eyes had grown accustomed to the light and they could see the people who accompanied them. Five men, dressed in T-shirts and jeans. Young men, brawny, with harsh faces and dead eyes.

And the two others, the man and woman whose voices Brad Adkins and Rick Taylor had heard in their cell. The man, stick-thin, was dressed in a beige desert suit with high boots. His face was covered by a silk paisley handkerchief. The plump woman had squeezed herself into a Laura Ashley dress. She also wore a straw hat with a scarf wrapped round its crown. Her dyed dark hair hung down under it, tossed gently by the wind. She looked like an old hippie. The wide brim of the hat cast a shadow over her face, and she was careful to keep her head low, but they could see her mouth, which was set and cruel.

The group encircled the two men.

'We'll ask you one last time,' the woman said, in her cut-glass accent.

'One last time,' repeated her male companion, whose voice was similar, rasping.

There was a silence in which the two men looked at one another in despair. Suddenly they knew what would happen to them if they could not, at this eleventh hour, provide an answer.

The only sounds were the whispering of the stiff stalks of the shrubs, the hot breeze and the tedious grating of crickets.

After a long minute, the man consulted his watch and looked at the woman.

'Silence is your answer, then?' the woman said to her captives.

'We have told you that we found nothing.'

'That's it, then,' said the man. 'I told you that days ago, but you never listen.'

'You are not in charge.'

'More's the pity.'

She laughed. 'We sound like a bickering old married couple.'

'Isn't that what we are?'

The woman stopped laughing, and turned to her henchmen. 'You know what to do,' she said. She and her companion walked back, still bickering, to the SUV, parked 75 metres away. Adkins and Taylor watched them. Had they really only walked that far? They couldn't remember when they had last eaten. They'd been given water to keep them alive, that was all.

One of the five men left behind supervised while the others divided into two pairs, each seizing one of the Americans and dragging them to separate rocks, to which they chained them. The walls of the valley craned down, enclosing everything, leaving only a blue slit of sky above, in which the white disc of the sun hung like an angry eye.

Then the fifth man approached, drawing a long knife with a broad, heavy blade. A butcher by training, he removed the men's hands and feet quickly and efficiently. He then took a smaller knife and cut out their tongues.

65

They were a few kilometres outside Edirne, way north-west of Istanbul, on the Bulgarian border.

On Detective-Major Haki's advice, Su-Lin had been left at the police station in town. That she had been allowed to come with them at all had bothered Graves, but Marlow convinced her that the archaeologist was sufficiently recovered. She kept her reservations about her colleague's fixation with the woman, and her own feelings, to herself.

Looking at the bodies of Brad Adkins and Rick Taylor, Marlow was glad they'd left Su-Lin in Edirne. Graves wished she had stayed behind herself.

They'd come to the place in two police Toyota Land Cruisers, Haki and his men in one, leading the way; Graves and Marlow in the other, with their driver.

Now the three of them stood by the corpses chained to the rocks, five metres apart, looking down at them in the flat light of dawn.

'You say they've been here three days?' said Marlow.

'A goatherd discovered them late yesterday,' replied Haki. There was no twinkle in his eye now. 'Three days is what our forensic trawl's determined. But it didn't take them that long to die. We think they must have been dead within the ten hours after they'd been put here.' It was a moment before he continued. 'Blood loss, dehydration.

Can happen quickly. Especially when you consider what was done to these guys.'

The overnight flight in the INTERSEC Falcon 7X from Paris to Istanbul had taken just under five hours, but Marlow had never felt less tired, even after the helicopter and car journey from Istanbul to Edirne, and from Edirne, over rocky and inhospitable terrain, to this site of slaughter. His senses were alert, the ghost which haunted him forgotten. If only it would stay that way. He'd told Su-Lin her colleagues were dead. He did not tell her the manner of their deaths.

'So they were brought here last Wednesday, and they've been missing . . .'

'Fifteen days,' supplied Graves. She was looking at the cadavers, her face abstracted. There was a connection here, something familiar about the manner of their deaths, if only she could place it.

Marlow and Haki followed her gaze in silence. In the short time since their deaths, the two men had shrivelled within their ragged clothes. Crows had pecked out their eyes and it was easy to imagine, in this heat, what incursions larvae had made in the tender recesses of their bodies.

The postures of the bodies showed that the two men, while life remained in them, had strained out towards one another.

'Move them, shall we?' said Haki. 'We've done all we can here.'

'Yes,' Marlow agreed. Turning to Graves, he said, 'Make the arrangements, and inform their families, and Yale. Do it through the New York office. Tell Leon to get Hudson to handle it. But keep it close, and don't go into detail. This mustn't get out.'

She nodded. 'What about Su-Lin? Do we go public on her?'

He looked at her impatiently. 'She has no family to tell, and she can't give us any names of friends.'

'Tyre marks not far away,' said Haki. 'And the headman of the village four kilometres away saw an unfamiliar black vehicle on a track not far from his place three or four days ago.'

'Any chance he recognized the make?' Marlow didn't hold out much hope.

'Oh, absolutely. Porsche SUV. He recognized it from an ad on his satellite TV.'

Marlow looked thoughtful. He knew the organization which had abducted Graves in Istanbul was responsible for this. But why kill them in such a way? Was a message being sent?

66

Istanbul, the Present

Alone with her, Marlow comforted Su-Lin as best he could. But she seemed inconsolable.

'Who could have wanted to kill them? What harm had they done anyone?'

'We'll find out.' He almost told her they had a trail to follow, but checked himself in time. He made to go.

'Are you leaving me?'

'I have to.'

'Don't leave me alone.'

He returned, took her in his arms, stroked her hair. 'You are perfectly safe here.'

'Stay with me!'

He forced himself to go. The need to keep her safe was paramount to him. If only they could close the last gaps in her memory. But something else troubled him. Su-Lin was making inroads into his loneliness. She was so vulnerable. But he'd have to keep her out.

They were not staying at a hotel this time, but in a flat above Haki's office for the night before returning to Paris. The day was been spent contacting Lopez at base, transmitting the details of what they'd found. Marlow returned to the Operations Centre with a heavy heart.

All day Graves had been distracted. Now Marlow found

out why. 'Baldwin of Flanders,' she said briskly, as he entered the room.

'What?'

'Baldwin of Flanders!'

'Take me with you.'

'Baldwin of Flanders was one of the leaders of the Fourth Crusade,' Graves said. 'He was the golden boy, the one they crowned emperor of the new Catholic empire in the East, after they'd taken Constantinople.'

'And ripped it apart between them.'

'When I saw the bodies, I knew there was something. Some connection.'

Marlow noticed the troubled look had left her face. She was focused now.

'Go on.'

'It didn't take long for the new empire to start showing cracks,' she continued. 'Boniface wasn't as useful to Dandolo any more, which was why Baldwin got the crown – that, and the fact that Baldwin was younger, less intelligent, less experienced – much more manipulable, in other words.' She paused. 'Boniface established his own territory around Thessalonika and carved out his own kingdom. There was no problem with Baldwin.'

'So Boniface did well.'

'Yes, but he was double-crossed by the Bulgarians, who didn't like so much power on their doorstep. They ambushed and killed him in the summer of 1207, only three years after the sacking of Constantinople.'

'Sure, but what has all this to do with our archaeologists?'

'Wait! The conquered Greeks of Constantinople

weren't out of the picture, and they allied themselves with the Bulgarian king, Johanitza, who didn't have any time for Baldwin either. Johanitza was Eastern Orthodox Christian, not Catholic, don't forget. There was a battle between Baldwin and Johanitza in April 1205, which Baldwin lost. The little emperor was taken prisoner. The battle took place – at *Adrianople*.'

Marlow knew immediately where she was going with this. 'And Adrianople is –'

'Modern Edirne. Exactly. And there's more. No one knows what happened to Baldwin exactly, but he disappeared from the face of the earth, and there's an enduring story –' Graves's voice faltered.

'Go on.'

'The story goes that his captors kept Baldwin prisoner, tortured him, and took him to a remote place in the countryside. They cut off his hands and feet, and threw him into a valley. The story goes that it took him three days to die.'

67

Over Christmas, 1924, Robert Koldewey invited General Erich Ludendorff to dinner. In the ten years since their first meeting, he and Ludendorff, sharers of the secret, had become unlikely allies. The dinner was a simple affair, as it always was in the archaeologist's rambling Berlin apartment, full of dust and books, cases and shelves of ancient pottery, side-tables holding unwashed whiskey glasses, the whole place smelling of good tobacco and damp tweed. After the meal, they sat facing each other in armchairs on either side of the hearth.

'So,' said Ludendorff. 'I imagine you didn't invite me here just to say *Frohe Weihnachten*.'

Koldewey didn't smile. 'As you know, the only other men aware of the existence of the tablet are Einstein and Max Planck. But they know nothing of its importance.'

Ludendorff had no idea how much Koldewey had chosen to tell the two scientists, but he was certain that neither of them had any ambition for personal power.

'Their insight, and their knowledge of astronomy, energy and matter have been invaluable.' Koldewey went on. He drew on his cigar before continuing. 'With their help, I have cracked the code of the writing on the tablet.'

'My congratulations,' said the general, though he had a feeling of foreboding.

'I am close to death,' the archaeologist went on in a matter-of-fact voice. 'I will perhaps last until February, but that is not certain. I must pass my knowledge on to someone. You are the only person, logically, for that role.'

Ludendorff hesitated. 'I don't know if I –'

'It is surprisingly simple. You will be able to hand the secret on, when the time comes. If it ever comes. I had considered letting it die with me, but' – he broke off, showing rare emotion – 'I find I cannot. Let me show you. A small experiment.'

From a leather bag on the table at his side he produced the tablet. Ludendorff was immediately aware, in the firelit room, of another light, a dull glow, which came from the little piece of clay.

Koldewey stood, raised it in both hands above his head, and closed his eyes. The room – Ludendorff could not believe it afterwards – darkened, but for the light from the ancient artefact. Ludendorff found himself standing too, and crossing the room to a case in the corner. It was as if something else – something outside him – had taken control of his will.

'Lift the lid,' Koldewey's voice said – though it seemed to come from within Ludendorff's own head.

He obeyed.

'Take out the pistol.'

Ludendorff removed a Luger Parabellum from the case.

'It's loaded. Aim it at me,' the interior voice, insidious, irresistible, continued. It seemed now to blend inextricably with Ludendorff's own thoughts and desires.

'Shoot me.'

This is insane, thought the general, but the objection in his mind melted away immediately as he cocked the gun and raised it. He felt his finger tighten on the trigger.

'Enough!'

As if someone had thrown a switch, the room returned to normal. Ludendorff saw that Koldewey was sitting back in his chair, and the tablet was nowhere in sight. The gun was gone too. He looked in the case. It was there again, as if no one had touched it.

The general felt a fear greater than any he had ever felt on any battlefield.

That evening, Koldewey told Ludendorff all he knew, and the general trembled at it.

68

No means had ever been found of opening the box found with the tablet which Koldewey had wrested from the dead right hand of Enrico Dandolo. Neither force, nor the most ingenious locksmiths had been able to penetrate it, but it had been preserved carefully, together with the tablet it had once contained.

On the archaeologist's death, two months after their dinner together, Ludendorff found himself the owner of both the tablet and the box.

For more than two years he had kept them in a safe, uncertain what to do with them. Many times he had considered destroying them. He had never been able to share Koldewey's awe of the objects, though the archaeologist had convinced him of the tablet's power. That conviction had never tempted Ludendorff to put the object to his own use. His experience at its mercy had left him a shaken man.

But during that time he had also watched the progress of the still-young man now sitting at the desk across the room from him. They'd been associates since the early 1920s, and together experienced, shoulder to shoulder, the abortive attempt to seize power in Munich late in 1923. The man, leader of a new political party, had gone to prison after the *putsch* had been nipped in the bud, but Ludendorff, already in his late fifties, had got off lightly, given his reputation as a war hero.

He'd admired the way the man had bounced back later, and he'd watched his progress, and the progress of his National Socialist German Workers' Party, with enthusiasm and interest. Ludendorff had little time for the dithering rule of his former colleague, now Chancellor of Germany, Paul von Hindenburg; and in the Nazi Party he saw a chance of his country redeeming itself from the dishonour and economic chaos it had brought on itself by the disaster of the World War.

Ludendorff stood in front of the desk in the ordinary little office. The office smelt of disinfectant, as if someone had been trying to get rid of a bad smell. There was a faint odour, the general noticed. Like the smell of pants worn for too long.

The man at the desk was a slightly built 38-year-old. He radiated enormous energy. Every muscle in his body was tense. The brown uniform he wore was cheap and badly made, and it hung in creases on him. He didn't look like a man who'd been awarded the Iron Cross in the war a decade ago. Ludendorff remembered that the recommendation for the honour had been made by a Jewish senior officer.

The man ran a nervous hand over the lank hair which fell across his left temple, and then moved it restlessly to scratch the toothbrush moustache, black as his hair, which grew beneath his strong nose, a little too large for his face.

The moment had come.

Ludendorff had thought long and hard before reaching

his decision. Ten years earlier, he'd refused to give up the Babylonian tablet to the man who'd gone on to create, even without it, an unshakably powerful Union of Soviet Socialist Republics. But Lenin had been dead for three years now, and power had passed to Josef Stalin. An unknown but dangerous quantity.

The tablet and the box were in Ludendorff's briefcase, carefully wrapped.

'I am glad to see you, General,' said the man. 'Please – take a seat. Can I offer you something? Herb tea? A glass of water?'

Ludendorff would have preferred a cigar and a cognac, but he knew the man neither smoked nor drank. It was said that he lived on a diet of fruit and steamed vegetables. And yet his body seemed weak, flaccid. Black, coarse hair, which reminded the general of the hair on an insect's legs, edged the pale, thin hands.

'No, thank you,' replied the general. He sat down.

'They tell me you have something for me.'

'As we discussed.'

'Ah.' The young man's eyes glinted for a moment before reassuming a mild look. 'Yes. I have thought about that. I am grateful to you for your confidence.'

'It is your cause that I believe in.'

'The cause is everything. It is my life's work. The redemption of our country.' The man hesitated. 'I know you share that ambition.'

Ludendorff nodded, stiffly. They had had many conversations leading up to this one. What he did now was crucial.

'May I see this – this artefact – we have spoken of?'

Ludendorff opened his briefcase and withdrew two packages, laying them on the desk, and opening them.

'The box once contained the tablet. We *believe*. We do not know what it contains now, since we have no means of opening it.'

'I will find a means,' replied the man, picking the box up and turning it over briefly in his nervous hands, before laying it aside and concentrating his attention on the plain little slab of clay which lay before him. There was no hiding the expression in his eyes now, as he touched it. 'And this is –'

Ludendorff knew that the man was convinced of what the tablet could do. He also knew that the man was a believer – no cynic. Any trace of a supernatural dimension to its capacity had been removed through the scrutiny and analysis of minds Ludendorff knew to be as searching as his own, if not more. But, unlike him, the young man was in tune with the occult. He consulted an astrologer, and he believed in his own kind of mystical destiny – something which it was beyond Ludendorff's imagination to comprehend. But Ludendorff respected the intensity of the young man's belief. He would have been proud to have had such a son.

'You must explain to me how it – operates,' said the man, raising his eyes to meet the general's.

'I will tell you all that Koldewey transmitted to me,' replied Ludendorff. He drew a sheaf of papers, arranged in a grey folder, from his briefcase. 'Here are the notes I have compiled, which will amplify anything I say.'

'Excellent,' said the man, holding the general's eyes with his in a way which made Ludendorff uneasy. He held the tablet firmly in his right hand, which shook slightly even then, with barely suppressed nervous energy, and, having gazed at it firmly for a moment longer, placed it in his left breast pocket, close to his heart. 'If this does what you say it will, you be rewarded.' He paused. 'Let us hope it will.'

'For the sake of the Fatherland,' said Ludendorff.

The man continued to look at him. 'Of course,' he replied. He slid the folder towards him, over the desk, and riffled through it. 'Much to learn here.'

'I will tell you more,' promised Ludendorff.

'That will be tomorrow,' replied the other man. 'At eleven. I hate the early morning,' he added, spitting the words out as if the early morning had done something to deserve his personal loathing. 'The sooner I am able to use this thing, the better. I will set aside two days for us to make a start.' He stood awkwardly, abruptly, reached out his hand. Ludendorff, standing himself, grasped it then took a pace back. The men exchanged salutes. The new salute. Ludendorff clicked his heels.

'The future of our country will be safe in your hands,' the general said.

As he left the building and made his way to his Maybach W5, where his chauffeur stood to attention at his approach, something deep in Ludendorff's heart suddenly misgave him.

But he ignored it. The die was cast. He would meet Adolf Hitler again, as they'd arranged, the following day.

69

There must be something Dandolo was missing – something defective in himself, for there could be nothing wrong with the power of the tablet which nestled, as always, close to his heart in a hidden pocket of his robe. Had he not delved fully enough into its secrets?

But Zara *had* fallen, that whore city, the army *had* reached Corfu, and the problem which confronted him on this pleasant little island was one he could rely on his own strength to overcome. Of that he was confident. Most of the Crusaders, in any case, were eating out of his hand. Only a handful needed to be brought to heel.

It was already early May. As all years now, this one was passing too quickly for him. His concern was with the journey still before them, the tides, the winds and the passing of the seasons.

'Consider your position,' said Leporo. 'You made sure that Pope Innocent lifted excommunication from the Franks. Why hasn't he lifted it from the Venetians?'

'The Crusaders are happy.'

'Not all of them.'

'As for the Venetians, I have taught them to regard excommunication for what it is – meaningless. The attack on Zara has been forgiven, despite the killing of priests, despite the sacking of churches. The pope needed his Crusade.'

Dandolo did not explain to the monk how he, guided by the tablet, had controlled the thoughts of King Emeric of Hungary, making him take no action in reprisal at the destruction of his vassal city. Nor had the pope, the co-protector of Zara. Dandolo's manipulation had seen to it that the pope's teeth were drawn. The tablet had shown him how. Its power seemed limitless. He consulted the writing and applied its message. But it was true: Pope Innocent had not revoked excommunication from his men. He knew he hadn't yet fully grasped the tablet's potential, but he knew he was within reach of his aim: controlling men's minds *at will*! To do that, he would have to draw closer to the tablet – become, he thought, one with it.

It didn't matter. The Crusaders' share of the loot from the destroyed city had come nowhere near paying what they still owed.

But, for the rebel Crusaders, all the news was good.

'Boniface has returned from wintering with his cousin,' Leporo reported.

'What news does he bring back with him from Swabia?' Dandolo was alert. The result of the visit was important. Boniface's cousin Philip was married to the daughter of Isaac, the deposed emperor of Constantinople.

'Isaac hopes to get his throne back. As you know.'

'Do we have their support?'

'Isaac's son shares his ambition. He is close to his brother-in-law.'

'But can he be trusted? Alexus Angelus is a callow boy.'

'He hates the uncle who's kicked his father off the throne. He hates living in exile at the Swabian court under his sister's protection.'

'Where is he now?'

Leporo smiled, eyeing his master. 'That is the best news of all. Boniface has brought him to Corfu, full of promises – 200,000 marks and 10,000 men – to support the Crusade, if we will only take back the Great City first, and replace him and his father on the throne there, as joint rulers.'

'Good news indeed!' If it hadn't been for those fucking malcontents. He squeezed the tablet under his robe. What was he missing? Almost full control, and yet . . .

'They've set up a separate camp, and they have established their own Council. They're obstinate bastards,' said Leporo.

'Their forces are too weak to attack the Holy Land by themselves. They will never drive a path through Egypt, never even get there, without a fleet.'

'They are desperate men. Our spies report that they plan to travel through Syria. The strait between here and the mainland is narrow. Many of the defectors who left us at Venice have reached Syria in Genoese ships or vessels hired from African corsairs. The rebels here plan to join them. If, together, they can get up enough of a force to mount a Crusade, the pope may shift his blessing from us to them.'

'They are still weak!' said Dandolo.

'If those that are here get away . . .' Leporo let his voice trail off, watching his master keenly.

But Dandolo was not looking at him. He caressed the tablet with his thumb. It *had* to hold an answer for him. But he didn't want Leporo around when he consulted it. He always, now, imagined that his work with the tablet took the form of conversations. Frid, with his doglike devotion, he could trust, because he did not need any more power than his own to control the Viking. Leporo was a different matter. Leporo was too like himself.

'Leave me,' he ordered. Already the ghost of an idea was occurring to him. But was it coming from him, or the tablet? 'Go and summon the leaders. Bring Alexus with them.'

Leporo bowed, gathering his papers together. He wanted to stay, wanted to see what his master did when he was alone, but had not yet found a way of spying on him with success. That Viking bastard Frid was always there. Dandolo's eyes, these days, far more than Leporo had ever been. The Norseman was standing in the shadows by the door now, immobile, but missing nothing. Why should he have the master's trust when he, Leporo, who had saved him, who had rescued the sight of his left eye, had not?

But he didn't believe his master had ever used the tablet to control him. Dandolo was too intelligent not to know he needed to share some of the knowledge.

But, he reflected grimly, he could be certain of nothing. He would only be that when he had the tablet in his own hands and could bend it to his own will. Universal Christendom under his iron dominion!

Once the monk had gone and Dandolo heard the heavy door close behind him; once Frid had moved to stand in front of it, arms folded, impassive, silent, the doge plucked the tablet from his sleeve. Holding it in both hands, arms crooked, raised above him, he peered up at it through the faint light in the room. And, as he looked, the room darkened. He concentrated, forcing his eye to focus on the letters which had been stamped on the clay two thousand years before.

The letters began to glow – a dark, dull red, so softly that Dandolo couldn't be sure that it wasn't a trick of his dying eye. But he understood its signal well enough.

He remained, rapt, alone in a universe inhabited only by himself and the thing he held before him, for twenty minutes, under the watchful eye of Frid. And as Frid looked at his master, he saw that a strange light enveloped the seated figure and sequestered him from the world, a light of so deep a crimson that it blended with the shadows of the room, dark as wine, and somehow alive.

Frid waited, patiently, confidently, for the time to pass. An old proverb came into his mind then: 'Man says, *Time passes*. Time says, *Man passes*.' And then, without warning, he felt a strange impulse shudder through him – what another man would have recognized as fear. Dandolo must not die. The doge must achieve what Destiny had prescribed for him.

Frid did not know that the power which swept through the room was affecting him too. Only his simple nature, his innocence, protected him.

Then, disappearing more quickly than it had arrived,

the strange light dissolved. The room resumed its normal appearance.

Frid shook himself like a water-spaniel. Dandolo faced him. The blind eye was a withered socket, a scar, the opening of a narrow cave in a yellow rockface.

But the other eye held him with a milky regard.

70

The camp of the rebel Crusaders was on a low hill, sloping down to the sea, four kilometres north of the town. It was late afternoon, and the sandy countryside turned golden in the light of the setting sun when the procession arrived at its gates.

All were on foot, their rich garments and their boots dusty from the road. At its head was the doge, stooping, weary with the effort of the walk, leaning on a stick, supported on his other side by the giant Norseman. Behind him, bareheaded, Count Baldwin of Flanders, the Marquess de Montferrat, and the emperor-elect, Alexus Angelus, walked, overshadowed by a giant cross, carried by five monks, with Leporo leading them. Twenty choirboys followed, chanting, their voices tossed away in the breeze, but singing on. No military retinue. No one bore arms.

Watching from the wooden ramparts of the camp, the rebels looked at one another uncertainly.

Ten metres short of the gates, the procession came to a halt. Dandolo raised his head to the men on the stockade.

'What is he doing?' whispered one.

'What does he see?'

Unease amounting to fear grew in them as the old man scanned their faces. Could he see them? It seemed he could. See them, and see through them. One of them thought he could detect a red glint in the depths of the black socket of the right eye, and recoiled.

His reaction was infectious. The rebels were already wavering. All consultations, all negotiations, had broken down in the last days. Anger had been replaced by uncertainty, uncertainty by inertia. But they had expected an attack and were prepared for one. But they got this – this embassy of peace. This pious procession.

Now, the hands that held their swords and spears hesitated.

'Open the gates!' someone inside the camp suddenly commanded.

The leaders, followed by their holy companions, walked slowly into the camp, and came to a halt in its centre. The circular stockade enclosed an open space like a parade ground, yellow earth floor, a handful of gaudy tents and hastily constructed wooden shacks for the cookhouses and washrooms. The rebel Crusaders gathered around the embassy.

They had not lowered their arms.

Leporo stood close to his master.

There were two circles now. Dandolo and his followers faced outwards, a loose formation with the choirboys, now silent, at their centre.

Dandolo stood furthest from the gate. Confronting him were the rebel leaders, among them the stubborn Guy de Chappes and the dour Richard de Dampierre. You could, Leporo thought, have cut the atmosphere as you might cut cake, it was so thick. They didn't even have armed backup hidden on the blind side of the hill, ready to move in at the first sound of a fight. He hoped Dandolo knew what he was doing.

Not a word was spoken. Then, very softly, the boys began to sing an Agnus Dei. The palisade provided a good acoustic for their clear voices, which rose through the darkening sky as if the sounds strained to reach heaven. As they sang, Dandolo flung off Frid's supporting arm and, leaning on his stick, sank heavily and painfully to his knees. The count and the marquess followed suit, heads humbly bowed.

With tears coursing down his cheeks, the doge raised his head towards Guy, Richard and the rest, and spoke, his old voice quavering in an effort to remain firm, in control: 'Do not leave us, companions in Christ's Cause,' he said. 'Do not leave us, I beg you, noblemen of France! I swear by the spirit of our great enterprise that I will never rise from this ground again — until you reassure us, comfort us, grace us with your continued allegiance. Our venture against the Great City is just: witness this innocent boy, Alexus, with justice also named Angelus, who has been barbarously deprived of his rightful inheritance, and who, if we aid him, will aid us in turn, with such recompense that Jerusalem will tremble at the sound of our approaching march. Shoulder to shoulder, comrades in Christ together, with a righted wrong to commend us further to Our Lord, our banners of the red cross will fly at last from the turrets usurped by the infidels!'

In the silence which followed, the rebel leaders looked at one another in consternation. Then Richard de Dampierre, his chain-mail stained red by the sunset, stepped forward and helped the old man to his feet.

They embraced, each man covering the other's shoulder with his tears. Guy de Chappes eagerly followed.

A great cry went up, drowning the voices of the choristers.

Dandolo clutched the tablet to him under his robe, and smiled.

A week later later, Geoffrey de Villehardouin and Conon de Béthune sat on horseback on a low rise above the harbour. They watched the fleet revictualling, and the busy sail-menders, ropemen and carpenters. Galleys, transports and warships teemed with sailors. On land, the army, after two days' drinking to celebrate its reunification, was cleaning and sharpening spears, swords and daggers, restringing bows and re-fletching arrows. Squires buffed mail until it shone bright as the sun. Horses were exercised with and without their armour on, rubbed down, fed apples, pampered and examined for the slightest defect, any sign of malady. The united Fourth Crusade, the Army of Christ Enthroned, in all its dazzling majesty, would embark and leave Corfu on St Theodosia's Day.

On the hill which sloped down to the shore, goats trespassed idly in the abandoned stockade of the former rebels, foraging. The only sounds were the dull clinking of their bells and the endless chirruping of the crickets. Richard de Dampierre, Guy de Chappes, clear-eyed, had forgotten the grudges they had held against the noble Marquess Boniface and Baldwin, the great lord of Flanders.

Geoffrey and Conon exchanged a look and a warm smile of comradeship. Above all, their minds were full of the piety and glory of their spiritual and temporal leader, the great Doge Dandolo, to whose forgiveness and compassion they owed their lives. They buckled down to the task of organizing their troops with a will, and with an inexplicable relief. Their way forward was plain now – a child could have grasped it, it was so simple: follow Dandolo. Follow him. Follow him always. Follow him into the very mouth of hell, if he commanded it.

Unquestioningly.

71

Paris, the Present

The weather had improved in their absence. The leaves on the planes which lined the boulevards were fresh and green. Locals and tourists crowded the café terraces, avoiding the cramped, dingy interiors despite news of another increase in street robbery and handbag-snatching from the marble-topped tables where *sacs à main* from Prada and Louis Vuitton were the preferred targets of the street kids from the *banlieue* who'd pounce like birds of prey and be off down side-streets before you had time to put down your *express* and raise the alarm – for all the good that did.

Su-Lin didn't show her disappointment when they told her she was again to be placed in the safe apartment. But her face fell when she learned that Dr Duff was to remain in attendance.

'I don't like that man,' she told Marlow as he helped her move back in. 'He digs too deep. There's nothing left to find.'

'There are still gaps to fill.'

'I don't know if I want to fill them. Not after what happened to Brad and Rick.' She looked at him.

Marlow wanted to put his arm round her. 'You're safe here.'

'But not from the past. What's going on? Why did my colleagues have to die like that? Why did they have to die at all?'

'That's what we're trying to find out.'

'Something we found in at the dig? Something whose value we didn't recognize?'

'We think so,' he said. 'But what it is . . .'

'That's what you want me to remember.'

'Yes.'

'What if I never can?'

'Then we'll have to find another way.'

Suddenly, she clung to him. 'I want to help.'

'I know.'

'Even more now. Now they are dead. I want to find the people who did it.' There was a vehemence in her voice he hadn't heard before.

'Try to remember what might have been taken from the tomb.' Marlow disengaged himself gently, but his nostrils were filled with her scent.

Su-Lin sat down, thinking.

'Cuneiform?' she confirmed. 'You mentioned cuneiform script, didn't you?'

Marlow waited.

She concentrated. But her face fell again. 'I cannot remember. Did you find anything?'

'We found nothing.'

She drew her long legs up. 'You still don't trust me, do you?'

'If we keep anything from you, it's for your own good. You know what these people are capable of.'

Silence fell between them again.

'What about the key?'

Her eyes were dark pools. 'Small. Iron, I think. The key to a box, a small coffer.'

'Anything else?'

'I can only think of what's happened! If I hadn't managed to get away, I would have shared the same fate as Brad and Rick.'

Marlow watched her.

At that moment they heard footsteps in the corridor outside; then there was a knock at the door. Marlow unlocked it, and Ben Duff entered the apartment.

'Just wanted to welcome you back,' said the psychologist to Su-Lin, while nodding at Marlow. 'But I see Jack's beaten me to it.'

He was holding a bottle of champagne.

'Duff's not going to get any more out of her,' Marlow told Graves later. 'And it was a mistake to tell her about her colleagues.'

'Then why don't we get rid of her?'

Marlow shook his head. 'Believe in strong measures, don't you?'

'Only what's necessary. She's been no use to us so far.'

'That's where you're wrong. She's focused on the key they found at the dig.'

Graves looked at him in surprise. 'Could she describe it?'

'It's the one.'

'Have we anything else?'

Marlow pressed his lips together, looked out of the window, down at the street. People were walking up and

345

down the boulevard, some hurrying; others – tourists – dawdling. There were several couples, some entwined, others talking. A plump, middle-aged woman dressed like a hippie with a tall, thin companion; a scrawny blonde on the arm of a short, slight man in a tweed cap that was too big for him; a pair of American teenagers, dumbstruck for a moment at the reality of a place they'd only known before from their computer screens. The Starbucks opposite full of men and women in anoraks and jeans consulting maps and guidebooks and looking around at the street-life.

All those people. Not twenty metres away. A different world.

'If we had a clue who we're competing with . . .' He was silent, then said: 'It's not another power, anyway. It's a private organization.'

Graves considered this. It was true that there was nothing on the grapevine that Leon had been able to trace. But she'd already decided there was a different line of approach. Not that she'd tell anyone yet. Not until she was certain of her ground.

'Chase Leon,' said Marlow. 'He ought to have something on that inscription by now.'

But two days passed before Lopez came back to them.

'There's nothing,' he said, as Marlow and Graves sat at the screen in the office.

'What do you mean – nothing?'

'They can't decipher it.'

'What are you saying?' Marlow exploded. 'They're supposed to be the sodding experts.'

'Not in this case. It's mathematical, in some way. They

346

think it's to do with astronomy but, beyond that, they say it deals with research which they're not familiar with. Hudson's been raising hell, but the people at Yale just close ranks, he says.'

'Hudson knows about this? In detail?'

'He *is* department head. He has a direct line to the Pentagon. And the Oval Office. He okayed Su-Lin, dammit. I had no choice.'

Marlow said, 'OK, Leon. See what you can do with the forensics from Haki on the deaths.'

'Already done. Confirmed manner and means. But no leads.'

Marlow had expected nothing else. 'OK.'

The screen went black.

'There's something wrong,' said Graves immediately.

Marlow looked at her sharply. 'Meaning?'

'Yale say they can't decipher it.'

'Yes?'

'Can't be true.'

'What?'

'Got any more out of Dr de Montferrat in the last two days?'

'Deaths of Adkins and Taylor have knocked her back.'

'We've got to give up on her,' she said.

'If I find I agree, I'll arrange for her to be put in protective custody in the States,' he replied crisply. What was it with Laura and Su-Lin? 'What makes you say Leon's Yale report can't be true?' he continued.

'Because I've cracked the code in the inscription. I watched what you did on the other code. Learned something from your methods. You've been a good teacher.'

'What have you got?'

She looked at him. 'We'd better think hard about just why the guys at Yale couldn't manage it. *If* they couldn't.'

'Explain.'

'Because it's dynamite.'

72

Back at his flat that night, Marlow nursed a Jameson's, smoked a rare cigarette and disentangled his thoughts. What Laura had told him brought a whole new dimension to the problem.

He'd told her to pass nothing on. No one else within INTERSEC was to know what he and she now knew.

Who else might know was the question that would keep him awake all night.

And could he even trust Laura? She seemed to be shaping up well. After the abduction, she'd gone on a week's intensive fieldwork retraining, but that hadn't been the real problem. There was something else he couldn't fathom.

Whatever it was, it had no bearing on her professionalism. And if it was personal, her training would see to it that she kept it separate. As they all had to.

To help him think, he dug out his chess board and set up the pieces on the low table by his sofa. A problem from Graham Burgess's *Gambit Book*. Black king's knight to check in two – mate, if he could solve it, in four. But he could see that the white king still had the opportunity to castle.

That was the trouble with playing against yourself – you could always second-guess; that was the liability, and also the asset, of solitude.

Despite the attempted discipline of the chess problem, his thoughts drifted. At the back of his mind, the demons still lurked. Why had she come into his mind, an unwanted tenant, at a moment like this?

There must be a reason. He'd measured the time that had passed since the break-up and compared his feelings now with what they had been. He knew she was losing her grip on him. He'd deleted the handful of emails she'd sent him afterwards, unread. What would she have written? What could she have written? And what was the point? She'd casually dropped a bomb on his love and now she was gone for good. She'd cared less than nothing for him, no matter what she'd said.

Trust. How it could mislead.

Impatiently, he put the thoughts away. It was time to stop poking the corpse.

He finished his whiskey and looked at the bottle. It was the same bottle he'd started a few nights earlier, hadn't touched since, and there were still a good two shots in it. He decided against it; it never helped. And the cigarette tasted dry and foul in his mouth.

But the taste in his mouth really had nothing to do with the cigarette.

He leaned over and stubbed it out, and suddenly realized why the image of that bitch of a lost love had come into his mind.

Whoever had succeeded him in her life had it coming too, sooner or later. The next victim. There are some people in the world who have a gene missing, a vital part of the machinery that makes a human being work properly – the gene that controls conscience. They use other people, then they throw them away, and find their own way of telling themselves that the shit wasn't down to them.

People incapable of expressing or experiencing normal emotions, normal humanity. People like her. Like one hell of a lot of politicians. Like criminals. Like spies.

Like the people he was up against now.

He snapped out of it and solved the chess problem. Later, after another two hours' work, he wandered into sleep, for he was shaken out of a bad dream – dead fish floating in dark water – by his phone.

He looked at his watch. Four a.m. The city was silent. He pushed himself out of his chair and grabbed the phone. The INTERSEC night commander's voice.

'Sir?'

'Yes?'

'You'd better get over here now.'

73

There was no sign of a struggle. Ben Duff had been hit hard once, on the back of the head, with something spiked. His cranium had one deep, neat hole in it. There wasn't much blood, but a little had trickled down on to the carpet. He was dressed in a bathrobe and looked, somehow, pathetic.

'Must have heard something, gone to the rescue,' said the night commander.

'Where were your guys?' asked Marlow. He was thinking of the bottle of champagne Duff had brought that other time, and of another possible reason for him to have been there, dressed only in a bathrobe.

'Everything was in place. But someone had cut the sensors, so Monitoring saw nothing. They raised the alarm immediately. I called you.'

'Took her out through a window in Duff's quarters. Unbarred there,' Marlow said. 'That your reading?'

The man was sweating. This could cost him his job. Demotion, certainly. Transfer to a desk at the Analysis Centre in Dayton. Or worse.

There was a cup of lemon tea on the coffee table. Untouched. Marlow touched it. Still warm. An hour? No more. 'Blanket search, fifteen kilometre radius. Airports, too. Don't involve the locals. Get one of our doctors over here,' he said.

'Already on his way. As for the rest, consider it done, sir.' The night commander withdrew at the double.

Marlow walked quickly along the corridor to the cubbyhole Duff had called home for the last couple of weeks. Matchbox office, bedroom, shower, kitchenette; nothing else. But it was round an angle of the building, and one window opened on to the rue Pernelle, the narrow street which flanked the block.

He looked around. It was possible they'd got in through the main entrance; he'd look at the CCTV tapes soonest. How they'd got any further would be up to Ops. to investigate, but how they'd got out was clear: down below a *monte-meubles* was parked, one of the crane-mounted flat-tops Parisians use to get furniture in and out of the windows of apartments in tall buildings when they move house. Must have had another car for their getaway. Pros. Had they drugged her? She was small, slight, easy to overpower.

He flipped out his phone, called Graves.

There was no reply for a long time. He was about to give up, send someone to see what had happened, break the door down if necessary, when finally, just before the call timed out, she picked up.

Relief undid the knot of stress that had been tightening in his chest.

'Get over here. The Centre. Now.' His voice was harsher than he'd intended it to be.

Now came the waiting. Doing nothing is the hardest thing *to* do, but Marlow had no alternative. Graves arrived dishevelled, apologetic. She looked dead beat. Had she even been to bed? Why had it taken her so long to answer her phone?

The call came at 5 a.m. Orly Airport. Iberia flight to Barcelona. INTERSEC fieldmen were in place.

The traffic was still light, so it took them less than fifteen minutes to get there, breaking every speed restriction in the book and outrunning one hysterical cop-car which pursued them down the avenue d'Italie but gave up soon after the Porte. Marlow knew there was no chance of the *flics* radioing ahead to colleagues, since their 5.5-litre, V8 AMG Merc CLS had unidentifiable plates. The driver only became law abiding when they reached the airport outskirts, but there was little traffic here either, the airport was just waking up, and in the terminal at Orly itself few people were about, most of them tired and grey under the dismal, draining light – lighting which airports specialize in worldwide.

Graves and Marlow moved carefully through the concourse, pistols loose in their holsters, and joined the leader of the team-in-place at a prearranged vantage point. They clipped on mics and earphones as they spoke.

'Where?' said Marlow.

'Three of them. Thin man, plump woman. Our subject with them, pliant, probably drugged. Row of seats near the Relay shop. Move in?'

'Let's have a look at them. See if we can do it without making a noise.' Marlow knew from the moment they'd got the call that something was wrong here, but he hadn't yet identified it.

He moved stealthily towards the spot identified by his

fieldman, and saw Su-Lin, empty-eyed, seated between a man and woman who answered the fieldman's description.

Their appearance struck a chord in his memory.

The man was reading a copy of an English tabloid newspaper, the *Daily Mail*, and the woman – who looked like she'd escaped from an Alan Aldridge album cover – was eating croissants from a Paul paper bag. Both were absorbed in their separate tasks, though the man occasionally glanced at the departures board, squinting as though he needed glasses to see it properly.

There was a soft leather bag at his feet. The woman's shoulder bag was at her side. Su-Lin, in black, and looking as if she'd dressed – or been dressed – hastily, continued to stare into space. At one point, when it looked as if he was in danger of her catching his eye, Marlow ducked out of sight, uncertain, but then Su-Lin half stood, with a little involuntary cry.

She wasn't looking at him. She was looking past him. She had seen Graves, who hadn't been as quick as he had.

Her two guardians were instantly alert. Moving quickly, they each took one of Su-Lin's arms and propelled her away from the seats towards the departure gates. The woman now held an automatic, a matt-white subcompact gun, a Glock, not easy to spot, maybe plastic-coated, looked like a toy. She'd conjured it up from nowhere, but she'd dropped her Paul bag. The gun must have been in there with the croissants. Marlow spoke tersely into his mic to alert the fieldmen, some of whom he could see out of the corner of his eye, gliding into new positions.

Graves had disappeared from view – she'd had the sense to get out of sight, at least.

None of the airport staff and none of the other travellers, now increasing in number, was aware of anything. Marlow saw that the field commander's men – five of them – had deployed themselves in a semicircle containing the target group from both flanks and from the rear. The man and the woman were corralled, and they knew it, but they showed no sign of losing their nerve, though up towards Departures the security people at the X-ray machines, even with their two-bit training, were becoming aware that something was going on. One of them, more zealous than her colleagues, started to approach, full of the power her job invested her with. You could see she'd just love to be in the police. Then she saw the gun in the hippie-woman's hand, and froze.

The man and the woman seemed amused. The man half turned his head, to look behind him, then looked at his companion and said one word, not loud, but loud enough for Marlow to catch:

'Abort.'

The thin man let go of Su-Lin with one hand, and of his bag with the other. But left in that hand was a Steyr TMP machine pistol, black and deadly.

The woman released Su-Lin's other arm and started to move, fast, through the travellers pushing trolleys. The man did the same on the other side. They made difficult targets in the crowd as they made their way back the way they'd come, outflanking the fieldmen. Su-Lin collapsed where she stood.

Graves rushed over to Su-Lin and picked her up, flashing a French DGSE card at the approaching security guards, and bundled Su-Lin away, out of sight, into the gathering crowd.

Not a shot had been fired. A dull silence, the silence of snow, had fallen on the concourse.

74

'There's your proof,' said Marlow, later. They'd taken Su-Lin back to his apartment. She was in the bedroom, sedated, being treated by an INTERSEC medic. They'd question her as soon as they got the OK.

'Proof of what?'

'That they want her as much as we do. We can't afford to let her back into the wild.'

Graves was silent a moment, pursed her lips.

'I almost screwed up.'

'Almost?' replied Marlow. But, seeing her expression, he relented. 'Everyone does, Laura. Nothing happened this time. And if she'd been killed, who knows? No good to anyone then. Neutralized.' But he thought about what they might have done to her if they'd got her away. He thought of Adkins and Taylor.

'Do you really think she's got any more to offer?'

'Yes. If they wanted her so badly.'

'They've got to the core of us. How?'

Marlow shook his head, then changed tack. 'Now let's get back to your translation of that inscription.' He looked at her admiringly. 'Incredibly good work, by the way.' He admitted to himself that Graves's standing in his eyes had climbed several tall ladders.

She smiled, pleased almost in spite of herself. 'Still

sounds unbelievable. The secret of total control. What does that mean?'

'Means, in the wrong hands, goodbye, cruel world. Means in any hands. If this thing is the key to absolute power, who isn't going to be corrupted by it?'

'What now?' she asked.

'You follow up on the inscription. Whatever background you can get. I'll organize a replacement for Duff. We need to know how far this experience has set her back.'

'If at all.'

Marlow didn't want to hear that. He went on: 'But we don't want a replacement here.'

'Where then?'

'New York. I'll get Leon on to it.'

'New York?'

'That's where we're going. Fast. Paris isn't the healthiest place to be any more.'

'Got you.'

'Pack your bags. Get the people at Centre to pack hers too. Bring them over here. And send everything new encrypted to yourself at your own place in NY. Not INTERSEC.'

'They'll want to see something.'

'Throw them a bone.'

She was on the point of pursuing that, but asked instead, 'What'll we do with de Montferrat until NY?'

'She stays here.'

Marlow looked in at the door of his bedroom after Graves had gone, but the doctor waved him away.

Marlow nodded and went back up the rickety spiral staircase.

The doubt still nagged him. He made coffee and found the makings of something to eat, a day-old *pain-au-chocolat* and some grapes. He drank the espresso, ignored the food, picked up a copy of the book he was reading, Alison Weir's life of Henry VIII – what a bastard he was – and flicked through it without being able to concentrate. He reached for *Le Monde* instead and found nothing but sombre articles about the unrest bursting out all over the developing world – but what else was there to write about? Sooner or later, Western Europe and the USA would find themselves in the same situation the Romans had, two thousand years ago, when the Goths and Visigoths, Vandals and Huns began to migrate into the fertile territories of the empire in search of food.

It had already started. An inexorable invasion. A colonization of the privileged by the desperate. History rolling over in its sleep. There'd come a day, Marlow thought, when the battles he was fighting now would look like the antics of a bunch of kids with peashooters.

He looked ruefully at the whiskey bottle. But no. He wasn't going down that path again. He turned to his chess board, but that didn't work either. He noticed that his shirt was buttoned out of synch, and redid it.

He heard the doctor climbing the stairs ten minutes later.

'She's OK. Awake, a bit groggy. No psychological damage that I can see. After all this time, they didn't get away with it. Give her one of these if she gets distressed.' He tapped a plastic container and placed it on the coffee table near Marlow. 'Do you want a nurse to stay over, or do you want to keep it tight?'

'Keep it tight.'

'You'll be OK?'

'Backup downstairs and next door.'

'I'll be back at 16.00 hours. Call me if you need me before then.'

'Can she talk?'

'You can try. Give her an hour.'

'When can we move her?'

'Tell you at four.'

Marlow worked on his computer until ten, and was about to descend to the bedroom when he heard movement below. Nothing suspicious. She was awake. He heard the faint sounds of her showering. It had been a long time since he'd listened to someone else getting up in the same place as him.

It was comforting. It told him that he didn't have to be alone for ever. When the sounds ceased, he imagined that she'd be waiting, wondering, uncertain.

He called her name and went down the stairs to the bedroom.

She was sitting on the bed, wearing a black T-shirt a couple of sizes too big. She looked up at his approach.

'Hello, Jack,' she said, smiling.

75

New York City, the Present

'Adler's got vast resources,' Sir Richard Hudson was saying. 'An international communications company, one of the big contenders. Damn it, he's got governments in the palm of his hand.'

'Then he's joined the club,' said Marlow.

'He's not asking for secure information, Jack. Nothing like that. Look on his money as an extra reserve. Public/Private Sector Enterprise. All that.' Sir Richard waved his arm. The movement wafted his eau-de-cologne in Marlow's direction. 'He doesn't even know who we are.'

'I should hope not.'

'We're using the INTERPOL cover. They're *au fait*. No danger of a leak, if he double-checks. Not that he will. Rich maybe, powerful, yes, but a simple businessman at heart.'

Marlow was silent. He looked out over the New York skyline through the big picture window in Sir Richard's office on the top floor of INTERSEC Central. Watery sunshine, high cloud. The lighting was warm and discreet. Thick-pile blue carpet. A mahogany bookcase covering the wall behind the teak desk. No trace of a computer or any other vulgar modern equipment. Just three telephones, red, white and blue, and a grey intercom to connect with the outer room. An original Dufy graced the end wall. Not a hint of cuts here.

'I've been in this business since Cambridge,' Sir Richard reminded him sternly. 'I was three years old when Burgess and Maclean jumped ship. Squeaky clean since then. More or less. They brought in James Bond as housekeeper.' He waited for his joke to strike home. When it didn't, he drew briefly on his cigar, and went on: 'Adler's deeply distressed at what happened to Adkins and Taylor. And' – he paused – 'at Dr de Montferrat's continued absence.' He looked at Marlow. 'Any news there, by the way?'

'Nothing.'

'Yale and Venice?'

'No more than what we know.'

'Which is all Adler knows, as well; though I can tell you he's made quite thorough investigations through the university boards himself.'

'Has he?'

'And he sent a team of his own to Istanbul. Much to Major Haki's consternation.' Sir Richard smiled. 'Adler's angry. Impatient. It'd be better to have him safely in the fold. We don't want any loose cannon rolling about, do we?'

Marlow considered. The press had been allowed to give the deaths front-page coverage, but below-the-line, with additional biographical background articles in the broadsheets, around page five. Hadn't lasted more than a day. There'd been vague speculation about a kidnapping gone wrong, about Islamist terrorists, but nothing more. Focus soon shifted to the latest coup d'état in Africa. That was where things were hotting up, ruffling feathers in White-hall, Washington, Berlin and the Elysée. Bad for business.

As for the recent suicides at Yale, and another in Ven-ice, there had been obituaries, but nothing more. No conclusions were drawn, or public questions asked.

'What help does he think he can give?' asked Marlow.

Hudson spread his hands. 'Use of his resources, with-out strings. The man has eyes and ears everywhere. Keeps a good cellar, too.'

Since this further attempt at levity showed no sign of lightening things up, Sir Richard went on to a different tack: fatherly this time, older brother at least. Sometimes worked, he thought to himself. Worth a try, anyway. 'Come on, Jack,' he cajoled. 'We can do with having all the help we can get. Isn't it good to have him on our side?'

'Have you read his file?'

Hudson nodded, and shrugged his shoulders just a lit-tle. 'He's head of a multinational. All his own work. Don't get to be that without cracking some heads.'

He waited. Marlow let him.

'After all, Jack,' said Sir Richard at last, 'I *am* the boss.'

Marlow nodded, forced himself to smile. Diplomacy, delicacy, these had always been Hudson's strong points. Marlow, seeing that he had no option, agreed to Adler's financial involvement, but no more.

It was a small price to pay for keeping Hudson's curios-ity at bay.

It bought him time.

Leaving the building, Marlow set off on foot, taking him-self down 5th past the Frick Collection and the Zoo, then across Grand Army Plaza as far as St Thomas's, where he turned right along 53rd and continued past MoMA. Left down 7th near the Sheraton, and south again until he reached West 48th and his destination.

A long walk, but he could be certain no one was following him.

He went in, checked the lobby was empty, and used his security card to operate the lift. It took him to the thirty-fifth floor.

He walked down the softly lit, soundless corridor to the last door on the right, pushed the buzzer briefly three times then let himself in with another security card.

She was waiting for him. Dressed in a purple silk sheath.

'Hello, darling,' said Su-Lin.

76

A cold January day, almost the end of the month, and it had been a long twenty-four hours.

But now the fruit had fallen into his hands – the fruit which had been the goal of his ten-year struggle, his *Kampf*.

Longer than ten years. Since the day of his birth in the little Austrian border town of Braunau, Destiny had chosen him for this path.

He thought of Ludendorff, an old man now, living in retirement, forgotten. The general had turned to God, writing books about the dismal fate of Germany and the world's ills. A changed man. The old fool had broken with him a year after the last meeting they'd had, when the general had placed the fate of his adopted country firmly in his hands.

Now, under his undisputed leadership, that country would be purged and, once clean again, go on to purge the world.

He was alone, looking out of his office window at the procession. It was thousands-strong, the SA men in brown uniforms and badges, their red-white-and-black armbands caught by the firelight of the torches they carried as they marched in celebration and in triumph. *Die Fahne Hoch . . .!*

Of course there were still snags. People who resisted him. But they would be broken. What had he said to Otto Strasser, when Strasser had had the temerity to ask him what the policy of the Nazi Party was? He smiled in pride at the memory of his reply: 'The policy is not the question. The only question is power.' Strasser had argued back, saying: 'Power is only the means of accomplishing policy.' 'No,' he had retorted. 'That is the opinion of the intellectuals. We need *power*. That is *all*.'

And now he had it. Soon, when the programme was in train, he would deal with Strasser, and his brother, and all the other left-wing, Jew-loving breed.

Ludendorff could have had no idea of the importance of what he had handed over. If he had, he would never have let the tablet go.

The man felt for it in his pocket, clutched it. This little piece of baked earth. It had taken him much study, much discreet consultation, but he had mastered it, as he would master everything else. Nothing stood in his way now. If there were a means of using it to control his enemies – the weak British, the pusillanimous French and the distant, aloof Americans – as well as it had enabled him to control his fellow countrymen, he would find it. Their turn would come.

For the moment, it would be the turn of Germany, the turn of Austria, the turn of Poland and, above all, the turn of the Jews.

Their power would be broken for ever; their fraud uncovered in the shining light of the New Dawn.

There was a knock at the door.

'*Herein!*' barked the man.

An excited young adjutant entered. 'First edition,' he said, 'Chancellor!'

Controlling his excitement, accepting his Destiny, the man took the proffered copy of the *Völkischer Beobachter*, the *People's Daily*, *his* newspaper; looked at the front page. Big picture of him, smaller ones of Frick and Göring, now ministers in the new administration.

He read the headline: *Ein Historischer Tag – Erste Maßnahmen der Reichsregierung* . . . 'A Historic Day – First Measures of the National Government led by . . .' and then *his* name. *His* leadership! *His* country. Above all others!

It was past midnight. January 31 now. The first day.

The First Day of the Third Reich.

77

New York, the Present

Leon Lopez became aware of the problem on an otherwise unremarkable late Wednesday afternoon.

He'd been looking away from his screen to rest his eyes, taking off his glasses and wiping them on his tie. It was going to be his son Alvar's fourteenth birthday the following week, and he intended to buy him the latest Ubisoft game, top of Alvar's wish-list.

He thought about Alvar, and Lucia, now rising eleven, how time flew, and of his wife, Mia. He allowed himself a contented smile.

Then he saw the icon flash on his screen, clicked, went to the inbox, saw the mail.

Perhaps it was Mia's Swedish connection that alerted him. There was something about the message that had come through, though how the hacker had managed to get as far as he or she had in order to place it was nothing short of miraculous.

The message itself made Lopez freeze.

He picked up the internal phone, and spoke briefly. The sector's systems were instantly locked down, and Monitoring went on full vigilance status.

Over the next hour there was nothing more. No

demand for money, no attempt to access any kind of information. Lopez studied the message.

I have something you may need. I know this because you taught me history of science and other skills. I am in need so I turn to you. The other skills you taught me let me see your recent exchange about the scroll with colleagues in Paris. I am sorry. Accident. I just want to be in touch with you. You were like a father. I always follow you. Maybe we meet.

Christ, thought Lopez. How can I explain this to Jack?

He decided to block the thing himself, nip it in the bud before anyone else in the sector knew. This job was well-paid and a welcome addition to his university salary. He wasn't the only academic to moonlight like this. He had colleagues, economists, who were in the pocket of big business. One made a fortune producing analyses in the financial press which were favourable to his client's projected investment ventures. That paid for the house in Malibu.

Lopez didn't want to lose this sinecure. But, now, he was vulnerable. He knew that if he hadn't isolated and neutralized this incursion by day's end he would have to come clean. If he didn't, and they found out, he'd be out of more than a job.

As he'd expected, there was no source for the mail. But the message contained clues. One was obvious, not even a clue, a statement. Whoever it was was a former student of his. The other was less apparent but clear to him because of the way Mia still spoke English sometimes, especially when she was agitated or needed to express a difficult concept. Whoever had written this was not a native English speaker, that was clear. The nuances suggested, equally clearly, that the person was Scandinavian, and probably female.

Maybe we meet. Fine, but how, when there was no way he could make contact to arrange it? The time before Marlow would start asking questions about the lockdown was limited. Luckily, Marlow was otherwise engaged somewhere and Graves was working from home on material she'd told him needed further processing before she passed it on to him for analysis.

He had, maybe, two hours.

Something told him that whoever it was wouldn't be long in getting in touch again.

He considered the position. It'd taken courage to make this first step in the first place, and now the person – she – would be careful, would make sure she wasn't led into any kind of trap. If he was being watched, he had to give some kind of assurance that he was alone. If he was putting his neck on the block, if he was laying himself open to some psycho, so be it. But he didn't think so and, anyway, he hadn't a choice.

One thing was certain – he had to get out of the office. The very walls oppressed him. He passed the work he was engaged on to his assistant, told her he'd be back in an hour, and made his way down through the hotel and out of the building. He walked a block, avoiding his usual coffeehouse, and made his way to another, on East 75th near the Whitney. It was dark, fake-Edwardian, a pastiche English gentlemen's club, all but deserted at this hour.

He chose a table in a corner, and a chair which faced the

door. He ordered an espresso and a bottle of Gize. They came accompanied by a porcelain dish of mixed nuts and fruits. He drank the coffee quickly then sipped the water, while his brain refused to come up with a plan and floundered constantly back to the hope that something would happen to take any decision away from him. Absently, he nibbled the fruit-and-nut mixture, unable to taste it.

He'd been there fifteen minutes and was beginning to fidget, hating to sit still, a world away from his normal, ordered existence. Then she entered. He knew she was the one from the moment he saw her.

She must have been hanging around near the office – she knew where it was, my God, she knew where it *was* – then followed him, waited some more, either uncertain or to make sure he was really without company. But then she'd taken the plunge. She was short, stockily built, had close-cropped brown hair, a tanned, big-boned face. She wore khaki chinos, black trainers and a parka that was too big for her. A leather shoulder-bag swung from one shoulder. She looked about as much at home here as a penguin in a desert. She'd seen him, of course, but she didn't approach, looking about uncertainly instead. A waiter was making his way towards her. The handful of other customers, all middle-aged businesspeople, paid little attention, though one or two of the women looked in her direction curiously.

Before the waiter could reach her, Lopez stood up, heart in mouth. 'Over here,' he called.

She nodded, sidestepped the waiter and came over to him. She still looked unsure of herself, but she also looked relieved. The last step had been taken.

78

The waiter came over.

'What'll it be?' he asked.

Leon looked at her questioningly.

She hesitated. 'A Schweppes?'

'And another coffee. Latte this time,' said Lopez. 'Decaf.'

'Coming up.' The waiter left them.

They didn't speak until he'd returned with the drinks and parked them.

'Got your message,' said Lopez.

'Thanks.' Her eyes were wary.

'Took one hell of a risk.'

'I know.'

He was trying to place her. How old was she? Maybe twenty-five. So she'd been in his class five, six years ago. Then it came to him. Surname at least. Lundquist. 'I remember you,' he said. She'd been one of his better students, maybe the best of her year. He'd taken her under his wing, taught her how to make a computer do everything but sing and dance, thought about recruiting her for INTERSEC, but she'd caught the hint and wasn't interested. Wanted to go on, do a doctorate, go home to Sweden, teach.

Annika, that was it. Annika Lundquist. But here she still was, and she looked very far from prosperous.

'You wanted to see me,' he said guardedly.

'Yes.' The tension, which had ebbed while he'd been talking, returned to her face. She looked around.

'You'd better tell me, and fast. Do you realize what a security risk you've become? Do you know what happens to people who've done what you've done?'

'Wait. It's important. I think. You always said, "Come to me if ever you need anything."'

He was silent. It was true. He'd learned since never to make such promises. But it was too late for this one. Besides, Lopez was intrigued. It was the first time in a while that he'd come face to face with the cutting edge.

'You said you were in need.'

'I am not doing so good. I need money.'

He sighed. Was that why she was still here, not back in Sweden, why she looked as if she'd been sleeping rough?

Drugs? Not like her, but who could tell?

'I want to go home.' She drew herself up a little proudly. 'I qualified. You can call me Dr Lundquist. But I had problems with a man. Not so good. And lost my job. Have to work in a cash and carry. To pay for little Mia.'

He wanted to ask questions, but something in her eyes told him not to. He inferred that Mia was her kid. Interesting, her giving the baby the same name as his wife. He felt his heart soften a little. And he was intrigued.

'Remind me, where do you come from – in Sweden?'

'Ystad.'

Down in the south. In Scania. Town on the coast, hemmed in by flat countryside. Like Manhattan once was. By the look of things, she'd be better off there than here.

'You want money to get back there?' he asked.

'Yes,' she replied. 'Start over.'

'Nice coincidence, your having something you want to sell me.' He saw her recoil at his tone.

'I was going to get in touch with you anyway. Then I saw a little of what you were looking for. That was the coincidence. But it doesn't matter. What I have may be of no consequence at all.'

'What is it?'

'My father's family is very old. He was so proud of it, as a little girl I would get embarrassed for him, talking to his friends too much, after too much beer, about his great-grandfather the engineer *this* and his great-great-great grandfather the general *that*. But it wasn't just boasting. There was a chest, full of papers. Some of them very old, should have been in a proper archive. But he took good care of them. When he was killed, my mother gave me some of them. I think she intended I should sell them if I ever got short of cash. We may be an old family, but we are not rich, and I am the only child.' She looked wistful. 'My father would have liked a son, but all he got was me. Not that there was a name to preserve any longer. His own father was the grandson of a daughter of the old family. There was little left to inherit, when his turn came, but the old papers and letters.'

The door of the coffeehouse opened and she looked round, alert. It struck Lopez that he might not be the only one she was wary of. But it was only a couple that entered, a plump woman with long dark hair, eccentrically dressed, accompanied by a business-type, a gaunt man with wet lips and pale eyes. Annika turned back to Lopez.

375

'I learned enough from you to work on very old documents. There is one in the collection written by hand on
good vellum, in Latin, dictated to a scribe in Sweden in
about 1210; the grammar and spelling are perfect but the
tone is of a man speaking rather than writing. The narrative wanders a little.'

Lopez leaned forward. 'What is it?'

'It's a letter, but it's also a memoir and a kind of last will
and testament. But there's a whole passage that I cannot
fathom. It seems to be written in code, or in another language altogether, strange to me.'

'Do you know who wrote it?'

She frowned. 'I told you, a scribe, near where Malmö is
now, but there's no way of telling, the city wasn't founded
then.'

'I mean, who dictated it?'

'It's signed – or at least there's a mark, and then the
name written in, added by the scribe.'

'Go on.'

'It's the name of our oldest ancestor. That's what my
father used to tell me. I doubt if anyone except perhaps
an aristocrat can trace their family back so far, but I don't
see how the document can have made it into that trunk of
my father's otherwise.'

'And what is the name?'

'Frid Eyolfsson. He was a man close to Enrico Dandolo.' Annika watched his face. 'I'd been reading about the
Dandolo Project in the professional journals. Then there
was that news of the deaths of those archaeologists. I
knew Dr Adkins briefly, I was at Yale as a junior lecturer
for a semester.' She smiled, half-mockingly, half-ruefully.

'He tried to seduce me. But he was always doing things like that. I don't think he meant any harm by it. He didn't ever take other people's feelings seriously.' She hesitated. 'Then I lost my job, and things got just too bad for me to handle, so I thought I'd try to contact you. But I couldn't reach you – even through Columbia. There were clues though – and so I set off in pursuit of you.' She looked at him. 'I was desperate. I just wanted help. To get away. But I'd already connected the Dandolo Project to something . . . something secret . . . you seemed to be involved with. And I remembered this document. I couldn't help it. My father used to hold it up often enough. "A piece of Swedish history," he'd say. "It ought to be in the *Riksarkivet*."' She slumped back, exhausted by her speech, which had spilled out fast, words tripping each other up, like a confession.

Lopez noticed she'd eaten all the nibbles. The waiter was on the other side of the room, serving the couple who'd come in earlier. Lopez waved him over, and ordered a plate of mixed sandwiches and a tall cappuccino.

'Can you show me this document?'

'Yes. But I don't have it with me.'

Lopez paused, uncertain. 'You're *sure* it exists?'

'I'm in need, not mad. You can come with me now.'

'No.' Lopez looked at his watch. 'I have to get back. Can I call you?'

She produced a biro, wrote a number and an address on a cardboard coaster, and slid it over to him.

'Thanks. Later today?'

'I'll be in all evening.'

'We'll arrange something, then.' He hesitated, reached

over, patted her hand. 'It'll be all right, Annika. You'll see. We'll sort this out for you.'

She smiled back wanly. He could see she didn't believe him, much as she wanted to.

The waiter reappeared with a tray. He placed the sandwiches, beautifully garnished, with the coffee, in front of Annika. 'Nothing for you?' he asked Lopez.

'Just the bill.'

He paid it when it came, but still sat for a minute. She was eating as if she hadn't eaten all day. He reached for his wallet again, withdrew $50, and placed the notes by her. She looked at the money, at him, mouth full, and smiled her gratitude.

'I'll call you in an hour. That good?'

She nodded.

'Until later, then.'

He stood, smiled at her, and left.

Outside, dusk was gathering.

When he got back to INTERSEC, he called off the lockdown. Security reported no queries in his absence. He was in the clear.

He was also alone with Annika's information. He considered his position.

But when, an hour later, he rang the number she'd given him, there was no answer.

79

Berlin, AD 1945

Late April, but it was as if spring had been strangled at birth. The city was a mound of debris, a grey pile between whose smashed buildings tattered figures flitted. Most trees dead and the Tiergarten a wreck.

Far underground, breathing pumped air, sallow from too many days of artificial light, the last representatives of the Thousand-Year Reich lived on. Uniforms were spotless, and routine maintained its brisk order. The Führer hardly slept, spent days and nights in the map-room poring over charts of the Middle East in the company of exhausted generals.

'Gentlemen, we need to secure the Persian oil. That is imperative for the counter-attack.'

They nodded their assent, knowing that the end wasn't more than two weeks away. The Russians were at the gates of the shattered city and, from the west, the Americans and the British were trundling east over Greater Germany. Those who could get out, had. Only fanatics were left – and those who had no other choice.

Adolf Hitler knew the truth: they had *betrayed* him. The very people he had sought to turn into a Master Race. At fifty-six, he knew his work was over. He had done what he could.

But one question tortured him. How had he exhausted the power that had been given him?

And now the tablet had disappeared.

His first thought was that it had been stolen. The box, too, which all the ingenuity of Nazi science had been unable to open. But how could that be? He had spoken of the secret to no one, not even Eva, soon to be his wife.

His thoughts wandered. He would take her to Valhalla with him. She was willing, and Blondi too, most faithful of his servants, the German shepherd Bormann had given him five years earlier. Blondi had had puppies recently, and he had named one of them Wolf, his favourite name. Didn't his own name, Adolf, mean 'Noble Wolf'?

It was only to Blondi that he had ever whispered his secret. Perhaps the gods had taken it back. It had served its purpose.

He knew he had never mastered the deepest secrets of the tablet. But surely the power of his own will had been enough, the tablet's power a mere ancillary. It had gone now – and he had no further need of it! Soon, he would be united with the warrior-gods of Valhalla. Soon, he and Eva and Blondi would be enthroned in the place which was theirs by right, and to which Destiny had led them.

And the world would never forget him – he would be immortal.

80

Unter den Linden, Wilhelmstraße and Friedrichstraße were rubble-fields, a few broken towers sticking up like the fingers of a dead man; but, as if by a miracle, the Kaiser-Friedrich-Museum had escaped with little damage.

A miracle, too, for me, thought Generalleutnant Hans von Reinhardt.

Reinhardt looked back with pleasure on his life. The scion of a modest aristocratic family from Pomerania, he'd used his title and contacts wisely, getting posted to the General Staff of the Regular Army early in his professional career. No front line for him, though there were times, he knew, when he fantasized about leading a platoon of desperate men into the thick of the gunfire.

In reality, he'd sat at an oak desk, held a pen instead of a Luger P 08; but he'd moved swiftly through the ranks to become one of the youngest generals on the staff. This was facilitated by a flair for administration, which led in turn to his secondment to Adolf Eichmann's sector of the RSHA.

After the big attempt on Hitler's life in July the year before, orchestrated by fellow officers of the General Staff, he'd played an executive role in Operation Thunderstorm. That purge had seen promotion for him, and privileges. But he knew that they had come too late to do him any good in the crumbling Third Reich. And the real downside was that he'd been pretty much forced, as a career move, to join the SS. But he would shed the unwelcome additional rank of Gruppenführer as soon as the war was over, and then – he would disappear.

Reinhardt had already laid plans. He'd heard good things about Argentina, but Neuquén in Patagonia looked right for him. Timber or cattle-farming. His family had been involved in such activities for generations, they were in his blood. He was already dreaming of his ranch. And of greater things than that. Perhaps even of a New Reich, a phoenix reborn. He'd always felt that his talent had never had a real chance to spread its wings.

The best thing to have come out of all this was that his slavish attention to detail in the great round-up and execution of suspects that was Operation Thunderstorm, had catapulted him into the Führer's inner circle. And now he found himself in this warren beneath Berlin, the *Führerbunker*, safe, but, at the same time, trapped.

Still, he'd been in worse traps than this and got free, and he'd laid plans. There was a flat in Potsdam, where civilian clothes and a forged Swiss passport awaited him. The passport was a work of art, done years ago by a master craftsman, Ernst Thalheimer, before they took him to Auschwitz. It was valid until June, 1950.

There too, was the box. He'd get money for that in the USA, his first port of call when he escaped. The box represented for Reinhardt a valuable antique which could be turned into cash for his onward journey and the purchase of land.

As for power, he was certain that all the power he would ever need lay in the tablet.

He'd stolen the box and the tablet from the desk in the

Chancellery the day before the move to the Bunker. Just in time, as it turned out. Had to steal the key to the drawer, get a copy made, replace the original, nothing missed; Blondi, the only other occupant of the office when he'd done the deed had barked a little, uncertainly, but he knew Blondi well, had made friends with her, and she liked him, trusted him.

As for the great leader, he had ceased to carry the thing with him all the time. The man was losing his grip on reality, they could all see that. Reinhardt knew how to make himself indispensable to the Führer, and he was pleased to see how the man clung to him, rambling on about the virtues of loyalty in the face of adversity. All the better that the Führer was getting vague. He talked to his god-damned dog, for Christ's sake.

But AH put his trust in Reinhardt too, kept him close, and had let enough slip, as the young general eaves-dropped on his meandering monologues to the dog, to alert the general to the potential of the little clay tablet he nowadays kept locked in that drawer of his desk.

It looked innocuous enough, but when he had held the tablet he felt an electric shock. He had no idea of its full potential, but he'd heard enough to know what it could do, in the right hands.

He'd deposited the tablet in the Kaiser-Friedrich-Museum. The director of Middle Eastern antiquities, an understanding man, had accepted it with a show of grati-tude, though Reinhardt, who had done his research, knew that his tablet was one of hundreds, if not thousands, already in the museum's vaults.

Safety in numbers.

There it lay now, wrapped in cotton wool, in a wooden case, among innumerable others, safe in a cellar of the museum, the only thing to distinguish it a discreet label: *On Permanent Loan by the Grace of the Freiherr Hans von Machtschlüssel-Reinhardt.*

Machtschlüssel. The key to power. His little joke. And he knew how to lay hands on it again, as soon as the opportunity presented itself, before he left the Fatherland, either for ever, or to return one day in triumph. But he needed additional surety.

It had fallen to him to travel on two secret missions to the American Office of Strategic Services bureau in Bern, Switzerland. These concerned secret negotiations between Heinrich Himmler and the OSS about a possible trade-off which would, Himmler hoped, save his skin when the Reich fell. But talks with the American secret service mattered little to Reinhardt. He took the opportunity to have a letter drawn up by a Swiss lawyer, proving his right to the tablet and describing how it could be identified. The lawyer's office kept a copy; another was placed in a safe-deposit box in the Bern branch of a private bank.

Satisfied that he had covered every eventuality, Reinhardt returned to Berlin. The Swiss lawyer, however, didn't file the letter in the firm's files but locked it in a drawer of his own desk.

The lawyer had another client: the Office of Strategic Services.

When he received a copy, the coordinating officer at Allen Dulles's Bern office looked over the letter. It appeared to refer simply to a more or less valuable artefact from Ancient Mesopotamia, legitimately lodged at the Kaiser-Friedrich-Museum by a member of the German General Staff. Family heirloom for safekeeping.

The coordinating officer had more important things on his mind. He had his clerk file the letter away, and forgot about it.

81

Leon Lopez knew something was wrong the moment he reached the corridor outside her studio-apartment in the downtrodden block in an anonymous street in the South Bronx. The front door was ajar, the flimsy lock unforced, worked open with a credit card, the oldest trick in the book.

Lopez was on his guard immediately, though his heart had been in his mouth since he'd started the drive up here to find out why she wasn't answering her phone.

He'd told nobody of his unauthorized field-trip. Part of his mind told him what a fool he was being, but something had tempted him to follow this lead for himself. Any connection to Dandolo was vital; it'd be a coup if he could bring new information into the fold, rather than just analyse what others had found.

They'd overlook any breach of discipline in the face of a new breakthrough.

But now, in the quiet apartment, with its threadbare furnishings, a bed along one wall, he felt misgivings.

There were untidy bookshelves, a desk and chair, and a small sofa with a plywood coffee table in front of it, angled to face a television in a corner.

He wasn't suited to this, he was unprepared, he hadn't got a gun. What had he let himself in for?

Off the main room was a cubby-hole with a lavatory, washbasin and shower. Empty, too. Across the living area from the bathroom, there was an open arch with a bead curtain stretched across it, which led to a kitchenette.

Picking his way cautiously across the room, Lopez felt his heart thump hard in his chest.

He lifted the strands of the bead curtain.

Annika lay curled up like a foetus on the square of battered beige linoleum tiles which covered the floor, hemmed in on three sides by waist-high cupboards, the tops of which carried a sink, facing a grimy window overlooking a grey wall ten metres away, across a narrow courtyard; and a collection of pots, pans, crockery, packets of cereal and pasta, and an elderly microwave. An equally venerable fridge hummed noisily between the cupboards. Lopez couldn't open the cupboards because Annika's body was blocking the doors. He kept his eyes averted from her face as he touched her. She was still warm, but there was no doubt that she was dead. There wasn't much blood, but the haft of a kitchen knife jutted from under her left breast.

It was a student's flat, untidy and cluttered; posters and reproductions on the walls made an attempt to relieve the dinginess; the bed was carelessly made. Hard to know whether anyone had searched the place, but, with mounting panic, Lopez searched it himself, steeling himself to shunt the corpse aside to peer into the kitchen cupboards. He did it all fast. He didn't know if Annika's killers would return, and he didn't know how much time he could allow himself. After half an hour, he resigned himself to the fact that there were no documents, ancient or otherwise, relating to what Annika had described in the coffeehouse a handful of hours earlier. There were no memory sticks, no CD-ROMs; and there was no computer either, though on the desk lay the power line which belonged to one, as well as a set of headphones, an iPod dock, a printer-scanner and a hub. He noticed a clearing in the dust on the desk where a laptop had been parked, leaving its out-line traced.

A drawer in the desk contained pencils and notepads, and the $50 Lopez had given her.

A light from the corridor came on and filtered under the door. He could hear footsteps slowly approaching. He froze, but the footsteps passed by.

Lopez felt sweat pour down his back under his clothes, and down his face. He took out a handkerchief and wiped his forehead and eyes. His glasses had steamed up, and he wiped them too.

It was time to go.

82

Straits of the Bosphorus, Year of Our Lord 1203

The day was fine and sunny, the wind mild and favourable; the ships had unfurled their sails to the breeze.

Geoffrey de Villehardouin, Marshal of Champagne, and the author of this work – who has never, to his knowledge, put anything in it contrary to the truth, and who was present, moreover, at all the conferences recorded in its pages – here testifies that so fine a sight had never been seen before. It seemed, indeed, that here was a fleet that might well conquer lands, for as far as the eye could reach there was nothing to be seen but sails outspread on all that vast array of ships, so that every man's heart was filled with joy at the sight.

Geoffrey, sitting on the warm stern afterdeck of the galley which had carried him here, stopped dictating to his secretary and looked out across the water. It was late afternoon on Friday, 12 July. They had arrived from Corfu a week earlier.

The marshal of Champagne knew they were in safe hands. They had dropped anchor, unopposed, within a few cables' length of the shore. This was the first surprise, since all the company had been ready for battle, expecting the Greeks of Constantinople, who had long since heard of the army's great triumph at Zara, to be well prepared for them. But there was nothing. There had been no naval resistance at all, though no surprise showed on the face of Doge Dandolo.

And he was the one to be trusted. Of old, they had learned, he had knowledge of this city, whose walls and towers looked like something from a fairy-tale, a magical idea of what a city should be like.

Dandolo's commands were obeyed without question. On his orders, the army quartered itself on the north shore of the great inlet which bordered the city on its northern side. No resistance there either, though the army of the Great City had the reputation of being one of the finest in the world. There were unprotected farms with granaries overflowing with grain, and rivers and streams where the fresh water was plentiful. A couple of hundred village girls were rounded up and pressed into service. Not enough to go round, but they would serve.

Geoffrey had come back to his ship to get cool, for the heat was fierce. There had been casualties already, five knights dead of burst hearts or struck down by the sun. They had learned not to exercise during full daylight, and to do so in light clothes.

But did they need to train for battle? At all?

Geoffrey thought back to the day of their arrival. In his mind, he started to compose the next part of his memoir, ready for dictation:

We'd decided to make an impression the moment they came within close range of the seaward walls. Trumpets were sounded, brass fanfares of defiance carried to the city on the wind, along with the thunder of their drums. The citizens were already on their rooftops and ranged along their walls, but for a time there was nothing else. Nothing except lines of people watching the fleet, but they were too far away for us to be able to see whether they were looking at the fleet with anything other than wonder and curiosity.

On that day, Dandolo did not hesitate. He gave the order immediately.

Transports were towed close to shore by galleys, the rowers sweating and straining at their oars. There was no hanging back – everyone was eager to be first ashore – and first were the knights, rushing down the gangways thrown on to the beach, their horses kicking up sand and pebbles. Infantry poured from the transports beaching behind.

There had been a show of resistance. One great gate swung open in the walls, and a troop of horse- and pike-men, silver and black, and red and yellow, appeared on the shore, on our left flank, charging towards us, a brave run, threatening to take us before we could wheel and face. But the discipline of our troops was strong and their morale flew higher than an eagle.

Geoffrey smiled at the memory. How those Greeks had broken and run! How they scuttled back, and how fast the gate had closed behind them!

Call that a fight? There were barely a dozen dead on the beach.

'We found ourselves – and all within an hour – in possession of an easy victory,' said Geoffrey aloud, and his clerk looked up and dipped his pen. But the marshal lapsed into silence, closing his eyes and letting the sun warm his face until it set behind the dark walls of the city and ceded heaven to the stars.

The walls cast their shadow over the water. They had stood for a thousand years. They had seen off greater enemies than these.

But their core was rotten.

83

New York City, the Present

Relief hit him the moment he closed the office door.

He'd started to feel safe as soon as he'd passed through the warm, well-lit foyer of the hotel which masked INTERSEC's operations.

He'd got back in one piece. No chase, no fight, no knives, no gunfire. Comfortingly, there were other people about in the building, night staff, hunched over blue screens, smoking cigarettes furtively near air-ducts, eating sandwiches and drinking coffee, concentrating on other jobs. But unaware of what was unfurling in Room 55.

Several thoughts fought for supremacy in his mind. He should report this, but to whom? What would he say? That he'd gone out on a limb and that the limb had broken?

He also thought: *how did the other side know?* Annika had been a master hacker. A few more lessons and she would have been his equal. Who had locked into her computer? Or had a different trail led the others to her? He was sure the connection with her ancestor, Frid Eyolfson, had opened a door for Annika. A door she'd wanted to lead him through.

He would never know now. She was gone, and so was her information. He had to report it. And face the consequences of not having told anyone sooner.

Shit!

Scrambling his private cell-phone, switching off the INTERSEC log-calls function, which he wasn't supposed to know about, he rang Mia again. He told her it looked as if it was going to be a long night. Her voice was resigned but irritated. Maybe she'd see him in the morning.

She put barbs on the 'maybe', and hung up.

He sighed. He went to his desk, clicked on his 12-core Mac Pro, and gazed emptily at the screen. He went to *Get Mail* just for something to do, to marshal his thoughts; he wasn't expecting anything. Then he stiffened. Something new, from a sender whose address was a cipher of numbers and letters. *No Subject*. He opened it, clicked on the attachment. His breathing thickened.

Fast as the machine was, the blue line at the bottom right of the page took an age to fill up. Then, there it was. Old writing on crumpled, dark-beige paper. A long document.

She'd scanned and sent it to him before ... What? Before anything happened to her? As a failsafe? Had she had some warning? Some premonition? He knew she would have erased anything connected to this from her hard drive immediately afterwards. She would have remembered to do that much. He sent a heartfelt thanks to that poor little corpse. He thought of her daughter, Mia, for the first time. Where was she? No evidence of a child in the apartment. With her grandmother? He could only hope so. He would find an address, try to contact the woman. Someone else would discover the body, alert the police.

He looked through the document and, as he did so, his

mind registered disappointment. Annika hadn't affixed any translation, and the letter was, as she'd said, in medieval Latin. And Lopez was no linguist. He could get by in French and Spanish, and that was it.

And someone else had the document as well, now, since it hadn't been in the apartment.

Someone they were racing against. Someone who had resources as great as INTERSEC's own.

The letter ended. He could see the bold cross plainly made – Frid's mark – and read his name written out beneath it, with another, that of the scribe.

But the writing on the scanned parchment continued. Not in the Roman alphabet, and in a different hand from that of the scribe. Something else, something strange, but distantly familiar. And at the very end, in a crabbed hand, a different person again had added a note in yet another language.

Lopez concentrated on the five lines that had caught his attention. Why was it familiar? Five lines of uncertain scrawl. Something Frid himself had copied out? It looked as if the writer had laboured hard in his task, there were crossings-out and corrections, but the whole matter looked complete. Hard to tell where one word ended and another started. Were they words?

Numerals! Numerals were more up his street.

Then it came to him. This was similar to the incised inscription they'd seen on the shank of the key.

He picked up the blue phone and started to tap in a number. But, halfway through, he stopped.

The temptation to crack this on his own was strong. But how much time did he have?

84

Vienna, AD 1946

The man in the dark-blue suit sat on the bed in his hotel room and looked at the box he held in his hands.

So far, so good. It had been a tough six months, but now it was January again, and much of the dust had settled. He could break cover. That meant facing new challenges, but it was still a relief.

Vienna was bundled in the misery of defeat; but what its cobbled streets and battered buildings concealed was an energetic renaissance based on a black market which carried on as if the four zones which Britain, France, the USA and the USSR had divided the city into had never been called into being. Austria stood in the middle of Soviet-occupied Europe, but it was unlikely that Vienna would suffer the fate which hung over Berlin; and the Hotel Sacher, on Philharmoniker Straße and just opposite the opera, was able to keep up appearances, depending on its ability to maintain the delicate balance between rationing and its black-market suppliers. The man had chosen to stay there not just because it was still the best hotel in town, but because spot checks were rare, and it was close to one of the American sectors.

The Swiss passport safe in his left-hand breast pocket, the wallet with its precious cargo of $500 in his right, he

396

stood up, and wrapped the box in a black velvet cloth. He placed it carefully in his briefcase then pulled on his overcoat, taking a grey trilby from the table near the door.

He checked his watch. A short walk through the drizzle north to Herrenstraße and the Café Central, where his contact would be waiting for him at 19.00 hours. He'd arrive precisely on time. The passport, its stamps correct and giving his name as Aloysius Guttmann, would sweep aside any obstacles placed in his path by the occupying powers. Aloysius Guttmann was a respectable Swiss art dealer, in early middle age.

He was what Hans von Reinhardt had now become.

His contact was already there, plump and sleek, in contrast to most of the other customers. Sitting below the vaulted ceiling with its white marble columns, he was reading the café's copy of *The New York Times*, and having difficulty with the stick-holder to which the paper was attached. In front of him on the table was a slice of *Sachertorte*, half eaten, a flute of Mumm and an espresso, made with real coffee.

As Reinhardt approached him, he rose politely, and the men shook hands.

'Herr Guttmann, good to meet you.'

'And you, Mr Lightoller.'

Harvey Lightoller, of Lightoller and Steeples, fine art and antique dealers of Madison Avenue, had a firm handshake and a look that gave nothing away. Reinhardt ordered a Stiegl *helles*.

'Pleasant trip?' asked Reinhardt.

'It had its moments,' replied Lightoller. 'The train from Salzburg took four hours.'

'Things will take a while yet to get up and running properly.'

'I daresay they will. Anyway, off to London in a couple of days, as soon as I've concluded our business here. God knows what the flight will be like.'

'I trust you'll be comfortable.'

'So do I.'

'At least it's safe to fly again, these days.'

Lightoller looked at him appraisingly. 'Your English is excellent, Herr Guttmann.'

'I'm working on it.'

They continued with more or less uneasy small talk until the beer arrived. The men toasted each other: '*Zum Wohl.*'

Lightoller was not given to small talk. He glanced at Reinhardt's briefcase, then at his watch.

'I think you have something which we might be interested in. Early thirteenth century, your telegram said.'

'As far as I can judge.'

'But the key is missing?'

'Unfortunately.'

Lightoller sat back, finished his coffee, washed the taste away with a sip of champagne, ignored the cake. 'That needn't be too serious.' He paused, briefly. 'Do you have it with you?'

Reinhardt took out the box in its velvet shroud, and placed it on the table. Then he sat back while Lightoller unwrapped it.

The dealer held it up to the light in delicate fingers. 'I

think it's earlier,' he said at last. 'Could be twelfth century.' He paused again, not telling Herr Guttmann that the box could have been made as early as the eleventh, which would increase its value by a vast amount. If L&S bought it at a good price, they should make a killing at auction.

'Very nice,' he continued. 'And the craftsmanship is beautiful. Far more sophisticated than one would expect in a piece of this age.' He sat back, still looking at the box, turning it in his hands. 'Yes, I think, with the right client, we might be able to do something with this. Have to have it verified, of course. There's an acquaintance of mine at the Albertina, so we should be able to conclude this quickly. I gather that is your wish? And that you'd rather we paid for it in dollars?'

'Yes.'

'I'd have to give you an order, to be drawn on the bank of your choice in the city of your choice, of course.'

'That will be satisfactory.'

Lightoller looked at him. 'Has it any provenance?'

'Family heirloom.' Reinhardt wasn't worried. He had the necessary papers already forged. He'd produce them when asked. Mustn't seem too eager.

'Indeed,' said Lightoller, his voice as delicate as his fingers. He rewrapped the box, tapped the velvet shroud with his fingers and sat back again. The judicious effect he sought was marred slightly as he was obliged to suppress a belch. 'Had you a figure in mind?' he asked, recovering his poise.

Two days later, Reinhardt boarded a train bound for Bern, via Salzburg and Innsbruck, with a change at Zurich. He was pleased with the way his business had been settled, and with the slip of paper from Lightoller and Steeples now in his wallet guaranteeing the substantial sum which would be awaiting him at J. P. Morgan's when he arrived in New York later that month.

After he'd collected the letter from the deposit box in Bern, arranged matters with the lawyer there and used the man to have his travel documents rubber-stamped, he'd be ready for the final steps: first, Berlin, to recover the last item of his luggage; then, Hamburg, and the liner that would take him to America. His business in New York and, afterwards, at last . . . the steamer to Buenos Aires.

He settled back, alone by the window of a first-class compartment, and opened the Spanish teach-yourself book to page 62, Chapter X: COMMON PREPOSITIONS. He started to read: *There are certain prepositions which require the insertion of* de *before the following noun* . . . His mind was contented. Everything was going according to plan.

But there are some things you cannot plan for.

There'd been a mix-up further down the line. Points had not been switched.

Reinhardt's train thundered confidently on, as did the *Zürcher–Wiener Schnellzug*, in the opposite direction.

The head-on collision occurred at 2.35 in the afternoon. Reinhardt hardly had time to hear the screaming of brakes and the rending of steel. He saw his book jolted out of his hands, saw it fly through the air. He felt himself flying, flying.

He never saw the flames.

*

The next day's *Wiener Zeitung* reported the news:

TRAGIC RAIL CRASH CLAIMS 17 DEAD, 49 WOUNDED

Herr Guttmann, incinerated in the crash, was never identified.

85

New York City, the Present

'Where did this come from?' Marlow asked. 'And when?'

Lopez adjusted his glasses. 'About an hour ago. Encrypted sender. No way to trace it. I called Graves immediately after I called you, and left.'

'And that's it? No one else in the office knows?'

'No one outside our section,' Lopez said. 'If that's what you mean. I put it on a stick, locked the computer down, got in a cab and came straight over.'

They were in Graves's loft in Greenwich Village. She was seated at the beechwood table in the airy living and dining area. Marlow and Lopez stood by the low arm-chairs and sofa which encircled a glass-topped coffee table.

Lopez hadn't been home. He'd decided to wait for day-light and, with it, came the realization that it would do no good to try to go it alone. There was no way he'd be able to translate the new information without Graves's help, and he'd realized after his moment of madness that the risks he was running wouldn't be worth the possible bene-fits. He just wasn't cut out for it. He recognized, at the same time, that he knew he was too scared to drive home in the dark. There might be watchers out there.

He'd rung Mia again, who was furious at being woken,

and waited until dawn. The light of day brought comfort and clarity. He knew he'd wasted precious time. He prayed that no one would catch him out in the lies he'd told Marlow to cover his tracks.

Lopez had arrived first, at 7 a.m., and Graves plugged the stick into her laptop as soon as he'd explained its content. She'd done a printout, and started work immediately.

Marlow arrived five minutes later, wearing an old Arran pullover and battered jeans.

'How long will it take?'

She looked up. 'Give me half an hour.'

Lopez thought: *They've got a night's start on us, and it's my fault.* 'I'll make coffee,' he said. He wondered if Annika's body had been discovered yet.

He busied himself behind the counter of the open-plan kitchen, glad of something to do. Marlow finally relaxed enough to sit down, but he was lost in thought and ignored the coffee Leon put next to him.

'How did you know this was important?' Marlow asked suddenly. His tone was friendly. Nevertheless, Lopez's heart jumped as he felt Marlow's eyes on him.

'I don't know – instinct, I guess. The manuscript looked as if it might belong to the timeframe we're looking at.'

Marlow said nothing more. Whatever he was thinking about absorbed him completely. From time to time he consulted his watch, and whenever he did so he also looked up at the old railway-station clock fixed high on one wall of the room, as if seeking confirmation from it.

The only sound was the gentle clunk of the clock's minute-hand. Graves would occasionally get up and take heavy tomes from her bookshelves, spreading them out on the table and consulting them, her pen scratching on a yellow pad.

At last she looked up, took off her glasses, rolled her shoulders to relax them and stretched her arms, out and up.

'Done?' asked Marlow.

'It's done.' She looked at Lopez. 'You were right about the code, Leon. It's close to the one on the shank of the key. Some variations, though – my guess is that it was created later by someone who had access to the key and managed to decipher what was written on it – maybe Dandolo himself.' She looked thoughtful for a moment. 'It still beats me why Yale couldn't do anything with –' She stopped herself as Marlow glanced at her. Her decoding of the inscription on the tablet – which Bishop Adhemar had mistakenly printed, giving him the mirror-image which he'd taken for a positive – had to remain between the two of them. Marlow's look had warned her.

Marlow cast a quick look at Leon to see if he'd picked up on the momentary tension in the air, but he was occupied in pouring coffee for Laura.

'Yes, and it's linked to the artefact, that's for sure. But as I said, it'll take time to unlock the other code.'

'Well, we're not going to ask Yale for help on this one,' said Marlow, looking again from one to the other of them.

Lopez thought he felt his boss's eye rest on him a moment longer than was necessary.

'I could sure as hell use a drink,' said Graves, pushing her coffee cup away. 'Leon, there's a bottle of Chablis in the fridge.'

'Tell us what you've got,' said Marlow. He noticed she

was wearing her emerald ring once again, and another, plain, on the little finger next to it. Plain, but broad enough to cover the little heart tattooed there.

Graves took a sip of the wine Lopez had poured her. 'This is what Frid writes,' she said. 'He was obviously close to Dandolo. As he was a Viking, he was probably a bodyguard. My guess from this is that he became a confidant because he was the one man around the doge whom Dandolo thought to be loyal *and* simple-minded enough to be trusted. This is a kind of will. But it's more than that. Maybe it's just that, at the end of his life, Frid needed to get things off his chest. By the time he dictated this, Dandolo was long dead. That's the background.' She paused, looking at them, then put her glasses back on and picked up her papers. 'He writes first about his personal bequests, and then hints that *there are greater riches still to be found if anyone should ever be bold enough to seek them.* He says he writes this *in contradiction of his master's instructions*, but only after a long struggle with his conscience. He says he would have made the journey to unearth the treasure himself, if infirmity hadn't prevented him from doing so.' She looked up. 'He was already old by the time Dandolo died, but he might also have been injured, wounded, who knows?'

'What riches?' asked Marlow; but he'd already guessed the truth.

'Dandolo ordered him to arrange things at his burial. He was to be buried' – she consulted her notes – '*with a certain box, with its key, and a tablet of clay.* These were to be secreted about his person, concealed in his robes, without anyone else knowing.'

'That would have been difficult,' said Marlow. 'Dandolo

must have invested Frid with the authority to oversee the burial. That way, he would have had total control of it.'

'Everything was buried with him, in accordance with his instructions,' Graves went on, 'and the funeral took place on' —again she consulted the papers she was holding — 'what looks like 25 June 1205, in Constantinople. *The doge was buried, again according to his instructions, in the aisle of Hagia Irina. Though the funeral was one of great ceremony, the grave was to be covered over, unmarked. Everyone approved of this as a mark of the doge's great charity, piety and modesty.*' She looked up. '*In the doge's hand lies the treasure I urge you to seek.*'

She fell silent.

'Falls into place,' said Marlow.

'Yes.'

'But no one knows where anything, other than the key, is now. The key was found by Adkins and his team, and taken from them.'

'But they can't have found the box or the tablet,' said Marlow.

'No.'

'So where are they?'

All three of them fell silent again.

'Can you make anything of the code yet?' asked Lopez.

Graves shook her head. 'The code will take a while.'

'You've done well so far,' said Marlow. 'Keep on it.'

Lopez thought, what if the others – the people who have the original – get there first? His stomach grew hollow, but he didn't dare level with his colleagues. All he could do was pray. There was something else. Marlow knew he was good with numerals. Why hadn't he been asked to collaborate?

'And the other writing? The stuff in Old Norse?' Marlow continued.

'It *is* Old Norse – you were right. It was penned by a kinsman of Frid's – someone who knew how to write, but only just – after Frid's death. It says he doesn't understand the Latin, but he's preserving the document, as it must be important, since Frid killed the scribe he dictated it to as soon as the job was finished.'

'Let's get on with the rest,' said Marlow. 'Leon, get back to INTERSEC. Trace whoever sent this to you. And – give this priority – do a search: museums and specialist antique dealers worldwide. We need to find that box.'

'OK,' said Lopez, happy to be away from them. All he wanted was for this nightmare to be over.

Marlow looked troubled after Lopez had gone, and Graves asked him why.

He shook his head. 'It's nothing. But Leon and I go back a long way – there was a bad business in Paris and I wouldn't be here now if it weren't for him. But he's holding something back. I can feel it.'

Graves shrugged. 'I think he's OK. He wouldn't go out on a limb.'

'Hmn.'

'He won't pick up that you didn't ask his help with the code?'

'Better that than him knowing what it is before we're sure he's solid. And what can he do? He knows he's covered,' said Marlow. 'And he has no copy.' A moment's pause. 'We need that box.'

'You think it still contains the tablet?'

'We can't assume that it doesn't. We need to locate it fast, before another Dandolo does.'

Marlow thought again about the Yale experts' failure to translate Adhemar's 'scroll'. 'Any further input from Dr de Montferrat?' Graves asked, just a trace of acid in her voice. 'You haven't mentioned her recently.'

Something flashed across Marlow's eyes before he answered. 'No progress. The new psychologist is good. Dr Shukman. She seems hopeful. But we've been there before.'

'Good luck with that.'

'Get started on this code right away. I'll be back to check progress after I've staved off Dick Hudson.'

'On to us again?'

'Fire down my neck.'

Graves tapped the papers in front of her. 'I'm on it.'

Marlow left her and, still troubled, made his way down to the street. But, once there, the direction he took wasn't the one which led to INTERSEC.

86

Berlin, the Present

It was just after dawn, but the newspapers were already neatly laid out on Adler's office desk, all the main European ones. He'd already seen the ones from Russia, India and China online.

Translations into German were appended wherever necessary. The papers from the US and South America would come later. And of course the news had already been slotted into the regular newscasts on his websites, and TV and radio stations worldwide.

He picked up the first paper, a copy of *Die Welt* so crisp he almost imagined the wretched Frau Müller ironed the things for him.

He thought about her briefly. Despite all her efforts, she really was getting too old and scrawny to be good for his company's image. He'd have to remember to fire her.

He read the headline on the first page of the business section with satisfaction:

MAXTEL OUSTS RIVALS IN KEY NICHES IN RUSSIAN, INDIAN AND CHINESE MEDIA AND ONLINE SECTORS. EYES FIXED ON BRAZIL AND IRAN.

The investment had paid off. The creditors were off his case. They weren't yet paid, and Adler knew his back would still be against the wall until they were, but it was time he threw his hat into the ring. It would send a warning to those who needed one, who needed to recognize this for what it was – a declaration of war.

Its downside was that he was gambling with chips he didn't yet have: everything depended on getting the one thing he needed to place him in full control.

India wasn't hard. China and Russia would be tough to bring to heel. But there were powerful billionaire oligarchs in all three countries now, not just in Russia; not to mention the politicians and the hardened criminals.

But he'd start with the oligarchs.

China was paramount, with its economic stranglehold on the West.

Adler squared his shoulders at the prospect. He was optimistic. He was confident that those who'd benefited from MAXPHIL's investment in the cultural and academic world would show their gratitude by coming up with a translation of the key part of the document, which Trotter and Sparkes had lifted from the Swedish girl, within the twenty-four hours he'd given them. These days, universities were more and more dependent on private charitable trusts for funding. They'd hate it if that money were withdrawn.

Adler was pleased that Annika Lundquist had left such a clear ethernet trail when she attempted to make contact with INTERSEC. His people hadn't been able to ascertain precisely with whom, but that didn't matter. The important thing was that the information had arrived in time for him to intercept her material, and the material looked promising. His people had assured him that she'd been able to pass nothing on, and he could trust his people. They knew what would happen if he found they had let him down.

But they'd done well already. The Latin part of the document was enough to be getting on with. So, there was a box, and the box contained the tablet, and the box was at least nine hundred years old. He was sure, now, that his rivals didn't have it, so the trail in that direction was cold.

Adler shrugged to himself. No matter. There were other directions to take. And he'd been getting ever more favourable reports from New York.

It was simply a question of waiting for the prey to enter the trap. And that wouldn't take long now.

87

New York City, the Present

Marlow woke in the middle of the night.

He was back at his own apartment. He had left Su-Lin late the previous evening.

They had made love with their usual hunger; but when it was over, something prompted him not to stay till morning. She'd been disappointed, had sulked a little after she had tried, and failed, to pull him back to her bed.

'It's your safety I have in mind. I don't want to leave you.'

'Then don't. I'm safe with you.'

'The more I visit you here, the higher the risk. Someone always notices in the end.'

'Then let's move – take me somewhere else. I can't be without you.'

But there was something cornered in his mind. Something he found it difficult to deny. He knew he couldn't hold it off for ever. His professionalism, everything he stood for, told him that. But he couldn't accept it.

At first, when he woke, he thought he was back in the Paris flat, but then the more familiar, reassuring surroundings asserted themselves. This was the real thing. This was home, as far as he had anywhere he could call home.

He got up and struggled to remember what it was that had awakened him.

But this was work. Nothing to do with his other misgivings, he knew that. Something to do with what he should be concentrating on. It turned on a question he'd overlooked, or which hadn't seemed important at the time.

He showered and dressed abstractedly, and was going through the motions of making coffee when it came to him. He looked at the clock on the oven. Four a.m. It would be 10 a.m. in Istanbul.

He hesitated between email and calling, but he needed to talk, to describe, and get an immediate response. The blue phone, the safe line, was in his living-room, concealed in a compartment built into the bookshelves. He made for it, dialled a number, and waited as he listened to the series of clicks which preceded his connection to INTERSEC's switchboard.

'Marlow,' he said when he was through. 'Section 15. Ultra-secure.'

Another moment while his voice pattern was verified.

'How may I help you?' said the preppy voice at the other end.

'Detective Major Haki, Istanbul.'

More clicks, then a profound silence. Seconds later, the ring tone. Three times, then the phone at the other end was picked up. A moment's further silence for the security check at the Turkish end. Then Haki's voice, genial as ever: 'Hello, Jack.'

'I want you to do something for me, Cemil.'

'I rather gathered this wasn't a social call. What time must it be where you are?'

413

'The gloves. The gloves you found at the dig. The ones your Forensics said were a hundred years old.'

'Yes. I remember them. They're still in our lab.'

'I want you to get them back to Forensics. Urgently. I want them to go to work on the gloves. Anything they can pick up. Traces on them, DNA –'

'That'd be a very long shot.'

'Never mind. Mineral traces, anything they might have touched, where they might have come from.'

'I'll get them to try. After a century, it'll put them on their mettle to find anything at all.'

'Get them to work fast.'

'Front of the queue. Now.'

Marlow, all thought of sleep shaken from him, went down to the basement to collect his car.

Room 55 was deserted, the desks and tables clear. Lopez hadn't left anything for prying eyes to see, but there was a message on Marlow's terminal:

There aren't many iron boxes the right size and period left in the world today. Iron rusts and rots with time, unless it is kept in optimum conditions. Those that are left fetch high prices on the market. One located in the British Museum, London, another was bought by the Getty Foundation three years ago. There's a third in the Hermitage, and a fourth in a private collection in Lausanne, which I've been able to access. The fifth is in Le Clos Lucé at Amboise, in France. The problem is that all have provenances which seem watertight, completely reliable, and none has anything which fits in with what we're looking for.

The dealers are a little more promising. One example in particular, which was bought from an unknown vendor by Lightoller and

Steeples of Madison Avenue in 1946 and resold by them at auction a year or so later. I've yet to trace what happened to it, but although L&S closed down in 1960, some of their transactions may still be on record at the Internal Revenue Service. Unlikely they've been transferred to the IRS computer centre in Maryland, so they may still exist in the vaults in Washington. Report on this follows.

There was a space, before Lopez's narrative continued, the time showing five hours later than his first entry.

Found it. IRS very helpful and there were fully descriptive invoices still on file for several items. This is ours: Iron box, 10 centimetres by eight, five centimetres deep, locked, key missing. Box had never been opened. Finely chased, decorated and inscribed. Probably French origin, date estimated: last quarter of eleventh century. L&S made a good profit on it, by the look of things. Their payment for it recorded but no trace of what happened to it or who might have picked it up. Was to have been drawn on Morgan's in New York, so will follow up. No other information. Investigation ongoing. Will send copy of original documentation soonest.

Marlow closed the message and dragged it to a safe file. It would auto-delete in twenty-four hours if he didn't countermand.

Marlow scented blood, but scenting it was a long way from tasting it.

88

Haki's return call came in the early evening.

'That was fast.'

'We're up to date here,' said Haki. 'CIA funded. They like to keep us chaps on the front line well equipped.'

Marlow didn't smile. If Turkey ceased to be a secular state, the West would have to brace itself. Fleetingly, he thought of the Ottoman empire. How the Turkish emperors had once held sway as far west as the gates of Vienna. That had been in the seventeenth century. A floodtide which Dandolo's action in Constantinople, four hundred years earlier than that, had unleashed.

'What have you got for me?'

'Verbal or shall I send?'

'Verbal.'

'Gist then. Full technical to Section 15, immediate.'

'That'd be good.'

'OK.' Haki paused briefly, and over the line Marlow heard paper crackle. 'Here it is,' Haki went on. 'The gloves were made in Germany, possibly Austro-Hungary, before 1914, but they're not much older than that. Very little material on them, after all this time, but there *are* traces of sand, and earth, of course – and what could be baked clay, a minute quantity, on the right and left thumb and index fingertips. There are also traces of what could be rust – red iron oxide – but they're microscopic particles, and we'll have to do further tests. Our people found them on the palms and the inner parts of the fingers and thumbs of both gloves.'

'DNA?' said Marlow.

'As I said, that'll be a long shot. But we're working on it.'

'Thank you. Anything else you get, send to me fast,' said Marlow.

'Flying-carpet treatment, dear boy.'

Haki was as good as his word, Marlow thought, when, two hours later, another call came from Istanbul – past midnight by then in the Turkish city.

But it wasn't Haki's voice on the line. It was a voice he didn't recognize. Urgent, bordering on panic.

'This is Colonel Demir. You won't be getting that full report you requested soon. There's been a bomb. Al-Qaeda, we think, but that's just first indications.'

Marlow went cold. 'Where?'

'Car on Defter Emini. Just outside Forensics. Massive explosion.'

'Casualties?'

'Three fatalities. Major Haki's one of them. God knows how they found the location. And why they picked that target. We'll keep you updated. But terrorists, for sure.'

Marlow, his throat dry, hung up.

He wasn't so sure.

89

Geoffrey de Villehardouin listened while his secretary ran over what he had dictated. He wondered how much he should leave in his final, official account. Much had happened. He wanted Doge Dandolo to be happy with what he had written:

> After the victory, and the coronation of Emperor Baldwin which followed soon afterwards, came the division of the spoils.
>
> The foul weather which had followed the victory had passed. The ships were no longer battened down, though the camp, where the foot-soldiers still lived, was a mire. But in the city, still wrapped in the remains of its magnificence, despite its rape, the mood was buoyant. Boniface, grim at first at not having been offered the crown, had emerged radiant after a meeting with the doge, and even suggested that he himself should place the imperial cope on Baldwin's shoulders – the crown, and the orb and sceptre, were to be presented by Dandolo.
>
> There were now two armies in the city. Boniface's, stationed to the south-west by the Golden Gate, was busy with its preparations for departure for Greece,

418

where a kingdom lay open for the taking. Baldwin's was occupied with repairing the fortifications they themselves had broken down, and entrenching themselves in readiness for imposing dominion over their leader's new empire.

Pockets of Greek resistance within and around the city had been mercilessly crushed. The main enemy leadership had withdrawn, to Bulgaria, Hungary and Nicea.

His secretary stopped reading and Geoffrey sat back, satisfied. But there was much that Geoffrey did not know.

The Venetians had awaited a break in the weather with impatience. They needed to overhaul the fleet.

Dandolo felt the sun on his face, and smiled. Work on the great, secret ocean-going warships would continue now. The secret ships, whose existence was veiled to the eyes of all but a few.

All thought of Jerusalem was forgotten. There were other things to think about now.

Hundreds of works of art had been melted down by the Crusaders and turned into coin to pay the Venetians the balance which was owed, and Leporo was busy, rescuing what remained, supervising their packing and transfer to the transport ships which would return to Venice with them.

'The religious trophies will provide us with a special glory,' he reported to Dandolo, on a day when the sun had finally banished the last of the clouds.

'Good,' replied the doge, his mind elsewhere. There was no further need to use the power of the tablet on

Leporo. He was already caught in the snare of his own greed. Dandolo was sure of that.

Leporo's value to him had diminished. Dandolo was thinking now of his conversations with Frid about the great voyage to the country far across the great sea to the west. The land there was wide, and open, and fertile. There would be riches beyond the imaginings of Europe. And God *would* grant him the time to harvest them.

Time. He peered at his hands. He could barely see them, and not at all unless he moved them. In five years, less, those hands would no longer exist. They would be dust. He would have gone. He would have *gone*.

The remains of a man, turned to dust, weigh no more than a new-born baby. Time.

'Abbot Martin has been collecting in St Pantokrator. And his monks have been busy in the Greek monasteries and churches beyond the city walls.'

'Excellent,' Dandolo said.

'Barely any need to threaten,' Leporo went on, needing his master's approval and hating himself for that need. 'Abbot Martin looks the part – a fellow prelate. The Archimandrite Nicanor at Pantokrator filled sacks for him. There is a reliquary with the very finger Doubting Thomas thrust into the wound of Christ. There is still blood on it.'

'Have it all shipped. Present the finger to the Vatican, with my humble respects. It will please the idiot who sits on the throne there.'

'Cardinal Peter is already sending favourable messages ahead.'

'I am glad of it.'

Leporo watched Dandolo. The doge was at the window of an opulent room in the Palace of Boucoleon, gazing out across the harbour below, where his great ships were anchored. Only the eyes of the seamen who worked on them, and the eyes of Frid, were not clouded by the power of the tablet. Dandolo had seen to that. Only they could see the true magnificence of those ships. The secret was safe from the others, including Leporo.

But Leporo's mind was not on the ships. His own eyes roved Dandolo's office, once a stately conference chamber of the old regime. His eyes wandered keenly over the surfaces of richly carved tables, rested on the handles of drawers and chests, on the dusty wall-hangings and draped silks and brocades still lying where they had fallen in the attacks.

He was taking advantage of the rare absence of Frid. Frid was at the harbour. Frid would have noticed, might even have guessed what he was looking for. Inwardly, Leporo cursed the Viking for the hundredth time, as his mind cast about for a way of bringing him down.

He could see no clue, and he didn't dare start a search. But he had to make his move before Dandolo sent him back to Venice with the booty. Or before the old man died.

The old man? Leporo was getting old himself. His own time was running out.

He knew Dandolo sometimes left the tablet locked in its box, in a secret drawer, though never for long. It was like a drug to him, though it seemed to Leporo that the doge was afraid it was drawing too much of his own remaining strength, his own will.

Was he carrying it now? Leporo eyed his master and, as he did so, saw the right hand tighten under the sleeve of the robe.

90

New York City, the Present

Marlow sat on the sofa, his old tweed jacket thrown across its back, across the coffee table from Graves. They were in her apartment. She sat on one of the low easy-chairs. She was wearing a skirt instead of jeans, and now she crossed her legs and leaned back a little. She looked dressed to go out. The grey skirt was close-fitting fine wool, and the black silk roll-neck she wore with it hugged her figure. The two together had cost a fortnight's salary.

'The code is the same kind as the one on the key,' she said, 'but it's corrupted somehow, either because whoever wrote it didn't understand what they were doing as well as they thought they did, or it's deliberate – as if the person *wanted* to make it impenetrable. There's a way in, there always is, but it's like feeling your way in the dark, through a maze.'

'Then let's think laterally.'

'There's another thing. I have to report to INTERSEC. My absence has been noticed.'

'You answer to me.'

She shook her head. 'Sir Richard is concerned. You haven't reported to him yourself.'

'That's where I'm headed now. I can't risk him alerting Homeland Security. They'll blow everything.'

Graves recognized the warning note in his voice, but said, 'He wants to know what's going on, Jack.'

'I wonder how much he knows already.'

Graves, thinking of the information Lopez had let slip, nodded.

'Damage limitation.' Marlow continued. 'All we can do.'

'I'll give him a progress report. Throw him some candy.'

'Do that.' He leafed through Graves's work on the code, frowning. 'Don't tell him we're on to Yale – why they said they couldn't translate the writing on the tablet.'

'If Yale knows – who might they be working for?'

'The CIA? Homeland? But what would they make of it? Big organizations like that always take time to filter things. And the politicians get underfoot. So we still have time on our side.'

Graves crossed her legs again. 'Hudson wants me there now. I'll keep on working on this as soon as I've shaken him off.' She took her papers back from Marlow, accidentally touching his fingers with hers.

'Good. Keep working on it. I'll join you again as soon as I can.' Marlow stood. 'Let's go. I'll give you a lift back to INTERSEC. Need to check with Leon and show my face.' He paused, though, irritated. 'Why's Hudson sticking his oar in now? This is what you should be concentrating on.' He waved at her dining-table, her laptop an island in a sea of books and papers.

'Girl's gotta have a break. Anyway, I'll work on it tonight.' A hesitation. 'Nothing else to do,' she added; but Marlow wasn't listening.

She secured the apartment and they left.

There was something new about him, she thought,

watching him. Something had changed, but she couldn't place what.

She looked at the tattoo on her finger, and caressed it ruefully.

Leon Lopez had made progress. '*If* this is what we're after,' he said, showing Marlow the webpage. But they'd scarcely entered Room 55 when a call came through from Sir Richard, summoning Graves to his office. Word must have passed immediately from the hotel lobby to his secretary. 'Do you want to wait for Graves?'

'Tell her after her audience with Hudson.'

'OK. This is it.'

The page was from the website of Sotheby's, New York, and it advertised a forthcoming sale of medieval antiquities. Lot 4249 was the iron box Leon had already identified as a possible candidate. It was described as a '(?) jewellery casket or coffer'. The description went on to mention that it was locked and that the key was missing; but there was still a hefty reserve price of $100,000. A small photograph of the box appeared, together with a short note of its provenance, which dated from 1946, with its acquisition by Lightoller and Steeples. Since 1948 it had been in the possession of the Ashworth Foundation, and displayed in its small museum in Pittsburgh. It had been sold when the foundation hit difficulties in the mid-1970s, and had since been part of a private collection owned by the industrialist George M. Bamberger. Bamberger had died the previous year and the collection had been broken up for sale by his two sons.

'What do you think?' Lopez asked Marlow. 'These

things are pretty rare. I haven't been able to locate a closer match.'

'When's the sale?'

'Friday.'

'Gives us about a week. We'll need a budget for this. If the reserve's $100,000 –' Marlow thought. 'Put in for $250,000.'

'That much?'

'We can't let this go.'

'Can we justify it?'

'I'll think of something. In any case,' Marlow added drily, 'Sir Richard has found us a new benefactor.'

'Who?'

'Rolf Adler. MAXTEL wants to be as closely involved as possible in getting to the bottom of this. MAXPHIL bankrolled the Dandolo Project.'

'I hope Hudson's not trading off somehow.'

'Adler thinks we're INTERPOL. And don't forget, he wouldn't have been able to do this without government approval.'

'International government approval.'

Marlow shrugged. 'I don't like it either, but MAXTEL's a multinational – and you know what governments are like about money these days. Any source is OK. Everything's for sale. Not that it'll do any good. We all know that we've already passed the tipping-point. Clearing debts in the West is just a pipedream, now.'

Lopez nodded.

'Though maybe all that's about to change,' said Marlow thoughtfully.

'The tablet?'

'Control.'

'Name of the game.'

'So who *is* after this tablet?' asked Lopez.

'Someone who believes it can be used to put the world to rights? Who knows? Someone with a vision of how to sort things out, if they're allowed to have their own way.'

'Order through dictatorship?'

'Brave New World. It wouldn't be the first time. Every civilization there's ever been is based on something similar.'

'But they've always crumbled, and people have survived.'

'There's a first time for everything,' said Marlow.

'We've got to find that tablet!' Lopez's mind flashed on Annika, sitting in the coffee-house. *Anything to make amends*, he thought.

'Find the box, and we're home. Maybe . . . You should just catch Accounts today. Spin them whatever line you like. We should be OK with this. We haven't had to call in the cavalry, and compared with the cost of one Tomahawk, we're a cheap date.'

'I'm on to it.'

Auctions are very public affairs, but Marlow intended to bid in person. He wouldn't use a front. He needed his people to see this through on their own, but he could hardly keep it under wraps, and he wanted Graves to be there with him. 'Tell Laura. Get her to contact me.'

'Where are you going?'

'Tell you later.'

'What about Hudson?'

'He can wait.'

427

'Where can she get you?'

'Secure cell. But later. There's something I have to do first.'

Marlow left the building soon afterwards. There was still the other, unfinished business.

He dived into the crowded streets, and made his way to the nearest subway. He took a train to 49th and 7th, and walked the rest of the way from there.

91

Berlin, the Present

It was the best news.

He was sitting at his desk. Night had fallen, and Berlin glowed beneath him, bathed in thousands of lights. The office, illuminated only by the desk-lamp, was wrapped in deep shadows. The red glow from the MAXTEL neon on the roof found its way into the room, and stained his face and hands.

He reread the translation he held in his hands. It had taken twenty-four hours longer than he'd hoped, but it brought him a step nearer his goal. The box had been traced. Meanwhile, his assistants in Venice and at Yale were working on the code in the Frid document, which they had, so far, been unable to break.

The code held the secret, Adler was certain. But if all went well he could manage without it. Once he had the box. No one had been able to open it, as far as he knew, since it was last locked, nine hundred years before. And he had the key.

He had gone to so much trouble and expense over those damned archaeologists. But he knew from their special qualifications that he wasn't the only one, apart from INTERSEC, interested in the box. He wasn't the only one who knew Dandolo's secret, careful as he'd been to cover the tracks of his own investigation. But the manner of their deaths would have sent a warning to his competitors. They'd know someone was wise to them.

But who were they? And was INTERSEC working for them?

But why worry? Once he had the box, and had opened it, any competition would be neutralized.

He looked at his watch, waiting impatiently for the call from New York. At last, at 8 p.m., 2 p.m. EST, it came.

The telephone barely had a chance to complete one ring.

'Yes?' he said, tonelessly.

The voice at the other end was measured. No panic, no urgent need to propitiate him before getting to the point. He liked that.

'I mentioned they had a lead,' said the voice.

'Yes.'

'They've narrowed the field down.'

'Tell me.'

'The targeted item is selling at Sotheby's on York Avenue here. Lot 4249.'

'Guaranteed what we want?'

'Worth the gamble.'

'Reserve?'

'$100,000.'

Adler came close to laughing. The box was as good as his. 'When?'

'Friday.'

'Time?'

'Ten a.m. 4249 is fifth up. Morning session.'

'We'll cover it. Who's bidding for them?'

'My guess is Marlow.'

'In person?'

'Yes.'

'Seems risky.'

'We know what he's like. He'll want to view the room. Look for us. No one knows him, he thinks. No photographs, no public ID anywhere.'

Adler saw that. A man like Marlow would have no traceable public documents; not a tax record, not a bank or any other account, not a driving licence, no birth certificate, no property deeds, nothing. But he had left clues about his life, despite himself. And exploiting those was Adler's main strength now. He congratulated himself on his success in that direction so far.

'Other bidders of interest to us?' he went on.

'Three big museums. Two important private collectors.'

'Check their limits.'

There was a pause.

'Are you coming over?'

'Yes,' said Adler.

'How will you bid?'

'Phone.'

'Won't you do that ex-Berlin?'

Adler smiled to himself. 'I need to be there.'

Adler hung up without saying more. The tension left his shoulders. He felt the elation he always felt when battle was about to be joined. But battles should never have unknown outcomes. He picked up the yellow phone, and tapped in a number.

He had to be sure this was a battle he would win.

92

New York City, the Present

The auction room was two-thirds full, but it was still early. Marlow and Graves sat five rows back, aisle seats with a view of the auctioneer and the lots. Graves had been to the viewing and examined the box. The lid had a raised relief of an eagle, its wings outstretched, its talons ready to clutch, and its head down, beak poised. Around the sides of the box, people and animals cowered in various attitudes of terror and prayer. Only one man, in the centre at the front, was bold enough to stand tall, his arms held up, his hands holding a small, irregularly shaped object. The box stood on simple ball feet. It gleamed under the halogen spot which lit it. It looked brand-new, not a trace of wear or damage. But for the artistic style of the moulding, you would not have guessed its true age.

Five INTERSEC agents, three female, two male, were seated elsewhere in the room, three discreetly scanning the bidders in the saleroom, two ready to watch the telephone bidders ranged along one wall near the auctioneer's lectern. Lopez sat towards the rear, away from them.

When Lot 4249 came up, the room had filled to 80 per cent capacity. Lopez recognized two department heads of big American museums, one of them the Met. He picked up German and French voices. The smell of money was palpable.

No sealed bids, and no online interest, or from the House. That was unusual, but Marlow let it go, for there *was* interest – strong interest – from seven or eight people right from the start, including three on the telephones, and within a minute the box had passed its reserve.

An elegant woman with dark-red, curly hair dressed in Vivienne Westwood raised a gloved hand a fraction, to bid $150,000. Marlow noticed she wore a hearing-aid.

'Do I see $160,000?' The crisp, English voice of the auctioneer, Marlborough or Wellington to his fingertips, rang out.

A bear of a German in a charcoal suit nodded discreetly.

'170?'

A nod from a smart girl on the first phone.

'180?'

A bearded man in tinted glasses shook his head and looked down at his catalogue, making a note with his pen. The redhead raised a fingertip once more.

'190?'

The price passed $200,000, and it was down to three in the room against two on the phones.

When it hit $250,000, one of the phone bidders hung up.

'We're done, too,' said Graves. But Marlow raised his hand again. The enormous German across the room hesitated, then raised his.

'We're done, Jack,' insisted Graves.

'No we're not,' he replied. He grinned. 'You know how it is – everything goes over budget.'

Graves looked over her shoulder towards the back of the room, hoping to catch Lopez's eye, but she couldn't see him. The room was now full, and the atmosphere was beginning to show heat.

By $300,000, only one of the phone bidders remained.

'310?'

A nod from the German.

'320?'

A fingertip from the redhead.

At $370,000, the German pursed his lips. At $400,000, he signalled that he was out.

Now the room was humming; the item had passed five times its reserve. It was between Marlow, the redhead and the phone bidder.

'They'll kill you for this,' said Graves, sotto voce.

'Perhaps.'

'Stop.'

'It'll go on Adler's bill. And how can we stop?'

Graves sat back, her face set.

At $750,000, the redhead, looking as if she'd just lost her mother, closed her catalogue and crossed her legs, sitting back.

'Are we sure?' asked the auctioneer.

The woman hesitated, momentarily putting a hand to her deaf-aid. Then she changed her mind, smiled, and the fingertip went up.

Still a three-horse race.

Adler, in the Grand Suite at the Pierre, followed the progress of the auction on the television link to his laptop, and scowled. Decision made, he reached for the yellow cell-phone, one of three on the table next to him. He spoke into it briefly. The Cottbus-boy in him wasn't going to part with that much money for something he could get for nothing. And there was another consideration. That *Scheißkästchen* Marlow was well past his limit, and he mustn't get the box at any cost.

The price had hit $900,000 when the telephone bidder hung up. The redhead had just raised her finger to up it another fifty against Marlow when the auctioneer faltered, his attention caught by a disturbance at the back of the room. Seconds later, a stutter of automatic fire shattered the plasterwork of the ceiling. It tumbled in chips and flakes on to the yelling people below, who parted like the Red Sea, stumbling over chairs and each other in a scramble to get out of range.

A broad aisle was created in the space vacated by bidders and spectators, an aisle which led straight down the centre of the room from the main doorway to the auctioneer's lectern and the podium on which it stood. The auctioneer grasped its sides, frozen. The attendant standing by the box where it lay on a small table covered with a plum-coloured velvet cloth, crouched down.

At the far end of the aisle five hooded figures in combat gear fanned out, two on each side, while the fifth made his way fast down the length of the room to the podium. Each had a nylon belt at his waist, attached to which were a Kevlar commando-knife and a holster from which projected the butt of a Walther P99. In the hands of the four covering the room were new Magpul PDRs, and it was from one of these that the rapid fire had come.

Marlow, bent low with an arm protectively round Graves's back, took in the weapons at a glance. These were no ordinary criminals. He risked a look round the room, but couldn't see Lopez or any of the other INTER-SEC operatives. He hoped they'd see sense. This was no place to start a gun battle, let alone against such formidable arms.

Two more salvoes followed, low over the heads of the cowering crowd, as the leader of the group reached the podium and snatched the box from the table, placing it in a soft black pouch slung across his shoulders. The attendant collapsed like a puppet with its strings cut, while the auctioneer, chalk-white, found time to thank God that the lectern he stood at hid from view the wet stain which had flowered at his groin.

A minute later, the attack force had gone, leaving a silence in the room as profound as the seabed. The redhead was nowhere to be seen; nor was the attendant who'd taken the telephone bid.

93

For two days the media had screamed about it. But there had been no deaths, not even any casualties, so the news wasn't hot. Who cared about an antique fought over by a handful of privileged people? A spokesman for Sotheby's appeared on Sky News, and the big German was interviewed by NDR and the *Frankfurter Allgemeine*. He'd been bidding for the Bodemuseum in Berlin.

'We've got to find it,' said Graves.

'And we've got to crack the code in Frid Eyolfson's letter,' said Marlow. 'We're not the only people working on it.'

'What do you mean?' asked Lopez nervously.

'Whoever has the original document your mysterious contact sent us knows as much as we do.'

'Or as little,' said Graves.

'That's a slim, slim chance and we can't make any assumptions based on it,' replied Marlow. 'They may know more already. The essential thing is, they've got the box and the key, which means they've got the tablet.'

'*That's* an assumption,' said Lopez.

'Everything links the tablet to that box,' replied Graves.

'But there's no evidence yet that anyone is using the tablet.'

Lopez was silent, thinking.

'No trace of who sent the document?' Marlow asked him.

'Nothing so far,' Lopez replied, thinking, *now would be my chance to tell them*.

'The INTERSEC backup at Sotheby's only knew what they had to,' Marlow said. 'If we have to do a major sweep, we'll have to be more candid than we have been with Sir Richard.'

'Can we avoid that?' said Graves.

'That's what I'm hoping. But I want you back at your apartment soonest, to report on those five lines of cipher. Go back to the inscription on the key. The codes must be linked. Sort out the bridge.'

'Who was bidding against us?' asked Lopez suddenly.

'One of them was a bad loser,' said Marlow. 'And it wasn't the redhead.'

'Why bid at all, if you were going to come in and grab the thing anyway?' said Graves.

'That was a last resort – we went too high for them.'

'There was the woman – the redhead,' said Graves.

'And there was the phone-bid, the last one left standing,' said Lopez.

'Neither of them showed any sign of stopping when the auction was interrupted,' said Marlow. 'Except for the moment with the deaf-aid.'

'What?' said Graves.

'The deaf-aid. She hesitated but then she continued – as if she'd got authorization to go on. And it wasn't a deaf-aid.'

'She was pretty distinctive,' said Lopez. 'We could give a description to the cops.'

'The hair was a wig – could have been, anyway – and

once she's taken off the Westwood outfit, she's as anonymous as she wants to be,' said Graves.

'Get someone up here to do a facial composite,' said Marlow. 'Then put it direct through a secure server with the FBI, see if they've got any matches if we haven't.'

'Jeez, how many people do you want to involve?'

'Use the INTERPOL cover. And see if we can trace the call. The phone bidder. There had to be someone on the other end of that line. It's possible there'll be an electronic record. And Sotheby's CCTV. Do they have an outside camera?'

'Sure thing.'

'The box was already close to ten times its face value when the bidder lost patience. And that redhead – who knows how high she was authorized to go?' Marlow paused. 'Something else: how did our competitor get wind of the auction, and make the connection as fast as we did?'

94

'There's material on the interior CCTV,' Lopez reported to Marlow later.

'Shoot.'

'Clear images, but they don't do us much good. Three of them were slightly built.'

'Women can handle those lightweight weapons as easily as men. They think more clinically too – maybe that's why the operation was so well handled. Have you thrown out a net?'

'Yes. But they'll be long gone by now. Better footage from outside.'

'Go on.'

'Arrival and getaway. Three motorbikes, all Vulcan 900s, got a number-plate on one. Tracked it.'

'You've got a *number-plate*?'

'Believe it or not. It's registered to Andrei Borovsky. He's a partner in a firm called Zwinger and Dels, with offices in the Bronx. Make leather goods – handbags, belts, wallets, that kind of thing. The senior partner's called Sergei Kutuzov. Russian new money, took over an existing German firm three years ago.'

'Some kind of front?'

'No links yet, so officially these guys are clean. The bike was stolen twenty-four hours ago. Borovsky reported it to the local cops, but not until 2 p.m. this afternoon.'

'Could be a connection. Check on them, especially this Kutuzov. Try the FSB in Moscow. Our embed there. Colonel Safin.'

'Will do. Should I get them to check out Zwinger and Dels?'

'Hold off for now. We don't want to frighten the horses. Anything from Laura?'

'She's gone back to the Frid code. Left what she had with me on the facial comp.' Lopez looked quizzically at Marlow. 'Something odd here. She thinks so too.'

'Go on.'

'She set up the facial composite deal OK. We got a pretty good likeness – as the woman looked when she was at the sale, as she might look with her hair dragged back, and dressed in a coat from Bershka. But the face *is* distinctive, strong. We tried different makeup applications, the effect of different-coloured contact lenses, and the face still shone through them. Eyes, especially. But here's the thing: we tried the FBI and the CIA, and both dragged their feet, claimed computer glitches, then, finally, said they hadn't anything like her. Think something's behind that?'

'Homeland, you mean?'

'Could be.'

'No. This whole deal is ultra-secure within our section.'

'Sure?'

Marlow was silent for a moment then said: 'What about *our* files? I guess you checked them first.'

'Sure did. And – go figure – a whole swathe cut through. Fifteen files missing – all women of the right age and ethnic group.'

441

Marlow closed his eyes, and opened them again. 'OK,' he said. 'Leon, you've got to give this your very best shot. There are too many players on the pitch.'

'Sure.'

'I'm going to see Hudson.'

'He's not here. Washington. Day conference with joint chiefs.'

'Shit – when was that called?'

'He left an hour ago. Emergency session.'

The blue phone buzzed discreetly. Marlow picked it up, pressed the flashing 5 button. 'Yes?'

'Laura. Got something. Maybe. Come over?'

'On my way.'

Lopez watched him go, and turned back to his work. He felt stronger now, surer of himself. If he could crack this, make even a little headway for them, he'd be able to erase some of his error. Things had gone too far. If his mistake came to light now, he wouldn't be looking at dismissal any more, he'd be looking at a coffin.

95

'There's more on the tablet here,' said Graves. 'Just a clue in the first couple of lines I've been able to decipher. The problem is that it's written in a kind of shorthand, which makes it harder to crack. You've got to understand the symbols, and then understand what they're abbreviations of. It's kind of a mathematical code which you have to get into before you can get at the letters, and they're encoded too.'

Marlow nodded.

'It proves the importance the tablet has,' continued Graves. 'The last three lines are beginning to look as if they contain a clue about where it ended up exactly, when Dandolo died, but the encryption there's got me, so far.'

'Give me what you have.'

'This is what Dandolo learned from the man who deciphered the writing on the tablet for him. An Armenian monk.' She pushed her glasses up her nose. 'At the time, they knew the tablet was very old – it was the Armenian who put Dandolo right on Adhemar's mistake. It was made in about 3000BC, which makes it five thousand years old now.' She looked at him. 'It was created somewhere in Mesopotamia –'

'Confirms everything.'

'Fertile crescent then. Where civilization began. There's more. They grasped far more than we thought possible about the principles of astrophysics and quantum mechanics, though they didn't see them in scientific terms, more as forces of nature – of the supernatural. But the formulae on the tablet show a man how to harness those forces to influence – control – people and events.'

'So, using this, you could create your perfect world?'

'Yes – a world shaped to your ambitions.'

'Jesus!'

'You can trace its progress. Long before Babylon fell to Cyrus the Great, the tablet must have passed into Egypt via the Assyrian campaigns there. The Great Pyramid of Giza was built in about 2500BC. It's built of 2,500,000 limestone blocks, but even more stunning is its alignment: the sides of the base match the compass points with a deviation of only twelve seconds of arc. How did they achieve such a thing so early?'

'Go on.'

'The Assyrians re-conquered Egypt later, much later, and the tablet came back to them, because there was a last flowering of Mesopotamia and Babylon under Nebuchadnezzar the Great, about two and a half thousand years ago. After that, it may have passed from the Babylonians – Belshazzar was the last nominal ruler – to Cyrus, when he conquered the country. This is speculative, but the Armenian was on the right track. He traces the tablet's progress through Cyrus all the way to Pericles of Athens in about 460BC, the Greek Golden Age, and from him to Alexander the Great and Julius Caesar. The trail goes on until it reaches Constantine, the Roman emperor who converted to Christianity in about AD350, and made all Europe follow him in the

Faith. Constantine was also the founder of a great city –'

'Constantinople.'

'It all fits.' Marlow drove a fist into his palm.

'It's speculative, but, yes. All the people I've mentioned who were connected with the tablet were bent on absolute global power; and, in their terms, they succeeded in getting it.'

'Though they never kept it.'

'That must have been when the tablet passed from them.'

'Or their power to use it waned.'

'Now that *is* speculative!'

'In the hands of any individual – any power – this would be an unimaginable force.'

'Childhood dream: the world you want.'

Marlow's face cleared. 'Business,' he said.

'What?'

'What rules the world now? Business. Big business. Banks. Multinationals. And how are people influenced?'

'Through the media?' said Graves.

'So who'd be best placed to benefit from knowing how to use this thing?'

Graves pondered this then replied: 'Unless a government – a powerful government – beat them to it.'

Marlow fell silent, and continued to pace the room, lost in urgent thought. 'Get on with that,' he said. 'Because, however Leon got that document, the original *is still out there somewhere.*'

96

The following day, Lopez reported back. 'We've got nothing on the woman bidder – dead end everywhere. I've traced our files – "glitch in the system", as you know – but they're all back in place now, and none of them matches our target.'

Marlow was looking through the files himself as Graves leaned over his shoulder. Two computer screens were set up in Lopez's laboratory area, one with Graves's facial composite, the other showing each of the fifteen INTER-SEC breakdowns on likely matches. Nothing. They went through them again. The third time, Lopez interrupted the sequence on number five.

'Wait,' he said. 'Someone's altered this. The date on this image doesn't tally with the date on the backup info.'

Marlow looked at the screen hard. The general backup information had last been updated fifteen days earlier. The date on the image was . . .

'Day before yesterday!' he said.

'That fits,' said Lopez. 'Someone's not as clever as they thought they were.'

They looked at each other.

'Keep on this, Leon,' said Marlow. 'Don't let it go, wherever it leads. But be careful.'

Lopez nodded. 'If they're watching, there's nowhere to hide.'

'Throw up a smokescreen.'

'If they make mistakes like this, they must be too confident for their own good.'

'Or they think we're more stupid than we look,' said Marlow.

'There's a better trail on the bike,' said Lopez. 'Colonel Safin came up with some interesting background.'

'Go on.'

'This Sergei Kutuzov. Money scattered around everywhere, mainly in tax havens. Registered business address in the Turks and Caicos Islands, but he's got clusters of companies in Liechtenstein, Guernsey, the Seychelles and Vanuatu. None linked to any identifiable parent bank accounts routed through places like Bolivia and Uruguay. Hard to pin down.'

'Globe-trotter,' said Marlow, reading the information Lopez had handed him. 'Quite a stash for a leatherware merchant.'

'He's a minor oligarch. Made a pile during the Yeltsin sell-off in the 1990s. Got a complicated partnership network. Safin came up with two principal names: an Indian software mogul called – wait a minute, name here somewhere –' Leon flipped through a battered brown notebook fished from a pocket. 'Vijay Mehta. And there's a Chinese associate, property developer, Shanghai-based, Guang Chien. Each of these guys is bankable at around $25 billion.'

'Memorize these notes and eat them,' said Marlow.

'About to do that very thing. And there's a fourth player in this game, Safin thinks. But whoever it is, he's got his tracks well covered. And Safin can only do so much without getting burned.'

'Anything on the bike you traced?' said Marlow.

'Still missing.'

'They'll have changed the plates anyway. Or got rid of it somewhere,' said Graves. 'Borovsky reported it stolen. Nothing to prove it wasn't.'

'We have another lead – of a kind,' said Lopez. *Somehow he still had to come clean to Marlow, but the longer he left it . . .*

'Yes?'

'Kutuzov has some unpleasant sidelines. One of them connects him with Medellín, way back, when it was still the crime capital of Columbia. Give you one guess what he was involved in.'

'Smack?'

'No toffee apple for getting that right. And guess who his principal partner was?'

Graves said. 'Gotta be one of the other players.'

'Mehta. But let's not leave out Chien.'

'Guang Chien? The Chinese?'

'He had another little scam going. Human organs. Mainly out of North Myanmar, the Lisu tribes in the Kachin hills. Gets them from children and adolescents. Weeded out by Chien's men, dressed up in NDA-K uniforms. The Lisu have a good, organic diet. Very healthy hearts, livers and kidneys. Rich kids in the West and Saudi are the main recipients.'

'Christ,' said Graves.

'No-risk business. What can the Lisu do? Take Chien to the International Court of Human Rights? And high profit, since he makes 100 per cent on everything, less overheads, of course. The other main source is in rural southern India – that's where Mehta comes in again. And, of course, the hinterland of Russia. So our little trio have a pretty well boundless line of supply.'

'Chien involved in the drugs?' Marlow asked.

'That's still an open question, but I don't think I'd die of surprise if we didn't verify. Safin tells me there's a couple of opium-poppy plantations in Pamir which even the maddest Taliban units don't dare go near.'

'You got all this from Safin?'

'Some. The rest, I picked up the scent.'

'Surely they've got enough,' Graves said wonderingly. 'If they're worth $25 billion apiece.'

'People always want more,' said Marlow. 'And the more they have, the more they think they're entitled to.'

'Narcissistic psychopathic infantilism,' said Lopez.

'What?' said Graves.

'Big egos, little maturity.'

'Sounds scary.'

'It is.'

'We need to tie these guys in with the box,' said Marlow. 'If they're after it, and that's their track record, God help us.' He paused. 'You mentioned a fourth player?'

'The Fourth Man, yeah,' Lopez replied. 'Or Woman. Nothing on him – or her – so far. But from what I can gather, the others take their cue from this person.'

'What's the name of this leather company?' asked Marlow.

Lopez checked his notes. 'Zwinger and Dels.'

'In the Bronx?'

'Check.'

'Address?'

Leon tapped a search into the Mac. 'There it is.'

'Time we took a look,' said Marlow.

97

This time there'd be no backup, and this time he'd go alone. Laura's lack of field experience would be a handicap, and Leon, while another pair of eyes and ears might be useful, was strictly a desk man these days. His presence risked being more than a handicap – it would be a liability. It was breaking all the rules, but there was no one else he could trust absolutely. No one he could trust at all. And now, now that he had let his heart rule his head, he wasn't sure he could even trust himself.

He selected a lightweight PDR – an FN-P90 submachine gun – along with his habitual HK USP Kompakt automatic, and he packed two ALS CS blast dispersion grenades.

He left it until past midnight to set off. Dressed in dark-grey combat gear and lightweight, rubber-soled boots, a black scarf round his neck, he drove the INTERSEC Q-car through light traffic for half an hour to his destination.

He parked the beaten-up-looking Toyota half a block south of his target and made the final approach on foot. His objective was in a deserted street in a rundown light-industrial quarter, an area occupied by warehouses and small manufacturers, more than half of which were closed, businesses shattered by the collapsing economy, steel shutters up, graffiti everywhere.

Zwinger and Dels was sandwiched between two concrete blocks and looked as firmly shut up as its two neighbours. The whole of the other side of the street was taken up by the back wall of a much larger concern, punctuated by loading bays, all closed.

Marlow approached cautiously, making no more noise than a shadow. The streetlights were widely spaced, intervals of twenty metres or so, and the electrical power in this district had been reduced, so the light they gave was feeble, pooling around the bases of the lamps in circles no more than three metres in diameter. Moving in close, Marlow noticed a small door in the huge entry bay which was the only point of access to Zwinger and Dels. There were windows, but high up, over five metres, and the walls of the building were sheer.

He made sure the PDR was slung safely across his back. One tug of the strap and it would be in his hands. He unclipped the guard on the holster which held the pistol. There were two security locks on the door, oldish-looking Adams Rite cylinder-operated flush bolts. Staying in the shadows, Marlow surveyed the building. No CCTV outside; maybe internal. There'd be an alarm, but he could see no sign of one. A keypad near the door. He'd disable it once he was inside.

He darted silently to the wall near the door and flattened himself against it. He listened, straining for the slightest noise, against the sound of his own breathing, which he kept shallow and light. He listened for a full minute.

Nothing.

He took out the small tool kit in its black case from the

bellows pocket on the left thigh of his trousers. The tungsten tools were small, precision, covered in a dark-grey nitrocellulose coating. The locks may have been old but they were top of the range and would take some work to pick. Noise was unavoidable, and there could be movement and vibration sensors. But he had no alternative. Marlow worked swiftly. No reaction. No alarms. The first lock gave after five minutes, the second after three. He tested the door. It swung noiselessly inwards. He listened again. Still nothing.

The interior was almost pitch dark, but there was enough light to give Marlow the impression of an empty space with the proportions of a small hangar. Steel galleries on two levels flanked three walls, accessible by steel stairways at each corner of the area and halfway down each long side. The central space was occupied by serried ranks of workbenches punctuated by pieces of machinery ranging in size from sewing-machine to small car.

Hugging the walls, he moved around the room and, looking back, he saw that the area above the main doors, where the windows were, was boxed off, an internal wall with another, narrower gallery running along it, and doors in the wall. There the offices would be.

A steel spiral staircase led up to them, reaching the gallery at its central point. Marlow made for it, keeping low, crouching as he moved quickly between the workbenches towards his goal. Once, he stumbled over some piece of equipment he hadn't seen in the dark, and it fell to the floor with a deafening clang. He became a statue, blending with the shadows, and waited. He strained all his senses but no impression came back to him that he was anything other than alone.

He'd be vulnerable on the staircase. You couldn't move fast on a spiral, and this one was narrow and caged in. He gripped the rail in a gloved hand, made sure none of his equipment would swing as he moved and, lithely as a cat, took the first few steps. The metal did not creak. Solid. Joints and holding bolts greased or oiled.

The gallery was narrow and high. Marlow had a choice of five doors. One was immediately at the top of the staircase. The other four, evenly spaced, two on each side, to his right and left. The whole gallery was maybe eighteen metres long.

He went to the right.

Both doors were unlocked and gave on to conventional offices: the usual desk – without drawers, however; two chairs, one on either side of the desk; filing cabinets; computer terminals; windows with Roman blinds overlooking the forlorn street outside.

Marlow checked the unlocked filing cabinets quickly but, as he'd expected, they contained nothing but reports relating to the legitimate business of Zwinger and Dels – orders received, in train, and dispatched; accounts and human resources files. Same on the computers. No trace of anything personal; no hint of the personality of whoever worked there. Not a trace, either, of what he was looking for.

The central door led to a larger office, the furniture similar but better quality, a carpet that reached the walls, pictures – copies of landscapes by Cuyp and Ruisdael – a cocktail cabinet, and a leather sofa with a coffee table in front of it. No computer here; three phones on the otherwise empty desk. The desk drawers, too, empty of anything but office paraphernalia, albeit of an expensive, even designer, kind. Marlow lifted each of the paintings, but no wall-safe was concealed behind any of them.

Outside again, Marlow made his way to the door on the extreme left of the gallery. A storeroom: boxes of A4, unused CD-ROMs, cartons of ballpoint pens, yellow pads, invoice forms, envelopes, memo-forms – did people still use those? – and copies of the firm's catalogue.

The door to the fifth room was locked. It took Marlow another five minutes to open. He looked at his watch: 1.30 a.m. He'd been inside half an hour. He had to get moving.

The fifth room was packed with computer equipment, all perhaps a shade more powerful than a modest leather-ware company might normally have needed, and there were two fax machines, side by side on heavy steel desks, drawers slung beneath them.

Behind the drawers, pushed against the wall, were two filing cabinets.

They were too heavy, too boxed in, to be moved. And they were locked. Marlow worked, straining on account of the difficult, cramped area he had to work in, forcing himself to keep his stress level down, listening keenly above the tiny sounds he was making as he manipulated his precision tools in the locks for noises from the street or from the cavernous space which yawned behind him, beyond the room and the gallery outside it. Another five precious minutes gone.

At last both cabinets were open. One had a false front, not drawers at all but a door, opening on to a cupboard space containing a new MacBook Pro. The drawers of the other cabinet contained telephone directories, but up to date, covering principal towns in the Baltic States, Colombia, India and China. There was also a directory in an alphabet Marlow recognized as Burmese.

He lifted out the laptop and opened it. As he'd expected, it demanded a password. He typed in the first word that came to his mind: DANDOLO.

He tried the numeric values of the letters.

No time to play games. He'd take the Mac with him. He placed it on top of one of the steel desks and reached into the back of the cabinet he'd removed it from. There could be memory-sticks, CDs perhaps, but he hardly thought it likely.

His fingers touched something.

98

He brought it into view. A plain steel box, slightly smaller than a shoebox. Locked. It was a combination. Built-in digital display, similar to the type used on hotel room-safes.

Marlow looked at his watch. Time to go. Neither the Mac nor the box was heavy, but he'd have to carry one under each arm, leaving neither hand free to go for a weapon.

Getting out was the hardest part, like getting down a mountain after you'd reached the summit. Getting out, you were in danger of dropping your guard, relaxing. Getting out was when –

He was halfway down the spiral staircase when the first burst of rapid fire clanged and sprayed all around him, angry orange flashes spitting up from the bowels of the dark vault below him.

The caged and narrow staircase made it almost impossible for him to manoeuvre. They'd waited for this moment. He'd walked straight into it. Now he was faced with a lightning choice. The laptop was under his right arm, the metal box under his left. His right flank was turned in the direction of the gunfire when it first started. His right hand was the one he needed to free.

He had to lose the computer but, even as he reached the decision, another vicious spatter of fire raked across the staircase in a horizontal line, bullets snapping off the high metal walls and speeding at nine hundred rounds per minute from the Magpul PDRs down there, hidden in the darkness. Some nearly found their mark. As Marlow released his grip on the Mac a burst hit it, smashing it out of his hand and sending it spinning and crashing down.

If he had let it go a split second earlier, his hip and upper thigh would be a shattered, bloody mess.

He wrenched his arm back to pull the FN-P90 round and into his grip. He propped the snub barrel between the crosswires of the stairwell's grille and, bracing himself, swivel-fired down into the void. In the brief pause which followed his counter-attack, he flung himself down the staircase, fighting against the vertigo he felt on moving down the spiral at speed.

Another burst from the factory floor hammered around him. How many guns? Three? Five? The five Vulcan riders? He paused to fire off an answering volley himself, and heard a scream in the darkness. Then he let the sub go, leaving it to swing from its strap, its light weight not enough to hamper him, and pulled the HK from its holster. He'd have to sacrifice the P90's 900 rpm for greater freedom of movement.

He'd almost reached the bottom when the lights flared on. He saw the target he'd hit: black clad; blonde hair clogging in the blood which fountained from her head. The woman's body writhed in agony, her gloved hands scrabbled to free themselves of the black gun-strap to reach the wound and staunch the flow.

He sprang down the last three steps and ran for the door, but before he reached it he could see it was shut. He dived for cover behind the nearest workbench as renewed fire battered and smashed around him. But the workbench had a solid metal frame and it was close to the wall behind him.

He put the box down carefully and knelt, bringing the P90 round again and placing his automatic within close reach. The lights were spots, facing him. He squinted past their piercing beams into the gloom they protected, red blurs in his eyes obscuring his vision as he fought to discern giveaway movement. If they were going to get him, they'd have to close in. On the stairs they'd had a clearer target. Down here, there was machinery in the way.

They kept up their fire. Marlow counted. Four. They'd try to come up on either side, pin him in. They knew he had only one exit and they'd sealed it.

If he tried to go for it now, he'd be dead before he got within two metres of it.

He watched and waited. One minute passed, two. They might have been years.

Then, movements. Two. Either side, as he'd thought. Shadows flitting. Marlow raised the sub and fired two clinical bursts.

More screams, louder this time, one a wail of anguish so great it tore a fibre from the brain. Two down, two to go. The agonized screaming went on from the left-hand side. The right was suddenly silent.

He must have raised his body too far in that fatal moment of relaxation. A single gunshot rang out. Different gun — sniper rifle, must have infra-red sights, he thought before the muscle in his left shoulder ripped painfully and he fell back. He felt the warm blood soak his jacket. Flexed the muscle. Snapped his teeth together to stifle a cry. But the torn muscle still worked, he could still use his left arm. Flexed his left hand. OK. Now he let out a yell. Deliberate this time. And ducked down, grabbing the automatic and holstering it as he did so; and grasping the box. The pain bit hard, but his hold held. He did not dare raise his head again, but now, in the silence which followed the firing, and despite the dulling reverberation the stabbing gunfire had caused in his ears, he heard the two people left standing approach. Cautiously, but less cautiously. That fatal relaxation again. They thought they'd brought him down.

One of them crashed into something metal and angrily thrust it aside. The sound echoed round the walls.

They were coming for him.

99

Marlow put the steel box down again, carefully.

He judged them to be about five metres away now. He unclipped and armed both the CS grenades, stood, and pitched them. He dived down, pulling the scarf from the neck of his jacket and tightening it round his mouth and nose. There was nothing he could do about his eyes. But he hadn't had the CS-gas explode right in his face, as they had.

In the background, the wailing had become a kind of keening. He became aware of it again as the other sounds, of floundering and crashing, cries of surprise and rage, then choking, mingled with it.

He scrambled over to the wall, kicking the steel box ahead of him. Then he drew his automatic, and stood. A draught from the door blew the gas away from him. He stopped squinting, and saw his two opponents flailing blindly.

The lights helped him now. He stepped close enough to get a sure aim, and raised the HK. He fired twice. The bodies flung themselves to the floor.

Marlow stood over them and fired one more shot into each exposed neck.

This time there was no screaming. This time the kills had been clean.

He waited for the gas to clear then looked at the bodies.

Both male, one burlier than the other. About twenty-five years old, maybe thirty. He frisked them, found keys on one, holstered his gun and picked up the box.

The keening had ceased too. He went over in the direction the sound had come from. She lay on her back, eyes open, mouth open, lips drawn back from the teeth, dark hair fanned around the agonized face. His bullets had ripped a line through the middle of her body just above the groin. Young woman, tanned, athletic-looking. Death had rescued her.

Marlow unlocked the door, and stepped out into what felt like clean air. He made his way back to the Toyota in a dream, only his throbbing shoulder and the now-cold wetness of his jacket reminding him that it was anything but. He slung the steel box on to the passenger seat and drove off. Back to INTERSEC's garage, where he left the Q-car, signing it in to the night-guards, without explanation.

He didn't go up to Room 55. He switched to his own Corvette Z06 and drove home.

100

4.15 a.m. Marlow knew that the first priority should be to call an INTERSEC medic, get his shoulder seen to: but that could wait an hour. It was a flesh wound, experience taught him that; no real damage, pain worse than the thing itself.

He washed the wound, tied a bandage round it and changed into a fresh T-shirt. He badly needed coffee, but he was too impatient. He pulled the steel box towards him. Its combination lock looked complicated. And he wanted someone else in on this. After a moment's hesitation, he picked up the phone. He had a result now.

He hoped, though he couldn't suppress the doubt which, like an unwanted tenant, had lodged in his mind, that his calculations had been right. The ferocity with which his incursion into Zwinger and Dels had been attacked confirmed they had been. But he was the only person able to play the cards in his hand. The decisions lay with him. No need for anyone else to know the details.

Once he'd sorted this out, he'd deal with the next item on his agenda. His heart wrenched at the thought.

But this first.

He tapped in Graves's number. He'd need her help with tackling the combination lock. Lopez's expertise in that particular field would have been greater, but Marlow didn't want to include Lopez, not yet. Graves answered immediately, fully awake. Fifteen minutes later she was there. Marlow used the time to make coffee, a major task, hampered by his shoulder. He wanted her to start work the moment she arrived, but she insisted on looking at his wound and calling a medic. While they were waiting, she interrogated him about Zwinger and Dels. He told her as much as he needed to.

The medic arrived. Marlow refused point-blank to go anywhere, but he allowed the woman to clean and dress the wound properly, and apply sutures. He was lucky they'd been using hard-nosed bullets, and none had lodged. The medic stayed half an hour, then left, after extracting a promise from Marlow that he'd stop by the clinic before midday.

Graves, meanwhile, had been addressing the problem of the steel box.

The lock required a five-digit combination, but the permutations were endless. They started with various possible numeric values of names associated with Enrico Dandolo. The first and then the last groups of letters of other names followed. All in vain.

'Maybe we're looking too hard,' Marlow said finally.

'Meaning?'

'It'd be unusual for anyone to put a code in here that was entirely unrelated to the contents of the box,' said Marlow.

Graves looked at him. 'You took one hell of a risk,' she said. 'You could have been killed. Easily.' A moment passed. 'With you dead, what would we have done?'

'I assessed the consequences. That's what you do. And that's not relevant now.'

'Whoever it was expected you.'

'Or someone else.'

'Anyone at the saleroom likely to have recognized you?'

'My mother wasn't there.'

'Think.'

'No one.'

'Then we're back to square one.'

'Unless we try a little more lateral thinking.'

'That requires coffee,' said Graves, leaving to fetch it.

Marlow looked at his watch: 5.30. He tried typing in numeric codes relating to the names of the dead archaeologists, and Su-Lin's name. But the box remained closed.

Graves appeared with the coffee minutes later, and reapplied herself to her work.

'Here goes nothing,' she said, and typed in: 13124.

The mechanism whirred, and the box clicked open.

'What did you set?' asked Marlow.

'13-1-24.'

'Which is?'

'Simplest thing in the world. You were right. Lateral thinking. All I did was type in the numbers that relate to the position in the alphabet of three letters.'

'That's . . .'

'Exactly.'

Marlow took this in then said urgently: 'Who knows?'

'Like I said, they were expecting you.'

Marlow shook his head. His heart was hammering, despite himself. 'Here goes.'

Turning the steel box so that its opening was facing away from him, to deflect any booby-trap blast, he flipped the lid open. Inside, nestling on a bed of crimson velvet, lay the box. Next to it, fixed in a niche specially made to hold it, lay the key, familiar to them from the photographs they already had of it.

'There could still be some kind of trap here,' warned Graves.

'We haven't set anything off.'

'Yet.'

'We've got to take that risk.' He looked at her. 'You'd better back off. Kitchen should be far enough. There isn't room enough in here for more than a small blast.'

'I wouldn't miss this for the world.'

Marlow swung the steel box round again, so that its opening was facing him once more. Gingerly, he tried the lid of Adhemar's box. It was locked. Cautiously, he lifted the key. Fitted it into the lock. He turned the key, and it moved as smoothly as if it were brand-new.

There was a gentle click.

Marlow lifted the lid.

The box was empty.

Graves and Marlow looked at one another, thinking the same thought.

'They've got it,' said Graves.

'Maybe.'

'Where do we start?'

'Finish deciphering that code.'

'Nearly there,' she said grimly.

'Don't forget that there's still no indication that they've used the tablet.'

'You think they haven't figured that out?' said Graves. 'Adhemar's mistake.'

'It's a possibility. We might still have a chance.'

'Why do you think they defended an empty box so fiercely?' asked Graves.

'I don't know. And why leave the key with it?' replied Marlow. 'To gain time? Or to mock us?'

'That'd be an expensive kind of mockery,' said Graves. 'To waste four lives.'

'We're not dealing with the kind of person who'd regard that as any kind of waste,' said Marlow grimly. 'But if the idea was to buy time . . .'

'The guys in the Zwinger and Dels factory didn't know that what they were defending was worthless?'

'They can't have done.'

'There's another possibility,' said Graves.

'Yes?'

'What if the tablet was never *in* the box?'

'Something isn't holding water,' said Marlow. He stood up, reached for his jacket. 'I'll find out. Contact you again in four hours.'

'No way I'll have it deciphered by then.'

'Short of a miracle,' said Marlow.

'Short of a miracle.' Graves smiled tightly. 'And you shouldn't be going anywhere.'

Marlow ignored that, but his cell-phone buzzed as he was leaving. Lopez.

'We need to talk,' he said. 'Urgently.'

'There's a coffeehouse on East 75th, near the Whitney. Can you meet me there?'

'That's close to INTERSEC. Is it secure?'

'It's the last place anyone will look. Eye of the storm.'

Lopez was waiting for him, hunched over an untouched espresso. Lopez had planned this moment. He knew this was the unique opportunity he'd have to confess and – if Jack would listen – redeem himself at the same time.

'What've you got?' Marlow noticed that Lopez's hands were sweating.

'There's something I have to tell you – and something I haven't told you,' he began.

Marlow looked serious, but not threatening. 'Shoot,' he said.

Lopez swallowed hard, and told him the whole story – about Annika Lundquist, the original Frid document, his visit to her apartment, and what he had found – and not found – there.

467

Marlow listened in silence and, at the end, remained silent. Someone knew where they were and what they were after. Someone had been watching them and watching anyone who made contact with them. Lopez had blown cover badly.

'Every action has its consequences,' said Marlow at last. 'The action you took should destroy you, you know.'

'I was trying to –'

'*I* know.' Marlow paused. 'The question is, what do we do about it?'

'I know what I deserve.'

'But I also know what you've done in the past – for the organization, and for me.'

'I don't expect that to count.'

'You saved my life.'

'That doesn't buy me anything.'

'It shouldn't. You know the rules.' Marlow paused again. 'On the other hand, your action produced results – important ones. And if anyone else knows you stepped out of line, apart from the dead girl and me, they aren't going to go running to Hudson with it.'

'I hope.'

'Whose interest would it be in?'

Lopez looked up. 'What do you mean?' He was thinking of Mia and the kids. If he died. He hadn't considered consequences thoroughly enough. Now he was at his friend's mercy; and his friend was a professional.

But Marlow had his own secrets. He too had been vulnerable, weak; and because of that, he would carry Lopez part of the way. He understood what Lopez had done, and why. The reasons behind his own actions were murkier. He snapped back. Some mistakes could be corrected. Some damage could be repaired.

He looked at Lopez. 'You're lucky. For the moment you're more useful alive than dead. You're getting a second chance. Only one. Step out of line again and you know what will happen.'

The tension in Lopez's neck slackened and his head dipped like that of a man reprieved.

Marlow broke the mood. 'Time to bring you up to date.' He looked round the room, checking it. Office people, preoccupied with keeping the machinery of business oiled. Preoccupied with their own lives. No one showing a hint of interest in them.

'Listen carefully,' he said. 'There isn't much time.'

He told Lopez about the recovery of the box. 'But we're stuck on the code.'

'That's why I called you,' said Lopez, playing his last card, but glad his friend had spared him before he had to play it.

102

In Room 55, Lopez unlocked his Mac and opened a series of encrypted files – boxes within boxes.

'It's Frid's five-liner,' he explained. 'I knew it was a code based on numbers, and numbers are my field. Laura would have got there, I guess, in time, but I needed to try as well – I needed to redeem myself.'

'You shouldn't have had a copy,' said Marlow. 'Where did you get one? I had your copy deleted.'

Lopez looked at Marlow. 'We go back a ways, Jack. I already knew, more than you did, just how little time we had.'

'I hope you're going to make me grateful.'

'You were right all along – the code's like the one on the key. The difficulty, why Laura couldn't get it immediately, is that whoever wrote it deliberately skewed its logic. Can't have been Frid; we know he was illiterate, and we can reckon that he was innumerate too. But what matters is that I've recognized it.'

Lopez adjusted his glasses. 'The numbers here don't correspond to the usual letters, but to their opposite number, if you like. And we're talking about a version of Aramaic with a basic 22-letter alphabet, so there's no single central letter. Look: *kaph* is letter number eleven, *lamadh* number twelve. Those are the two "central" letters.'

'And the code?'

'In the end, it's simple. It's another mirror-image of what it should be. The first letter of the alphabet here is given the value eleven instead of one, so the eleventh letter, *kaph*, its value is one, not eleven. In the second half of the alphabet, the last letter doesn't have the value twenty-two, but twelve, so it's *lamadh*, the twelfth letter, that has the value twenty-two.' Lopez looked up. 'It's skewed. But when you apply that to the numbers in Frid's five-liner, you get this.'

Lopez tapped in a series of instructions on his keyboard. The screen, which had been showing a cleaned-up version of the uncertain script on Frid's document, now dissolved and resolved itself into a pattern – letters related to numbers, according to Lopez's theory. The computer had transposed the letters into the Roman alphabet, and separated them into words, which Marlow recognized as the same dog-Latin that the clear-text part of the manuscript had been written in.

In part, he could read it, but he couldn't make sense of it alone.

'Call Graves now,' he said.

She arrived within fifteen minutes. The five lines of code had rendered a short paragraph of text. She was able to translate it quickly.

'If you were right, this may be a reprieve, of sorts,' she replied. 'I think this must be something Dandolo – or an aide other than Frid – encoded and copied down somewhere; the original is lost, I guess, but Frid must have had it, and copied it into his "will", either as a safeguard or as a reference for his own future use – assuming he knew what it meant.'

'You said something about a reprieve.'

'Yes – the tablet wasn't in the box – it never was.'

'What?'

'This is what it says.' Graves cleared her throat. "'I, Enrico, Doge of Venice, Master of Constantinople and of the Great Tablet of Power, state that through the agency of my loyal and trusted servants, Father Leporo de Monteriggioni, and Frid Eyolfson, late of the Emperor's Varangian Guard, am laid to rest in the Church of Saint Irina in the Great City, and that according to my inviolable instructions which are unalterable under pain of my curse, I am buried in my ducal robes, and that the Tablet shall remain where it last lay, in the grip of my right hand, to lie with me for ever, hidden from the sight of Man and God, its Power to cede to no successor."'

She looked up. Marlow remembered the doge, as he lay in the open tomb in Istanbul. He remembered the broken fingers of Dandolo's right hand.

'The box must have been taken by archaeologists. There were plenty of digs going on in the early twentieth century. They must have missed the key,' Graves said. 'The three artefacts were separated. The locked box, we now have. Whoever stole it from the auction already had the key –'

'– which they took from Montserrat, Adkins and Taylor.'

'But they can't have found the tablet. Like us, they must have thought it was still in the locked box which Bishop Adhemar had made for it,' added Marlow. 'And there's the

472

question of the gloves Major Haki had dated for us – a hundred years old.'

'The Germans had a lot of influence in Turkey around the First World War,' said Graves. 'And the Kaiser was a keen patron of archaeology. Several important finds were made at about that time in Turkey and Mesopotamia.'

'Like the Gate of Ishtar,' said Lopez.

'Discovered by Robert Koldewey, who was an expert on ancient Mesopotamia,' added Graves. 'And the Gate of Ishtar is now in Berlin.'

'I can throw some light on that,' Lopez said. 'You asked me to research the history of the box before it came into the hands of those New York dealers – Lightoller and Steeples.'

'Yes?'

'The IRS came up with some stuff, remember? Nothing's computerized or been put on any kind of electronic file, but there was an incomplete archive of Lightoller and Steeples's transactions which went to the tax authorities after the business was wound up, and they let me access it. It contains more details. Apparently, Harvey Lightoller bought the box from someone called Aloysius Guttmann in Vienna in 1946.'

'An Austrian?'

'Or German. The name Guttmann may have been assumed anyway. There were a lot of senior SS and Gestapo trying to get away in the mid-1940s, turning precious objects which they'd either looted or requisitioned into cash to pay the fare to South America and set them up in new lives.' Lopez paused. 'This Guttmann disappeared without trace, but he may have been one of the three unidentified fatalities of a train crash between Vienna and Zurich which occurred a couple of days after the transaction. There was also a note in the paperwork giving the address of a firm of lawyers in Bern. It's long gone out of business, but its records are intact. The firm was wound up after the senior partner, Anton Hoffmann, was shot dead by an intruder at his offices in 1949. That's all a matter of record, it was just a question of following it up.'

'But it still brings us to a dead end,' said Marlow. 'The German connection's a long shot, though it's worth pursuing. Too many "maybes", Leon.'

'Not necessarily. It seems from the 1949 Bern police reports that the intruder who killed Hoffmann wasn't after the cash in the safe. But Hoffmann had certain connections, and papers in his keeping may have compromised them. Some of the papers he passed on to, let's say, confidential clients with special interests in them. But he kept copies, as a kind of insurance.'

'Which was bad news for him in the end,' said Marlow.

'It looks like it.'

'We've still got to find the tablet,' said Graves.

'I wonder if Robert Koldewey took it,' Marlow said, thinking of the gloves. 'I wonder if he knew what it was.'

'Which would mean that it could have ended up where?'

'In Berlin.'

'There's a lead I can follow,' said Lopez after a moment's thought.

'Where does it go?' asked Marlow.

'Can't say yet, but if I'm right, it comes very close to home.'

103

Berlin, the Present

Now? Now they were going to withdraw support? Now, when he was so close to his goal?

'I have told you repeatedly,' he said to the three men once again assembled before him, but this time in the windowless conference room on the eighteenth floor of MAXTEL's office building in Berlin, 'this is not the moment.'

'Our principals are not happy,' said Vijay Mehta. 'We have all invested deeply in your project because of our long association with you. It is time to cut our losses.'

Rolf Adler held the Indian's eyes for a moment before turning to the others. Both Guang Chien and Sergei Kutusov returned his gaze steadily, hard-eyed.

'By pulling out now, you risk losing everything we have worked for,' said Adler. 'Almost within our grasp is the instrument which will give us total control. No market fluctuations, no wars – *nothing* – can possibly affect us again; and natural disasters can be predicted with accuracy, their consequences planned for in advance.'

'The key word in that little speech is "almost",' said Chien.

'After all, we have only ever had your word,' added Kutuzov. 'The effectiveness of your business makes us take you seriously. But we are beginning to think that your project is mere fantasy.'

'Is unlimited business control – the control of nations – so fantastic? It has been attempted before in history with great success.'

'Never lasting,' said Mehta.

'This time it *will* be lasting. And we can hand it on to our chosen successors. The East – the countries you represent – holds the key to the future. The economies of the West have passed the tipping-point. We all know that. In the past, men looked towards the West for new opportunities; now, it is the turn of the East.'

He had not told them all he knew, of course. He needed their support right up until the moment when he could turn on them and discard them, along with their worthless and narrow-minded visions of mere financial control. Adler knew what he wanted – to control Destiny itself. After that, MAXTEL, its satellites already in place above the earth, would replace God, through its radio, internet and television arms, for a grateful and obedient world. That world would become his plaything.

He thought back over his researches. Adhemar had partially understood the meaning of the tablet. Even he, with his meagre comprehension, had achieved some success. Dandolo had gained more, but could not dominate every dissident voice. Adler did not know into whose hands the tablet had passed, since – as he guessed – it had been unearthed a century ago. Perhaps it had lain forgotten in some vault, not understood at all. Not finding it among the discoveries of the archaeologists Adkins, Taylor and Montserrat, he'd guessed that Dandolo's tomb had been opened before, and his researches had led him to suspect the interference of the archaeologists of the colonial period. British? No, not British. They had never held more than a precarious position in Asia Minor; but Germany, his own country, had. The tablet was close, perhaps even, and in mockery of his own frustrated search, in this city – his city!

And *he* understood the tablet fully, better than anyone before. He had had the benefit of eight more centuries of knowledge and research to draw on.

It was so close. He could feel it. But these three henchmen who now came crying to him because their creditors were on their heels for the money they, in turn, had lent him threatened to ruin everything. MAXTEL, unknown to anyone but them, had taken a serious knock in the fiscal crisis of 2008. But it would recover. It *had* recovered, though there was still work to do. Hence his need for these wretches in the first place. But, within days now, he was sure, he need never fear the unexpected again.

He had to give a sharp pull on the reins of these people. Fortunately, he still had it within his power to do so.

'May I remind you, gentlemen, that our joint ventures over the years have included operations which, if exposed to public view before we have complete control, would be enough to bring us – or rather, you – down, as disastrously as Icarus fell when he flew too close to the sun.'

The men looked at each other. They knew what he was talking about.

'You wouldn't dare – you are as compromised as we would be, in such a case,' said Mehta.

'I think not,' replied Adler. 'I think you will find that there are no records anywhere to connect either me personally, or MAXTEL as an organization, with any of the ... hobbies ... we have indulged in together.'

'Rubbish,' spat Kutuzov. 'There is nothing more obvious than your club in New York, Zara la Salope, to begin with. That alone, linked to your name, would send your stockholders fleeing.'

'You do not have access to any of my accounts or business histories,' rejoined Adler. 'On the other hand, your interests, and yours, and yours,' he continued, turning to Chien and Mehta in turn, 'are less secure. Your companies are not as strong, even together, to be a match for MAXTEL.'

Kutuzov threw him a sceptical look. 'Bluff,' he said.

'Do you wish to call this bluff?' asked Adler. 'I can give you chapter and verse on everything you do. Let me down now, and you will fall.'

'You have no proof of anything,' said Chien.

'You are right to be sceptical,' replied Adler. 'You each have a computer terminal in front of you. I invite you to enter the name of any one of your companies, and you will see it linked to sexual exploitation, drugs, the trade in human organs, under-the-counter arms deals with the most insalubrious regimes. It's all there, gentlemen. MAXTEL, on the other hand, is inviolable. You were too greedy to question me when you needed backing, and that was your weakness. You trusted me. I have learned that, to get what you want from a creature as fickle as a human being, you need to rely on something rather stronger than trust. You need to have something on them. You need to rely on their own sense of self-preservation. That is the only factor that counts.' Adler watched them, changing his tone judiciously. 'But don't take my word for it. After all, that would mean trusting me, wouldn't it? And you don't want to fall into that trap again.'

He watched as each of them reluctantly applied themselves to the glass-thin terminals neatly placed in front of them on the huge conference table.

It didn't take them long.

'We still have to *trust* that this project of yours will repay us,' said Kutuzov sullenly, after a long pause.

'And with dividends,' added Chien. Mehta had been plunged into a gloomy silence.

'By all means,' said Adler. 'And, of course, a share in the glory, if you stick with me.'

'I'm not sure that my creditors –' began Mehta.

'They will agree to another month,' said Adler. 'That is all I need. Look at the return you are offering. No one gets that kind of percentage in the present economy. And, believe me, they'd question it, if they themselves weren't as greedy as you are. But their greed is your friend. Master it, and you've mastered them.'

'What if some won't comply?' asked Kutusov.

'Sergei, I'm sure you don't need lessons in how to deal with people. Individuals don't sink the boat. Small holes, we can plug. And if anyone wants to pull out, well, we can make an object lesson of them for the others, can we not? After all, in a very short time we need not worry about being accountable to anyone, ever again – not politicians, not governments, not the law, not even reforming revolutionaries, military juntas or mad dictators.'

'People will still have an idea of freedom,' said Mehta. 'Of individuality.'

'My dear chap, do you really think so?' asked Adler evenly. He looked at them. 'We're agreed then?'

Sullenly, his associates nodded.

'Good! I do so hate it when there is any kind of disharmony.' Adler concealed his relief. He didn't have the power to do more than bully and outmanoeuvre as yet, but he hadn't risen from the gutter to the heights without knowing how to crush people into submission, regardless of their feelings. Of course there was still the question of time, and the question of where he put his own trust. He hated the thought of his position being compromised, but he knew his key operatives were loyal. He allowed himself a moment's satisfied reflection on how things had gone in New York. At first, he had been bitterly disappointed in what had happened there, and he had lost control of his temper when he found that the box was empty. One should never lose one's temper. A sign of weakness.

Luckily, there had been someone to vent it on.

Poor Frau Müller. No amount of work could disguise the wrinkles that made irrevocable inroads round her eyes, on her cheeks and neck. She might have striven to hold her weight at 48kg, not much for a woman 1.68m. in height, but it was all in vain. A skinny old blonde was all that remained, distasteful and unnecessary. And he could dispense with her loyalty now. She had served her purpose.

Meanwhile, he awaited more information from New York, as it became available. He was confident.

It was an intellectual process, really. Quite simple. And soon, the irritating unpredictability of success would be completely removed. No one would stand in his way.

As for the box, he congratulated himself on the little trick he had played on Marlow. Mr Marlow and his colleagues would never catch up with him now – and in fact they'd been rather useful to him. It didn't really matter that Marlow hadn't died, and Adler's own operatives for the Sotheby's heist and the Zwinger and Dels job were skilled, but not indispensable. If there was any fallout, it would come to rest on Kutuzov's shoulders, did the man but know it. As for the unlocking code for the steel box, Marlow would be sure to get that message. It had been a risk – *MAX* – but Adler knew he was too well-connected for it to worry him unduly. Besides, he liked to gamble, a little.

The episode had not only amused him, and sent another little message to his competitors, similar to the *coup de théâtre* he'd brought off in the killing of Taylor and Adkins; it had also bought him time. And that was the important thing: *Time*. How they must have kicked themselves. They must have been convinced that they'd got what they wanted at last. He'd make a friendly, concerned, call to his friend Sir Richard when the time was right. To see how things were going, to see if they'd made any progress, if they'd located Dr de Montferrat yet.

He looked benignly at his associates and pressed a discreet button laid into the surface of the wood on his side of the table. Moments later, a tall blonde woman, elegantly dressed, and in her late twenties, entered the room with a black-lacquer drinks trolley.

Frau Müller's replacement was shaping up well. Frau Müller herself was currently convalescing in a clinic he owned near Gstaad. When she had recovered he would see that she was generously provided for, during what he was sure would be a short retirement.

He eyed his new secretary appreciatively as he said: 'Gentlemen. I think this calls for a drink, don't you? And I'll propose a toast: to mended fences.'

Inwardly, he smiled. He had told them nothing of the old Viking document. He hadn't told them that even the heavily encoded part had now been successfully deciphered by his experts, always grateful for the donations and endowments of his philanthropic organization, MAXPHIL.

He hadn't shared with his associates what he'd deduced from his findings, either.

Just one more piece of the puzzle, and the picture would be complete.

104

Marlow took the call on the secure line in his apartment at midnight. The INTERSEC operator had already told him who it was.

'We've done the impossible,' the crisp voice of Colonel Demir, Detective-Major Haki's superior in Istanbul, told him.

'The DNA on the gloves? You've traced it?'

'No. We went through every databank at our disposition and our people crosschecked with yours. It was always a very doubtful undertaking, in my view. There's no record of any DNA which matches the sample we were able to extract. So we crosschecked something else. Turkish Security Services and Foreign Office records indicate that in 1915 there was a German excavation at this site, conducted by the then world authority on Babylon, Robert Koldewey.'

'Yes?' said Marlow, registering the familiar name.

'He was looking for an ancient temple which existed centuries prior to the building of the Church of Hagia Irina, on the same site. But he found something else, and the German authorities, in the shape of General Erich Ludendorff, were called in at his request.'

'I see.'

'Very few people were permitted on to the site. Koldewey worked alone after the initial excavations had been made, and a crosscheck with his DNA, which is on record, was negative. It is therefore highly likely that the gloves were used by General Ludendorff.'

'And what became of the findings – whatever artefacts they may have discovered?'

'Normally, they should have stayed within Turkey, or within our jurisdiction. But the country was in turmoil at the time. There was a war going on and, within the country, the old regime was crumbling. The administration then in power permitted Koldewey to remove the artefacts to Germany.' Demir paused. 'That is what we have for you.'

'You have indeed achieved the impossible.'

'A full report is being prepared, and will be sent within twenty-four hours. But I thought you'd like to know the results of the findings as soon as possible. It was most fortunate that the damage done to our forensics department was less extensive than we at first anticipated.'

'Good.'

'But we do not now believe that the attack itself was Islamist-inspired,' continued the colonel. 'Any relevant information our investigation reveals will be communicated to you.'

'Thank you, Colonel,' said Marlow.

There was a further pause. Marlow checked his watch.

'You may like to know that the funeral of Detective-Major Haki has taken place. He will be much missed by colleagues and friends.'

'He was a fine man,' said Marlow. 'We are indebted to the work he put into this mission.'

'Goodbye,' said the colonel, his voice still as crisp and formal as before.

Marlow hung up then immediately dialled a number. He spoke briefly then dialled another.

He grabbed a coat, went down to the basement garage where the Corvette was parked and drove over to Graves's apartment.

Lopez arrived five minutes after him, and Marlow briefed them both.

'That places the tablet pretty much in Berlin,' said Graves when he'd finished.

'Supposition.'

'More than likely. Something to go on.'

'Even if it were there,' said Marlow, 'we'd still have to know where to look.'

'But if the link is with Koldewey, we can narrow the field immediately,' said Graves. 'Give me a moment.'

She walked over to her computer and did three fast searches. She looked up from the screen minutes later: 'There's a 99.5 per cent likelihood that any artefacts Koldewey unearthed would have ended up at the Kaiser Wilhelm Museum in Berlin, which later changed its name to the Bodemuseum. But there's a snag. The Bode had a major refit – a massive overhaul – between 1996 and 2007, and all ancient artefacts were transferred to another place, the Vorderasiatisches Museum – what used, until recently, to be called the Pergamon. My guess is that's where it'll be.'

'Jesus – that's still a big haystack. Didn't you brief me that there were over thirty thousand Babylonian tablets in the British Museum alone – and wasn't that just the unclassified stuff? What if the Pergamon's got a similar-sized collection?'

'There may be a way of narrowing that down,' said Lopez suddenly, his eyes keen behind his glasses.

Marlow looked at him. 'You've got that other lead?'

'Maybe.'

Lopez and Marlow exchanged another look: Lopez had redeemed his error; no need for Graves ever to know. Lopez signalled back: was it OK to speak of this in front of Graves? Marlow nodded.

'I said there was a link close to home,' Lopez began. '*Possibly*. I've followed up on the Swiss lawyer, Anton Hoffmann. You remember I told you he was killed by an intruder in his Bern office in 1949?'

'Yes.'

'This guy Guttmann, the one who sold Adhemar's box to Lightoller and Steeples in Vienna, was a client of his. I've verified that now.'

'Who with?'

'Bern police. The Swiss never throw anything away.'

'Not even stuff relating to a murder committed over sixty years ago?'

'Still a cold case. They never found the lawyer's killer. And the intruder got away with what must have been a suitcaseful of confidential records. What most of them were, we'll probably never know. But the police impounded what documentation was left, as evidence, and they've still got it. Not much, but there's a kind of ledger, a list of transactions, noting the dates of certain papers and dossiers, letters and so forth.'

'You've accessed this?'

'I played the INTERPOL card, and they scanned the entries for 1946. There's one dated 4 February.'

'Go on.'

'Guttmann left a letter with the lawyer. There's a note attached to say that another copy went into a safe-deposit box at a private bank's offices in Bern, but we may not have to follow that copy up.'

'Isn't that the most obvious thing to do?' asked Graves.

'That might attract attention,' said Lopez, 'and we still don't know who we're up against. In any case, there could be a simpler route.' The thing is, this letter is registered in the lawyer's ledger as "Aloysius Guttmann/General Hans von Reinhardt."'

'So it's possible that this Reinhardt was a Nazi fugitive?' asked Graves.

'It's not only possible, it's actual,' replied Lopez. 'Reinhardt's listed as having died in Hitler's bunker when the Russians took Berlin in 1945, but no body was ever found. He was a senior staff officer who built a career on the back of the Nazi regime and rose quickly. In the end, he was one of Hitler's closest associates.'

Marlow and Graves remained silent as that fact sank in. Each knew what the other was thinking.

'Then you mean he . . .?' Marlow started to say, letting the question hang.

'It's a possibility.'

'But it's a long shot.'

'Not if Reinhardt knew the box was empty when he sold it. It was certainly locked, but he didn't have the key. No one did then. It was still in Dandolo's tomb.'

'So, if he did know the box was empty, he might have known where the tablet was,' said Graves.

'We need to know what was in that letter,' said Marlow.

'That means we have to get authority to open the safety-deposit box, if it still exists after more than sixty years.'

'I told you there was a simpler route. And, as I said, it's close to home.'

'Meaning?'

'The intruder who killed Hoffmann was one of ours. By 1949, things were winding up. Tracks needed to be covered. And there was a certain amount of house-cleaning to be done, especially in quarters which weren't regarded as 100 per cent trustworthy.'

'And Hoffmann was one of them?'

Lopez nodded. 'Links to the Commies, apparently. Never proven, but better, I guess our colleagues from those days thought, to be safe than sorry. As it was, Hoffmann had kept records which would have compromised us if they'd ever fallen into the wrong hands.'

'You say this intruder was one of ours?' said Marlow.

'Hoffmann worked for the OSS. From as early as 1943, he was passing certain documents to it, which he thought might be connected to Axis powers war criminals.' Lopez leaned back. 'And all the OSS files – which would have included that kind of material – found their way eventually into the archives of the organization the OSS eventually became.'

Graves drew in her breath. 'The CIA,' she said.

They looked at each other.

'You're wasted at Columbia,' Graves said to Lopez.

'Just part of the job. I'm shit at field-work.'

'You've never tried it.'

Marlow and Lopez exchanged the briefest look.

'Anyway, I'm better off the way I am,' said Lopez. 'Moonlighting like this.'

'So we'd better get on to Langley,' said Graves.

'Yes,' Marlow agreed. 'But for that we'll have to go through Sir Richard. I can't pursue things in that direction without his authority. This is just too hot. And too urgent.' *Which means I'll have to trust him*, he thought.

'You want me to draw up a request?' asked Graves.

'I'll see him personally,' Marlow replied. To Lopez he said: 'You're certain no one else has seen this information? You haven't had any of it routed through an open computer?'

'Initial information only.'

'What, exactly?'

'Reinhardt's identity. The existence of the letter.'

'Could anyone armed with that information do anything with it – as you did?'

'Not if they hadn't made the connection, and I don't see how –'

'Bern police?'

'Nothing we can do about that.'

'Yes there is. Tell them to shut down access. Now. Full INTERSEC authority. Even the Swiss will have to bow to that.' Marlow paused, thinking. 'And nothing on paper or on file about this. Nothing in the computer system. Lopez, trash anything you've got that's in an open or official INTERSEC channel. But put it all on a protected stick before you do and keep it safe. Put it under Alvar's mattress, or Lucia's. Hide it in a computer-game box.'

'That's about the least secure place I can think of,' said

489

Lopez. 'But I'll manage.' His eyes said, *You trust me again — thank you.*

But Marlow was looking out of the window at the night city. He had to know, now, who they were up against. Whatever it took, however great the risk, he had to flush out the enemy. Bring them into the open so they could be shot down. Getting to the tablet first wouldn't be enough. His enemy was cunning, baffling and powerful. He would never give up while he still had cover.

There was one line of attack open to him. It tore at his heart to take it, but he'd have to face the truth, and redeem himself, as Leon had, one day, and it had better be now.

105

Rule number one of the hunter: lull the quarry into a sense of security, lull it into thinking it is in a position it can trust.

Then strike.

Everything was in position. The few discreet questions he'd asked her had established that INTERSEC's adversaries were not in possession of the Babylonian tablet. The questions had not aroused any suspicion. She still thought she was safe, and in control.

Only Leon knew the whole truth, and he needed Leon. Leon had set up the surveillance and could follow anything that happened from its source to its destination. It was that simple. And he could trust his associate, because Leon was in his debt.

When he'd told Leon of his suspicions, his friend had been first wary, then shocked. In the telling, Marlow, taking stock of himself, had been shocked too. Out in the open, the truth sounded so naked, so banal.

Marlow raised himself on one elbow in the bed and looked down at her. Asleep, she looked so delicate, so vulnerable, that he could still hardly bring himself to believe what he knew to be the truth – any more than he could believe that his loneliness and his broken heart could have induced him to such folly. But it was done, it could be corrected, and the bonus was that he could turn it to his advantage.

Still, he had to tread carefully. The sound of the snapping of the smallest twig underfoot, and the quarry would bolt.

This wasn't revenge. Just business. His business. He had no room in his heart for revenge. It was too numb for that.

She must have sensed his gaze on her, if she had been sleeping, for now she stirred, and her eyes opened. She looked at him with those eyes, which he had, until now, thought enigmatic and charming. He had been blind. Her eyes weren't enigmatic, but blank; they revealed nothing.

He wondered if her hand might come up to stroke his cheek, but it stayed where it was, immobile. Hands which could be so voraciously explorative when they were making love were as incapable of tenderness as the eyes. He now faced what he had long realized: no matter how ferocious – even aggressive – her lovemaking had been, there had never been any warmth in it. In fact, they had never *made love*; they had simply fucked. From her, there had, after all, been no giving, only taking. Only the truly vulnerable would fall for that, and Marlow, seeing that clearly now, as clearly as a drunk emerging from an alcoholic haze looks back on his folly, inwardly cursed himself for the chink in his armour.

'I missed you,' she said, smiling. The words were inert. The mouth that smiled now had been voracious, too.

'I missed you too,' Marlow replied, trying to inject some warmth into his voice. What a sham.

He knew now, of course, why his enemy had been able to keep pace with him. But this time he had fed her – his enemy's source all along – enough information *deliberately*. This time she would be tracked. Tracked, and trapped.

The question remained of not only who she was working with, but why.

He mustn't underestimate her intelligence; he had to keep one step ahead. The opposite side had organized everything exquisitely well. Everything, from the sham memory-loss and the pretended vulnerability to his seduction had been done with a ruthless efficiency. Only a consummate actor or a psychopath would have been able to carry it all off so convincingly, and it had been helped by the mock-abduction which had resulted in the murder of Ben Duff. It was clear now that INTERSEC had been allowed to thwart it; it had been stage-managed to allay any ghost of suspicion. Just like the set-up at Zwinger and Dels – a delaying tactic which might have signalled his own death.

But Marlow had the advantage now. His meeting with Sir Richard had gone well. Hudson, after only the briefest of interrogations, had passed on INTERSEC's request to his opposite number in the CIA, who had responded with speed, undertaking with Sir Richard to override the usual bureaucracy. Hudson had warned his counterpart of the urgency of the transaction, but Marlow knew that no secret service was ever as efficient in reality as it was in books. Nevertheless, he had extracted an agreement that the Reinhardt letter was to be forwarded directly to him at Room 55. INTERSEC had an internationally backed remit. It was their case. They should have first call on the document.

The problem was that he knew that, from the moment

he had the letter in his hands, he'd be closely watched. If Lopez was right, the Reinhardt letter would give them the location of the tablet.

But he already had enough information, based on Graves's deductions, to feed his enemy. He had told Su-Lin just enough, allowing her to coax the information out of him, to whet her appetite – and the appetite of whomever she served.

If there were a de Montferrat connection with Boniface, Dandolo's henchman, it would come out now.

He was taking a risk, and a big one.

Above all, he mustn't awaken any suspicion in her. He had to give her time to communicate with her contact before he made his own move. Lull her. Lull her into a sense of security. Keep her thinking she still had the upper hand, even though that meant he couldn't have her arrested immediately. Therein lay the risk but, without it, he'd never catch the main prey.

He ran his fingers over her cheek, but her lips didn't even move to kiss his fingertips. The pity of it, he thought. But his heart hardened. This was no Desdemona.

'I have to go soon,' he said.

'Must you? I get lonely. Even Ellen doesn't come to see me every day any more.'

'That's because you're cured. We'll be able to let you go soon.' Marlow thought of Ellen Shukman, the psychologist who had replaced Dr Duff, and whose own life could well have been in danger – Marlow's fault, *his* responsibility, again.

Her eyes sharpened at his words. 'What do you mean? You'll let me go? Back to Venice? Won't I be in danger?'

'Very soon, there will be no more danger,' he lied. But he could sense her mind working: *has my cover been blown? Was* she thinking that? He would have to tread carefully.

'Not until we are absolutely sure,' he said soothingly. Did she really take him for such a complete fool? Well, she was right to. But now it was his turn, though he had to be careful not to turn this into anything personal. Small danger of that, though. He may have made a bad mistake, but he still knew his business, and now he was wide awake.

She sat up, smacking him playfully, her delicious breasts swinging seductively, her lithe arms throwing the duvet aside as she swung her legs out to sit on the side of the bed. It all looked too beautiful to be true.

'You raise my hopes, only to dash them,' she said. 'I am getting so bored here.'

'Not for much longer, I promise,' Marlow said. 'Where are you going now?'

'To make you coffee.'

'Not lemon tea?'

'I know what you like.'

She smiled at him, but not with her eyes. Never with her eyes.

106

Catholic Empire in the East, Year of Our Lord 1205

Early spring, and the renewed year brought little stability. The rows between the Crusader leaders had held up his plans for the great voyage to the West; he could not leave a volatile situation behind him.

It came to him that he should have taken the crown himself – but then he could not have undertaken the voyage west, and he had to acknowledge that his own days were numbered and had to be consecrated to what was most important to him. He was ninety-five years old. Boniface was the choice he should have made. Strong and mature, he would have been a worthier heir than the pliant Baldwin, but it was too late. Boniface was engaged in fighting an alliance of the Greeks and the Bulgarians, united in their Eastern Christianity, and they were proving themselves difficult to subdue.

And Baldwin was dead. After his defeat at the battle of Adrianople, to which he had set out at the head of the finest of the Crusaders, he had been captured.

Dandolo recalled the report of the captain who had made his way back to Constantinople, leading a ragged and dusty troop of survivors, released by the Bulgarian king, Johanitza, in order to bring back the news and thus lower the morale of his enemies further. The captain and his men had been forced to witness Baldwin's end. The new emperor had been stripped of all but a loincloth and bound loosely at the knees and elbows, allowing him just enough freedom to crawl. Then, with a battleaxe, the victors had roughly severed his hands and feet and thrown him, bleeding, down on to the floor of a rocky gorge a few kilometres from the city of Adrianople itself. There they had left him. His death could not have been quick or kind.

And Dandolo had not been able either to prevent it or to rally his troops to take an immediate and ruthless vengeance. His strength was waning and, with it, his hold on the tablet of power, though he clutched it ever closer to him in his right hand under his robes, concentrating on the voyage he willed himself to make.

But a part of his otherwise indomitable spirit – an increasing part – was whispering doubts to him now, and those doubts were growing into certainties with every day that passed. There had been days – three he knew of at least – when he had neglected the tablet. Three days when, suddenly, he was aware that his right hand held nothing in it! True, the tablet returned there, the good Leporo had retrieved it – left, he had reported, on a desk, or in an unlocked drawer. That was cold comfort, though, in the face of the doge's unwilling acceptance of the fact that his own mind was beginning to fail, just as his flickering eyesight was failing – and failing fast.

He tried to calculate how long it would be before his left eye gave out for ever and consigned him to eternal darkness, even before death was ready to do the job. Would he see light again after death? Would Christ reach out to him and bid him join the great company of the blessed? Would he be strong-limbed and hawk-eyed once more, in the Elysian Fields? How he would have liked to have clung to that thought, and believed in it. But there was only the here and now. And the here and now brought little comfort. Even if he reached the great land in the West, he doubted if he would see it, see the green fields and the tall trees and the soft, rolling hills which he already saw in his imagination.

Would the journey itself even be made? his faltering spirit asked him. Yes! It had to be! And there was hope, some hope. Baldwin's brother, Henry, had taken over as emperor and he was a good and firm administrator. The new empire here and, with it, the interests of Venice, were safe, at any rate for now.

Should he pass on the secret of the tablet to Henry? Again, Dandolo's mind misgave him. He needed it for the journey. On the voyage, he would study it harder. He had been too hasty when he drowned the old Armenian who had opened the door of its secrets to him. He wished that old man with him now, but it was too late. Too late, once again. Time had played a skilful game of chess with him, and it looked as if Time had him in check.

But not checkmate! Not yet! Not yet!

But what if he died during the voyage? Or before it? Should he entrust the secret to Frid? Could Frid handle it? The Viking's loyalty was beyond doubt, Dandolo believed. But did Frid possess the mental fortitude to complete the great mission? Had he the strength of will to control such incomparable power?

As for Brother Leporo, who had been with him for

countless years: no. Leporo had not the vision. Leporo was a follower, not a leader. Leporo was too prone to jealousy to embrace a massive destiny, however much he might have thought he had it in him to do so. If the tablet were to fall into his hands, it would be a black day for the world, for he would be within its power, instead of having power over it. That was why Dandolo had been so worried at the temporary loss of the tablet – and so relieved and reassured when Leporo returned it to him. Despite the physical manifestations of its power which the millennia had imbued in the ancient tablet, it was the correct interpretation of what was written on it that gave its owner supremacy. Hadn't it worked, if only partially, for Bishop Adhemar? And he had made use of a flawed copy! His 'sacred scroll'!

So the tablet had better remain safe with him. He would not let it out of his grip again – ever. If its power should slip away from him, he would see to it that no one else would have the opportunity to inherit it. And what if a cautionary voice in one of the backrooms of his mind whispered that the most prudent course would be to destroy it? That he could not do – that would be asking too much. That would be like tearing out his precious left eye. He and the tablet had become one. One power, one destiny. The rolling millennia had decreed that they should be fused together, the right workman with the right tool, and never separated, for all eternity.

His head cleared. He knew what he would do. He would leave instructions that the tablet should be buried with him. In his grip. And that his grave should be on Holy Ground, but unmarked. Marked, if anywhere – and for a man as important as himself there would have to be a monument – in another place, to throw the curious off the scent. Only Frid and Leporo would be privy to his plan and, as an extra surety, he would place a curse on anyone who had the temerity to try to disturb his bones. There was an afterlife, and his spirit would watch over his dust with a keen eye. A man of God like Leporo and a man of devotion like Frid would heed such a warning, if nothing else.

Dandolo rose from the table in his rooms in the Palace of Boucoleon where he sat alone. Frid was organizing the finishing touches to the secret fleet; Leporo was supervising the final lading of the transports which would sail on the tide of the following dawn, taking the second consignment of precious and holy artefacts of the great city home to Venice. He looked out of the window and could just make out the four bronze horses, taken from the hippodrome here, on the deck of the largest ship, glinting in the afternoon sun as the deckhands lashed them down.

He snorted contemptuously. He could still – just – make out the outline of the horses' backs, see their shape. His left eye would not fail him yet. He was a fool to give in to pessimism. He would win yet – he would win, and his name would go down in history as a conqueror whose might would eclipse that of Alexander and Caesar.

107

New York City, the Present

'We've got some more on Zwinger and Dels,' said Lopez.

'Tell me,' replied Graves, looking up from double-checking the Montserrat family tree. Su-Lin was still getting under her skin. And it irked her that Marlow was keeping her wrapped in cotton wool. As far as she could see, the archaeologist had contributed very little to their work, despite her evident willingness, though Graves had to acknowledge that, from a professional point of view, the pretty academic had to be protected, for her own safety, and for the security of their operation.

'Looks like our little leatherwear company fronted two kinds of distribution network,' Lopez continued, looking up from his own screen in the main section of the Room 55 suite. 'Took a hell of a long time to deconstruct their accounting system, but any business, whatever it is, has to have records somewhere. These boys made leatherware all right, and good stuff too – some of their belts retailed for $250, and the legit. turnover at wholesale level ran to a respectable $1 million a year.'

'Still small potatoes.'

'As you say. I've had my guys do an inventory of their equipment – not the machinery, that's OK – but the electronic and software side is way above what they'd have needed. And after Marlow's own version of the gunfight at the OK Corral the place has been a desert – no employees, no management, nobody. All the birds have flown the coop, and someone wiped most of the slate clean, computer-wise. But I have ways of making computers talk, and one little hard drive on one little laptop kept its neck out of the noose.'

'Keep talking.'

'The big deal was in distribution of snow and smack, on a very ambitious scale, raw produce coming in from Columbia mainly, and really high-quality stuff from, believe it or not, Afghanistan: they had connections with US troop suppliers so import was made easy.'

'But that's –'

'We'll get to that. First things first. Processing here, in a plant just outside Baltimore and another in Colorado. Zwinger and Dels was the main clearing-house for distribution throughout the Land of the Free and Western Europe; main shipments to Germany and France. Huge markets in those countries – one thing the local geeks aren't economizing on, it seems. Redistribution centres in Berlin and Marseilles. The other little business they've got going is a massive internet-porn interest. So hard-core it'd melt your eyeballs, and all tastes catered for, especially the ones that'd send you straight to jail if you didn't cover your tracks very carefully.'

'So what else is new?'

'What's new is the list of directors. Or main shareholders. It's all very kosher, the way they run these businesses.

Pity for them that their technicians aren't quite as good as ours.'

'So what have you got?' asked Graves, urgency in her voice now.

'You remember the guy Andrei Borovsky? The guy whom one of the Vulcan 900s was registered to? The getaway vehicles from the attack at Sotheby's?'

'Of course, the junior partner at Zwinger's.'

'And remember the name of the other partner we unearthed?'

Graves thought for a moment. 'Sergei Konitsev?'

'Sergei Kutuzov. Our guy in the FSB, Colonel Safin, got us some dirt on him. Kutuzov had two identifiable partners, an Indian called Mehta and a Chinese called Chien – they both figure on the board of Zwinger and Dels. Now what on earth do you imagine they'd be doing on the board of a two-bit operation like a leatherworks, even one which sells belts at $250 a bash?'

'I see where you're going with this.' Graves reached for the phone.

'What're you doing?'

'Calling Sir Richard.'

'Why not Jack?'

'He isn't around right now.'

'Wait up. Mehta and Chien are in on the drugs and porn rackets, sure, and their names are linked to two other tasteful little operations. The human-organ traffic we knew a bit about, but there's also a very private club here in New York which they have an interest in.'

'And?'

'This club has an owner.'

'Most clubs do.'

'This took forever to dig up. I couldn't believe it when I saw it, but I double-checked, triple-checked, and there doesn't seem to be any doubt.'

'Hit me.'

Lopez was on the point of replying when he checked himself. 'This is a really big one, Laura. Maybe I'd better run this by Jack first.'

'Have you tried him?'

'Yes, and he's not responding.'

'And he isn't here,' Graves cried in frustration. 'Surely you can tell me. And if it's as important as you say, we should go straight to Hudson.' She pressed on. 'Is this the guy who may have the tablet? Who knows what it is, and who may be able to use it?'

Lopez spoke slowly, softly. 'I believe there must be a connection, yes.'

'Then tell me! You've given me all the rest of the shit, why not the punchline?'

Lopez seemed to have firmed up his decision. 'Jack first,' he said.

'This isn't the time for games, Leon.'

'I was never more serious.'

The lock on the outer security door buzzed and the door clicked open. The two of them turned to see Marlow appear behind the glass inner door, which opened for him after another few seconds.

'Where the hell have you been?' said Lopez, the tension breaking out in his voice. He scarcely noticed how haggard his chief was looking, and how much more than usually unkempt.

But Graves said: 'What's happened?'

'The trap's set,' Marlow said to Lopez.

He took a seat. He looked dead beat, but his eyes held a fire neither of his associates had seen there before.

'What's happened?' Graves said again.

'I've got a report to read. From Dr Shukman. Take me five minutes. But I'll fill you in. What have you got?'

'Leon has something – I think,' Graves said drily.

'Laura wanted to take this to Sir Richard,' Lopez explained. 'I thought, keep it in the family to begin with.'

'That's good.'

'He didn't want to tell me at all,' said Graves.

'Not before me?' said Marlow, still preoccupied. 'Better come out with it,' he said, looking at Lopez and adding, in answer to the question in Lopez's eyes, 'Laura needs to be in on whatever you've got. Now more than ever.'

'Question of trust,' put in Graves acidly.

'This is big,' said Lopez seriously. 'And I apologize to my colleague. Laura, you and I couldn't have run with this alone. And it has a bearing on Sir Richard.'

'Not my fault he's been calling me into his office because I haven't been at my desk here and he wants to check up on me. I'm not sitting on his lap, you know.'

'OK, Laura,' said Marlow. 'Leon?'

'I've got the Fourth Man,' said Lopez.

'Background?' asked Marlow, and Lopez ran through what he'd told Graves.

'So who is he?'

'Take a look for yourself.'

Lopez swung the screen of the nearest terminal round

and touched it, pulling a text loaded with figures and references into view. 'This is a digest of the paperwork,' he said. 'And it all points – here.'

He touched the screen again and dragged a picture into view – a large colour photograph of a smiling Rolf Adler.

108

Dr Ellen Shukman's report on Dr Su-Lin de Montferrat was concise. 'It's partly conjectural,' she'd said as she handed it to him, 'but mainly based on observation. It bears out your suspicions, and I'm glad I'd already written it when you came to me with them. Otherwise you might be accusing me of reacting to suggestions you placed in my mind. I just hope it isn't too late.'

Marlow, alone in his office, read Shukman's report, half disappointed to have his worst fears confirmed, half relieved that his suspicions were, after all, well-founded.

Given your directive that the memory-loss may have been faked, we can confirm that, in certain circumstances, such a piece of acting could be undertaken by the subject in such a way as to be convincing even to herself. Thus the subject, if properly controlled by a dominant Other who understood enough of her condition to manage it, would provide a useful and almost wholly reliable tool in the hands of that Other.

The subject has, in the light of our interviews and researches, indicated that she has passed a psychological boundary, freeing herself from what we might call normal inhibitions – indeed that she is almost certainly incapable of experiencing or expressing normal emotions. [The last phrase struck a harsh chord with Marlow.]

In one sense the subject inhabits a grey area in which all moral aspects are blurred, and any rules are of her own making. Her goal is exclusively the furtherance of her own ends or those of her Controller. Nothing else, no other consideration, plays any role at all. Salient 'qualities' in this context include ruthlessness, callousness, selfishness, faithlessness and mendacity. These 'qualities', coupled with a highly developed manipulative function, enable the subject to function flawlessly within a world created by a flawed psyche. Downsides for such a subject include: humourlessness, friendlessness and isolation; such a subject is emotionally immature and shallow, and also, having physical beauty, vain. Such a subject will not suffer any sense of personal defectiveness or inadequacy. To sum up, we are looking at an aspective borderline personality disorder with high psycho-/sociopathic elements, among other dysfunctional strains.

Marlow read through the summary twice, sighed, and fed the pages of the report through his shredder. All he had to do now was watch and wait, and he didn't think he'd have to wait long. He was certain that Su-Lin had not only picked up on the information he had fed her but, as he had hoped and intended, she'd decided that he suspected her, and would prepare to bolt.

All mechanisms were in place for her to succeed in escaping without realizing that her flight was being facilitated. Mechanisms were also in place to have her closely followed in whatever direction, and by whatever means, she might take. The computer to which she had had access was being closely monitored by one of Lopez's assistants.

The blue telephone rang at four that afternoon. It was the commander of the watch squad on surveillance duty at the 48th Street safe-house.

'Mr Marlow?'

'Yes?'

'Subject is on her way. Taxi to Kennedy at 15.55. Pursuit implemented.'

'Keep her in sight, but don't get too close. Seal the apartment until the forensic team arrives. Await advisement.'

'Sir.'

The phone went dead. Marlow sat in thought. He'd wait until her destination was certain before he joined the pursuit himself. He tried not to think of the risk he was taking.

But there was not much time for reflection. An intranet message appeared from Graves asking him to contact her immediately. He made his way to the main section of Room 55.

She was waiting for him, her face rigid. 'We may have a glitch,' she said.

'What?'

'I've just had word from Hudson: there's a delay on delivery of the Reinhardt letter. He asked me to relay. You're to see him now.'

'What's the problem?' Marlow asked on entering the cigar-and-eau-de-cologne-scented office.

Sir Richard, though impeccable as ever, nevertheless for once looked ruffled. 'Nothing serious. Administrative, really.'

'What?'

Hudson spread his hands. 'It seems Homeland's got wind of this operation. Worried it might affect national security. Need to vet the letter before forwarding it.'

'How long will that takc?'

'They say twenty-four hours.'

Marlow felt cold. Jesus, friendly fire at this stage of the game. 'Haven't you told them what they're jeopardizing? There'll be more than fucking national security to worry about if we don't get there first.'

'Don't worry. The letter's perfectly secure.'

Marlow thought of the other copy, on the Swiss safety-deposit box in Bern. Christ, he hoped that was secure.

'I'll nudge them to get it to us more quickly.'

Marlow could have throttled the suave bastard. This wasn't a fucking diplomatic game. This was gloves-off, blood-on-the-canvas stuff. 'Do that,' he said.

He made his way back downstairs, sweating. Once he regained Room 55 he went straight to a blue phone and rang the watch commander for an update.

'She's arrived at the airport. Following her in.'

'Terminal?'

'One.'

Marlow thought. Terminal One. Aeroflot, Air China, Lufthansa. Among others. Quite a choice.

'Keep me posted.'

'Sure.'

'Soon as you know her flight, get someone on it. Get airline clearance for an inflight communications line too.'

'On it.'

Marlow hung up. Su-Lin was a lifeline now. If her trail

led to Adler then, provided Marlow had the location of the tablet in time, he could spring the trap. But if he hadn't . . .

And there was the ever-present possibility of third-party interest in the tablet. Marlow hadn't forgotten the reluctance of Yale to play ball over translating the Adhemar manuscript.

Was Homeland Security really interested in the Reinhardt letter?

Why the delay *now*?

His mind raced. He saw Graves watching him, and gave her a tight smile. He didn't want to talk.

Lopez entered from his lab.

'Jack – Christ, I'm glad you're here,' said Lopez. He held a sheaf of papers untidily stacked in a blue file in his hand.

'Tell me it's good news.'

'I don't think it is.'

'What?'

'I thought you were in your office. I was about to ring.'

'With Hudson.' Marlow looked at Graves, including her. 'Delay on the letter. Twelve hours min. Homeland.'

'Shit.'

'So tell me.'

'I've cleared all sensitive info. from the electronic files. About to shred this stuff.'

'But?'

Lopez shook his head. 'Jeez, Jack, I don't know how to tell you this.'

'Go *on*!'

'Someone got there first. Christ knows how they tapped

in. It was only unlocked for half an hour. My premier assistant –'

'What did they get?'

'Enough to know our thinking on Reinhardt.'

'So they'll have as close an idea as we have about the location?'

'Not the precise location, but –'

'Without the letter, they can't know that.'

'– but they will know the letter exists. And they'll know about the copy still in the deposit-box in Bern.'

All my fault, thought Marlow. All my fault. Got to put this right.

The blue phone rang again. It was the watch commander at Kennedy, checking in.

'News?' Marlow barked.

'No scheduled flight. Private jet. Long-haul. Gulf-stream V.'

'Got its flightplan?'

'On its way.'

'Fast as you can.'

'On it.'

'Know who owns it?'

'Licensed to a big company. MAXTEL.'

'Jesus, he must be confident.'

'What?'

'Nothing.'

There was a buzzing on the line. 'What?' the watch commander was saying to someone else. Then he was back on. 'Destination's just come in,' he said.

'Hit me.'

'Berlin, Germany.'

'Good. I'm going there. Your contact here will be Graves. Liaise with me through her. I want registration, ETA, anyone travelling with her, everything.'

'Got it.'

Marlow hung up and looked at his associates. 'The game's afoot,' he said. 'Laura, I want you to organize an INTERSEC long-range for Berlin as soon as possible.'

Graves looked expectant. 'But I'm coming too.'

'Not yet. I need you here. Leon, as soon as that letter comes through, gut it and send me the details ultra-secure – through Laura.' Marlow looked at her. 'OK with that?'

'I'm here. Soon as you need me, just whistle.'

'I'll do that.'

Marlow looked at them both. 'Walkdown time,' he said. 'Please God.'

109

'You have done well,' said Rolf Adler, sitting on the sofa in his office in Berlin.

'Thank you.'

'Pity your cover's blown – but then, you can't have everything.'

Su-Lin, perched on the armchair near him – it was so large and deep it would have engulfed her if she had sat back – pursed her lips. 'I have brought you everything you requested on this mission. I expect to be repaid, not criticized.'

Adler watched her. He was unused to being spoken to in such a way, but it amused him and, in Su-Lin's case, he accepted that he was in the company of an equal partner. Su-Lin's de Montferrat and Venetian connections had first brought him into contact with Doge Dandolo. His business connections with her late father had paid him an unexpected and incalculable bonus when he had discovered the daughter, an ambitious little mouse who longed to be a lioness. A stormy and short affair had ceded place to a much more satisfactory business partnership, and he had managed to identify and handle a capricious, ruthless and entirely amoral temperament. The girl was an ideal foot-soldier – she was entirely free of the slightest scruple.

Without her, he would be in ignorance of the great destiny life had prepared for him. Without her, he would not have the means to attain that which he now held virtually within his grasp. But he knew what she expected. The deal was that once the tablet was theirs, they would rule in unison. Adler did not trust her any more than he imagined she trusted him, but he knew her limitations, and he had a bone ready to throw her.

'Five million Swiss francs are already lodged in your name in an account with Kleinwort Benson in Geneva,' he told her. 'As an initial token of my gratitude.'

'But we are not there yet.'

'We are, as the poet said, winning near the goal,' Adler replied. 'But we are, you're right, not quite there yet.' He paused. 'This General Reinhardt,' he continued. 'I'd like to know how the tablet came into his possession.'

'That's immaterial.'

'He was close to Hitler. It makes me wonder . . .' Adler had pondered this already. Hitler had failed. But even Hitler had not had his detailed knowledge of the workings of the tablet. Hadn't Hitler driven out the very Jewish scientists who might have helped him, had they not been relentlessly pursued and victimized, or driven into exile? It was ironic, and what a fool the man had been. All he had done, quite apart from his clumsy destructiveness, was create an enormous loss in Europe, and an enormous gain in the USA. To control people, you had to lull them into a state where they were unaware that they were no longer thinking for themselves.

'We have enough information to know that the tablet is here in Berlin, and not only that, that it is lodged somewhere in the collection now housed at the Vorderasiatisches Museum. We also know that a copy of Reinhardt's letter exists in a bank vault in Bern. That letter will give the precise location of the tablet,' said Su-Lin crisply.

'Getting the thing from Bern can be arranged,' said Adler drily. 'I have people in Switzerland who have influence with that particular bank and, as we know that the general left us long ago, a close relative with the right papers in his hand can be organized to pick up his remaining effects even at this distance in time. We don't have to resort to violence or robbery, and the expense that would entail. But we must move fast. Marlow will be on its track already.' He thought for a moment. 'What we need is someone who can decipher the tablet for us when we have it. Someone who is guaranteed to have that knowledge and produce results quickly. She was within our grasp once, but Marlow rescued her. Fortunately for us, as it turns out.'

'The Graves woman?'

'Precisely.'

'We know where she is. Springing her might be quite an undertaking.'

Adler smiled. 'You underestimate me,' he said.

'Whatever is to be done, it must be done now.'

'Alas, I should have liked to use you. But I am afraid that, as you say, your usefulness in that connection is at an end.'

'My work has been impeccable.'

'And rewarded.'

'For the moment.'

Adler looked at her. 'You are comfortable in your apartment here?'

She returned his gaze, guardedly. 'Yes.'

Adler spread his hands expansively. He had installed his aide in a penthouse not far from Charlottenburg, with its own exclusive elevator and his own security firm guarding it. The last detail she did not know. If she had known, she would also have known that she was a fly already caught in a web. 'I have put a car and driver at your disposal. I suggest you relax for a couple of days, enjoy yourself. As soon as Ms Graves has been successfully delivered to us, I'll bring you in to help persuade her to . . . advise us. I'm confident she'll come round.'

'It'll take you a couple of days to get her?'

'Less, I hope. But these things take a little organization.'

'INTERSEC's already organized.'

'Don't worry about INTERSEC,' Adler said curtly; but he saw her expression change at the snarl he'd been unable to keep out of his voice, and recomposed his face into a bland smile. 'Where are my manners? We should be celebrating your achievement.'

'Have we time for that?'

'Indulge me,' replied Adler, keeping a close rein on his patience. He rose and, crossing to a concealed refrigerator, produced a bottle of Dom Perignon from it, and two cold flutes. He placed them on the table, opened the bottle and poured the wine, then crossed to his desk and, unlocking a drawer, brought out a small black box. This he placed by Su-Lin's glass.

She looked at him suspiciously, but opened it. It contained a Cartier wristwatch in white gold.

'Time will, I hope, always be on our side from now on,' said Adler.

'Thank you,' she said, rising and giving him a peck on the cheek. He resisted the urge to recoil. But he knew that the watch she was now placing on her wrist would not stay there long.

'The pleasure is all mine,' he replied, grinning broadly.

'What do the British say? "Here's to crime"?' She managed a cold smile.

'Very witty, Dr de Montferrat.'

They clinked glasses, and drank. The slightly nutty champagne was delicious.

After she had left, Adler summoned his new personal assistant.

'Little job,' he said. 'Little tidying up to do.'

The PA's face was expressionless. 'Do you wish me to contact Trotter and Sparkes?'

Adler waved a hand. 'No need for that. This doesn't really require special skills. The boys from Pankow should be able to handle it. It concerns Dr de Montferrat.'

'When, sir?'

'Tonight at the latest. By the way, she has a Cartier watch, which I shouldn't mind having retrieved. And freeze that Kleinwort Benson account as soon as the job's done.'

'Sir.'

'I do need Trotter and Sparkes for another job,' Adler continued. 'So get them here immediately for a briefing.

Tell them to pack an overnight bag, and organize the Gulfstream for them. They'll be bringing a guest back with them.'

'From where, sir?'

'Oh,' said Adler. 'New York.'

110

New York City, the Present

Graves sat in her apartment sipping a glass of Chablis and watching the dusk wrap its cloak over the New York skyline.

Shortly before leaving INTERSEC, she'd relayed the information provided by the watch commander about Su-Lin to Marlow, now in Berlin. She tried to imagine him there, wondered if he'd be sleeping, if he'd have time to sleep.

It had been a long day, of tension, of waiting. Waiting for news from Switzerland which, they hoped, would confirm that the copy of the Reinhardt letter in the bank vault in Bern had not been removed. The latest news from the bank had been that it was secure, but there was a rather stiff rider to the bank's email to the effect that their responsibility was to hand it over, if requested, to anyone with the correct authorization. There was no way, they had said, rather more formally, that their client confidentiality would be compromised, no matter how much time had passed. Graves had spent that afternoon organizing an injunction to be used against the bank in case of need, forcing them to hand the letter over to INTERSEC.

As for the copy lodged in the OSS files and later transferred to the CIA archive, Sir Richard, for once, had been as good as his word. It had arrived at INTERSEC after a delay of only nine hours, and Lopez had quickly confirmed that it contained, in precise, somewhat dated, German, not only where the tablet was, but how it could be identified. It was some comfort that their deduction that it would now be in the Vorderasiatisches Museum was correct but, more disquietingly, the letter itself imparted authority to its bearer to demand the tablet's immediate release by the museum's director. It was unclear whether the letter they had in their possession, or the one in Bern, or both, carried weight in such a scenario. For security, the letter they had was being couriered over to Marlow now, in a diplomatic bag carried by an INTERSEC field operative on Sir Richard's immediate staff. Maximum priority and super-ultra-security. That important.

Graves wished she had been selected to be the courier, but INTERSEC feared that, after her brief capture by the forces they were now able to identify as 'most likely adversary', her profile was too visible, and she should travel separately. She had to accept waiting until the following day, when she'd fly to the German capital on an INTERSEC Falcon to join Marlow. The rendezvous in Berlin would be sent to her via an encoded SMS on her arrival.

It was still early evening, but her flight left at dawn, and she was exhausted. She finished her wine and switched on the television, where an episode of *Frasier* was airing – Eddie was suffering from some mysterious depression which was affecting Martin and the whole household. She left the TV to play and, undressing, prepared to shower and go to bed with an apple and a good book. She was determined to finish *The Princess of Cleves* before she left; she found the formal, old-fashioned style soothing. She already knew it would end badly. Honour before self-gratification. But either course would lead the heroine down the tubes, poor thing. Sometimes you just couldn't win.

It was after her shower, after she had towelled herself dry, put on her favourite kimono – white silk, with a golden dragon embroidered across its back – and wandered back into her living room, that she sensed something was wrong. The TV played softly on, everything was in its place, as it had been. But . . .

She stood quite still in the centre of the room. Her automatic was in her briefcase by the side of the sofa and her INTERSEC-dedicated cell-phone lay on the coffee table next to last month's edition of the *New Yorker*, open at a review of a Pollock retrospective at MoMA. For some reason, both seemed far away, separated from her by a dangerous journey of just a few metres. The shadows had deepened while she'd been taking her shower and she hadn't yet switched the lights on. Daylight had faded and the only illumination in the room came from the electric cityscape beyond her windows.

Silence. Nothing. Yet she sensed – she was sure – that she was not alone. What was it? A slight odour? Patchouli oil? Something that reminded her of her mother when she herself had been a little girl. Her mother had been at Woodstock. She'd also been involved in the student demonstrations in Chicago and, later, at Kent State – she'd been standing near Allison Krause when the National

Guard gunned the kid down. Her mother would have been horrified if she'd known what Graves did for a living; she wouldn't have understood it.

Why were these thoughts coming to Graves now? Now, with the smell of patchouli oil and the sense of impending danger?

In the shadows, someone sniffed, and a light went on. An Aram lamp which hung over the sofa, its light spreading just enough to reveal the form of a plump woman in a flowing dress covered with flowers. She wore a straw hat over long dark hair. Graves could see nothing of the face but the mouth.

It smiled. 'Don't be alarmed, dear.'

'Who the hell are you?'

The woman chuckled. 'Your travel agent.'

Graves made a quick calculation. There was no way she could get her gun out of the briefcase, but if she could grab the briefcase itself and swing it, she just might –

Even as she started to lunge forward, an incredibly strong, bony arm wrapped itself round her throat from behind and pulled her close to a body which, under its clothes, felt skeletal. A faintly sour, antiseptic smell. 'Sweet dreams,' said a male voice close to her ear and, as she struggled, she felt a hypodermic needle thrust hard into her upper right arm.

III

Berlin, the Present

The nine-hour delay caused by Homeland, and the extra time it took for the INTERSEC courier to get the letter to him, had counted for a lot. Just how much was clear to Marlow the moment the curator of Mesopotamian Antiquities at the Vorderasiatisches Museum expressed, with some embarrassment, his regrets.

'You must understand that there was nothing we could do,' he said. 'The conditions of the loan were perfectly clear, and we were presented with impeccable credentials.'

It was four o'clock in the afternoon. Outside, the sun shone brightly in the clear Berlin air, in mockery of Marlow's dark mood.

The tablet had been handed over to a young woman presenting herself as Frau Birgit von Machtschlüssel-Reinhardt the previous evening; after half a day of checking references, all of which had been confirmed with extraordinary speed. The transaction must have taken place soon after Marlow had landed in Berlin. As soon as the letter was in his hands, Marlow had gone to the museum, to be confronted by the news that the tablet was gone.

'It was very sudden – quite irregular. Unique, in my experience; but the tablet in question was not on actual display, and the lady was insistent. She said she only had limited time in Berlin, so we had no alternative.'

Marlow was silent.

'She left an address, contact number, email, of course.'

Marlow remembered the combination on the steel container that had held Adhemar's empty iron box and its key: 13-1-24. M-A-X. MAXTEL.

Adler would know that he was in pursuit. Would the tablet even still be in Berlin? And how much time did he have? If Adler already knew how to use the tablet, he had no time at all.

But he still had to try.

He drove back the short distance to INTERSEC's Berlin base, where he'd established a modest operations centre. Something else was nagging at his mind. Why wasn't Graves here yet? She should have made contact by now, even allowing for the time difference. The time difference, he reflected as he tore through the nascent rush-hour, ignoring outraged horn-blasts from other motorists — that was another factor to Adler's advantage, as it bought him another six hours, easily time for him to have sprung the copy letter from the Bern bank, which, with his influence, must have been a simple task.

At INTERSEC base, there was more bad news. Worse, if possible, than he'd just had.

In response to the message waiting for him, he immediately put through a priority call to Lopez.

'Thank Christ,' said Lopez, as soon as he heard Marlow's voice.

'What's happened to her?'

'Our people went to her apartment at 4 a.m. to collect

her for the flight. They called ahead and there was no response. When they got there, there was no response either. Of course they had a set of duplicate keys to her place, but when they got in, nothing.'

'*Nothing?*'

'Not a trace. Nothing disturbed. Nothing at all. Her case was half packed at the side of her bed, but her bed hadn't been slept in.'

'OK, Leon.'

'We're following every lead. Forensics have gone over the place. One or two small elements, fibres from clothes, a couple of fingerprints, but I'm not optimistic.'

'I don't think we need Forensics to work out what's happened to her,' said Marlow, his throat dry. 'And we need to find her, not how they managed to get to her. What happened to her security cordon?'

'In place, but hell, she's not the only person living in her block. And you kept it low-level in order not to draw attention to us. The third party, remember? The other guys you think are interested in the tablet, apart from MAXTEL?'

Marlow was silent.

'What do you want me to do?' Lopez went on. 'Come over?'

Marlow thought. Lopez was the only other person, apart from Graves, to be fully in the know. He could use him here, in Berlin. But was that outweighed by the need to keep some kind of anchor in New York.

How deliberate had that nine-hour delay been?

And he couldn't afford the time it'd take Lopez to get there, even if he boarded a plane immediately.

'We have one chance,' he said. 'Graves is still equipped with a homing implant, isn't she?'

'Yes. If Adler hasn't second-guessed it.'

'Activate it.'

Marlow hung up. He glanced round the functional room he sat in. Plain white walls, grey woodwork, a plain blind covering the square window. Cold, flattening light. For a moment he felt helpless.

Unless Adler had specialists in his pocket – and Marlow already suspected the translation delay at Yale hadn't originated from him – then Graves was the one person in the picture apart from himself and Lopez who had guaranteed knowledge of the tablet, and she was the only person who could interpret it. If Adler had all the data he needed, except the vital means of using the instructions which would open the door of unlimited power to him, then it followed that . . .

Wherever she was now, the tablet, and Adler, would be with her.

Adler had planned this every step of the way. If he knew about the tracker in Graves's arm, they were lost.

112

The room was dark, wood-panelled, the only light – whether natural or artificial, she could not tell – filtering from windows which were mere slits high up in the walls. An indeterminate light. She couldn't tell from it what time of day it was. It seemed slowly to be waning. It might have been approaching dusk.

She didn't know how long she'd been there, didn't know where she was. She estimated that she'd been conscious for maybe ten minutes since the drug they'd pumped into her had worn off. She was still groggy, but her eyes were able to focus and the headache she had was manageable. She was still dressed in the kimono she'd been wearing when they'd taken her, and her naked body felt vulnerable beneath it.

The room was simply furnished. There was a plain table, two simple wooden chairs, and the single bed on which she was lying. A cell, she thought. They've put me in a cell.

She had already raised herself on one elbow, and now she got unsteadily to her feet. Her head swam a little, but she kept her balance. She started to explore what little there was to explore in the room but, after a few steps, she had to sit down on one of the chairs. She'd noticed that there was one door, made of steel, with no handle or any other feature. The slits of windows were two metres above her highest reach, even if she'd stood on the table, too narrow in any case for anyone to pass through, and had thick glass panes with no sign of any catches to open them.

So she was trapped.

She could guess who had captured her, and why. All she could do was wait.

She didn't have to wait long.

They must have been watching her, for soon afterwards the door opened soundlessly, and an elegant man of perhaps fifty entered. Impeccably dressed in a charcoal-grey business suit. Not a hair out of place, and fine, delicate hands whose fingers tapered to immaculately manicured nails. He carried a small black leather case, which he placed on the table. She knew his face. It did not surprise her.

He was followed by the plump woman who'd been in her apartment, and a tall, bony, impossibly thin man. Both were incongruously clad in grey nylon boiler suits and wore surgeon's gloves. Plastic goggles hung round their necks and their heads were covered in nylon surgeon's caps. The man was carrying an oilcloth or tarpaulin, the kind you lay on floors to protect them when you're decorating.

The door swung to behind them, and closed with the softest of clicks.

The man in the suit carefully unzipped the case he'd been carrying, and from it drew a grey velvet bag, from which he took a small oblong object which seemed to be made of terracotta. This he placed on the table before her, on top of its little bag. She knew immediately what it was.

'If you're counting on being rescued, don't,' the man said at last. 'But I haven't much time. I need your help. A little translation work.'

'You won't get it,' Graves replied.

'I think I will,' he replied. 'I could tell you that we are already watching your mother's house in Mount Vernon. I could even tell you the house number and the name of the street. But you might still think I was bluffing, and that she could not be in any real danger. So . . .'

He reached into the case again and from it took two more objects, which he placed near him on the table. Graves looked at them and flinched. A scalpel and a pair of jeweller's pliers. Behind her, she heard a discreet noise, and half turned to see the bony man shake out the oil-cloth and spread it neatly on the floor.

'My associates are rather expert with these simple tools,' said Rolf Adler. 'Take off your kimono.'

'Let me help you, dear,' said the plump woman, coming forward. The smell of patchouli oil was overpowering in that confined space. 'Don't struggle.'

She pulled the gown clear of Graves's body and left it draped behind her on the chair. Graves tried to retrieve it, to stand, but she was still unsteady, and could not collect her thoughts. What little strength she'd regained now ebbed.

Adler regarded her gravely for a moment. Then, delicately, he picked up the pliers and handed them to the gaunt man, who stepped forward in turn to receive them and pulled his goggles up over his eyes.

'Now,' he said to Graves again. 'I need your help.'

113

'We've got a signal, but it's faint,' Lopez told Marlow. The secure New York/Berlin line was poor, and Marlow had to strain to catch his associate's voice. 'Shall I send it to you?'

Marlow moved to the window of his hotel room in a vain effort to improve the reception. 'Tell me,' he said. He didn't want to involve his INTERSEC colleague in Berlin too closely. He was no longer sure how well any information could be contained. He looked at the large-scale map of Berlin and its immediate surroundings, spread out like a coverlet on the bed.

'Place called Bönigsdorf. Tiny. About fifteen kilometres south-west of Potsdam. There's a mansion just outside the village. Not a big place, but old. Very thick walls. Kind of mini-fortress. Modernized recently, stands alone in a walled garden, big, couple of acres. Nothing on security there.'

'That's where he's gone to ground?'

'That's where Graves is, as far as the tracker is concerned.'

'Do you think he's wise to it?'

'Jesus, I hope not.'

Neither of them voiced the fear they both shared. To separate Graves from the implant, Adler would have to cut it out of her arm. But he'd have to find it first.

'I've got the place,' said Marlow, pinpointing it on the map.

'You could need backup.'

'If I need it, I'll call for it. I'll check it out alone first.'

'You'd better hurry.'

'She won't collaborate.'

'He won't give her any choice. And what if he doesn't need her?'

'To translate the thing? No, he had this planned. It'll take him too long to get someone else he can trust to do it. He's let us do all the groundwork for him.'

Marlow hung up. He swiftly changed into dark clothes – black jeans, soft matt-black boots, a rollneck of the same colour, over which he strapped the harness for his automatic. He clipped a Kevlar knife in its sheath to his belt and pulled on a black suede bomber jacket, stuffing black leather gloves into one of its pockets. Into the other he put a small spray canister. Then he went down to the garage and picked up the car he was using, a gunmetal-grey Porsche 911. From its boot he removed a PDR, his usual FN-P90, and two blast dispersal grenades.

He took a south-western route out of the city, into the light of the setting sun.

Once outside the city limits, the gathering darkness engulfed him and the roads became lonely. He drove fast but steadily, and had reached his destination by mid-evening. The place was as Lopez had described it. Marlow parked a hundred metres away, and walked down the country lane which led past the house. Everything was silent except for the gentle rushing of the faint breeze in the branches.

His senses were on full alert, but he was not challenged, nor could he detect any hint of anyone watching him.

He reached the wall and skirted it until he came to the gate. Very gently, he tested it – locked – and through its grille made his survey of what he could see of the house.

It stood on its own; he had not passed another building in the last kilometre, and there was no other he could see as he scanned a countryside which looked monochrome, shades of grey, in the light of a three-quarter moon. A square house, unornamented except for a modest portico surrounding the front door. Another door to the rear, and a third, on the west side, bricked up. Two floors of tall windows, and one upper storey where the windows were smaller; narrow slits of windows towards the base of the building, which indicated a basement or cellar of some sort. No visible outbuildings except for a double garage. The place was surrounded by a wall about three metres high, in which there was one entrance, an iron double gate from which a short drive led through neat gardens planted with dark-green trees and shrubs to the front door and the garage to the east of it. The gate and the garage doors were closed, and there was no sign of light in any of the windows, as far as Marlow could see, and in many places his view was impeded by the wall. He could not see the north side of the house at all.

It seemed impossible that there should be no guards, but it occurred to Marlow that Adler may have come here with only a skeleton crew. Like Marlow, he would want to keep his discovery close until he was completely sure that he could use it. But there would be electronic surveillance. Marlow would have to take that risk. From what he could see, there were no cameras in the trees, but he'd have to take a chance on passive magnetic field detectors, microphonic or H-field systems.

The bars of the gate were set too closely together for him to squeeze through them, but the wall was scalable, and it wasn't topped by razor wire or any other deterrent. Marlow walked round it until he was at a spot which he judged to be out of the sightlines of most of the windows. He bent his knees and leapt, succeeding the second time in getting a grip on the wall's parapet, and with an effort he hauled himself up until he was straddling it. He crouched low, collecting his breath and listening keenly, just a shadow among other shadows. After waiting a full two minutes, he swung his outer leg over and, after a second's further pause, dropped on to the grass below.

He remained crouched there, then cautiously made his way forward, using his spray canister to search for infrared alarm lines. There could be fibre-optic detectors, as well, but he could see no E-field poles and there was still no evidence of CCTV cameras.

Silently as a cat, he came closer and closer to the house. He began to scan the windows for a possible way in. He'd have to keep as silent as ever and, even if the garden wasn't wired, the house certainly would be. He was well armed, but he was alone. His only ace in the hole was the element of surprise.

He was ten metres from the nearest wall of the house when two low, dark shapes came hurtling round the far corner towards him. Low and silent, and very fast.

Dogs. Adler had chosen the oldest and most effective defence mechanism in the book.

There was no point in running. Too far to get back to the wall, the dogs would be on him in seconds. And no Mace spray. Marlow could take out one dog silently, but not two. He drew his automatic and crouched in readiness.

He was lucky. The leading dog came in for the attack first. Both Dobermans, long-muzzled beasts, which made his job easier, but vicious and lethal as Lugers. Marlow raised his left arm to give the dog something to go for, rising slightly as he did so and bracing himself for the weight of the animal's body as it threw itself on him, jaws open, ready to latch on to the proffered target. As soon as it had, and Marlow felt its teeth worry at the thick leather of his jacket as it sought to bite through it to the flesh, he brought the gun up and smashed its butt down on the dog's muzzle, up at the top, between the eyes. The beast died instantly, without even a yelp, and Marlow shook himself free to deal with its companion, which had been worrying his ankles, snarling, but not barking. Now the animal sensed danger and hesitated, looking Marlow in the eye, but not jumping up, as he had hoped it might. Impasse. Swiftly but steadily, he re-holstered the gun and drew the knife. The dog knew that it was not feared, and it showed doubt. Only seconds had passed. Marlow had to take advantage of the brute's hesitation and strike, but the dog kept low.

Then it was too late. The animal reached a decision, turned and bolted back the way it had come.

Moments later, there was a confused sound of men's voices. Rough voices, calling to each other in – what language? Slavonic, in any case. Lights came on in the house and, as Marlow flattened himself against the wall, dark shapes appeared round the corners of the house on either side of him. Someone barked an order and in an instant the whole garden was bathed in the glaring, flat whiteness of searchlights. There was the ominous clicking of sub-machine-gun bolts.

There was nowhere to run. Praying that the glass of the window behind him wasn't reinforced, Marlow smashed the stock of his PDR into the nearest pane. It shattered easily; old glass, maybe even the original glazing. No need to worry about setting off alarms inside now.

As the machine guns started to stutter, he hurled himself inwards through the low-silled window, shattering more glass and delicate wooden struts with his weight as he rolled over and over across the polished oak floor of the room beyond it.

No one there. Yet. He rose fast and turned back to the window. The guards, thundering up, were still bellowing at each other in what Marlow now recognized as Serbian. Not trained mercenaries; not for this kind of work, anyway. Far too incautious. He crouched by the window until he could tell his pursuers were close. Then he stood abruptly and brought the FN-P90 to bear, hammering out an arc of withering fire at face level and at point-blank range.

The silence after the deafening noise had echoed away was as deep as the sea. Somewhere in the silence, it seemed about a hundred kilometres away, the surviving Doberman whimpered in fear.

Five bodies lay sprawled and broken under the window. Only one moved, but no sound came from the contorted face, as his whole jaw had been shot away.

Marlow listened in the silence, but there was nothing. The dog stopped whimpering, and then the only noise which re-established itself was the sound of the wind in the trees. The white light bathed everything in an eerie glow.

Then there was another noise. Creaking, whirring. Electric doors opening.

The garage doors.

Marlow craned through the window. To his right, he could see the main gates opening. Then the noise of a car. A black Porsche SUV roared out of the garage and, as it sped up the drive and out of the gates on to the lane, he caught a glimpse of the passengers: a plump woman at the wheel, and next to her a thin man, both dressed in what looked like boiler suits.

He sprang through the opening, gun ready, and made for the garage.

Its interior was illuminated. There was a second car there, a burgundy-red Rolls. Near it stood Adler, a gun in his right hand. His other hand held Graves's upper left arm in a vicious grip as he manhandled her towards the car.

Marlow stepped into view, drawing out his HK but wary of lining up a shot as Graves's body was between his line of fire and Adler. Graves saw him, and Adler followed her line of sight with his eyes before she could dissimulate. Swearing, he swung his weapon round and fired wildly. One of the three rounds he got off found its mark in Marlow's shoulder, in the same place as his earlier wound. Marlow was knocked off balance as he felt his collar-bone smash and went down. Adler was wielding an

AutoMag V and the .50-calibre bullet had done a hell of a lot of damage. By the time Marlow had raised himself to one knee and levelled his own gun with a shaking hand, Adler had had time to bundle Graves into the car, hitting her neatly over the back of the head with the automatic's barrel to subdue her, and had taken his place at the wheel.

Marlow fired at the tyres as the Rolls' engine kicked in, but his aim was wide and his bullets hammered harmlessly into the wing. The big car turned heavily on to the drive, slowly picking up speed. You can't hurry a Rolls.

But then something happened. The main gates began to close. Adler accelerated to beat them, but a woman had appeared, framed by the gateway, in the middle of the drive, caught in the light. A thin woman in late middle-age. Adler drove straight for her, but she made no attempt to move. Instead, she raised her right hand. It held a tiny gun – a Ruger LCP. She brought up her left hand to steady her right and fired just before the car was on her. The .38 bullet was enough to shatter the windscreen. The big car swerved at the last moment, catching the woman and flinging her to one side before smashing into one of the gateposts. Flames burst under the bonnet in an instant.

Marlow ran, his heart battering his aching ribs. Once, he stumbled, turning an ankle, but he forced himself back to his feet and ran on, reaching the car and wrenching the nearside rear door open, using his good arm and all his strength to drag Graves's unconscious form out by her legs, pulling her free and across the grass as far as he could before he collapsed. On the other side of the drive, he could see the shape of the woman, dressed in a fawn mac. She lay still. Over the roar of the fire in the car Marlow could hear Adler's screams, could see the flailing arms and the twisting body as the man struggled to get out, could see his head catch fire and turn into a burning skull, the jaw still snapping open and shut as the fire ripped flesh and muscle from it. Then it gave a last convulsion and slumped on the ivory leather seat, like a puppet with its strings cut, as the flames closed in on it and covered it like a shroud.

Frau Müller had taken her revenge.

114

New York City, the Present

'What will happen to her?' Graves wanted to know.

'Does it matter?' Marlow smiled, and shifted his position in the armchair at Graves's apartment. The effort sent a shooting pain through his heavily bandaged shoulder, and he winced. 'In any case, you don't have to worry about Frau Müller. She'll be in a wheelchair for the rest of her life, but she'll live, and we're not taking any action against her. No one is. It's not worth it. She's not worth it.'

'Isn't she a risk?' asked Lopez, from the other armchair.

'No. Without Adler, she's nothing. When he fired her, her life was over.'

'But she was a willing aide. In all those projects of his . . .'

'She's already told the police everything she knows. She's implicated the three international businessmen we know of, one Chinese, one Indian and one Russian, but it'll be one hell of a job to bring any kind of case against any of them. They're just too powerful. Even if we did get them, there'd be others like them, but as far as these guys are concerned, without Adler and without MAX-TEL, they're nothing. They'll have the police watching them for ever; their teeth are drawn.'

He thought of the other two accomplices, the middle-aged couple in the car who'd got away before Adler. God knows who they'd been. Domestics? Aides? Rats deserting the sinking ship? They'd probably thought an army was descending on them. But he'd never know who they were now. The German police and EUROPOL had drawn a blank. They'd vanished. There was nothing to pursue.

'Memories are short,' said Graves, interrupting his thoughts.

'So is life,' said Marlow. 'The important thing is, they don't have this.'

The other two followed his gaze to the little clay tablet that rested innocuously on the coffee table between them. Marlow had picked it up from the scorched grass where it had fallen from Adler's burning hand and transferred it quietly to his pocket in the confusion of police cars, fire engines and ambulances that had invaded Bönigsdorf in the wake of what the international press later reported as 'the tragic loss of billionaire entrepreneur and philanthropist Rolf Adler, in a freak auto accident at his country seat outside Berlin'.

No one breathed a word about the other circumstances. House cleaners had arrived and done their work well before the press was let near the site. As for the public services, they turned the blind eye they always did when called to similar scenes.

'So what's to be done with it?' said Graves, picking the tablet up and turning it over in her hands.

The other two were silent for a moment.

'We know what it can do,' said Marlow.

'If the whole thing isn't a myth,' said Lopez.

'A myth? You mean it only worked because they believed that it did? Is it worth putting that to the test?'

'It could be a major force for good,' said Lopez, guardedly.

'What do you mean – we could use it as a force for world peace?' Marlow's tone was mocking. 'I don't think even this tablet's that powerful.' He paused for a moment. 'In any case, the risk of its being used for other reasons is too great. And that is a greater likelihood, whoever gets their hands on it.'

'We're the only ones now who know what it does, how to use it,' said Graves thoughtfully.

'I hope so,' Marlow replied. 'But just in case, I decided to buy this.' From his shoulder-bag, which lay at his feet, he pulled a plastic bag, and from it, an ordinary hammer. A large one.

'You can't be serious,' said Graves, alarmed.

Marlow ignored her. 'Leon,' he said, turning to him, 'have you done what I asked you?'

Lopez nodded gravely. 'All data on this thing has been erased from every file we have.' He looked at Graves. 'I've hooked into your system and done the same there,' he added. 'Sorry. Orders. All INTERSEC files are blank now.'

'And the ones in Istanbul? Haki's stuff?'

'Not enough to put two and two together.'

'So the secret's safe?' said Graves.

'I hope so,' said Marlow again.

'You'll get hell from Sir Richard.'

'Will I?'

'I take it you didn't consult him before taking this decision?'

'Should I have done? It was always my department's responsibility.'

'It got bigger than that,' said Graves.

'I know,' said Marlow. 'And I knew for sure from the moment we found ourselves unable to trace that woman in the Westwood coat who was bidding at the auction. She was working for Sir Richard, wasn't she? Or for the CIA. Or even Homeland Security direct.' A pause. 'You're expecting him, aren't you?'

Graves was silent.

'Any time now,' Marlow prompted her.

'Yes,' she said, biting her lip.

'I kind of knew – as you must have done – that people other than MAXTEL were interested from the moment Yale baulked at translating the document you found at the Cluny Museum.'

'But I translated that for us.'

'You did. But then you wondered. And, quite rightly, you double-checked. And you decided we couldn't handle this on our own.' Marlow leaned forward. 'Then there was the delay on the delivery of the Reinhardt letter. That clinched it. The Land of the Free thought the best place for this thing would be in its custody.'

Graves was silent again, as Lopez looked at her in silent astonishment. 'I didn't tell Adler anything,' she said to Marlow at last. 'He was going to torture me, but I wouldn't have told him.'

'You weren't working for him. You are a good operative. But you were supposed to be working for me. Not Sir Richard. Not the CIA. Not Homeland.'

'I did what I thought was right!'

Marlow sat back. 'Each of us owes the others one hell of a lot,' he said. 'More than you know. And we won. Kind of. So, if there's a hatchet to be buried, let's bury it now.'

'Shit,' said Lopez. 'I'm going to open a bottle of Laura's Chablis.'

But he was interrupted as they heard movement outside Graves's door, then a key in the lock. A scent of cigars and expensive aftershave. The dapper figure of Sir Richard Hudson entered the room.

He looked at the three of them in mild surprise, then at the tablet, which lay in the centre of the table.

'I see he has a key to your place,' said Marlow evenly.

'I'll take that,' Sir Richard said, indicating the tablet. 'Ms Graves —'

'Sit down,' said Marlow.

'I beg your pardon?'

'Sit.'

Dumbfounded, but clinging to his dignity, Hudson did as he was bidden.

'That artefact is in my custody now,' said Sir Richard. 'It represents a potential international security threat. Heaven forbid that it should fall into the wrong hands. The damage could be incalculable.' He paused, for effect. 'I am here to ensure that it is properly contained.'

'Good,' said Marlow. 'So am I.'

He took the hammer in his hand and, concentrating against the pain in his left shoulder as he made the effort, swung it, smashing it down again and again on the tablet, on Adhemar's Sacred Scroll, on Dandolo's key to the destruction of the Eastern Roman empire, on whatever other evil the thing had served since it left the hands of its creator, until it was a mess of rubble, and the coffee table beneath it, an expensive piece of furniture which Marlow would have to replace, was a total wreck.

In the silence that followed, Sir Richard smiled aridly. 'The best-laid plans of mice and men . . .' he murmured, half to himself.

'What do you mean?' said Marlow sharply.

Hudson spread his hands. 'I mean that we misjudged you. It's a pity. You played your role almost perfectly.'

Marlow shared a look with Lopez.

'I'd better explain,' Sir Richard went on. 'We knew about your little upset with that ghastly blonde. We knew how much you'd been hurt and how vulnerable that had made you. We thought that might be useful. Neat, too – turning an Achilles' heel into an instrument for us to use.'

'You *knew* about Juliet?' Marlow's mind hurtled back to sunlit days in Paris, over a year earlier, and a needle went into his heart even now.

'The HR woman? Yes. And what she'd done to you. The first time in years you'd been able to trust somebody completely and she blew up the bridge you were on. So there you were. On the other hand, we'd had our eye on Adler for a long time and we knew how he played the game.'

'You were taking one hell of a risk – didn't you think perhaps there were too many imponderables?'

'We couldn't be sure how things would pan out, but our game is a little bit like chess, don't you think – a mixture of anticipating your opponent's moves and hoping for the best? That was why, when it came to the question of a new person to head Section 15, I thought of you, though of course I had you covered.' He paused. 'And it almost came off.'

Marlow looked at the shattered pieces of terracotta on the floor. 'But it didn't.'

'No – at the last minute, you took the initiative.' Hudson rose. 'But don't worry. We're not going to turn you loose. You're too good a soldier. And, anyway, we couldn't afford to. Turning you loose would also have to mean terminating your contract permanently.'

Marlow knew what that meant.

'You don't have a choice if you want to live. So this is what is going to happen. The new section head is Ms Graves. You will work to her orders from now on.' He smiled at Marlow and put out his hand. 'Come on, Jack – that's the business. No hard feelings, eh?'

Epilogue

Brother Leporo sat in chains on the deck of the corsairs' ship, thinking. The wind chilled him under his habit. He hadn't eaten properly in a week.

First, he thought about the attack. He brooded for long hours about the attack every day. Had God's hand been in it?

After they'd buried Dandolo with all due ceremony, Leporo himself assisting the new cardinal and the papal legate at the altar of St Irina, the monk had hastened to complete his arrangements for departure. His ship was ready, and the heavy transport, laden with goods for Leporo's own new monastery close to Padua, was taking on its last riches. Of course, Frid was there all the time. It had been Frid who'd seen to it that the old doge was buried in precise accordance with his wishes, the tablet clenched in his right hand. Frid who had stood over the coffin as it was lowered into its vault with its treasures, to make sure nothing upset the arrangements. Frid who had kept him, Leporo, under a stony and watchful eye.

But Leporo didn't mind that. He had watched the Venetian fleet fit up and depart for its home city. He saw – for Dandolo had never successfully blinded him to them – the great ocean-going, secret ships, broken up under

Frid's command. It didn't matter. With the power he had now, once he had learned it, he could rebuild. What was destroyed could be restored. What was broken could be mended. What was dead could be resurrected.

Even now . . .

They'd been three days at sea when the corsairs' sails appeared on the southern horizon, red and white, like Viking sails, only lateen-rigged. By mid-afternoon they were within an arrow's flight of them. The battle had been fierce but hopeless and, with the heavy freighter, it had been impossible to outrun them. Frid, of course, had fought like a demon, and after the fight he had disappeared, along with his half-dozen Northern countrymen. Leporo hoped he'd been killed or drowned, but a boat was missing from their ship, and the sad truth was probably that he'd managed to get away once the tide of the fight had turned irrevocably.

Leaving Leporo and the surviving Venetian crew to be taken prisoner.

All that a week ago. But now they were sailing slowly along a dusty coast. North Africa. What a dump it looked. A waste of sand and dunes and scruffy grasses growing in untidy clumps. Sailing slowly, because of the freighter, *his* freighter, stolen from him and now in the hands of a skeleton crew of Moorish pirates.

He'd considered escape but abandoned the idea. He was old, he acknowledged. His back and his chest ached all the time, his knees cracked when he walked, his penis was a shrunken walnut between his legs, even his piss came in nothing but a dribble these days.

Acknowledgements

Huge thanks go to the people involved with this book at Penguin, Alex Clarke, Sarah Day, Nick Lowndes, Alice Shepherd and Anthea Townsend, for their unswerving support and invaluable input. The same thing goes for my friend and agent, Mark Lucas. My wife, Marji Campi, not only put up with me with patience while all this was going on, but carried out the raw editing with all the rigour it required. I want to thank as well: Daniel Campi; Charles de Groot for advice on financial aspects of the story; and – especially – Peter Ewence.

I found the following books (among others) helpful in preparing the background:

Chronicles of the Crusades, by Jean de Joinville & Geoffroy de Villehardouin, translated by M. R. B. Shaw; Penguin Classics, Harmondsworth, 1963
(*I am indebted to M. R. B. Shaw [1890–1963] for the passage from her translation of Geoffroy de Villehardouin at the beginning of Chapter 39*)
To the Finland Station, by Edmund Wilson; Orion Books, London, 2004
The Great Betrayal – Constantinople 1204, by Ernle Bradford; Hodder & Stoughton, London, 1967
A History of the Ancient Near East, by Marc van de Mieroop; Blackwell, Oxford, 2007

Hitler, by Joachim C. Fest, translated by Richard and Clara Winston; Penguin Books, Harmondsworth, 1983

Without Conscience, by Robert D. Hare; The Guilford Press, New York, 1999

But he still had time.

He clutched the tablet under his habit. They hadn't found it in their cursory search. *His* tablet. True, a copy, and hastily made, but a good copy, made with care in five hours when the old doge was sleeping. A miracle that Dandolo had slept so long. And the panic when he woke and found the tablet missing. Leporo had restored it to him with reassuring words. The old man's mind was going by then. His eyesight, in those last days, had flickered out at last.

The tablet. Leporo knew only the rudiments, but he would learn more. There were documents in Venice, left behind by Dandolo. He would get back, he would read them. They would ransom him from Venice, surely. Dandolo was a hero there, and everyone knew that the monk, Leporo, had been his right-hand man for four decades and more.

The train of his thoughts was interrupted by the rising sun, which soon warmed his back, banishing the night breezes which had robbed him of sleep. There was activity on the deck, sailors bustling and running, most making for the prow. Leporo struggled to his feet and peered ahead. Glimmering, glinting in the sun's first beams were the domes and minarets of a city.

All the preparations on board now indicated that this was their destination. He caught a word: 'Algiers'. He had heard of this place. A rich country, as far as he remembered, despite its dismal coastline. As long as he was ransomed and not sold into slavery, all would go well.

The captain appeared on deck, bare-chested, but wearing a silver turban and trousers of the same material. Dressed for disembarkation, thought Leporo, as he watched his fellow prisoners being roused and organized into ranks, sailors feeding them dry bread and cold water. Fifty of them, all seamen, like their captors. One or two of the Venetians spoke Arabic, and appeared to be getting on well with their Muslim counterparts. They'd get off lightly, if they played their cards right.

Leporo accepted his own bread and water, drank from the wooden beaker, chewed the bread with his old, unsteady teeth.

Just give me the time, he prayed.

A senior officer approached with a colleague, two sailors in tow. A weeding-out of the prisoners was taking place. The most unfortunate, the mortally wounded and the diseased among them, had been thrown into the sea immediately after the battle.

Leporo recognized the senior officer, who did not return his smile.

The corsairs spoke in Arabic. Leporo strained to catch words any words he might understand, but failed.

'This one?' asked the senior officer, indicating the monk.

'One of their mullahs,' his colleague replied.

'Explains why he's still alive,' answered the senior officer, prodding him. 'Too old to be worth anything.'

'Ransom?'

'What makes you think that?'

Leporo longed for an interpreter, but all his bilingual fellow-countrymen were too far away, on the other side of the ship, and he could scarcely demand one.

'What are we going to do with him if we land him?' said the senior officer. 'He could turn out to be a liability.'

'We've fed him all week.'

'Time to cut our losses, then. We can afford to, there's a king's ransom on that transport.' The senior officer came to a decision. 'Throw him overboard. Do it discreetly, don't want to upset the others.' Then: 'You say he's a mullah?'

'Yes.'

'Show some respect then, some mercy. Cut his wrists first. Make it quicker.'

The two sailors were given their orders and took Leporo aft, away from the others, and down a deck, close to the waterline. They unshackled him and pulled his hands free of his robe. As they did so, a small clay tablet fell to the deck. Leporo gave a cry, and stooped for it.

They held him back, firmly. One pinioned him, the other drew his knife and opened the knotted blue veins. Leporo watched as if in a dream. This was not really happening.

Then he felt a rush of cold water, refreshing, strange, and he still couldn't believe this was happening as the blue sea closed over his head.

The sailors watched for a moment. Then one of them picked up the tablet.

'What's this?'

'He dropped it.'

'Looks worthless.'

'Probably one of their relics. Might get a couple of dirhams for it.'

'Not worth the bother.'

'All right. Cross to the port side. We're close enough to the shore. I bet you two dirhams you can't throw it hard enough to reach the beach.'

'I accept!'

They regained the upper deck and crossed to the port side.

The sailor who had picked the tablet up took a good look at the shore, barely a slingshot's distance away, and concentrated. Then he raised his arm, and hurled the tablet towards the land as hard as he could.